An Instant in the Wind

André Brink was born in a small South African village in 1935. Since 1961 he has been lecturing in modern literature and drama at Rhodes University, interrupted by several sojourns in Europe. He is the author of seven previous novels, and one work of non-fiction, *Mapmakers*. He received the Martin Luther King Memorial Prize and the French Prix Medicis Étranger in 1980; was three times awarded the most important South African literary prize, the CNA award; and has been twice runner-up for the Booker Prize.

*Available in Flamingo
by the same author*

Looking on Darkness
Rumours of Rain
A Dry White Season
A Chain of Voices
The Wall of the Plague
The Ambassador
States of Emergency

André Brink

An Instant
in the Wind

Flamingo
Published by Fontana Paperbacks

First published in Great Britain by
W. H. Allen & Co. Ltd 1976
This Flamingo edition first published
in 1983 by Fontana Paperbacks
Third impression October 1989

Flamingo is an imprint of
Fontana Paperbacks, part of
the Collins Publishing Group,
8 Grafton Street, London W1X 3LA

Set in 10 on 11½ point Plantin
by Buccleuch Printers, Hawick

Printed and bound in Great Britain by
William Collins Sons & Co. Ltd, Glasgow

For BREYTEN
such a long journey ahead
for you and me

And so it was I entered the broken world
To trace the visionary company of love, its voice
An instant in the wind (I know not whither hurled)
But not for long to hold each desperate choice
–HART CRANE

We live in a disoriented, deranged social structure, and
we have transcended its barriers in our own ways and
have stepped psychologically outside its madness and
repressions. It is lonely out here. We recognize each
other. And, having recognized each other, is it any
wonder that our souls cling together even while our minds
equivocate, hesitate, vacillate and tremble?
–ELDRIDGE CLEAVER

Who were they? The names are known – Adam Mantoor and Elisabeth Larsson – and something of their history has been recorded. We know that in 1749, the last year of the rule of Governor Swellengrebel, Elisabeth accompanied her husband, the Swedish traveller Erik Alexis Larsson, on a journey into the interior of the Cape of Good Hope where he died some time after; that she was eventually discovered by the runaway slave, Adam; and that they reached Cape Town together towards the end of February 1751. An interesting trifle, a mere footnote adding nothing to one's knowledge of the land or the course of history.

Who were they? A few more facts may be added by tracing, with much trouble and some luck, the long list of the dead composing their genealogies.

Adam Mantoor   In 1719 Willem Lowrens Rieckert, a farmer near Constantia, entered the birth of one Adam in the Slave Register of the Cape. The mother was reported to be Krissie, also known as Karis, a Hottentot woman. But as Hottentots were not generally kept as slaves in those days, additional research is required to explain that she was booked into Rieckert's service in 1714, at the age of ten or eleven, after being discovered, with a number of other children, by an expedition to the Olifants River soon after the epidemic of smallpox which had ravaged the colony the previous year. The name of her child's father was registered as Ontong, a Cape slave also in Rieckert's service, but sold soon afterwards to one Jeremia van Niekerk, farmer of Piquet Berg, for 800 rixdollars.

This Ontong appears to have been a child from a liaison, in 1698 or 1699, between a male slave, Afrika, imported from Madagascar, and a slave woman, Seli, brought from Padang at a barely nubile age. It seems likely that this Afrika was the same slave who, in 1702, was executed in front of the Castle on a count of sedition and the murder of his employer, one Grové. For his services the executioner would have received a bonus of sixteen rixdollars – four for the use of the irons, and twelve for breaking on the wheel without administration of the death-blow.

9

Forty years later Afrika's grandson, Adam, also fell foul of the law by disobeying the instructions of his master, the aforementioned Willem Louwrens Rieckert, and by assaulting the latter with a piece of wood. For this crime he was sentenced, after a fair trial, to flogging and branding, followed by banishment to Robben Island. In 1744 his escape was recorded without any further particulars, and for seven years no more was seen of him in the colony. Finally, in March 1751, he was flogged (three rixdollars) and strangled (six rixdollars).

Elisabeth Larsson For some reason it has always been assumed that she arrived from Sweden with her husband. But in the Cape Archives the letter, dated 17 May 1749, has now been discovered (*Ref. no. C41, p. 154*) in which Governor Swellengrebel gave permission for the journey into the interior. In this letter the members of the expedition are listed as Hermanus Hendrickus van Zyl, Free Burgher of Stellenbosch; Erik Alexis Larsson of Göteborg, Sweden; and 'his housewife Elisabeth Maria Larsson, *née* Louw, of the Cape'.

The founder of this line of the family, Wilhelmus Janszoon Louw, arrived at the Cape of Good Hope in 1674 as a soldier of the East India Company, accompanied by his wife and two young sons. One of the children died during the passage from Texel in 1694; the other, Johannes Wilhelmszoon (b. 1668) married a Huguenot girl, Elisabeth Marie Jeanne Nourtier (b. Calais, 1676). At that time the father Wilhelmus had already obtained his discharge from the Company and started farming in the district of Stellenbosch. His son and daughter-in-law settled on the same farm, presumably because the father's state of health had become too precarious for him to cope with all the work.

From the marriage of Johannes and the French girl six children were born: Jean Louis (1696 – deceased six months later), Elisabeth Marie (1697), Marcus Wilhelm Johannes (1698), Aletta Maria (1701), Anna Gertruida (1703), and Jacomina Hendrina (1704). It seems that Johannes played some part in the insurrection of the colonists against Governor Willem Adriaan van der Stel, but that he died in 1705, before the struggle had reached its climax in the deportation of the Governor. After his death his widow remarried one Hermanus Christoffel Valck and gave birth to three more children.

The only son of the family, Marcus Wilhelm Johannes mentioned above, returned to the service of the Company where he was soon promoted from clerk to bookkeeper and eventually to keeper of stores, or *dispensier*. In 1721 he married Catharina Teresa Oldenburg (b. 1703), daughter of a distinguished Company inspector who visited the Cape from Batavia in that year.

Two sons born from the marriage – in 1722 and 1724 respectively – both died soon after birth, leaving Elisabeth Maria (b. 1727) as the only surviving child. It may be of interest, however, that between 1740 and 1748 Marcus fathered at least five more children from three different female slaves in his service; at his death in 1750 all five were listed as assets in his estate.

Elisabeth Maria probably met the Swedish traveller Larsson very soon after his arrival at the Cape in February 1748. A year later they were married on the eve of their departure on that fateful voyage into the hinterland. One reason why the journey drew very little attention at the time must have been the fact that Larsson consistently represented it to the authorities as a simple hunting expedition (his licence was for shooting elephants, rhinoceros, hippopotamus and 'exotic beasts') rather than as a journey of exploration. Not only did the Company at that stage – unlike a couple of decades later, during the visits of Larsson's illustrious compatriots Thunberg and Sparrman – frown on explorations by foreigners, but it seems reasonable to assume that Larsson himself would have tried to prevent others from forestalling him in the execution of his main project. This was the collection and cataloguing of plants, birds and animals unknown in Europe; and, above all, extensive geographical observation aimed at the definitive mapping of the interior.

After her return to the Cape Elisabeth Maria Larsson, *née* Louw, remarried (the Marriage Register mentions only her maiden name, which explains some of the confusion obscuring her historical identity for so long). Her new husband was an elderly neighbour, Stephanus Cornelius Jacobs (b. 1689), and the ceremony took place in May 1751. In August of the same year she gave birth to a son. Soon afterwards her husband died. She never married again.

Classified under the name of Elisabeth Jacobs there exists, in the Cape Archives, a handwritten *Memoir* of eighty-five octavo pages, in which, ostensibly for the benefit of her son, Elisabeth gives a brief survey of her life. With great objectivity and reticence, remarkable in her circumstances but intensely frustrating for the modern historian, she includes an outline of her Cape journey: 'Left the Cape in April 1749, with two tent wagons, crossed Hottentot's Holland Mountains, proceeded to the Warm Baths' – and more in the same vein, describing the customary coastal route as far as Mossel Bay, and over the Outeniqua Range; and from there quite far north, with a wide semicircle through the Camdeboo to the hinterland of the Winterberg and the Suurveld in the Eastern Cape. The account suggests that the newly married woman found it interesting in the beginning, but that excitement soon gave way to boredom and finally to 'unbearable revulsion'. Her husband devoted nearly all his time and interest to his feverish scientific activities, pressing flowers, shooting and stuffing birds, preparing animal skins, collecting reptiles, and meticulously mapping their progress.

There appears to have been trouble with Van Zyl, who had joined the expedition as a guide but very soon got hopelessly lost. Things came to a sudden head when, after a violent quarrel, he ran into the bush and blew out his own brains with a pistol. Soon afterwards a band of Bushmen stole twenty of their oxen, forcing them to abandon one wagon. Later, all their Hottentots deserted the expedition, taking with them all but two of the remaining oxen. And then Erik Alexis Larsson quite simply walked off into the wilderness and disappeared. At that stage they were encamped in a bushy region somewhere along the tributaries of the Great Fish River. And there Elisabeth was discovered by the runaway slave.

The *Memoir* contains very little on the first part of the return journey to the sea, but, fortunately, reveals rather more about the rest of their trek, which one can, with a certain amount of conjecture, reconstruct through the north-eastern section of the Tsitikama forest and across the mountains to the Lang Kloof and the Little Karoo, over the Swart Berg or 'Black Mountains', through the Karoo and so back to the Cape.

But even this information is scant, almost insignificant. And it is only the final sentence which strikes one with sudden, subtle meaning after so many dreary facts, when Elisabeth writes:

This no one can take away from us, not even ourselves.

Quite by accident, in the course of a completely different research project, a vital new discovery has now been made in Livingstone House, the headquarters of the London Missionary Society: the badly deteriorated but still decipherable journals of Larsson himself. How on earth these three folio volumes in sturdy leather binding ever landed in the hands of the LMS is impossible to tell. The only explanation, in itself far-fetched, seems to be that wandering Hottentots may eventually have found them in the desolate farmhouse where, many years before, Elisabeth had made the final entry, and delivered them to the missionaries of nearby Bethelsdorp.

The major portion of the journal is in Larsson's own handwriting –

extensive, clinically accurate notes on their progress, observations, discoveries, conclusions and expectations. There is, for example, a detailed catalogue of everything taken with them on the two wagons with which they left the Cape. The first wagon was loaded with six large chests (on which the couple's mattress was unrolled at night) and two smaller ones containing

clothes
white candy sugar
coffee
tea
10 lb chocolate
a jack, nails, iron rods, and assorted bits of iron
pins, needles, cotton
stuff for bartering: glass beads, copper tinderboxes, knives, rolled tobacco, Indian scarves, combs
500 lb gunpowder in small barrels, wrapped in wet sheepskins to preserve the contents watertight
1 ton lead and tin, with a complete set of casting moulds
16 blunderbusses, 12 double-barrelled pistols, 2 sabres, 1 dagger
10 reams paper for pressing plants
scientific instruments, including a compass, a hygrometer, a dipping needle, a yard-long barometer in a box, with additional mercury in an earthenware bottle

The second wagon contained two large empty boxes intended for scientific collections of specimens, insects, etcetera, as well as the following

2 tents
1 table and 4 chairs
1 iron grill
1 large frying pan, 2 kettles, 4 saucepans, 2 coffee cans, 2 teapots, 2 washing tubs, 3 washbasins
4 halfaums of brandy, two for storing specimens, the rest for bribing and encouraging the Hottentots and winning friends in the country
a collection of porcelain plates, dishes, cups and saucers

The trek was accompanied by thirty-two oxen, four horses, eight dogs, fifteen chickens and six Hottentots.

Every day the distance covered was calculated and the weather noted. One is struck by the numerous references to wind – 'Windy today' – 'Windy again' – 'Very windy' – 'Elisabeth complains about wind' – 'Gusts of wind' – and once a longer reference, the nearest Erik Alexis Larsson ever approached to poetry in his journal: 'The whole interior is like a sea of wind on which we toss and drift unsteadily'.

There is a daily catalogue of new discoveries. Every buck or beast of prey shot was measured and dissected and described in detail. With just as much precision, events of importance were recorded:

'Attacked by wounded lion and saved just in time by Hottentot Booi, who was bitten in the arms before the animal could be killed. Interested to note that Booi's flesh under the skin was exactly the same colour and texture as that of a white man.'

It also transpires that Larsson perfected a highly ingenious method for shooting birds without damaging them, so that they could be stuffed for his collection. This method, 'rediscovered' years later by the explorer Vaillant, consisted of pouring a small quantity of gunpowder into the gun (the exact amount to be determined by the size of the bird and the distance from it) and securing it with a plug of candlewax, afterwards filling the barrel with water. In this way the bird was merely stunned by the impact, and its wet feathers prevented escape.

There are very few references to personal circumstances. Occasionally there is a brief note: 'Quarrelled with Elisabeth' – 'Elisabeth, sadly, has no faculty for scientific understanding' – 'Elisabeth very demanding last night, again this morning; not conducive to concentration'.

His final entry (dated 3.1.50) is followed by some empty pages before the journal is resumed, without any dates, in Elisabeth's handwriting. Her inscriptions are, on the whole, longer than his; her tone much more personal than in the *Memoir* of so many years later. There is an unfortunate lack of explicit detail, and some of the experiences which, judging from the urgency of the tone, were most significant to her, remain distressingly cryptic. But there are occasional remarks in which one suddenly glimpses an existence beyond history:

Such a long journey ahead for you and me. Oh God, oh God.

Who are they? The *Memoir* and the *Journals* are presently being prepared for publication in annotated editions, the latter subject to final permission from the LMS. Then history will claim them for itself. But history as such is irrelevant. What is important is that phrase, *This no one can take away from us . . .* Or those other words, *Such a long journey . . .*

It is to this end that the crust of history must be scraped off. Not simply to retell it but to utterly expose it and to set it in motion again. To travel through that long landscape and back, back to the high mountain above the town of a thousand houses exposed to the sea and the wind. Back through that wild and empty land – *who are you? who am I?* – without knowing what to expect, when all the instruments have been destroyed by the wind and all the journals abandoned to the wind, when nothing else remains but to continue. It it is not a question of imagination, but of faith.

He finds her huddled on the driver's seat of the wagon among the wild fig-trees, late in the afternoon, with the birds already settling in the branches for the night. She is surrounded by the remains of her trek, the relics representing in this wilderness the achievements of her civilisation: unloaded rifles (fired off last night and this morning) and bags of lead and powder, dried flowers between sheets of stained white paper, stuffed birds and delicately boned skeletons, drawings of animals and trees and camping sites beside hills or rivers, small reptiles preserved in alcohol, the long tube of the barometer still upturned in its bowl of mercury, kettle and cooking pots at the fire, hand-embroidered sheets spread over bushes and a dried aloe stump, clothing still crumpled and damp from last night's storm, a grill marked with new rust, crockery; and the map on one of the boxes behind her, its outlines suggested by early Portuguese and defined by a century of shipping, a narrow patch from left to centre inscribed and covered with the contours of hills and rivers, mountains, plains, longitudes and latitudes, heights above sea level, climatic zones, prevailing winds – surrounded by white emptiness containing only a few tentative lines and dots, open and exposed, *terra incognita*, great and wide.

For a long time he remains standing in the opening of the rough shelter of branches surrounding the wagon, holding the dead hare by its hindlegs; from the nostrils tiny drops of blood stain the trodden grass. She doesn't look up.

He can still turn back. She won't even know that he has been there; the last dogs have disappeared long ago, with the Hottentots. What is it that drives one from one's familiar wilderness to the ultimate outspan of a trek like this? What is it that compels one to follow a wagon for weeks on end, tracking it like a dog or a beast of prey? What is it one cannot annihilate in oneself, which forces one to circle a camping site restlessly, endlessly, drawing ever closer?

He can still go away. But he stands looking at her, like many times

17

in the past weeks, only so much closer now, and openly. Her long dark hair is loose over her shoulders, which are narrow and hunched, as if she has grown younger and much more weary overnight, no longer a woman but barely a girl. The blue dress with white embroidery and without any trace of the padding and stiffening and hoops of the Cape, now crumpled and dirty. Last night she slept in it and today, for the first time on the journey, she hasn't changed or washed herself or even combed her hair.

Here I am. Five years has been enough; too much.

Something finally makes her look up: not sound, but silence. The wind which has blown steadily through the days, raging past the camp last night, tearing branches from the hedge, tugging the wagon sail from the plaited reeds of the bodywork and shredding it to bits, has suddenly died down.

'Who are you?' That is the first thing she says as she notices him and draws back on her seat, after the initial shock about his clothes.

'My name is Adam Mantoor.' He doesn't move, except to readjust his grip on the hare's legs.

'Who are you?'

There is something almost comic about the situation. He comes a few steps nearer to reassure her, but misinterpreting his move she grabs one of the blunderbusses and jumps up.

'Don't move!'

He hesitates, and gives another step.

She pulls the trigger, but nothing happens. Dropping the gun, she looks round in bewilderment, then picks up one of the long pistols and hurls it at him. He has to duck, or else she would have hit him. Now he knows for sure. Calmly he comes to the wagon and puts down the hare. She begins to retreat under the canvas roof, her hair clinging to her cheeks. He grabs the gun. After the briefest of struggles she lets go, too scared even to try and hide.

From one of the open bags Adam takes a handful of powder, weighs it in his palm and, under her wide-eyed stare, pours it down the barrel, gently secures a plug, then rams down a measure of lead. Cocking the gun so that the flint stands up like a snake ready to attack, he offers her the rifle, the ornate butt turned towards her.

Without removing her eyes from him she takes the gun.

'What do you want?'

He shrugs. The jacket is too large for him.

'Wait,' she says suddenly, withdrawing into the tent and returning after a few seconds with a copper mug in her hand. 'Brandy.' She motions to her mouth. 'Drink.' Repeating, with more emphasis, as he fails to react, '*Drink.*'

Adam shakes his head and puts the mug on the front seat beside the dead hare.

'You must go away now,' she orders, reassured by the loaded gun in her hands. 'My husband will be back at any moment.'

'No. He got lost.'

'He'll shoot you dead if he finds you here.'

'With his gun full of water?'

'How do you know . . . ?' she asks, taken aback. Then, with renewed resentment, 'You watched him! For how long have you been spying on us?'

He makes a vague gesture which draws her attention back to the broad cuff of his brocaded sleeve.

'Those are his clothes. You killed him and stole all his things!'

'I've had these clothes for a long time.'

No, Erik Alexis was not wearing this outfit when he left yesterday morning, following the scarlet bird. But ten days ago, a fortnight perhaps, it's noted in the *Journal*: they thought the Hottentots had stolen it.

'So it was you.'

Another shrug.

'They belong to my husband.'

'What about it?'

'Who do you think you are speaking to?'

Yes, he's thinner than Erik Alexis. Same height, more or less, but much thinner. Actually he looks ridiculous wearing that expensive blue jacket and the floral waistcoat and those breeches, with neither hat nor stockings to go with them, and those rough buckskin shoes. A clown in the wilderness. I don't know what you've come for. I don't want you here, I'm scared of you. But I need someone to help me. He stayed away all day yesterday. It wasn't the first time he has wandered off like this in pursuit of some exotic bird or beast but he's never stayed away a night before. And such a night.

And yet she did sleep. Probably through pure fatigue and fear, hardly conscious of the storm that raged. The dogs disappearing one by one: two in a fight with the lion, another dragged off by a hyena, others shot by the Bushmen they tried to pursue, the rest treacherously running off with the Hottentots. Van Zyl becoming more and more unmanageable, stealing brandy and picking quarrels, hiding behind

19

shrubs to catch glimpses of her changing or bathing; then running off into the bush; the pistol shot. 'The Hottentots can help me bury him. You stay away, it's not a pretty sight.' So considerate. But what of the nights or early mornings? The sight of the back of your head in the yellow lantern light, writing your Journals, drawing your map. You're as bad as old Mr Roloff. If maps could cook you might have married one. You wouldn't miss the rest. It's I who have to slake my thirst, and burn. Is this what I left everything for, travelling into the wilderness with you, one flesh? One map, one journal – flesh is much too uncertain and unpredictable for your scientific precision; too indecent and too terrible. The only thing you trust is the length of your barometer, the mercury rising or falling the breadth of a hair. How you punished that Hottentot who broke the spare bottle. You had him stretched out between the wagon wheels, and stood watching as they flogged the life out of him, your pale Swedish hands trembling. And that very night they all deserted us. Are you surprised I slept so well last night? My fear was also relief, release. In the heart of the storm I was safe and protected, much more than ever in your company: in all that violence nothing could touch me. But now another day has passed and tonight I won't be able to sleep at all. You must be somewhere. But why didn't you return in answer to my gunshots, until I'd fired off the last one and this savage had to come and load it? I hope you found your beautifully plumed bird after all.

'Where do you come from?' she asks.

He turns back with a vague, sweeping gesture including most of the dusky world behind him: tall, gentle slopes bending over into sudden deep ravines overgrown with tangled brushwood: trees she doesn't know, shrubs she doesn't know, named by Erik Alexis Larsson, Latin names, meaningless to her ears.

How apt that you should merely motion, saying nothing: for this land has not yet been given a name, certainly not a Latin one; it does not yet exist. And it's yours, all right, you may have it. But what am I doing here? I must have come in search of something, beyond the Cape and its farthest known mountains, but not this: more mountains, more plains, more valleys and rivers; wind and rain, drought, silence. Not this, it means nothing to me.

Adam moves; she tenses. But he only picks up the hare, this time by the ears, and goes to the grey and black ashes of the fireplace washed out by rain. She watches him intently. He squats down, his back turned to her – I could shoot him now, with the gun he's loaded himself

– takes out a knife and begins to skin the hare. Rapid, neat flicks of the blade which fascinate her, from the white paws down to the armpits, and across the breastbone towards the stomach. *The same colour flesh.* She sits down on the wagon seat again, keeping the gun across her knees; but he doesn't look up once. From the barrel beside the wagon he takes a kettle of water to the fire, as if he has been familiar with the place for a long time. Under the belly of the wagon he finds dry wood. With his back to her he kindles a fire. How? Gusts of whirling smoke, an acrid smell of herbs which suddenly makes her feel nauseous. The smell of the land. He scorches the grill and arranges the hare meat on it.

The sun is down, the sky still glowing. It is impossibly quiet. Behind the nearer hills are farther mountains, different from the porcelain blue ridge of Hottentot's Holland, larger, bulkier, like vast animals asleep.

While the meat is roasting and the kettle boiling on the fire, he brings in the two remaining oxen and begins to tidy up and strengthen the wind-blown kraal. He is aware of her watching him. He need only look up to see her. But what would there be to say if he did? I know you? I don't know you? Who are you? What are you doing here? You don't belong here. We don't want to know about the Cape here.

It's not true. For five years I've been talking to myself in the wilderness; for five years I've never been able to banish the memory of that Mountain and the bay. The best view by far is the one from Robben Island. They bury you in the sand up to your neck and urinate in your mouth. Through their widespread legs you can see the Mountain. Mother is singing in the vineyard: *Rock of ages, cleft for me* . . . And Grandmother, huddled in her crocheted blanket, mumbles about Padang and about the red and green of hibiscus and shivering touch-me-not leaves.

She has her food on the wagon; he stays beside the fire.

After the meal she puts down her plate and looks up.

'Bring me some water for washing,' she orders. Behind her, under the canvas roof of the wagon, a lantern is burning, suspended from a short chain.

He doesn't move.

'Did you hear me?'

'Fetch your own water.'

Even in the light of the fire he can see how pale she has become.

'I won't let a slave speak to me like that!' she says angrily.

21

'I'm not a slave.'

'What are you doing here?'

'I thought you needed help.'

'Don't cheek me.'

'Why not?' He gets up quietly.

'I don't want you here,' she flares up, a touch of hysteria in her voice. 'I can manage perfectly on my own.'

He stands watching her while, pale and with teeth clenched, she climbs off the wagon and comes to fetch the kettle of boiling water from the fire next to him. As she returns to the wagon, she looks back and says viciously: 'You don't seem to know your place.'

He makes no response.

'As soon as my husband comes back . . .'

He turns back leisurely and begins to feed the fire with logs for the night. Moving away from the smoke, later, he can see her shadow against the canvas of the wagon tent. She must be close to the lantern, for the shadow is grotesquely large, yet he cannot look away. He's never been so close before. She is undressing. Bent over a tub, she begins to wash herself, her arms and body freed from the ample dress. In profile he can see the movement of her breasts, no longer a mere bulge covered by lace and frills, but round and defined.

White, with your black shadow. For five years I've been reduced to talking to myself, or to small bands of wandering Hottentots, men-of-men, in the freedom of the wilderness I freely chose. That night when I returned from the island, stumbling out on the sand, half drowned, naked under the sliver of moon, the wind clammy against my shivering body: that night I chose, and knew: this was the way to freedom. Somewhere there it lay in wait for me, ever receding. Beyond what mountain does it begin, across what river? Where does the South stop tugging at one like a tide, back this way, back to people, back to one's childhood? And there you're standing with your shadow against the canvas. You're not even aware of it, unless you despise me so much that you don't care? – brushing your hair, moving your shoulders and arms. If you turn I can see the points of your taut nipples. You: the ultimate *thou-shalt-not*, the most untouchable of all, you: white, woman.

Around them lies the thin circle of the kraal and the wild fig-trees. Surrounded by the infinite and determined by it, reduced by it.

In the dark, soon after the light on the wagon has gone out and the warm smell of the wick has vanished, the animals start up. Outside the fire has died down to a glow. Last night, in the storm and the howling wind there was no sound of animals. But tonight they're back, distant at first, but approaching until they are quite near. Jackals laughing. Wild dogs barking. And the sound she fears most, the eeriest of all: the cry of hyenas, starting low down and rising to a pitch, like exclamation marks in the dark. The moon is not out yet. Erik Alexis Larsson would have known when the moon was due to wax again, and wane, and disappear. Erik Alexis Larsson would have known everything.

Are they feeding on him tonight? Or are they on their way here, through the futile little fence, past the fire – perhaps even lured by the fire? Hippos will leave the water to come to a light in the dark. Beside a river you named on your map, we were sitting at our small table playing chess that night, the lantern between us, when suddenly the huge thing appeared. You grabbed the lantern and began to run in wide circles, followed by the hippo, until the Hottentots shouted at you to drop the light. You hurled it away from you fleeing in the opposite direction, and the animal stormed the lantern and crushed it into the earth and went away. All you noted in your Journal afterwards was: 'Discovered that some animals, e.g. the hippopotamus, are lured by light instead of being scared.'

Pushing herself up from her bed she crawls to the front of the fastened tent and opens a corner of one flap. The night feels cool on her face; it's stuffy inside. After a while she recognises his dark shape beside the fire. She feels an urge to call him, but what is there to say or ask? Her voice is unmanageable in her throat. There he is, but it's so dark she cannot even make out whether he is looking this way or not. Is he going to keep watch like this all night? Why should he? She doesn't want him here. He is a threat to her independence, her silence; a threat to her. Yet if he hadn't been there, like this, tonight, she would surely have died of fear. Should she offer him a gun? Or is it sufficient for him to simply sit out there, dressed in her husband's Cape clothes which hang so loosely on his tall, thin body? That dark man in the dark.

Elisabeth secures the corner of the flap again. Her hands are trembling, the palms are moist. He's there, outside. She pulls the embroidered sheet up to her chin. Her eyes pressed shut, she remembers the mulberry tree, the fruit bursting with redness and ripeness. Tonight, oh God, these hyenas will never stop calling. It's not a pretty sight, he said. And her face is burning like that day in the tree.

*

23

He is the first to return to the camp among the wild fig-trees, emerging from the narrow overgrown kloof which runs through the greenish brown hills. It is still hot, even more so in the clothes he hasn't grown used to, and he has been walking since early morning. In a folded buckskin over his shoulder he carries a small hoard of lightly speckled eggs, carefully removing them at the fireplace where he arranges them in a hollow.

Looking up, he sees her approaching through the trees on the opposite side, tall, with her long dress flapping loosely round her long legs, and strands of dark hair clinging moistly to her forehead and cheeks. As she comes nearer, he notices that she is disturbingly pale, with a bluish hue around her mouth and specks of perspiration on her upper lip. She is not conscious of him at all. Walking right past him she goes to the wagon where she stops, panting lightly, pressing her hands against the splashboard and resting her head on the inside of her elbows. Her sleeves are rolled and he can see the delicate lines of light on the tiny hairs of her forearms.

It is only when he finally gets up that she becomes aware of him, jerking up her head in fear; then, recognising him, she relaxes, her head dropping as before.

'Would you . . .' she begins, but stops again, breathing with some difficulty and clenching her teeth. Without completing the question she goes to the back of the wagon and scoops up some water in a jug, pours it into a cup and comes back. This time she sits down on the grass, leaning against the front wheel. And all the time he stands watching her detachedly, perhaps with a touch of malice.

'The sun too bad for you?' he asks after a while.

'No,' she says stubbornly. 'It's nothing. It's only . . .' Then her body seems to contract. She gets up hurriedly and runs round the wagon where he can hear her vomiting. It startles him, makes him feel guilty. To occupy himself, he starts breaking wood for the evening fire, but abandons it after a while. At last she returns.

'You ill?' he asks.

'No.' She sits down, leaning against the wheel as before. She has untied her hair; it is long and soft and dark round her shoulders.

'There must be something wrong,' he insists.

'I'm expecting a child.' In sudden anger she sits upright. 'He has no right to leave me at a time like this. He's never cared for anyone but himself.' But she is too weary to remain angry. After a while she says, 'You didn't find anything, did you?'

'Not a trace. I've been up all the fingers of the kloof. The storm washed away everything.'

It is still early, but he decides to make the fire after all and boil a kettle.

With a tone of complaint in her voice, a tone she loathes, she says, 'At any other time I wouldn't have minded the sun at all. It's just because I . . .'

He stays silent.

'In the Cape I used to walk for miles,' she goes on. 'Whenever my mother turned her back. She always wanted to send a sedan chair along. Once I even climbed the Mountain, all the way.' She waits for him to react. 'I often went up the Lion's Rump, of course, and the Head too. But I climbed the Mountain only once. It's strange, the way it looks all flat from down below, while it's so uneven up there, isn't it? All rocky and craggy and covered with shrubs. There's a sort of fruit, like small pine-cones, with a springy feeling if you press it in your hand.' She is still pale, but with colour slowly seeping back into her cheeks. When the men went up, they always brought some of the fruit back and asked us to close our eyes and open our hands. All the screaming and giggling and coy laughter, I couldn't stand it.

There was wind up there. And the mottled grey cliffs all the way down to the sea. It seemed to stretch out to the ends of the earth, that blue sea. A peculiar sensation standing there, a feeling of recklessness, as if one might do anything one would never dare to do otherwise. I might have taken off my clothes if I had been alone.

She opens her eyes, almost startled to find him there; annoyed.

'I know the Mountain,' he admits grudgingly. 'I went up many times.'

'You also looked at the sea?'

'I saw it, yes.'

'I didn't want to come down again.' Why is she talking to him like this? – with all the breathlessness of a Cape girl at a ball, trying to hold the attention of some young officer from a visiting fleet, some official on his way to or from Patria, by blowing up, out of all proportion, her small adventures: picnics and excursions, the flurry of letter-writing and preparations when the cannon booms over the bay and the flags go up and the tavern women start diluting their wines with water.

'We used to fetch wood on the Mountain,' he continues, still reluctant, resentful. 'Then we stayed out all day and only brought back our bundles at sunset.'

'It must have been hard work carrying the wood.'

'Not at all. We rolled the bundles downhill, then tied them to poles and carried them like that.'

Her eyes are inscrutable. 'You're a slave,' she says.

'I'm not!'

The water is boiling.

'You can come and fetch your tea,' he says, in sullen antagonism.

'What did you come to the wagon for?' she asks with renewed suspicion. 'What do you want of me? I've got nothing.'

'Why should I come for anything? I just saw the wagon in the bushes and came to see.'

You were spying on us. You stole his clothes. You lured him away from here.'

'You said he was following some bird.'

She leans back again, avoiding his eyes. 'You'll have to take me home,' she says. 'I must get back to the Cape.'

'The Cape?' he asks. 'Why should I go back there?'

I can't stay here, can I?' She holds the cup tightly between both hands. 'I must find people. I can't . . .'

'There are bands of Hottentots that way.' He points.

'What use are they to me?'

He glares at her in silence. Why should I pity you? I should have stayed clear of the wagon altogether. Don't think because I'm here . . .

'I'm on my way to the sea,' he says, averting his eyes. 'Perhaps we'll find a farmhouse or a trek on the way.'

The sea, anywhere near the sea, rather than this endless undulating land.

'But we can't go before we've found him,' she protests. 'He must have hurt himself or something. Suppose he comes back and finds I'm gone?'

'He left you.'

'No, he didn't. He was only following a bird. He'll come back.'

'Will he pull the wagon for you?'

'He'll know how to get us out of here. After all, he's a man.' Resenting herself for saying so. Hearing again the cry of the new-born baby behind the door as her father came out with hunched shoulders, stopping as he saw her. 'Where have you been?' she asked in quiet accusation. 'Why do you want to know?' he replied. She could feel her face burning: 'Is that another of your bastards? And what's going to happen to him?' 'Mind your tongue, Elisabeth,' he said. 'It's none of your business.' She snapped at him in rage: 'You think a slave is nothing but a woman!' Thinking: and a woman no more than a slave. The impotent anger in his tired eyes. 'Go up to your room, Elisabeth, and stay there till tonight.'

'We have to stay here,' she insists. 'In case he comes back. Afterwards, all right.' Oh God, the sea.

He thinks: In summer, the warm semen smell of the milkbushes on the beaches of the Cape. All that I've given up. And now, after all these years.

Dusk has begun to fall. Down in the valley the hadedas are crying, coming up over the hills.

'Why do they cry like that?'

'Why not?'

'It's terrifying. Like a scream of death.'

He laughs derisively.

'Where do you live?' she asks on a sudden impulse.

'Nowhere.'

'I want to *know* why you've come here,' she demands with some vehemence. Continuing, as he remains silent, 'I know you're just trying to catch me off my guard.' She gets up nervously and begins to rearrange the guns and pistols on the wagon. 'You're waiting for a chance. But I warn you, I'm watching you. And if ever you dare . . . Even if I have to kill myself . . .' She swallows back a sob choking her voice. 'You understand? You have no right. I'm pregnant. And you're just a slave.'

He watches her in silence. A small twig snaps in his hand. The short sharp sound hits her like a gunshot. He is breathing deeply, trying to control himself before he replies.

'Slave,' he says after a while, 'slave! That's all you can say. But I've had enough of it now, you hear? "No right"!'

You may have the right to chop off my leg. But then to tell me I have no right to walk straight – that I won't allow. Watching her, he sees her trembling. Then he turns round abruptly and walks off towards the opening in the fence.

'You can't go away now!' she says. 'It's getting dark. You can't just leave me here like this. You've got to take me home, you've got to. Come back.'

Adam looks round. 'You scared?'

She doesn't answer.

27

You're trying to order me around because you're shit-scared, because you have no say over me. Not much authority you've got here. Suddenly he feels almost sorry for her.

'You want eggs for supper?' he asks clumsily. 'I robbed some nests in the kloof.'

The day of the loft. Where we always went after the day's work or games, Lewies and me. The other children of the Baas were too small for us. Long days of summer, naked in the cold mountain stream beyond the silver trees and the newly planted oaks. Riding on the wine-wagon to the Company's shed in town. Setting snares for the small grey buck trampling the wheat and barley in the early morning. Bareback riding on the calves behind the farthest wall of the kraal, tumbling in dust and dung. And then, always, up the wooden stairs to the high loft with the sweet smell of raisins we'd helped dry in autumn, from the bursting-ripe *hanepoot* grapes. Squatting in the fragrant dusk among processed hides and piles of bush-tea and the two yellow-wood coffins, ever ready, crammed with dried fruit, telling him all the remembered stories of my grandmother. At first he'd always accompanied me to the backyard to listen to her telling them, stringing the musical names on the threads of her memory, Tjilatap, Palikpapan, Djocjacarta and Smeroes, Padang and Burubudur; but after her hands had grown gnarled with arthritis and useless for any work, the Bass had freed her and she'd gone down to town, to a little shack of wood and clay and grass high up on the Lion's Rump. And since then it was I who had to retell her stories to Lewies sitting up there in the loft eating our sweet raisins. There was nothing secretive about it; the loft had never, like the cellar, been forbidden to us. It was part of our day's routine, with its smells of cinnamon and buchu and salted fish and dried fruit, of wild sour-figs and tanned hides. That was why I couldn't understand it all, that day Lewies had gone to Hout Bay with his father and a stranger from Patria: towards four in the afternoon, coming from the mountainside where I'd been robbing birds' nests, I felt hungry, so I went up to the loft and took some raisins; and on my way down the ladder the Madam stopped me.

'What have you got there, Adam?'

'Raisins, Madam.' I showed them to her.

'Where did you get them?'

'Up there, Madam. In the loft, Madam.'

'Who gave you permission?'

'But, Madam!'

That was all I could say to him, too, when the men returned at sunset and she gave me up to them:

'But, Baas! But, Baas!'

'Won't one ever get this streak out of you people?' he said. 'Well, then you'll have to learn the hard way.'

I still didn't understand what was happening, not even when two slaves were called to spread me over the wooden wheelbarrow and tear the clothes off my body. I began to cry as the thongs round my wrists and ankles gnawed into my skin.

'But, Baas, I always went up there with Lewies for raisins!'

He turned round to Lewies who was still holding the horses. 'That true, Lewies?'

'It's a lie, Pa.'

That's what he said, my inseparable pal of the mountain stream and the wine-wagon and the calves behind the stone wall. *It's a lie.*

'You're still young, Adam, and you've got a lot to learn. So we'll make it only one pipe.'

And then he sat down on the bottom rung of the loft ladder and lit his pipe, watching detachedly while the two yard-slaves used the good hippo-hide sjamboks to cut my thighs and buttocks and my back with blow after blow, as neatly as if a knife had done it, causing the warm ticklish blood to run down my sides. Afterwards the Madam brought the small brown box to rub salt into the cuts, while I screamed and pissed into the wheelbarrow.

'But, Ma, it's him,' I sobbed that night, shivering with cold-fever on my heap of skins while she tended the wounds with gentle herbs. She wasn't crying, not she. She was as calm as always. 'It's Lewies who always took me up there with him, Ma. He never said I mustn't. And now he told the Baas I lied. It's not right, Ma!'

'How do we know what's right?' she said soothingly. 'Look at me. I was born a Hottentot, by rights I should be free. But the Honkhoikwa, the White men with smooth hair, they know better. It's them what decide, it's us what got to listen.'

'No, Ma!'

'You better listen, 'fore you got no skin left on your arse.'

'But I don't understand, Ma.'

'Who is us to understand? Quiet now, Aob. Shh. The Baas said you must start early in the morning.'

Aob. That was me. That is my name. The one she gave me, the one not known to anybody but her and me. Adam to the world – but Aob to us while her hands are soothing my body in the dark, Aob when she tells me about her people roaming free in the wilderness over the mountains, following their cattle and their fat-tailed sheep as the seasons come and go, stopping at the many stone graves of the great Hunter Heitsi-Eibib scattered across the land. And Aob here, now. But to her I said: Adam Mantoor.

And that was the day when, for the first time, I discovered the difference. There was one *I* for the Honkhoikwa; another secret *I* for myself and my mother: that name she brought with her from that nameless land across the many mountains.

'I can suck the poison of the snake out of you,' said the old woman who found me beside the anthill; spitting it out over my shoulder. 'That's easy. But there's nothing I can do about the poison of the Honkhoikwa.'

'Your eggs are ready,' he announces.

She is sitting on the wagon. Behind her, under the arched canvas roof, hangs the lantern; her face is as dark as his own. Stiffly, proudly she comes to fetch her plate at the fire, hesitating just as she is about to turn back.

'Listen,' she says. 'I didn't mean to . . . When I said . . . It's just that I don't know what's going to happen any more. I felt so sure we'd find him today.'

'Tell me about the Cape,' he interrupts her brusquely.

'What do you want to know about the Cape? Why do you ask?'

'That's what I've come for.'

'But there's nothing I can tell which you . . . It's so long ago we left, I can hardly remember. When I do think back it's of long ago, childhood things.'

'I want to know.'

She sits down. After a while she begins to speak, right past him, as if he isn't there at all. 'Sundays in the big church. Mother always wanted to get closer to the pulpit, but the seats were allocated in a fixed order. And then the Castle. We went to all the receptions. The streets filling up with people when the ships came in. Evenings on the stoep, before supper – the grown-ups with glasses of white wine with a touch of absinthe or aloe, my father sometimes allowed me to taste it. After supper, the women and girls together in one room, talking or playing games; and the men next door, or back to the stoep in summer, with the slaves taking them pipes and tobacco and arrack and *sopies*. I always tried to slip out to watch them and listen to them. Their great voices booming outside in talk or laughter, so much more interesting than the women with their dainty little coffee-cups and their Moselle with sugar or aqua seltzer.' She looks away, the way she did before when she forgot about his presence; as if she hasn't spoken for a long time and finds it impossible to control herself any more. 'Once there was a bullfight at the Castle, it was a Sunday afternoon. They partitioned off the courtyard and chased in a bull, an enormous animal, all black, with great shoulders and wild horns. I can still remember the muscles moving under its skin, it was like hares running. And how it snorted and kicked up the dust and stormed the partition with the sound of wood splintering and women shrieking. And then they chased in the dogs and they charged the bull. As soon as they grabbed him by the nose he would fling them into the air like old rags. But there were too many of them, they attacked him from all sides. His shoulders, his thighs, his belly, his tail, his nose, everything. The noise was quite deafening, all that barking and yelping and bellowing. Once he stumbled and fell down. Some of the dogs tore pieces of flesh out of him. It was terrible, and the people seemed to go mad. Then he got up again. His nose was all torn and bleeding. But he kept on swiping at them. Once or twice he caught a dog on his horns; their guts were wrapped around his head and there was blood pouring into his eyes. I wanted to leave, I simply couldn't bear to look any longer, I thought I'd be sick any moment. But my legs were too lame to carry me. I began to cry. They were all shouting and screaming so much that nobody even heard me. And when I looked again, after a long time, the bull was on the ground and they were fighting one another and tearing him to pieces. There was nothing left of his beautiful black skin and all those moving muscles, everything was covered with blood and sand and dung. I never knew dying could be so sordid. And so unnecessary. He'd been so powerful, his muscles had moved so. But in the end it was just a mess, that dung and sand and blood, nothing beautiful, nothing strong, just a horrible mess.' She has started crying. Her hands are grasping the plate so tightly that he is afraid it may break.

'Why did you tell me all this?' he asks, bewildered.

She shakes her head. Slowly she recovers, and blows her nose. For a long time she sits looking down at the food on her plate. You don't even know the worst, she thinks, depleted. This, that when we went home I was no longer feeling upset or depressed. There was a wonderful lightness inside me as if I'd resolved everything that had ever troubled me. I felt quite dizzy, like the few times my father had

31

offered me a sip of arrack. It was as if I'd been involved in something very beautiful.

Her eiderdown lies spread out on the grass. On it, one side held in position by jars of brandy containing lizards and a couple of small snakes, the other pressed down by her knees, she has opened the large map drawn by Erik Alexis Larsson – the map with its narrow segment of lines and signs and detailed inscriptions surrounded by a white expanse bearing only the tentative information suggested by Kolb and De la Caille and elephant hunters, and Hottentots bribed with copper or beads, brandy or a few lengths of chewing tobacco. This and this I know for sure, look, it is drawn and inscribed very precisely; there is no doubt at all about this river's course; that mountain range with all its foothills I have explored and noted; on these plains the summer rainfall is low. But the rest? There may be literally anything, Monomotapas, regions inhabited by white men with long smooth hair, fabulous animal kingdoms, gold, Africa.

'Come here!' she calls, and he approaches. She smoothens a crease on the map. 'Show me the way to the sea from here,' she says.

'The sea?' He turns back and motions with his arm, that way, very far, to the right of the morning sun.

'No, I want you to show me here,' she says impatiently. 'On the map.'

He kneels down opposite her, frowning, studying the map with suspicion and curiosity.

'This is where we are.' She points. 'Here is the curve of the sea. But what route are we going to follow, in which direction?'

He shakes his head, rises on his knees and repeats his gesture to the south-east.

'Haven't you seen a map before?'

He looks at her suspiciously, sullenly.

'This is the Cape,' she explains tensely. 'Here are the Hot Springs. Then Swellendam. These are the Outeniqua Mountains. This is the way we came. Now show me . . .'

'Why do you ask me?' he says fiercely. 'You call this your land?' He grabs the map and pulls it from under the jars; a couple are overturned and start leaking into the grass. He flings the map down again and spits on the ground. 'You can crumple it and throw it away. You think it makes any difference to the land out there?'

'Leave my map alone!' she says sharply, amazed by his sudden explosion, by the unexpectedness and the violence of it; shocked by it; threatened. But she will not be intimidated. She has never allowed it before, why should she now? Her father often said, and in spite of their occasional flare-ups he was closer to her than anyone else, 'I don't understand you at all, Elisabeth. You should have been a boy.' For she had that in her which others easily mistook for a sign of 'masculinity': nothing hard or angular, but a core of silence inside her, an untouchable quality behind her unassuming gentleness of manner; a fierce will to be left in peace and to preserve for herself what she regarded as her own.

Finding that silence threatened, she still refuses to yield.

'It's a waste of time to argue with you,' she says haughtily. 'You're an idiot.'

'All right!' he flares up again. 'So your map brought you here. Well, let it get you out of here too!'

Just because you can read a bloody map! Does that make me a slave? I don't carry a bit of paper around with me. My land I've seen with my eyes and heard with my ears and grasped with my hands. I eat it and drink it. I know it isn't something there – it's here. And what do you know about it?

'If I'm an idiot, then look after yourself.'

She bends down and, picking up the map, begins to roll it up carefully.

'I've managed all the way to this place,' she says after a while, her voice strained, 'with my husband.'

'He managed so well that he's now gone and lost himself.'

'He'll come back.'

'It's nearly a week already. For how long do you still plan to sit around here?'

'How can I leave if he doesn't come back? For the rest of my life I'll go on thinking that he may have returned and that I wasn't there to wait for him.'

'Is he so helpless without you?'

'I'm married to him.' He hasn't been expecting a reply; certainly not this reply, so quiet, with her head held high. He looks away from her. She is breathing deeply. *What happened between us, is of no concern. Whether we made a mistake or not, is of no concern. And it's irrelevant, too, whether I love him or despise him. But he is my husband. He is the father of my unborn child.*

'If you think it's been easy for me to wait here all this time . . .' she

33

says. Her tone has changed, but there is no self-pity in it. 'If you think it's been easy to trek through this country . . .'

He glances at her, but her eyes force him to turn away again and he goes to the wagon. Perhaps it has started for you too, now. One thinks one can escape this land, but sooner or later it catches up with you.

She follows him.

'What are you going to do?' she asks behind him, climbing on the wagon to put the map away. 'What do you want us to do?'

'I'm going on to my sea,' he says. 'I'm tired of waiting here. It's time for me to go, and I'm leaving in the morning. You can follow your map if you want to.' He looks up. 'Or you can come with me.'

'And suppose he returns tomorrow? Or next week?'

'You want to go on with that child inside you, or do you want to stay here waiting for a dead man?'

'He is not dead!'

With a shrug he takes a gun from the driver's seat, together with some powder and lead.

'Where are you going?' she challenges him.

'Find some meat.'

'Who gave you the right . . . ?'

Although he is conscious of desolate revolt in her as he leaves the shelter of branches, he doesn't look back. Leaving the cluster of wild figs behind, he goes down the first grassy slope, green after the recent rains, with red trenches gashed into the earth by the torrent. Farther down the bush grows denser. Following a game path among euphorbias and cycads, he wades through the stream at the bottom and tackles the opposite hill, knowing that there are usually game grazing on the ridge above. He feels oppressed. How is he going to get her and her child to his sea? Do you know how far it is to the Tsitsikama? And how are you going to reach the Cape from here? It is impossible for you to stay here, I know. But how will we trek from here? This is not what I was looking for when I came to your wagon. Surely not this. All I wanted was – what? How must I know? I only wanted to hear about the Cape. After all these years in the interior: animals and silences, stones and harsh shrubs, the occasional band of Hottentots. One learns to find one's way, to get along; and yet. Now I cannot leave you here at all. The shock of sadness with which I recognised, in you, the Cape I hate, still numbs me. How can I let it all slip away again?

Who, he wonders, is in whose hands? Who needs whom?

Now they must go on. Every time, in going on, there is something of the first venture. Gathering useful bits of wood on the island, in those stolen minutes between the breaking of stones, and gardening, and fishing; until there was enough for a small raft and oars. For months on end. Waiting for the moment – for occasionally there was relief from the chains and the foot-irons. It must have been a holiday, for they were given brandy and there was much reading from Scripture; and with the guard in a drunken stupor, the chains loosened, he managed to get away and hide in the shrubs for the few hours until dark. The sound of the waves, the grating of shingle on the beach; then the rhythmic liquid sigh of oars in the water, moving in the direction of the faint glimmering of light on the coast, the dark mass of the Mountain; the stars in the expanse of sky above. The wind was contrary, the sea abnormally rough. But it was his only chance. Soon the waves grew so unruly that he had to abandon the oars and cling to the raft so as not to be washed away, feeling the boards creak and part and clash together and suddenly break loose. Now he would have to swim, keeping one broken plank wedged under his chest. If only one could see the waves in time. He swallowed water, feeling himself grow heavy like a sodden sail; losing his sense of direction, going under, coughing, gasping. He wouldn't make it. His arms were numb with cold, his chest was burning. Simply to go on and on, in the watery imminence of death. But suddenly he was belched out on the shore. Perhaps it felt like this to be born. Crawling dumbly out of reach of the tide he lay shivering and twitching on the sand, a dying fish.

'Remember,' the Baas had said, 'you've been bred for this land.'

This you, land? Then hold me tight, I can't fight any more, the water is trying to steal me back.

And then, after the single night in the mountains, the stealthy return to the farm beyond; and the flight on horseback. For if daylight trapped him on the Cape Flats it would be the end.

I lift up mine eyes unto the hills, that's what they'd taught him as a child; for he'd been brought up with religion, oh yes, with Jesus Christ and Heitsi-Eibib and Grandmother Seli's tales of the Prophet all confused.

Hiding in the dense bush through the endless hours of the day. And then, on the third night, up the steep slopes of the mountains, leaving the exhausted horse behind.

From up there he could see the whole wide curve of False Bay in the moonlight, terrifyingly beautiful; and Table Mountain in the

35

distance. – My mountain, my bay. That's where I was born, that's where my mother lives and my grandmother lies buried. And the father I never knew? On the square in front of the Castle my grandfather was broken on the wheel, his name lives on. Mine, all mine, I can shut my eyes and recall it very clearly. Silver trees, flamingoes and vineyards; the bare plains; the white houses; I can smell the stench of the slave quarters in town, and the sour young wine of the farmyard; I can see the coaches driving past in a cloud of dust and dogs. For all this, said the Baas, I have been bred. Now I must thrust it from me like an old blanket riddled with fleas, redolent with the familiar stench of many years; one even learns to love one's itches. To start again beyond this range, to learn everything anew; this is a stone, this is a tree, there is a buck, there is a poisonous adder. My land, my desolate wilderness: now it's you and me.

Tomorrow they will set out to hunt me. They'll saddle their horses and call their dogs and polish their rifles and weigh off lead; and they'll hunt me like a jackal. For now I've become a wild beast, less than a wild beast: a fugitive thing. Cain, at least, my pious mother told me, had a mark on his forehead to protect him. My only marks are on my back, not for protection but for damnation. All right, then, hunt me: try to run me down; see if you can wear me out, see if you can reach me. From now on it's me and you. My Cape, I hate you for what you've done to me. I cannot live without you. Now I have to. For now I'm free. And this is what freedom really means: that anyone may kill me. –

The moment he sees the young buck appearing among the trees ahead of him he raises the rifle to his shoulder and aims for the neck. In his haste to reach the kicking animal he nearly treads on the beautifully spotted puff-adder baking among the warm stones; jumps aside instinctively reaching for a stone, and kills the thing; red blood on the golden skin. Then rolls his dead buck over, cuts open the belly with swift flicks of his knife, tears loose the guts and shakes out the inside blood before he swings the body across his shoulders.

The sound of the shot shocks through Elisabeth waiting at the wagon. For a moment she feels sick, unable to move. My God, so he's returned, he isn't dead after all! She hurries to the opening in the kraal and stops there, too dazed to go any farther. Several minutes drag by before she sees Adam appearing far down among the bushes, slightly stooped under the weight of the buck. It's only you, not him at all.

She sits down. From shock; from relief. She feels ashamed to admit

36

it to herself, but it's true. Unbearable relief that it isn't Erik Alexis Larsson coming up that slope.

'And this is Mr Larsson. My daughter Elisabeth. We've heard so much about you, we really couldn't wait to meet you.'

A large man with a full, neatly trimmed, reddish-blond beard; middle-aged, his skin surprisingly white – she'd expected him tanned – with almost feminine ruddy cheeks; large white hands with red hairs bristling on the fingers and clear, abstract, mildly surprised blue eyes.

He bowed briefly; she nodded. No one said anything. Her father kept on talking but they did not really pay attention; then her mother called him away to attend to other guests. There were people staring at them, young girls.

'Your father insisted on introducing me to you,' he said, uncomfortable. Perhaps he meant it to sound flippant, but it gave a different impression. 'I've been told you are an accomplished pianist?'

'All the girls in the Cape are accomplished pianists,' she said. 'They also sing. And dance. What else should they do to pass the time?'

'You make it sound rather awful.'

'The Cape is a very small place,' she said. 'It will soon bore you. But, of course, it needn't bother you – you can always go away again.'

'I have no intention of leaving very soon.'

'The girls will no doubt be pleased. Most strangers just come and go.'

He did not react. With an intensity she found surprising, and in the accent she could not but find charming, he said: 'You must realise the world is getting rather small for explorers like me. After the discovery of Peru there is very little that remains. It's really only Africa.'

'The Cape isn't Africa.'

'But one can start from here.'

She remained stubborn. 'It's not easy to get the Governor's permission for an inland journey.'

'You almost seem to blame me.'

'Why should I? I don't even know you. It's no concern of mine what you intend to do. But it's better to be prepared, isn't it? One gets entangled in many trifles here in the Cape, and people don't try to make it easier for you. The Lords Seventeen must give permission for every single thing. And they . . .' She shook her head angrily. 'They'd like to keep us here, confined between the mountains and the sea. I suppose they're scared of what would happen if we started moving inland. They may lose some of their authority. I can see you don't believe me, but it's true. And my father is one of their officials.'

'Why should you worry about the Lords Seventeen? You're well established here?'

'Oh, very well indeed!' she said viciously. 'It's a disease we'll all die from one day.'

'Have you never been away from here?'

'Yes, I spent a year in Holland, with my mother. We visited all her relations.' She was silent for a moment, then added cryptically, 'Holland isn't a very big place either.'

'But full of life!' he insisted. 'It's a gathering-place for all the world.'

'Of course I enjoyed it. The concerts, the parties. And Amsterdam is beautiful. But it's – it's all so different. They're my mother's people, not mine.' Smiling a bit more confidentially: 'Do you know what I enjoyed most of the whole journey? It was on our return, in the Bay of Biscay, when there was a terrible storm and everybody thought we were going under. They wouldn't allow me on deck, but I went and I stayed there, clinging to the railings and getting drenched. It felt like the end of the world, it was wild and beautiful.'

'You seem to be yearning for an apocalypse.'

She left him for a moment, returning with a bowl of fruit. 'I'm neglecting my duty towards a guest,' she said with formal courtesy. 'Try one of the small red figs. They're delicious. Specially brought from Robben Island. My mother gets her cauliflower from the island, too, you'll taste it later tonight, no doubt. And, for special occasions, we order our water from there. It's supposed to be the sweetest in the Cape. You see, everything that's good here comes from elsewhere.'

He scrutinised her for a long time without saying anything, his blue eyes distant.

'Well?' she challenged him with sudden violence. 'Will I merit a paragraph in your diary?'

'Pardon?' he asked, shaking his head as if he had just awakened.

'You've been staring at me so intently.'

'Please forgive me,' he said, fumbling. 'I'm not really used to conversing with young ladies.'

'Don't feel obliged to waste your time in my company.'

'No, please, that's not what I meant at all,' he objected, with a touch of consternation. 'I think I'm boring *you*. I'm so clumsy. I'm more used to landscapes than to people.'

It was his silence, she thought, his stern reserve, which had prompted this rebellion in her, to force him to react, to reveal some of his secrets, this man containing a world enclosed in himself which he refused to share with her Cape; explorations and nights, beacons, mountains, high seas, aborigines, animals, exotic landscapes.

'Don't you think people are landscapes too to be explored?' she asked defiantly.

'You make it sound like a challenge,' he replied.

'On the contrary, Mr Larsson,' she said coolly. 'I'm only a very small bit of land in between the mountains and the sea.'

Accompanying him, a week later, in a hired coach on the winding road beyond the Mountain to Constantia, the landscape unfolding below them in valleys and marshes, she watched him intently: how his eyes took in every trifle, how a touch of excitement caused his cheeks to burn: exactly like this he must have travelled through other countries, through regions never explored before; and she felt an urge to break open that something in him so that she, too, might see it and experience it and know what it meant to have this fever inside one.

Round a bend in the road just beyond the town a large pack of baboons scattered before their coach; the dogs accompanying them burst into frenzied barking, giving chase up the slope towards the cliffs.

'Today they're scared of us,' she said, amused. 'But the last time I came this way there was one old male that broke away from the rest and tried to attack me on my horse. It took some hard galloping to get away from him.' She laughed and pushed back her hair.

'Do you come here often?'

'I try to. Although my mother doesn't approve, of course.'

'Isn't it dangerous?'

'I suppose it is. There are still leopards in the Mountain. And vagrants and runaway criminals hiding in the bushes. But if one really had to consider everything that might happen, you would never leave your house at all. And it's very beautiful round this next bend, you'll see.'

Below them, as they came round the Mountain, there were large flocks of flamingoes scattered across all the shallow pools of the marshland; one flock, frightened by the noise of the coach, took to the sky, exposing the brilliant pink of their outstretched wings.

'You see?' she said, ecstatic. 'To me this is the most beautiful sight of the whole Cape.'

'*Phoenicopterus ruber*,' he remarked pensively. 'They belong to the same group as the cranes, the *grallae*.'

39

She turned her head sharply, but he had no more to say. The road sloped down towards a sandy plain.

'In winter one can't get through here at all,' she told him. 'The road is under water then. If you're still around this coming winter, you must come and see.'

Gradually the patches of wild flowers on either side expanded, more and more luxuriant, until there seemed to be no end to them; large fields of heather dotted with proteas. Some of them he pointed out to her – *ixia* and *melanthia, monsonia, wachendorfia* – names she had never heard before; once he ordered the driver to stop so that he could collect others strange to him. Returning to the coach, he held an enormous bunch of them up to her, with a sudden smile which made him look much younger than usual.

'Thank you,' she said, delighted and surprised, taking the flowers. 'They're lovely.'

But as soon as he resumed his seat beside her, he took back the flowers. She realised that she had misunderstood his gesture, and bit on her lip, embarrassed and annoyed.

'I'll press them as soon as we arrive,' he explained. 'To think that not one of them has been named yet.'

'How do you find names for them all?' she asked, not without a hint of sarcasm.

'I only name them provisionally,' he said. 'Later I dispatch them to Sweden. I have a friend there, Carl, who is working on a system for naming all the plants in the world.'

'And what happens once you've systematised them all?'

'Wherever I go, I collect plants for him,' he continued, without listening to her. 'In the Amazon, in Surinam, in New Zealand, everywhere I've been.' For the first time there was undisguised enthusiasm in his voice. 'Sometimes one is completely overwhelmed by a new place, you feel quite helpless because there is so much all around you; you would like to take it all with you, you wish it were possible to gather it all up inside you. It's as if your eyes and ears simply cannot cope with it all. But then you set to work, naming things, trying not to look too far ahead but to concentrate on one thing at a time. And suddenly it's all done, and you discover that it no longer overwhelms you. Now you can handle it, it belongs to you. Nothing can take it from you again, even if you are miles and oceans and hemispheres away. Now you possess a small portion of the earth.' He carefully hid his bunch of flowers under his seat. 'You see? I'm assembling a portion of Africa too to take away with me one day. Something of this vast continent which will be my own.'

For a moment he was not strange to her any more; for a moment she understood his silence and his aloofness, responding to it with something she had recognised in herself. He was no longer a reserved foreigner rebuffing people with his stern reticence, no longer a traveller in a Cape coach, but a man intimately acquainted with worlds which, to her, existed only in the music of their names: Guyana and Surinam, the Amazon, Pernambuco, Tierra del Fuego, New Zealand, Fiji; names like gods or prayers. It stirred up a thirst inside her which left her breathless. And suddenly, illogically, she wanted to beg him: Here I am, explore me. Don't you see? I am a prisoner here.

'I'm going to marry Erik Alexis Larsson,' she announced to her parents, months later. 'He has asked me to wait until he comes back from his journey into the interior, but I told him I preferred to get married first and go with him.'

'Do you think it's wise?' Marcus Louw enquired cautiously.

'It's completely out of the question!' said her mother. 'I've never heard of such madness.'

'Well, I'm going to,' said Elisabeth.

'Use your authority, Marcus,' Catharina ordered. 'What will our friends think of it? A woman in the interior!'

'What's wrong with a woman in the interior?' asked Elisabeth angrily. 'What's wrong with a woman anyway? Is it something to be ashamed of? You make it sound like a crime to be born a woman. If a man can go on an expedition, why shouldn't I?'

'You will bring shame on us if you do this. In my family . . .'

'When you married me and decided to settle in the Cape,' Marcus reminded her quietly, 'your family also wanted to deny you. Have you forgotten how you used to be just like Elisabeth? Never satisfied, quite untamed.'

'And what came of it?' she asked, resentful, complaining. 'Married to a man with no ambition. Two children in the grave, my two sons who would have made all the difference. Bruised by this land, broken by it. But you refused to budge. There have been many times you could have had a transfer to Batavia or to Patria, but oh no: Marcus Louw was born here and he'll die here. So how can one expect Elisabeth to be any different? But this time you're going to put your foot down!'

'When my mother fled from France,' he said, 'it was no use anyone

41

trying to put a foot down.' Passion, of which he so seldom gave evidence, burnt in the network of tiny purple veins covering his cheeks.

'That was different,' said Catharina. 'She had no choice, the Huguenots were persecuted. But nothing forces Elisabeth to go away from here. Why on earth should *she* flee into the wilderness?'

'One doesn't have many options staying here,' said Elisabeth with quiet fury. 'You can either die or go mad, that's all. Neither appeals to me.'

'There is no need to be insulting,' her mother said sharply. 'Madness or death! What else awaits you among the savages and the wild beasts in the wilderness?' Her tone changed back to sulky complaint. 'It's all right for a man to go in search of adventure. Even so I should have thought Larsson was old enough to know better. It's the younger ones who must get something out of their system. But you, Elisabeth: you're used to a decent way of life, you're held in esteem, you're an example to others.'

'You make it sound as if I'm descending into hell. It's only the interior. Mother, can't you understand I can no longer bear it here?'

'You have more than enough to occupy yourself with.'

'Oh yes! I attend every party and every ball and every picnic. It helps to pass the time. But for how long am I supposed to go on like this? Until I've caught a decent man and can start breeding in a decent way?'

'Mind your language. Marcus, say something!'

'My father rebelled against his Governor,' he said, looking down at his glass.

'To his everlasting shame, yes!'

He banged down his glass. 'Perhaps it is to *my* everlasting shame that I crawled back to the service of the Company against which he rebelled. It was such a safe haven. It offered security to my whole family.'

'Are you also planning to go on an expedition?' Catharina sneered.

'No, I'm too old for that. But if she wants to go, it's for her to decide. If she really loves the man.' He looked at her with anguished, piercing eyes.

Elisabeth bowed her head. After a long time she looked up at him again. 'I've made up my mind. I want to get married and go with him.'

'That's gratitude for you,' said her mother. 'But if that's the way it has to be, at least we'll make it a wedding the Cape will never forget. But then we'll have to wait for the next fleet.'

'How far do you plan to go?' asked her father when, later that evening, the two of them were alone, playing chess in the drawing room, his glass of arrack beside the board.

'As far as possible,' she replied. 'It's impossible to predict. He is trying to plot a route, but he can't find a reliable map anywhere and everybody comes with different information. He's now heard about a Mr Roloff at Muizenberg . . .'

'I hope it works out.' He gulped down some arrack and sighed. 'Are you sure you're doing the right thing, my girl? Do you really love him so much?'

'I'll go with him as far as he wants to go, Father.'

And from here she will go on alone. It was no rational decision at all: it simply happened inside her when, after she'd heard the shot, she saw Adam coming through the bushes at the bottom of the hill. And now there is no turning back.

'What are you doing?' he asks as he drops the buck on the ground and squats down to start skinning it. She is busy on the wagon; feverish activity.

'If we are to leave for the sea tomorrow I'd better start sorting and packing now.'

His eyes narrow, watching her. She goes on working, too urgently, perhaps.

One box of clothes can stay behind untouched. Unless Adam can find a use for some of it? But she refrains from asking him, afraid that he may say yes; and she prefers not to open the box at all. The second box contains her own things. On the long journey here she used to change twice or even three times a day, what with all that dust and heat. There were enough Hottentots around to do the washing; and since they deserted the trek, she has been able to cope herself. Even before leaving the Cape she had to select her clothes with such care, there was so little space. What will she do now, with only two oxen left to carry everything?

Having skinned the buck and salted the strips of meat, Adam comes to the wagon to watch her work. It's easy for him, she thinks; there's nothing personal involved. To him it's a simple matter of going on.

'What's this?'

'His journals.'

He pages through the heavy leather-bound books, uncomprehending; then throws them aside.

'No, they must come with us,' she orders apologetically. 'I must take them back to the Cape.'

He sneers. Under his silent, defiant eyes she feels unsettled. If only there were something she could send him to do, to be rid of him; but she knows beforehand that he won't obey. It is as if he has taken over momentarily, a quiet supervising master. Resentful, she goes on sorting her belongings, refusing to look at him.

All right, so the journals will go along. That is her small victory. But there is no room for the innumerable stuffed birds, and the dried flowers – provisionally named until they could be sent to Sweden. Even their arms and ammunition must be severely restricted: two blunderbusses, a single pistol; a small quantity of powder and shot and lead. One jug of brandy for comfort in case of illness, or to buy help or friendship along the road; a small roll of tobacco; blankets. Tea and flour and sugar, salt, and what has remained of the chocolate. Most of the rest is luxury, even the beautifully hand-embroidered trousseau sheets, the iron curlers, and the pressing irons, the cologne. There may be room for one bucket, for a kettle, a pan, a minimum of cutlery; it's already too much.

Now sort it through again, he orders; throw out some more. And gradually a passion of destruction is kindled inside her, to discard, to strip herself, to rid herself of possessions. What are one's needs: what is the utter minimum one truly requires? After all, he arrived here with nothing whatsoever, except for the clothes stolen from her husband.

All the rejected stuff she repacks, with unnecessary care, in the boxes on the wagon, tidying everything meticulously to prevent its destruction by the wind should another storm break out: but the canvas of the wagon is torn already, and what about animals, what about marauding robbers?

Now that she has reached this point, she wants to free herself from everything that has kept her here, retaining nothing. To be virginal to any adventure which may lie ahead: anything; everything.

But afterwards, once Adam has moved out of sight, she reopens the boxes and begins to take out things again, adding them to the bundle of indispensables: cotton and needles, soap, and the cologne, her dark green dress – to wear when she arrives back home, one needs something decent.

Adam has selected the speckled ox for loading, tying it to a tree, the thong fastened to a short stick through the animal's nose to keep it still; and at the first signs of daylight streaking up from the mountains

44

he places two large hides across the back of the ox and begins to pack all their belongings on these. Elisabeth gives him a hand to fold up the flaps – a few more things have to be discarded, dear God - so that he can secure them. The thongs are tied under the animal's belly, so tight that they cut deep folds into the skin.

'Doesn't it hurt?' she asks.

'It's an ox.'

They have a final meal. Then Adam puts out the fire and tramples sand over it, as if that is necessary.

'Will you manage?' he asks, leading the second ox to where she can get on its back.

'Of course.' She looks him in the eyes.

'You sure you'll be all right?'

'I won't fall off if that is what you're thinking.'

He takes the rein of the pack-ox and tugs at it. She digs her heels into the ribs of the animal carrying her. They move through the opening in the tattered fence.

Now she has to clench her teeth, too overcome with emotion to look back.

He's gone. He isn't dead, he has simply disappeared. The land he wanted to explore and possess has devoured him. I'm free of him now. But there is still the child. For his sake I must get back to the Cape.

The ox has an uneasy movement, much clumsier than a horse. But I suppose one will get used to it. One gets used to everything. Or doesn't one? Does one keep on resisting? One of these days you will begin to stir inside me. We have no choice: we shall have to get used to each other's rhythms and space, you to mine, I to yours; and both of us to that of the ox and the land.

Down the slope and up the opposite hill.

'Are you sure you know the way?'

'Yes.'

'How long will it take us to the sea?'

'Long.'

He stops briefly to look back. And now she turns her head too. Faint among the wild figs opposite is the greyish white stain of the wagon's roof. There are birds overhead. She can see them flickering among the leaves. Are they sugar-birds, weaver-birds, finches? She doesn't know their names, and suddenly wishes she had paid more attention.

She shifts into a more comfortable position, and as they move

45

on sees the camp growing smaller and smaller behind them. Now it seems like a final haven her heart clings to. There is so much one has to leave behind, she thinks; hope, above all. For ahead there are only the billowing shapes of hills and mountain ranges, on and on.

Adam looks back, looks at her. He wants to speak to her. There is so much to say, to ask. To touch her, to penetrate her silence, to break into her. But all he can say, when at last he dares to speak is, 'Tell me about the Cape again.'

The town itself is the only one in the whole colony and is properly called the Cape, though this name is often injudiciously given to the whole settlement. The above-mentioned town is situated in an amphitheatre bounded at the back part by Table Mountain (*Tafelberg*), to the westward by Lion Mountain (*Leeuweberg*), and towards the east, in some measure, by Devil's Mountain (*Duyvelsberg*), so that it is most open towards the southern and eastern sides, facing Table Bay. According to the latest measurement the shore of this bay is 550 *toises* above the surface of the sea, and 1344 *toises* in length, when taken from east to west; the middlemost part of it being situated south-east of the town and 2000 *toises* from it. The hills surrounding the town are in great measure bare and that part of Table Mountain that looks toward it is pretty steep. The bushes and trees (if they may be so called), which here and there grow wild, are stunted partly by their own nature, and partly by the south-east and north-west winds. Hence they often look dried up, with pale blighted leaves, and on the whole have a miserable appearance. Some of them, sheltered by the cliffs, and at the same time watered by the rills that run down the sides of the Mountain, may perhaps be somewhat more healthy and vigorous; but they are universally deficient in that lively verdure which adorns the oaks, vines, myrtles, laurels and lemon-trees planted at the bottom near the town. Still farther on the dry heathy lands and sandy plains on the strand contribute to give the country an arid and barren look. It must be owned, indeed, that a considerable quantity of the most beautiful African flowers are scattered up and down in different parts during the fine season of the year; and the verdant plantations, together with a few acres of arable land lying round the town, make a striking appearance, opposed to the African wilds and deserts with which they are surrounded. To the nature lover the real surprise lies in travelling from town past the

Devil's Mountain towards Constantia, where one's pleasure in discovering so rich a collection of unknown, curious, and beautiful vernal flowers, in so unfrequented a part of the world, is easier to be conceived than described: divers *ixias, gladioluses, moreas, hyacinths, cyphias, melanthias, albucas, oxalises, asperugos, geraniums, monsonias, arctotises, calendulas, wachendorfias* and *arctopuses,* in addition to fields overgrown with a great many different sorts of heath and other shrubs and bushes, with some small trees of the *protea* kind. The entrance to the town, from the Castle on the shore, surrounded by its high walls and deep ditches, offers a superb view. To one side lie the Company's gardens; to the other, the fountains fed by water running from Table Mountain down a ravine or kloof visible from town. This is the source from which all the inhabitants draw their water-supply; and from the same source the batteries are daily supplied by a two-wheeled water cart. The gardens are 200 *toises* broad and 500 long, and consist of various quarters planted with kale, and other kinds of garden stuff, for the Governor's own table, as well as for the use of the Dutch ships and of the hospital. Fruit-trees are planted in some of the quarters, which, in order to shelter them from the violence of the south-east wind, are surrounded with hedges of myrtle and elm. Besides this, the greater walks are ornamented with oaks thirty feet high, which by their shade produce an agreeable coolness, and are much resorted to by the strangers that visit the port, and choose to walk in the heat of the day. At the end of the pleasure-garden and to the east of it, is the menagerie, palisaded and railed off, in which are shown *ostriches, casuaries, zebras,* and sometimes different sorts of *antilopes,* and other smaller quadrupeds. The town itself is very regularly built and quite small, about 1000 *toises* in length and breadth, including the gardens and orchards, by which one side of it is terminated. The streets, cutting the quarters at right angles, are broad, but not paved, this being unnecessary owing to the hard nature of the soil. Many of them are planted with oaks. None of the streets have names, excepting the Heerengracht, which runs alongside the large plain opposite the Castle. The houses, mostly uniform in style, are handsome and spacious, two storeys high at the most; the greater part of them are stuccoed and white-washed on the outside, but some of them are painted green: this latter colour being the favourite colour with the Dutch. A number of the best houses have been built from a peculiar sort of blue stone hewn by prisoners from the quarries of Robben Island. A great part of their houses are covered with a sort of dark-coloured reed (*Restio tectorum*) which grows in dry and sandy places. It is somewhat more firm than straw, but rather finer and more brittle. The popularity of this thatching in the Cape must be ascribed to an effort to avoid the grave accidents which may result from heavier roofing being ripped off by the notorious 'Black South-easter' winds raging in this region.

'Is that me?' Kneeling on the rock she leans over her reflection against a background of trees and drifting clouds. She has taken off her shoes. The pistol lies on the flat rock beside her, with the bundle of clean clothes. Shallow and still and clear the long pool lies in the narrow stream, but there is a barely perceptible trembling on the surface disturbing the reflection. Tense and surprised, she stares at the image looking back at her: Don't you recognise me then? the face seems familiar, but . . .

It's only three days they have been trekking now. Is it possible that one can become a stranger to oneself so soon? On the wagon, on that long journey, there was enough time every day, more than enough, for arranging her hair in front of the mirror, for attending to herself. Back home in the large house: the mirrors surrounding her, everywhere, even, on her insistence, in the bathroom: why not, if one's only function was being beautiful? Her mother would have been satisfied with the way she kept it up during the voyage: even in the wilderness one can retain one's dignity.

She has brought the small hand-mirror with her, but these past three days she's been too tired to use it at night, too busy in the morning preparing for the new day's trek. A plodding pace, but exhausting enough. Her body aches. Sometimes she can feel her stomach contracting in small cramps, perspiration breaking out on her face. She has maintained her nightly ablutions, of course, even if it meant that Adam had to lug the bucket of water for a mile or more – with that arrogant sneer on his face which frightens and infuriates her, and makes her powerless. But washing herself like that, hidden behind bushes, has been a furtive and perfunctory affair, simply to cool off and to rid herself of the worst grime of the day, no more, however passionate in her the urge for abundant water. (The mulberry stains, the stripes along my legs.)

This afternoon she felt too tired to go on. He probably noticed it, although he didn't say a word; and when they reached this stream he stopped to outspan. She could feel the resentment in him. He has the sea in him now – the sea! – like her. But she can't go on like this. Now he has gone in search of wood to make a fire and build a shelter for the night. She watched him walk off with his thongs, far across the next row of hills; and then she came down here - 'For God's sake keep the pistol with you!' – where she could guess the secret water. Knelt down on the broad flat rock, pressing her face in cupped hands brimful of water. Now she looks down at herself, into her own eyes, an obscurer blue than usual, but that may be due to the water. Moist hair clinging to her face; dust on her temples, in spite of that first immersion; thin lines of mud running down her cheeks. Are her cheekbones more angular, has she lost weight?

'Is that me?' she hears her own voice asking, strangely wondering. 'And if it's me – who am I?'

For it suddenly strikes her, like panic: that she should be here, she. In the Cape, on the social rounds inspired by her mother, she was well known – it was all one small, gossipy family – and instantly recognised at parties or balls: over there in the mustard dress, that's Elisabeth, you know, the daughter of the Company's keeper of stores; her mother is from Batavia. And on their journey: the wife of the white explorer. Now, quite suddenly, there is no one in terms of whom she can be recognised. No one, only herself, here at the water; in this space through which the late birds fly. What am I doing here? Who is this I who looks like this? She peers at the reflection, fumbling with her fichu: the delicate white lace is red with moist clinging dust; the stiff edges of her white cuffs, attached to the amber sleeves with bows at the elbows, are drooping and dirty. She wants to deny herself; she refuses to look like this. She is too pale, and from lack of sleep last night there are shadows under her eyes. She tries to rub them off with water, but in vain.

Impulsively she gets up and goes back up the hill to make quite sure. There is indeed no sign of him. He's gone far away, it should take an hour or more before he brings the wood. She is completely alone. It hits her in the pit of her stomach in a luxurious onrush of anguish. In the past, whenever he went away, the camp remained around her, the wagon a familiar tortoise shell. Even the day following Larsson's disappearance her isolation was not as complete as this, for she was expecting him to turn up at any moment: and previously, on their journey, there had always been somebody in the vicinity. After all, one couldn't leave a woman alone in the bush.

Returning to the water where, thoughtlessly, she has left the pistol with her shoes and the neat clean bundle of clothes, she looks down at herself once more, now standing, farther removed from her face, separated from it by the crumpled folds of her dress.

Her feet are dirty. She lifts the dress to her knees and wades into the water, cool round her calves; soft squelchy mud stirring under her soles and slithering between her toes. Her fear subsides, changes. She allows the hem of the dress to drop down into the water, feeling its slow sogging weight tug at her. She is alone. Undoing her fichu, she remains standing for a moment, her hands covering the *décolleté* of her dress in numb and sensual guilt. Then, with hurried determination, she unfastens the ribbons of her bodice and pushes the dress down over her hips into the water, allowing it to drift round her knees in a wet mass, sinking slowly. She steps out of the petticoats, freeing herself with small deliberate kicks. The clothes remain motionless on the shallow muddy bed, unaffected by the gentle movement of the water. She wades in deeper, feeling the greedy caressing coolness reach up over her knees and the sensitive insides of her thighs, past her hips and the gentle curve of her belly, until it reaches her breasts. In sudden exultation she dives in. Emerging again, feeling the heaviness of her wet dark hair, she swims across. Only after a long time does she return to the rock to fetch the soap and wash herself, then immerses herself once more in the voluptuous innocence of the water.

She has no desire to get dressed again; the day is still warm in the late sun. On the flat rock glowing with inner warmth she stretches out, her body pressed against the burning stone, cleansed and glistening wet, strangely moved, and moaning with urgent passion; turning on her back and tense, with knees drawn up, touching herself, caressing herself, opening, moistening, heaving, assuaging the violence of her need, swaying her head from side to side, bringing herself to ecstasy, hearing her own voice crying out, subsiding into silence with a final sob.

After a very long time she rises and, astride on the edge of the rock, surveys her reflection once again with brooding wonder. The face with its burning eyes, the small breasts rather fuller than they used to be, the nipples tender to the touch of her fingertips and the aureoles slightly – just slightly – darker; the gentle beginning of a belly swelling, the small tight angle of love-hair above the swollen suture of her still distended sex: all these things which are she and which she hasn't studied so intently for months, all of it suddenly inexplicable:

50

beautiful, strange, vaguely terrifying. Are these the contours of myself? And if something changes, if my breasts should swell and my belly bulge, my hands grow thinner, if my sex should ripen like a fruit, or my ribs become more visible: will it make any difference to that self, does it expand or shrink accordingly? Where does it reside, that elusive I? Above me, unquestioning, unanswerable, the sky, the white clouds slowly drifting, and the sun; around me stones and red earth, grass and tangled brushwood.

Subdued, she kneels and reaches for the sodden clothes; but leaning far forward to grasp them from the water, she catches a glimpse of a movement on the far side of the pool and stops, petrified. Sick with shock, she is too scared to look immediately: but when she finally manages to lift her head – thin droplets running from her hair and moving like a shudder down her shoulders and her back – it is only a *duiker*, a small doe with long wide ears and enormous eyes, staring back at her, quite motionless. There is something in the silence of that gaze which strips her more naked than the removal of her clothes has done, exposing her in her total vulnerability, moving her so deeply that she wants to cry. On long, delicate legs the doe stands motionless, reflected in the water, surrounded by the bush: and it is as if, in those great black eyes, earth and water, sky and world are all transformed into primordial, guileless staring. Amongst the trees of the garden I hid myself because I was naked.

Unable to do anything else, she raises her hands to cover her breasts, and the wet dress plunges back into the water.

Instantly – a single sweep of movement, a flickering of light – the little doe turns round and disappears. Gone, as if it has never been there at all.

With practical haste Elisabeth gets up, puts on the clean clothes she has brought with her, tying up ribbons, fastening hooks. The broad lace cuffs covering her forearms irritate her. She tears them loose and flings them away. With great care she tucks the dress in round her legs and kneels down to finish her washing.

He is gathering wood. The long collarless jacket hangs from a branch, tattered by thorns; the waistcoat was discarded on the very first day of their trek. Wearing only the pants and the dirty white shirt with its elaborate lacework, he piles up the branches he has gathered. The smooth hills of the past few days have risen slowly to a final sharp ridge with scaly cliffs close by. Below, the slope is almost bare of vegetation, the grass yellower than before, a different climate; further on it fans open into gently ribbed plains more even than the country they have passed through so far. Two more days – three, perhaps, with her – to the Hottentot village where he sometimes stops over. He has meant to go much farther today, down this long slope at the very least; but she tires more easily than he has expected. She probably won't admit anything herself, but he noticed the pale circle round her mouth and, after last night, sleepless in the drizzle, in the dark patches under her eyes. Now they're camped beyond the ridge, up there, near the stream.

Tonight they'll need less shelter than in last night's rain, when everything had to be unpacked so that they could cover themselves and their most precious possessions, the ammunition and her books, with the skins. Even so they were drenched. Three days now. It's different from the time they spent in the camp among the wild figs: they are more closely together day and night, separated only by the fire when it's dark. And she must be aware of him watching her.

– I'm watching you. This is our first night on trek; it is, indeed, something of a first night. I'm watching you, and I want you. With all the accumulated frustrated lust in me I'm aching for you, I want to grab you and feel you against my body, invade your silence. All I have to do is to stretch my arm across the fire and touch you. Are you asleep, or merely pretending? Are you aware of me? Dare you be aware?

So why don't I? Is it because of the child in you? But why should that deter me? Your body is still light, there's barely a hint of swelling. Would anyone have spared my mother for the sake of the child in her womb? –

My white master of the past, appointed by God: to him the world lay open and the law was silent. He had his wife, he had access to all that was white – but also to us, quite freely. All those trips on the wine-wagon to the Cape. We used to finish off-loading early in the afternoon, then hang around the taverns – I waiting on the wagon – until sunset, the dark time when the white men were allowed into the women's quarters in the slave lodge. To improve the quality of the local slaves, they explained. A necessary service. Half an hour; then the watchman with his lantern made the rounds, time gentlemen, and locked up for the night.

Don't ask so many questions, my mother said. Don't ask. At peace with the world in her dumb, serene way. She never bothered to understand, why should she? Her people had all died in the Great Sickness – if she had to die as well, let it be so – and only the handful of children were brought back by the hunters, and booked in, and taught about the Lord-thy-God of the House of Bondage, meekly resigning themselves to it all. Sitting quietly against the kitchen wall puffing at her pipe, that frail body with the bird-like wrists and ankles, a girl, a waif, it seemed in passing. But a mother: mine. Wrinkles covering her face from early adulthood. My people age easily, it's like a dam drying up, mud cracking. But Heitsi-Eibib always rises again on the dusty plains, she assured me: you'll live again. Praise the Lord.

You must be taking after your grandmother, she said. Your father's folk. It's always them landing in trouble for being so unruly. For talking and wondering and asking too many questions. That's why. What's the use of questions, hey? No peace of mind, that's for sure. We're all under the same yoke, accept it. It's only when you grow too old to be useful, like your Grandmother Seli, that you're freed to die. Until that day comes God and the Baas will provide for me.

Seli, my Grandmother Seli, tell me your stories, I want to know where I come from.

On the slopes of Padang, she said, one finds the touch-me-not, shrub upon shrub as far as the eye can see. You touch one slender leaf, and the shudder spreads across that whole wide slope, curling up all the myriads of trembling leaves. Don't let them touch you, my boy. You close yourself up tight. Remember your Grandfather Afrika: now that's a man in our eyes. Didn't utter a sound when they tore the flesh from his body with the red-hot tongs. Didn't bat an eyelid when they broke his bones on the wheel. I took him water that night – he didn't want anything to eat – and the sun was out before he died. Don't worry, he told me that night. He found it difficult to speak by then, but he never groaned once. Don't worry about the pain. There's only one thing that counts, and that is not to give in. Never to give in to them. You got to go on.

Let them hurt me now, he said. That's even better. You see, if you want to hurt a man you must know he's there. You can't hurt a man who's not there. In dying I become a man.

And do bring some wood from the mountain when you go up again, said Grandmother Seli. The days are getting cold, and I'm not so young any more. Is it tomorrow you going up?

Yes, I said, it's tomorrow I'm going up for wood. I'll bring you some, don't worry.

But in the early morning the Baas stopped me. Don't bother about the wood today, he said, I need you on the wine-wagon. Someone else can go for wood.

Was it my fault she died the next day, frozen to death in her windy shack on the Lion's Rump?

It was exactly two days later I heard my mother singing in the dry vineyard where she was pruning with the other slaves. 'Rock of Ages cleft for me', like the white people had taught her.

– Thou shalt not, thou shalt not: and opposite those dull red coals she's pretending to be asleep. She's woman, though she's white. Who knows but that she's burning for it too? So what restrains me? It's only her and me in this wide world, no one will know or care: does a tree care if a bird's nest falls from it? Does wood care if it burns?

Or is it the very fact that we're alone, that there's nothing beyond her I can violate? There's nothing I can avenge myself on. Only silence. And her closed eyes. And, if I listen breathlessly, her quiet breathing.

How can she be so peaceful? Is it because she knows I'm keeping watch against the beasts? Because she knows I'm taking her to the sea? *How* does she know? Because she believes me, because she has no choice but to believe me? Because she's wholly in my hands?

I can take your body and force it and break it, I can tear a scream from it: a scream of life like that other scream of death. But even so you'll be untouchable. Your eyes. Somewhere inside your body, beyond my reach, you have secured yourself in your whiteness. Perhaps I hate you too much. –

Then I took her smooth dark body in the dark, surrounded by the breathing of all those others, animals or moving hills. Her sea-smell. And the warm milk-bushes of the beach. I love you; I love you. And her gentle open palms on my shoulders after the grasp of her nails has slackened, the movement of her cheek against my neck. What is it that makes it happen? Body into body, that's easy, and quick, and done. But *this*: you and I, world without end? And less than a month later the Baas sold her. Good price, 400 rixdollars. Of course, she was very young.

He drags the bundles of wood back to where the oxen are grazing, and begins to construct a rough shelter of branches. Inside, a small hollow cleared for the fire. They still have salted half-dried strips of meat. While he is working, she approaches from the stream in her fresh blue dress, her hair still damp, and spreads the washing on her shrubs.

'Still tired?' he asks, in spite of himself.

'Not really. I had a swim.' He looks at her. And she goes on talking, trying to hide her embarrassment at the memory, her consciousness of him. 'There was a little doe, I suppose it came to drink. It gave me such a fright. At first I thought it was a lion or something.'

'You've been travelling for months. Aren't you used to the land yet?'

'Does one ever get used to it? He was always there to protect me.' She always refers to him as 'he'.

'You should have stayed in the Cape.'

She shakes her head with suppressed violence.

He starts breaking firewood. 'Then you wouldn't have been here now. In a shelter like this. You must be used to something rather different.'

She shrugs.

'What did your house look like?' he asks, as if he hopes to force a secret out of her.

'Why do you want to know?' She sits down on a fallen trunk. 'Thatched roof. White walls. A large garden.'

'Big house?'

'Two storeys. Yes, it was big.'

'You had your own room.'

'Of course.'

'Of course!'

'Why do you always ask about the Cape?' she demands suspiciously.

'What else is there to talk about?'

'But you never seem to be satisfied. What on earth could I tell you which would interest you?'

'You're scared to tell me anything. You want to keep it all to yourself. You think I'm a slave.'

'You *are* a slave.'

'Not here.'

'How can a place make any difference to what you are?'

'I was kept as a slave. I never *was* a slave,' he says, smouldering.

'And then you ran away?'

He shrugs.

'Why did you run away? You always question me. I've also got a right to know.'

'Who gave you that right?' He looks at her in rage. She feels an urge to cover her breasts with her hands again, as she did when the buck gazed at her, but she is too afraid.

55

'All right,' he relents, unexpectedly. 'I'll tell you.' As he breaks a branch on a large stone a splinter cuts into his palm and he curses. 'My master was a wine farmer, you see. In Hottentot's Holland. Made a lot of brandy too. He used to say it was the best in the Cape. He drank so much of it himself, one might well believe him. Whenever he was in a stupor he forgot to lock up the barrel. So I helped myself too. My people are made like that. In the end I decided it was better to run off, before the temptation killed me.'

Her pale cheeks are flushed with anger. But she controls herself for a long time, looking down at her hands in her lap, before she says: 'It's all lies.'

'Oh no, it's the honest truth.'

'You're a liar!'

'Of course I'm a liar,' he says quietly, deliberately, looking into her face. 'You're not expecting to hear the truth.'

'Why shouldn't I?' she asks, humiliated, on the defence.

'You're too white for the truth.'

He looks at her. She looks back. He can see her clench her teeth, lifting her head slightly, with that old haughty fierceness in her eyes. Then, still sitting as she does, with her knees pulled up and her arms folded round them, she drops her head on her elbows and shuts him out. He cannot make out whether she does it to confirm her independence or because she has to hide a sudden girlish weakness. Do not tempt me, he thinks: do not provoke me. You're white, and I am brown of my own brownness. Do not let me think you're no more than a woman. Do not plunge us both into the abyss.

And, standing there opposite her, she sitting on her stone, rounded and complete, they both, simultaneously, become aware of the silence as all sound stops. Not the gentle, gradual ebbing away of sound in the dusk, but an abrupt shock of silence imposed upon the world as if the birds and the beetles, the insects in the tall grass, even the leaves in the trees, have suddenly been clamped in an invisible, enormous hand. She looks up.

'What's happened?' she asks. 'Why is it so quiet?'

'Something has died,' he says. 'That's the way it happens. Everything goes quiet all of a sudden; and then you know.'

They found him on the afternoon of the second day, on the far side of the long plain, where the foothills of the next range began. Since early morning, emerging from their shelter for the night, they'd been watching the vultures, the almost invisible specks drifting on the highest currents of the wind and slowly spiralling downwards among the hills. No more than three or four to start with. Then, appearing from nowhere, another ten or twelve; until the sky was black with them.

On this side the plain was much more densely overgrown than before. The earth was dry, with bare parched patches in the shallow gravel ditches eroded by the wind, and clusters of dry branches blown in among the brushwood. Yet, from a distance, it appeared luxuriant, for the gnarled, thorny shrubs were green from the moisture sucked up from very deep down: white-thorn and tanglewood, hedgehog euphorbia and naboom, aloes, kiepersol and karee and cross-berries, assegai wood, the pale blue of plumbago. An indestructible wild, fierce landscape, its thickets so dense that, every now and then, the oxen found it impossible to force a passage and had to make wide detours in search of game paths and half-hidden trails. If it hadn't been for the vultures they would never have discovered the body at all.

As it was, they had to swerve far off their course to reach it. Yet neither of them even considered the possibility of not going. Even from ten yards away there was nothing to be seen, except for the vultures covering the ground and the thorn-trees, some of them with wings half-spread, the hideous bare necks stretched forward, the yellow eyes eager and evil. Reluctantly they flapped out of the way as the intruders approached; a couple even dared to follow them with ridiculous little flopping hops, cowardly aggressive. But in the end they all retreated to more distant trees.

He was lying under a shelter of branches. The first they noticed was the pathetic gaiety of small torn patches of clothing fluttering from the dead branches and the long white thorns – next, the black three-cornered hat, its proud plume broken and dishevelled.

'Stay here,' said Adam.

But she slid off the back of the ox and followed him.

A sudden squawk made them stop in their tracks. Two of the vultures had trapped themselves under the branches covering the body and were trying to break out with a thrashing of wings and claws, their beaks and throats and breast-feathers stained and slimy with blood.

Feeling death approach, he must have covered himself with the branches he'd gathered days before. If he hadn't done that, in his

57

efficient, calculating, Swedish way, there wouldn't have been anything left for them to see.

It was still not a wholesome sight. Most of the face had been torn away; the long maroon overcoat was torn to shreds, some of the shining steel buttons missing; the waistcoat with its gold embroidery was tattered, leaving part of the chest exposed, a couple of ribs horribly protruding through the mangled flesh.

Elisabeth forced herself past Adam. He tried to ward her off, but there was something in her attitude as she took his arm and pushed him aside which made him yield.

'I must see it,' she said quietly.

The Hottentots had deserted them; the cattle had been stolen; Van Zyl had shot himself and had been buried without really involving or concerning her. But this one was hers, this one she dared not avoid. This was what they'd travelled through the hinterland for; for this she had given up the Cape to come with him.

In spite of the stench she went closer and began to pull the branches out of the way. There was a sudden flurry among the surrounding vultures, as if, for a moment, they all meant to charge and converge on her, but Adam noisily scared them off. Farther back, the oxen were stamping and sniffing anxiously.

Strange, all she could think of was the lion hunt. How he'd hit the female with his first shot, stopping her for a second before she resumed her charge with a shattered shoulder. The Hottentots screaming, dropping their guns, fleeing in all directions. You dropping on one knee to take aim. The sickening dead click of the flint. And then, in a brownish, yellowish, roaring streak, the lioness jumped on you and hurled you to the ground. But in mid-jump there was the sudden report from a Hottentot's gun. And as the beast came down on you, Booi was beside you to grapple with it and pull it away. The great jaws locking on his shoulder and upper arm. Now it's all over, I thought. But the lion was already dead, and while Booi rolled aside and went on screaming, the animal remained motionless on top of you. After a long time you began to move under it, crawling out. You looked in my direction but your eyes were blank. Suddenly you started running, away from me, towards the nearest tree, a mere sapling. Like a baboon you scrambled up that bare, slender trunk, but the moment you reached the top, it suddenly bent over and deposited you back on the ground. You didn't even seem to be aware of it. You simply started climbing again. The same thing happened. Three times you climbed the sapling, and three times it bent over and dropped you back on the ground. Only then did you stop to look round, discovering that the lioness had been dead all the while.

Erik Alexis Larsson: Who are you? This disgusting, bleeding, tattered thing cannot be you. Who were you, calculating latitudes and longitudes and heights above sea level so precisely, stuffing birds with such consumate skill, naming all the plants and animals of the wilderness? Who were you and how did you get here? Tell me, I want to know, I am your wife. I have a right to know, I'm bearing your child. I want to know. My God, can't you say something?

Adam remained a short distance away from her, among the branches she'd scattered to reach the body. Here it begins, he thought, feeling the sun beating down on him. Here you will start learning too. Knowledge of death, that's the inevitable start. The day the snake bit me and the old woman sucked out the poison, rubbing in herbs, reviving me. And then that other time when I was dying of thirst on the cracked bed of the dried-up river, mirages dancing in my eyes: the old Bushman with his hollow reed, sucking water from the *gorreh* where there hadn't been anything; spitting it out on my tongue and into my mouth. 'You could have died here, right on top of this water. Why don't you keep your eyes open? What are you doing here? If you can't look after yourself, you must stay away from here.' Muddy water in my throat; the taste of life.

'You can't stay here,' said Adam.

For the first time it seemed to penetrate her consciousness. She got up quickly from where she was sitting beside the body, and hurried away, and quite suddenly began to vomit, pursued by the sweet stench wherever she went. Her stomach continued to contract, retching wildly, drily, long after it had emptied itself on the hard ground.

'We must do something,' she whispered at last, deathly pale and numb with cold in the heat, stumbling back towards the oxen and leaning her head against the load.

'What can we do?'

'We can't leave him there like that.'

Impulsively he said: 'You want to bury him in a ditch like a Hottentot?'

'I don't want the hyenas to get at him.'

'They've already been at him,' he said with deliberate cruelty.

'Oh my God, can't you do *something*?'

59

'The ground is too hard and we have nothing to dig with. We can cover him with stones and branches. But it'll only keep them off for a while.'

'Well, cover him then. The sun is so hot.'

This time she didn't follow him. She sat beside the oxen, in their meagre shade, watching him struggle with huge stones and heavy branches; from time to time she shooed off the protesting vultures half-heartedly. They would flutter off into the sky, but in the end they always came back. For them there was no need to be impatient.

Once again her stomach started heaving and she bent over to retch, but nothing came out. For a moment she was blinded by pain. Then the convulsions eased and she sat up again and watched him pile up the burial mound.

There is always a first night. After the feast – after the dancing and the meal at the long table: hams and partridges and venison, hares, fish pie, suckling pigs with mouths agape round yellow oranges; slaves rushing this way and that, soundless on their bare feet, serving Bordeaux and cool Moselle, nothing indigenous – after the feast we retired to our rooms, the guests still carousing downstairs. You apologised and went to the small salon to finish some work. I don't know what it was, I didn't ask, probably notes or calculations of some sort, something, sitting under the lamp. You briefly kissed me on the cheek and said: 'Perhaps Mrs Larsson should go to bed, I'll still be occupied for some time.' I wanted to sit with you and watch you work, but I was afraid to be a nuisance. Mother sent up two slave girls to undress me. Poor things, they'd been awake since five in the morning and it was already past midnight, with no prospect of going to bed soon. As they undressed me and loosened my hair and washed me, I closed my eyes, trying to pretend to myself it was you caressing me. I thought, deliberately: My bridegroom. But it sounded silly. And after they'd left I took off the long white nightdress with its lace frills and embroidery, and lay down naked, waiting for you. The day was breaking before you entered.

'I thought you'd be asleep.' You sounded surprised, almost annoyed.

'I've been waiting for you.'

I turned away so that you could undress without embarrassment, but all the time I was watching you in the little side-mirror: how large and white your body was, how strong, shaped by lands and voyages, and I tried to imagine how you would hurt me and cause me to bleed. I wanted to bleed, mulberry blood for you, for my own sake too: to know what it meant to be a woman, to be transformed into a person by you. You climbed in beside me, and kissed me, then turned round and were asleep instantly. And when you took me the next night that was precisely what it was: you *took* me, and used me, and then it was done. It wasn't even painful, with barely a show of blood.

'Is that all?' I asked.

'What?'

'Is that all – just this?'

'I don't understand you.'

'I don't either.'

And then you slept again. Not I.

Now I would wish to ask again: 'Is that all?' But once again you give no answer. Is that all? This pointless, ridiculous, sordid little bundle of rags on the plain – like a bird that has fallen and rotted, its feathers scattered by the wind? It's nothing at all.

Or everything? I know now: it is not the death of a man that is terrible. That is commonplace. What is terrible, is the death of everything you have believed in, everything you've hoped for, everything you thought you loved.

Rest in peace, Erik Alexis Larsson. There is always a first night.

That night, among the hills where they have made their little camp, her cramps grow worse.

All the way from where they'd found the body, until late afternoon, they went on without speaking. He glanced at her from time to time, but she didn't even seem aware of his presence, moving through the world like a piece of driftwood on a dam, unconscious of her own motion. The light was startingly clear: no haziness on the horizon, no mystery in the kloofs among the hills: each object defined in light, revealed in light, stone as stone, and tree as tree.

She was conscious of pain all the way, like the previous days, a constant companion, almost trusted by now; but nothing particularly bad. Since they halted for the night, it has become more definite, individual aches outlined like the trees or stones in the landscape; but she bit on her teeth and said nothing. But now, in the dark, for the first time, it has grown so bad that she cannot suppress a groan.

Adam wakes up immediately.

'What's the matter?'

'Nothing.'

'I heard you.'

Through clenched teeth she utters another groan. 'Oh, God, if only I were back in the Cape. Somebody would have known what to do.'

'What's wrong?'

'It's here.' Holding her belly, rubbing it slowly, pressing down. A secret tremor seems to start again inside, throbbing outwards, like the shudder of an earthquake. But she feels no urge to vomit like before. This time she knows, almost biologically, that her body is trying to rid itself of part of her, of the child.

Perhaps, if I lie very still, it will go away.

'Bring me the brandy.'

He hands it to her and she swallows a mouthful.

'We'll reach the Hottentot village tomorrow,' he says. 'Do you think you can hold out till then? They'll know what to do. We'd have got there today if it hadn't been for . . .'

She gulps down some more brandy. 'What difference will the Hottentots make? They're useless. Just a filthy lot.'

He doesn't answer.

But after a time – the stars have moved across the nearest hill with its grotesque silhouettes of aloes and dead tree-stumps – she begins to sway her head to and fro on the hard ground where she is lying, both hands pressed against her stomach, contracted with pain.

'Do you really think the Hottentots can help me?'

'They'll know more than I do.'

'How far is it?'

'Not too far.' He gets up to fetch the oxen. 'It won't be easy in the dark, but we can try.'

An hour later she nearly slips from her ox. He notices it just in time to catch her. She has lost consciousness. Only then does panic strike him.

Clumsily he forces some more brandy between her teeth and helps her to mount the ox again.

'Hold tight. I'll walk here beside you. It's not so far now.' His voice sounds pleading.

She groans again. The brandy has slightly dazed her but it is also nauseating.

Now she is no longer conscious of separate events. There is only the uneven hobbling of the ox swaying under her; the pain pressing down on her until she's breathless, then lets go; sweat on her face; branches tearing past when they do pass too closely; an occasional curse or muttered comment from Adam. Slowly it is getting light, a greenish dull glow in the east; sunrise; then, suddenly, dogs barking, cattle lowing; voices, people.

She is too befuddled to take any notice of the settlement. It is a village of some thirty or forty circular huts scattered round a palisaded cattle kraal in the centre; to one side, isolated from the rest by a clump of trees, a few more huts reserved – which she won't know, of course – for the sick, and for unclean women. Amidst the bleating goats and yapping mongrels, people approach, excited and half-asleep: young girls with beads and skin aprons; old women with caps and long cloaks and painted faces; half-naked young men wearing beads round their necks, brief aprons over their buttocks, jackal tails in front; shrivelled old men huddled in goatskin *karosses*.

They recognise Adam. He speaks to them, pointing at her. In a curious throng they surround her, all talking at the same time and trying to touch her. Then some of the old women chase off the others with loud imprecations, haul her from the ox – she is drawn up in pain, smelling the pungency of the rancid fat and buchu covering their bodies – and carry her off to one of the huts beyond the trees. Inside it has been severely swept, the earth is hard and smooth, a single reed-mat spread over it. Lying down she looks up at the simple pattern of plaited slats and folded cowhides covering the framework of the hut; overhead is a vent, revealing a bright segment of sky. She feels another spasm gripping her, but they're holding her arms and legs. Some of them force her to sit up, tugging at her clothes. She tries to help them unfasten and undress her, feels all clothing peeled from her; lies down again, trembling with cold fever. Someone lifts her head and presses her mouth against the edge of a calabash. She is overwhelmed by the strong smell of herbs, but cannot move her head. Strange hands cover her naked perspiring body with animal skins. Fierce spasms shake her. She can no longer control her body. Until it subsides; until everything is torn from her, bleeding, and the women bring water to wash her, to cover her up again and leave her, dimly conscious of birds chattering in the trees and slowly drifting into sleep, wishing she would die.

Where sleep ends and consciousness begins again, she cannot tell. In front of the hut, or among the trees near by, someone is blowing a monotonous tune on the long stiff feather of a *ghoera*, and the low sad tone intrudes upon her dreams. Sometimes there are shadows shuffling in or out. There is an ancient woman watching patiently at her side, a cap of zebra skin covering the bird-like skull, the shrivelled face cracked like the spiderweb patterns on a dry river bed, the breasts elongated and narrow like two old empty bags with a fistful of mealies in the bottom of each; puffing away quietly on her long pipe, emitting small clouds of bitter-sweet hash-smoke. Thin and distant, dogs are barking, goats bleating, children crying or laughing, sounds from another, remote existence.

'Drink,' says the old woman, holding a skin bag to her mouth. She is sickened by the smell, the sweet and sour of curds and honey; but too exhausted to resist she acquiesces dumbly. Cool and thick it slithers down her throat. But her stomach revolts. There is a fire burning in her guts.

The worst should have been over by now, but it seems to be only a beginning. They're trying to poison me, she thinks. Because I'm a stranger, and they don't trust me: I'm white. But why don't you choose stronger poison, why didn't you kill me swiftly and effectively? Can I help it that I'm white?

Too white for the truth. Those were his words. How does he know? A slave! He thinks lies and deceit are good enough for me. Does one really trek all this way in search of a lie? It's always different from what one expects. Don't torture me any more. You and the likes of you are stretched out on the rack in front of the Castle: it's clear-cut and easy for you. There are other forms of suffering, unending. But perhaps it leads to the same end for all of us. Ultimately we're all broken. It's this land: my mother knew it long before me. She should know, she has buried two children. Her two sons. And I remained, the girl, the lesser, the least, the not-a-son, the not-what-I-wanted. A woman in the interior, have you ever heard of such madness? She, too, was once young and undaunted; she too thought she'd conquer the world. That's what he said. She gave up everything she had, her family, Batavia, comfort, class, to marry a man from the Cape. Leaving France to settle among savages; but free. To cling to you, one flesh. Is that all? I can do it better with my own hand! Now strike me with madness if you wish. Poor young Van Zyl, he desired me. That, suddenly, made you jealous and aggressive: now he's dead. Now we're all dead. Except for old Uncle Jacobs in the Cape, he may still be waiting. 'Just grow up nicely, my child. If no one else wants you, your old uncle will look after you.' Playing chess with Father under the mulberry trees, for hours on end. 'Let me teach you, Elisabeth, we'll give your Pa a thrashing.' Touching, when no one sees, the inside of my thigh under the dress; fingers stroking upward, furtively. Poor old Uncle Jacobs, who caused me to lie awake at night, sinful and shaking with fear – now I'm missing even you. There's no sin left here: God hasn't come all the way with us. Somewhere along the road, I presume, he turned back to the Cape. The bleak new church, the house parties, the slaves serving almonds and figs: the sweetest ones, the purply red ones, are brought from Robben Island. Do try them, Mr Larsson. And the sweetest water is drawn from the prisoners' well. Strange, if you think about it: to find sweet water if you dig a hole on an island. Why not salt, with all that sea around? I was there once, remember, with my father. It's the best view, by far, of the Mountain. I almost envied the prisoners.

One has the same view entering the bay from Patria. A mountain like a psalm, I shall abide under the shadow of the Almighty. Provided you stay this side of the Hottentot's Holland range, it's so much safer. For a woman. Never to be able to do what you really want, because you're a woman; never to be allowed to become what you desire, because you're a woman. Like those dwarf-trees imported by the Governor. They too, I'm sure, would have wanted to grow tall and broad for nests and birds, giving shade to people and animals below: but they're forced to remain small and stunted, hideous little pretty trees for useless ornaments on window-sills or overmantels. But this once I refuse to obey them, I shall break free. This once I'll trek into my own wilderness.

So in the end I really was nothing but a curious little mammal to be noted in your diary. You must have had some satisfaction finding a name for me. Naming, you said, didn't you, was your way of possessing a part of the earth.

You thought I was a barrel or a wagon or a cow you could possess? Two wagons, five boxes, two frying pans, sixteen guns, nine Hottentots, one woman. How many rixdollars does that amount to? And will the Company ever compensate you for the loss? They're so damned stingy, sir.

Perhaps it would have been easier to be possessed after all. A possession needn't worry about eating or drinking, about tomorrow, or happiness, or love, or faith. Even a slave is given all he requires, food and stripes at the appointed times. So why couldn't I yield myself? What is there in me which refuses to be possessed by another? Here in this wilderness without end, I am alone. Even if I have to die: no rest in peace; unmourned. Just a heap of stones on the plain. Sooner or later the jackals and hyenas will dig you out and devour whatever can be torn off you.

A skeleton is what one should be allowed to be, clean and bare, bones. Discovering it in the veld you can't even tell whether it was man or woman. It's pure bone-being; human thing. No wonder Eve was created from a rib. There's more bone to us, we are more indestructible. He is all bloody, dust unto dust. Who possesses whom? You the earth, or the earth you? *Phoenicopterus ruber*, a species of *grallae*, if I remember well: I've never had – how did you put it? – a faculty for scientific understanding.

The old woman returns with curds and with *ghom*, squatting beside her and mumbling words Elisabeth does not understand: *tkhoe, kamgon, tao-b, gomma*. Passive, she listens, unable to grasp what is happening. When, once, she dares to speak, the old woman only laughs, baring her toothless gums, and goes away. Behind her, in the doorway, stands the tall shadow of a man. He remains for a while. But when she tries to push herself up on her elbows, she finds he's gone.

You, dark man, death or life: who and what are *you*? You with the terrible truth of your lies, you who have bedecked yourself, lean and strong, with my husband's outlandish clothes – what are you doing here with me? Why do I fear you? I used to order the slaves in our house without reflecting on it; when I bathed in the mountain stream, the slaves kept watch. I wouldn't even have minded if they'd seen me without clothes; the dogs and cats of the household staring.

I'm afraid of you. All right, in this darkness I'm prepared to admit it. The only way to control you is to command you. To be the white Cape woman whom I loathe. Fear is more imperative than one's little dignity. But why should I fear you? I'm not afraid that you'll violate me – you've had more than enough opportunity for doing that, it's too obvious, too ridiculously easy. What else? That you dare look at me without averting your eyes when I look back? That you're so silent? But not with the impertinence of a slave who can be flogged to teach him his rightful place. *What* is your place? Have you any place – or do you come and go like the wind?

You said we were going to the sea, 'your' sea, and I'm following meekly. Obeying like a dog, forced back into womanness. Why don't you abandon me? Why don't you let me die peacefully on my own? Let me be, I'm tired. I do not want to think any more.

When she opens her eyes again the old woman is back in the hut with her. It takes some time before she realises that her nurse is wearing one of her dresses, the yellow one. It's obvious that she didn't know how to put it on, so she resolved the problem by tying it round her waist with an ox-tail.

'It's mine,' complains Elisabeth. 'Mine. Give it to me.'

The old woman grins with glee.

She tries to sit up and take it back; she begins to cry. You have no right to take everything from me. But a new attack of fever sweeps through her, shaking her body; followed by a coldness which makes her teeth chatter. The old crone goes out, returning with a couple of younger helpers who pile up some twigs and branches on the floor and set them alight with a glowing stick brought in by another attendant. The sudden bright flame of paper burning. Smoke fills the hut and swirls round the women, obscuring them.

Paper? Once again she raises herself and crawls closer, rescuing a crumpled piece from the fire, peering at it with painful eyes. It's a fragment of the map.

They cannot understand what she is saying and reply by laughing uproariously and nodding with great conviction. The old woman mutters something which sounds like *kom-hi* and *kz'oa*; then they all file out again, Elisabeth remains behind, restored to silence, her eyes tearful of smoke.

If I can crawl up to the fire I may be able to set the hut alight. It should burn easily. Then it will be all over. I can't go on. This must be the end, they can't do this to me.

But she doesn't move. She is too tired even to make an effort. And frightened; and cowardly.

The little old man with his watery red eyes and heavy spectacles, in his shack assembled from bits of wreckage on the beach. Old Mr Roloff and his innumerable maps under the yellow lamp. But we're not allowed to take one with us: we'll have to draw our own as we go on, mile after painstaking mile. A yellow lantern swinging through my days. You sit there entering details on your map, compiling the catalogue of the completed day, writing in your journal. *Elisabeth very demanding last night.* You didn't know I was reading it behind your back, did you? Women are such treacherous creatures: to this you have degraded me. And for that, I think, I can't forgive you.

Swinging, swinging, slowly. Is it the motion of the wagon which causes it to move like that, or the turning of the earth? Watch out, it's buckling, it may throw us off. Turn down the flame, it's smoking, I'm choking, one can't go on like this. Why doesn't he come to help me? He's gone off long ago, of course. I was a burden to him, that's all, on his way to the sea. He must have arrived there by now. Perhaps he has discarded my husband's stupid clothes, wandering naked on the beach, brown among the brown rocks, diving into the water. If he looks up, there'll be a buck staring at him. He'll recognise the little doe with her enormous eyes: the long hair, tender breasts, the swollen belly. And he'll wade out, not caring about the doe watching him; large and strong, and stiff as a bull. Then they'll set their dogs on the bull. He'll toss them up, sending them flying like dirty rags. But in the end, in the end they'll get him. They'll grab him by the nose and pull him down and tear him to pieces while he's still alive. One is always betrayed.

They're dancing outside, it must be dark. Is there a moon? She can hear the clapping of their hands, their feet stamping on the ground; the *ghoera* and the wailing flutes; through her throbbing head reverberates the beat of *tkoi-tkoi* and of sticks. In Amsterdam there was chamber music, clavichord, and the great booming of the organ in the Zuiderkerk; and carillons. The controlled ecstasy of the modern composers, Mr Bach in Germany; the Italians Vivaldi and Scarlatti. *This* is civilisation, says Mother, contented and with great conviction; for the first time since I've known her she has no ailment. *This* is civilisation, it's as predictably beautiful as the gables of Amsterdam – oh, those frolicking red children in the snow, like Breughel – it's proper and tidy, like Steen and Vermeer. I don't like Rembrandt so much, she says, he's too dark, too brooding, it makes one feel uneasy. Oh, Elisabeth, if you had any regard for your mother, you would marry a good Dutch merchant and settle here.

Let's go to the gypsy woman in the Kalverstraat, they say she knows everything. She merely glances at your palm before she translates: a dark man – a son – a long voyage.

Forget about that long voyage. Why return to the godforsaken Cape? But it's not godforsaken, Mother, it's very religious. No allocated seat in the Groote Kerk is ever empty on a Sunday; even a bullfight is opened with a prayer. It's only beyond those mountains that the heathen world begins, banished into oblivion.

Last night I dreamt I saw God. Then I dreamt he spoke to me. And then I dreamt I was dreaming. Did I accuse him of taking away my child? I'm sorry, I was quite wrong. (Forgive me, I'm only a woman. You made me one.) He had nothing at all to do with it. He simply withdrew himself. It's not a cruel land, just apathetic. It takes from you what is redundant: wagon and oxen, guide and husband and child, camp and shelter, conversation, help, imagined security, preparation and presumption, clothes. Whittling you down to yourself. I'm tired. Let me sleep.

When she wakes up her head feels cleared for the first time; and he is standing in the doorway. In her sleep she has thrown off the animal skins; now she hastily pulls them up to her chin again.

'What do you want?' she asks, on her guard.

'Are you still ill?'

'I thought you'd gone off to the sea already.'

'I came every day,' he says. 'But you were all confused. I thought you were going to die.'

'It would have saved you a lot of trouble, wouldn't it? I didn't mean to be such a nuisance.'

He shrugs, withdrawn into silence.

'For how long have I been here?'

'A fortnight.'

'I'm still to weak to ride an ox.'

'Get well first.'

'Why don't you go to the sea on your own?' she asks in weary protest. 'If you run into people, you can tell them I'm waiting here.'

'You don't even understand the language,' he says impatiently.

She lies still for a while. Then, complaining: 'They stole my clothes.'

'No. They were only curious to see what you had. I gave them a few things you don't need.'

'The map!'

He grins derisively, but says nothing.

After a time he asks: 'Is there anything you need?'

She shakes her head.

'Then I must go. They don't like men visiting a sick woman.'

Much later the old crone returns. For the first time Elisabeth willingly accepts the curds and honey. The old woman clicks with satisfaction and goes out with the calabash, her empty dugs swinging. And the next morning a number of young girls come round to wash her and clean the hut. They chatter and laugh without a moment's rest, but she doesn't understand a word.

'Bring my clothes,' she orders at last.

The girls giggle uncomprehendingly.

'Clothes,' says Elisabeth, louder and more deliberately, but they still do not understand. Irritable, she sits up and makes explaining gestures to her body: I want to cover myself, I'm naked, bring me . . .

It causes great mirth among them, and they laugh and whisper together before one girl is sent out with a great amount of nudging and gesticulation. After a while she returns with Hottentot clothing.

'I want my own!' demands Elisabeth angrily.

But they only laugh at her and manage to pull her to her feet. For a moment she tries to resist; then, tired by the effort, she resigns herself to whatever they want to do to her. Soon, in fact, she begins to be affected by their glee, smiling back at them, almost relieved by their silliness after all these days of illness and isolation. With a curious voluptuousness, as if she were back in her own room in the Cape surrounded by mirrors and slaves, she abandons herself to their hands. Of what concern are they to her? They're servile and comical, tying a few strings of beads round her neck and her waist, and rushes round her knees, fitting a copper ring round one ankle.

The young girl who has brought the clothes and taken the lead laughs with uncontrollable joy, her magnificent white teeth sparkling. She's very young, quite lovely, with the small firm breasts of bare nubility. Once, without warning, impish and impudent, she puts out a hand and touches Elisabeth's pubic hair, pointing, laughing. Elisabeth frowns, not understanding, defensive.

Unexpectedly, while the others collapse in smothered laughter, the girl removes her own minuscule pinafore and takes up position directly in front of Elisabeth, her legs widespread, her young pointed hips thrust forward, forcing her to look at the peculiarly elongated inner lips protruding from her almost hairless cleft and hanging down in long pink lobes, like the wattles of a turkey.

Surprised by the girl's unabashedness and her own frank curiosity, for one brief moment woman confronting woman in total innocence, Elisabeth stares at the girl. Look: this is me. This is the most intimate thing of myself I can show you. It's sweet and funny, isn't it? What about yourself? Once again the girl puts out her hand to touch her mound. Immediately the spell is broken, the frankness gone. Blushing, Elisabeth turns her head away as if she is the one to be ashamed, experiencing again something of the gaze of the small doe. Hurriedly, almost in anger, she undoes the beads and rushes and removes the copper ring, and hands them back.

'I want my own clothes,' she demands. 'Bring me my dress.'

Still they fail to understand; giggling and whispering and nudging one another, their small breasts bobbing, glistening with grease.

'My dress.' She explains with emphatic gestures.

They confer with their backs to her, glancing over their shoulders, controlling their mirth. At long last some of them leave the hut, returning, soon after, much to her amazement, with the dress she

70

wore when she arrived: crumpled, but obviously washed and dried in the sun. With a haste she herself finds inexplicable she grabs it from their hands and puts it on, ties up the bodice and arranges the fichu. The girls watch her, now silent with curiosity, before thronging out back into the sun. She tries to comb her matted hair with her fingers. But soon she finds the effort too much and lies down again, half propped up against the back wall so that she can look out through the oval doorway, past the cluster of trees to the distant darting movements of children and goats in the village.

I'm recovering, she thinks. I thought I would die, but I am recovering. At home, if Mother felt dizzy, there was always someone at hand to sponge her temples with vinegar water or to offer her sel de corne de cerf. But here there hasn't been anything apart from the revolting stuff in the old hag's calabash. And yet I'm recovering. I'll be able to go on. I, alone. For the child has died.

The night the Bushmen came. The first they knew about it was when the dogs began to bark, and the wailing yelp when an arrow struck one. The cattle milling round in consternation, the Hottentots cursing and jostling each other in their scramble to hide under the wagons. *Sonkwas! Sonkwas! Sonkwas! Sonkwas! Koetsri! Koetsri!*

Larsson fired a shot into the air. By that time the cattle had already stampeded into the dark, surrounded by the Bushmen, with their shrill calls, like birds of prey. In the confusion he grabbed a gun and jumped on a horse to gallop after the marauders, accompanied by the two Hottentot foremen, Kaptein and Booi, the latter still with his arm swathed in heavy bandages. Their shots thundered in the night; the sounds of the cattle grew silent. After an hour or more the men returned. The Bushmen had disappeared; but they'd managed to save ten of the oxen. The trek could still go on.

Lying on the bed in the wagon she heard them coming back, but felt too sick to get up, a nausea which caused the wagon to revolve round her. The yellow lantern ducked and swerved. It had overcome her several times during the previous week: she'd ascribed it to something she'd eaten, or to bad water. But that night, in the midst of all the excitement, the terror, the din of the raid, the shots and galloping hooves, she realised in stunned silence: it was a child she had inside her; that was why.

And now they've burnt or buried it; or covered it with stones, like him. Two sons she buried. That was what broke her. But I didn't break. Try me, test me. I shall not yield. I refuse to give this barren

71

land my body. I'll cherish my fertility, it's mine. Let the earth keep its barrenness to itself.

He sits watching her. She's busy with those damned journals again. She must be doing it deliberately to affirm her superiority. What would happen if he were to get up here and pluck them from her hands and destroy them? How often has he felt the urge to do just that. Swallowing, just as often, his rage in dull resentment. Why? Poor creature: don't you think I can see how lost you are, hiding so desperately behind your heavy books? She is inside the shelter, while he is keeping an eye on the oxen as they graze. He has brought them up from the river a little while ago; soon he will tie them up inside the narrow kraal. He doesn't feel at all easy about the lions. The bastards have been trailing them all day long and found no game to distract them. It was quite early in the morning when he noticed them for the first time as they were crossing a hill; in the afternoon he could hear their low, patient growls in the distance from time to time. He hasn't said anything to her. She's still weak. And who knows, there may be game down at the river tonight. The lions are bound to go there first. In that case there won't be any danger.

She goes on writing. But from time to time she looks in his direction. Is she writing about me? he wonders resentfully. The Baas used to have books like those: punishment books; wages books; wine books. That was the first she asked for when, still unsteady on her feet, she left the sick-hut in her long blue dress and came to him, escorted by the women: 'Where are my things? Where are the books?' He showed her. He'd distributed the brandy and tobacco among the people, and one of the guns and some ammunition; also a few of her dresses. The map, of course, had been used to make fire. But the books were intact, no one had shown the slightest interest in them.

During the long days of her convalescence she paged through them interminably, reading, or simply leafing aimlessly. He was watching her then as he does now. Was she looking for something? What was there in the books to disappoint her, or shock her, or surprise or anger or excite her as they so obviously did? What dark secret did they enclose? The everlasting damnation of the words of God?

'My husband wrote down everything,' she explained when finally he dared to ask. 'About our journey.'

'Everything?'

72

To his surprise, she blushed, then said, slightly flustered: 'Well, everything that seemed important to him.'

'Why do you keep them? They're heavy.'

'You won't understand.'

After a few days she started writing in them too. He was still watching her. She always appeared selfconscious about it, glancing up at him every now and then. Or staring in front of her, thinking.

She remained dreadfully pale, her skin an almost translucent white. After washing her hair several times, she'd taken to plaiting it to keep it tidy, causing her to look several years younger, a mere girl. It troubled him; it made him aggressive. He didn't want to be saddled with her like that. What would he do if something happened to her? But, which was worse: what would he do if nothing happened? If she simply stayed with him like that, vulnerably young, girlish and dependent, attainable, yet at the same time so independent and aloof, protected by her Capeness and her books?

Then why didn't he simply leave her? Why waste those precious days waiting for her to regain some strength? He could have reached the sea by now. All these years his coming and going depended on no one but himself: that was how he'd come to define his freedom. Yet he'd approached her wagon of his own free will when he'd seen her stranded in the wilderness. How could he have known what would come of it? On the other hand, how could he remain bound to what he'd done so impulsively, that first day? (First day? And impulsively? For how long had it been shaping inside him? For how long had he hesitated, following the wagon, weighing his liberty against his loneliness?)

The moon waned, then waxed again – the Heitsi-Eibib of his mother's talks dying and reviving – and although she grew stronger, she remained pale, detached and listless, as if being alive didn't matter so much after all. Only on rare occasions did he notice a feverish glow on her cheeks again, usually when she was working on the journals; and once when twins were born in the village and the men took the girl – the other baby was a boy – wrapped in skins, to expose her on the veld. Elisabeth didn't immediately grasp what was happening, obviously regarding it as some sort of baptismal ceremony. Only the next day did she question him about it, and then she wanted to go and look for it and bring it back by all means. He had to forcibly restrain her. She wouldn't have found the baby, anyway. Moreover, the people might have reacted violently if she interfered with their affairs.

73

The strange thing was that from that day she seemed to recover faster. Although she remained pale, she made deliberate efforts to move about and restore her energy. She'd had enough of the village. Now she wanted to get away.

In the end it was the Hottentots who left first. One morning, as they got up, there was an abnormal commotion in the village. All the huts were stripped and broken down, the skins and reed mats rolled and tied in bundles, the poles and beams of the frameworks and of the palisade were heaped up and set alight; also the huts of the unclean women were burnt unceremoniously. Only Elisabeth's hut was left intact. The villagers came round to greet her, with much waving of hands and dancing and gusts of laughter, and then they were gone, men and women and children all, young and old, with cavorting dogs and lowing cattle and bleating goats and sheep. After the dust had settled in the distance there was nothing left of the village, apart from the smouldering heaps and the bare ground, and, of course, Elisabeth's hut.

She found it inexplicable. He merely shrugged. 'Why should they stay here? They always trek like this, from season to season.'

'But how could you have been so sure, then, that you'd find them here?'

'I know them.'

'And where are they going now?'

'Depends on the rain, and how soon it gets cold. Up to the Snow Mountains, I suppose. They may even cross the Great Fish River.'

'But what about all the old people they have with them? How can they go so far?'

'Those who get too old or weak to keep up are stuffed into porcupine holes.'

'But they can't do that!'

In no mood for an argument he left her and walked off on his own; when he came back, he saw her writing in her books. All right, he thought, write it all down. Write about the baby exposed on the veld and the old folk on the road. If that'll make you feel any better. Get it out of your blood: let me be.

It was strange, that night, to be alone again. During the day the bare patch where the village had been was still alive with memories, but at the onset of the evening there were no fires as before, no noise of homing cattle, children screaming, the shrill voices of women, the darker merriment of the men gathered round the *gli*-root calabashes.

74

They were alone again, just the two of them. But because they'd grown accustomed to the presence of people, this solitude was much more unsettling than before. Khanoes rose in the sky, followed by the other stars. There were jackals crying in the distance.

They sat on opposite sides of their fire, without speaking. But he was watching her. The lovely smoothness of her throat, where the collarbones joined below the little hollow; the frailness of her white hands, her eyes burning dark blue, much larger than before in her pale narrow face.

'The old woman who nursed me,' she said suddenly, staring at him through the flames, 'she was very old, wasn't she?'

'What about it?'

'She'll never survive such a long trek. Will they bundle her into a hole too?'

'I suppose so, if she gets too weak.'

'But how can they?'

'It'll be better for her than to go on walking.'

After a long time, when the fire had burnt down into smoky coals, she asked: 'What did they do with my child?'

'It wasn't a child yet.'

'What did they do with it? Did they bury it?'

'I don't know. It was the women who nursed you.'

'Or did they expose it on the veld like the twin girl?'

'I tell you I don't know!'

'Why didn't they give me the girl if they wanted to get rid of her? I could have taken her back to the Cape.'

'What for? Like they did with my mother? To be your slave?'

She stared at him with her large eyes, and said nothing. Only, finally, 'I'm going to sleep now.'

She got up and walked off to the hut. But she stopped at the entrance, gazing into the night, her head turned sideways as if listening intently. What was she trying to hear: a baby crying? Or was she simply waiting for him to do something?

The lion utters another deep moan, not far away now. The shadows are very long and black. It's time to take the oxen into the flimsy enclosure of branches. Jerking their heads and sniffing, they trample the ground uneasily. She is still holding the book on her lap, but she isn't writing any more. Perhaps she has also heard the lion.

The next day they loaded the ox and set out from the forsaken village.

'Are you sure you're really going to the sea?'

'I told you I'd take you there.'

'How far is it?'

'A long way. But we're getting nearer.'

She was still unsteady on her feet. The only reason she insisted on starting again probably was that she felt too exposed in the village after the Hottentots had left. Their presence had been a form of protection. In this new silence there was too much time for brooding; they were too conscious of each other. So it was better to move on, even if the laps were shorter than before and their progress slower. He supplied food – roots, fruit, berries, eggs, meat – and once again he had to provide enough water for her copious daily ablutions. She seemed to have an obsession about water, about washing herself and her clothes, as if the dust covering her was poisonous. Once, when she sent him off just after he'd spent half the afternoon collecting firewood, he lost his temper and flung his bundle down.

'Go and find your own bloody water!' he shouted.

'Do as you're told,' she ordered furiously.

He kicked a piece of wood out of his way. 'In the Cape I would have had to obey you. Here it's up to me to decide.'

'In the Cape I would have forced you to obey me.'

'Oh no. The Cape would have forced me, not you. Otherwise you would have been able to do it here, too. Who are you anyway? What are you?' It was like that early day when he'd lost control about the map. 'Just a fucking woman with tattered clothes. That's all!'

She stared at him in silence, then turned back to where they'd offloaded. For a while he stood watching her, his arms folded on his chest: how she sat down on her bundle, very still, her face turned away in profile, looking into the distance. It was that which moved him in the end, in spite of himself: her pride; and the pathos of her dignity.

He returned with the bucket of water to find her occupied with thread and needle, sewing up a dress. She looked up as he put down the bucket. He didn't look at her. Neither did she thank him. But while he was fastening the oxen for the night he noticed that she, back from her bath behind the trees, was making the fire and boiling water and, for the first time on their journey, preparing supper.

He prods the obstinate oxen through the opening of the small enclosure and ties them to a tree with doubled thongs. Then he blocks the opening with branches. Why the hell didn't those lions find themselves a prey at the river?

The book still lies open on her lap.

'Why did you take so much time with the oxen?' she asks as he kneels to make the fire.

'Just because.' He looks at her anxious face. 'Don't worry.'

'I know there's something wrong. Why won't you tell me?'

'There's nothing.'

He can see the tension in the corners of her mouth; the stubborn chin, the strong line of her jaw. The face she offers him is proud and defiant. But in spite of himself he feels something like sympathy for her: how can he be sure it's pride? What does it demand of her to go on like this and never to show any fear or wavering? It would be easy to put out a hand and touch her shoulder, reassuring her. Don't worry, it's all right; nothing will happen. It's not disdain which keeps me from telling you the truth, only concern that it may upset you too much, and unnecessarily. You may sleep in peace tonight, I'll keep watch. Tomorrow we'll be on our way again to the sea. There you can rest.

But he dare not touch her. And when, finally, he decides to speak to her his voice sounds neutral, even accusing.

'What have you been writing?'

'Nothing in particular.' She is quite withdrawn now.

Her resistance prompts him to open attack. 'There are lions near by. And you just go on writing.'

'Why didn't you tell me before?' she asks, very pale.

'Would you have written about them too?'

She makes a move to close the book, defensive now; but with an impulsive angry gesture he grabs the leather binding. '*What* is it you wrote in here? I want to know.' Before his eyes incomprehensible phalanxes of letter-ants march, motionless, across the page.

For a few moments they persist in a tug-of-war before he lets go, ashamed. She slams the book shut and keeps it pressed down on her knees, covered with her arms, like a baby she tries to protect.

'I've got to write down what happens. To take it back to the Cape with me.'

'Why? Will you forget if you don't write it down?' He wants to force more from her than mere answers, to open something of herself the way the book was open, but she remains tense and stern, unyielding.

'It's easy to forget.'

'What you forget isn't worth holding on to anyway.'

'You'd really like to know what I'm writing, wouldn't you?' she

77

suddenly taunts him. 'You must find it terrible not to understand a thing of what I'm doing.' Now it's she who is attacking, no longer he. 'I can sit here and write anything I want to. And you won't understand a word of it.'

'What do *you* understand?' he asks blindly. 'You only trekked along with your husband. In search of what? You certainly didn't find anything.'

'What did *you* find, wandering through the land all these years?' she asks quickly.

'That's my own business.'

'Why did you leave the Cape?'

'You always ask the same questions.'

'Because I want to know.'

'If I were to tell you the truth . . .'

'Why don't you trust me?' she asks desperately.

'Trust you?' he sneers. 'It sounds as if you're trying to convert me. Next thing you'll start praying for me.'

'I'm long past praying.' She looks in his eyes, with open defiance.

'I couldn't stand my master,' he says briefly, challenging her. 'That's why I left.'

'Why couldn't you stand him?'

'Because he was my master.' In spite of his resentment – perhaps because the descending dusk is urging confidence? or because of the nearness of the lions and the oxen straining at their thongs? – he abandons his defiance for a moment. 'One day,' he says, facing her squarely, 'the day he appointed me over his household and made me *mantoor*, he said: 'You've been bred for this land. Malgas for strength; Javanese for intelligence; Hottentot for endurance. You see? You belong here.'

'What's wrong with that?' she asks. 'Haven't I been bred in the same way? Hollander, and Huguenot, and three generations at the Cape . . . ?'

'It's not the land we've been bred for at all!' he answers angrily. 'You've been bred to be one of the masters, and I to be a slave. That's all.'

'Is that why you ran away?'

Ignoring her, he adds more wood to the fire, trying to make out where the lions are lurking.

'And are you happy now?' she demands. 'Now that you're free?'

He utters a short laugh, so harsh that the oxen raise their heads in snorts of fright. 'Do you really think this is what I wanted? Roaming through the wilds?'

'In fifty years all this land will be civilised,' she says.

'Civilised? What has that got to do with it?'

'I don't understand you,' she says, confused.

Suddenly: her breasts – that first night in the wagon. He has to struggle against the memory and the violence of the passion it stirs in him.

'How can you understand?' he answers. 'You're white. I'm only a slave, aren't I? I'm two hands and two legs, I'm like an ox or a mule. You're the head, you're the one who is allowed to think. I'm just a body. I'd better stick to my place. It's presumptuous for me to think. For twenty-five years I accepted it. But then it was enough, I couldn't take any more. And now I've had five years doing nothing but think, in this godforsaken wilderness. It's not written down in books, it's all here, inside me. But what can I do with it?'

'You're mad!' she whispers, shocked, but almost with compassion.

'Then allow me to stay mad and to go on thinking!' He has trouble controlling his voice. 'You're trying to protect yourself. You would prefer to keep me down here, in my "place", and despise me because I can't think. But it's useless.'

All she can say in the silence following his outburst is his name: 'Adam. No.'

He gets up quickly to break more firewood, almost sensuously conscious of his own strength: as if he deliberately wants to be a body, pure body, nothing but brute force. The rest is madness. Why did you force me to speak like this tonight? Let me go, leave me in peace – I'm free! – I want to be free.

In near despair he looks at her. She is still beside the fire, staring at him.

Turn your head away! Can't you see I'm naked?

If it had been day now, or only a different night, he would have left the enclosure, if only for a couple of hours, just to move about in open space again, to draw reassurance from the world surrounding him. But tonight everything is enclosed by the dark in which the lions are lurking; tonight infinity surrounds them. There stretches the Milky Way; there are the six lights of Khuseti. All that is familiar in this small flickering enclosure. It is impossible to get out; the ubiquitous animals are too dangerous. All they can do is to mill round here, round and round, along the endless spiral inward, in to him and her.

He has just returned to the oxen to test their thongs after a renewed threatening sound immediately outside when suddenly the growls erupt in roars. The earth seems to tremble under his feet, the oxen rear up, bellowing with fear. He hears her calling, 'Adam!' Even before he gets to her he hears the breaking and snapping of branches. Reaching out to take the gun which she is holding out to him – amazingly calm, pale and self-contained – he sees the black-maned male bursting right through the fence.

Without bothering to take proper aim, Adam fires.

'Load it again!' he shouts, flinging the gun towards her.

A large body tramples him to the ground. The lion, he thinks. But it's one of the oxen. They have broken loose, stampeding this way and that, the lion clinging to one's shoulder. Then they break out, trampling the branches of the enclosure to bits, thundering off into the night, the lion still holding on.

Grabbing the gun from her again, Adam rushes after them. It's only when he reaches the border of the light, among the scattered thorn-tree branches, that he discovers her beside him, tugging at his arm.

'Don't be stupid!' she screams. 'Stay here!'

He shakes her off and runs on; but barely ten yards further he realises that it's useless. Aiming in the general direction of the distant noise, he fires another shot. There is a sudden anguished burst of bellowing somewhere in the dark. Then silence.

With hunched shoulders he comes back to the broken kraal.

She looks at him, but neither says anything. In silence, together, they set to work to rebuild the fence before they return to the fire, panting. He adds yet more wood. A spray of sparks is scattered over them. Weird shadows dance over their faces in the brilliant light.

In spite of the fire her teeth are chattering.

'What's wrong?' he asks.

'Nothing.' She begins to sob, struggling against it until it becomes too much for her. But it doesn't last long. Then, clenching her teeth, she wipes away the tears. 'I'm sorry. I didn't mean to.'

'You didn't seem afraid at all,' he says clumsily.

'It was too sudden. It's only now . . .'

'Go to sleep. You're exhausted. I'll make you some tea.'

'I won't be able to sleep.'

'Try to.'

'Suppose they come back?'

'Not tonight,' he assures her. 'They've got what they wanted.'

'What are we going to do now? Do you think they got both?'

'I suppose so.'

'But how are we going to trek on?'

'We'll see tomorrow.'

It takes her a long time to doze off; and every now and then she twitches or mumbles in her sleep, or utters small moaning noises. He stays awake beside the fire, keeping it going, looking at her, listening to the night. But everything remains peaceful – although he knows that something is being devoured, somewhere. Only when the morning star comes out he pulls his skins over him and lies down.

Long before her, in the first warmth of the sun, he is awake again. He rekindles the dull, half-ashen coals, puts on the kettle, takes the gun, and goes off. Down at the river he takes off his clothes – the frilly shirt, by now discoloured and torn, and the frayed blue trousers – and dives in. The water is icy cold, reviving him from his gloom. With new energy he pulls the clothes on his wet body and walks in among the trees – redwood, white elms, wild cherry – in the direction the oxen took last night. Cautiously, since the lions, however well fed, are bound to be in the neighbourhood, he begins the search. Not far from the camp he notices the first vultures and climbs a tree from where he can look out. In a patch of grass among the sparse trees he spots the carcass of the ox, two legs jutting stiffly, ridiculously upward. Two lionesses are still feeding lazily with deep contented throaty growls; some distance away the male is dozing in the grass, occasionally flicking his huge mane to scare off the flies. Of the other ox there is no sign.

With rather more hope than before he starts exploring the vicinity in search of traces: dung, broken branches, flattened grass, hoof-marks. Even when, at last, he finds what he is looking for, he represses his excitement. The ox may have run too far to be found again. But patiently he follows the track, grunting with satisfaction when, from time to time, he finds new hopeful signs. He eats as he goes along – berries or juicy leaves, roots and bulbs, tubers, fruit, all available in abundance at this time of the year. Whenever he does stop for a moment he remembers, almost furtively, almost ashamed, last night's conversation. In the strong naked light of day he finds his words disconcerting; hers too. Whatever possessed him to reveal so much? He can only ascribe it to the night and the nearness of the lions; to remorse, perhaps, for having deliberately humbled her so many times; even to a protective urge towards her white vulnerability. But it was wrong, it was dangerous. It dare not happen again.

Quite unexpectedly he comes upon the ox grazing on the far side of a clearing among the hills in a small thicket of *kiepersol*. It still has a length of leather thong round its neck, half-choked by it. The moment Adam appears, the animal jerks up its head.

He begins to talk to it in low, caressing tones, inching closer. The ox gives a warning snort.

'It's all right,' Adam says soothingly. 'Don't worry. I've come to fetch you.'

Suddenly the ox swings round and begins to canter off. But a hundred yards further it stops again, looking back over its tall hump. There is dried blood on its flanks.

'Come!' Adam calls softly. 'Come on, now. Come.'

The ox replies with a plaintive sound. This time it allows Adam to come right up to it and pat its shoulder. The loose red skin twitches nervously. Fortunately there's nothing serious wrong with it: the marks on the flanks, caused by claws or thorns, are superficial scratches only.

'Come on,' he orders again, picking up the end of the thong and loosening the tight noose.

In the early afternoon they reach the camp again. Elisabeth jumps up, dropping her journals to run to the opening in the kraal where she waits until he brings in the ox.

'Did you have to go very far?' she asks.

'It wasn't too bad.'

'Is he hurt?'

'A few scratches, that's all.'

'You must be tired,' she says, with concern in her voice. 'I've made you some food.'

'Thank you.' He glances at her. There is a touch of colour in her cheeks today. He averts his eyes again. 'We must move on soon,' he says brusquely.

'Why?'

'It's better to get away while the lions are still feeding on the other carcass.'

'We'll be slowed down a lot from now on,' she remarks quietly.

'No. You can ride on this one. We'll throw out some of the unnecessary stuff.'

'There's nothing unnecessary!' she protests. 'We have little enough as it is.'

'What else can we do?' he asks, resentful.

'You can load everything on the ox as before. I'll walk.'

'You're still too weak.'

'I'm strong enough.'

He studies her, hostility brooding in his eyes, but not without a hint of approval.

'Surely it can't be so far now?' she asks.

'Not if we went straight to the coast.' He looks straight at her. 'But my sea is much farther on.'

'Why can't we take the shortest way and follow the beach from there?'

'It will take months to cross all the river mouths and overgrown dunes and stretches of rock.'

'Time isn't important, is it? As long as we reach the sea.'

'No. We're going to *my* place.'

'But . . .'

'I told you,' he says calmly, and with finality.

This is the real reason, he thinks. Not those river mouths and dunes and rocks which may impede their progress. But the need, the necessity, to remain in control. To subject her to his decisions. To keep her in her place.

She knows it too. She can see it in his eyes. But instead of bursting out as he expected, she says nothing: not acquiescence – that is evident from the unyielding posture of her head and shoulders – but the more formidable, equivocal opposition of silence.

I won, he thinks wryly. My decision will prevail. We'll follow my route, to my sea. But it's only provisional, a mere postponement. For last night has indeed changed something. And now it is merely a matter of time.

The episode at the river. She is sitting on a boulder at the edge of the water. The new footskins he made for her after her Cape shoes had worn right through, lie beside her as she bathes her feet. A few yards downstream he is watching the unloaded ox drinking. These last few days they've had to cross countless small streams, sometimes struggling for hours on end to find a shallow drift or simply to extricate themselves from thickets of tangled wood on the banks. This river is wider than most of the others, with a swift current down the middle, and clusters of rocks forming long deep pools connected by small foaming waterfalls. The ripples caused by the drinking of the ox disturb the clear reflections of the opposite trees; without this move-ment it would have been impossible to distinguish between things and their reflections. Lower down a flock of wild geese is drifting serenely on a pool; there are ibises among the driftwood of the far bank, and storks strutting stiff-legged on the marshy grass. The birds barely look up when they arrive with the ox.

'Strange to think,' she says impulsively, 'that I'm probably the first person ever to come here.' With a small laugh of surprise: 'I'm making history!'

'I'm here too,' he says with brooding rage. 'And many Hottentots come this way.'

'I only meant . . .'

'I know damn well what you meant.' In fierce, rough strokes he starts drying the ox with handfuls of dried grass. Once again the peaceful moment is disturbed. Exasperated, she presses her forehead against her fists on her drawn-up knees. Why must this happen every time? Why must she always say the one thing she shouldn't? Or is it his fault, deliberately finding provocation in her most innocuous words or gestures? It is exhausting, much more exhausting than their endless plodding through the days.

'You think you're taking history with you wherever you go,' he says with a sneer. 'I suppose history, to you, is what happens to the people of the Cape.'

'Well, it's from the Cape that this whole land is being civilised,' she retorts.

'And civilisation is history? The Cape with its churches and schools and gallows, is that all that matters to you? How do you civilise a land? And how do you know when you've gone too far?'

'I wasn't referring to that at all.'

'No? Why else should you imagine you're the first person to come here? History is what *you're* doing! It's everything that makes the Cape more prosperous and powerful. Isn't that civilisation? But don't you think history can happen here too, without you? – with every weak old Hottentot bundled into a porcupine hole, with every nameless wanderer crossing this river?'

Elisabeth gets up quickly. 'I don't know what's got into you,' she says. 'There's something twisted in you. No matter what I say, you always find a reason to attack me.'

'Because everything you say has been made in the Cape. Because you can never get away from your Cape way of thinking. And because I'm sick and tired of all your shit.'

'Why don't you go on alone then?' she asks, heated. 'You were the one who said you'd take me to the sea: I didn't ask you to.'

'What will happen to you if I leave you here?'

'It has absolutely nothing to do with you. I can look after myself. Even if I died, it would be no concern of yours. I'm not forcing you to stay with me. If I'm a burden to you, then for God's sake leave me alone. But if you do decide to stay, then at least have the decency to respect me.'

'Yes, Madam,' he taunts her.

Rising, she restrains the impulse to explode, and walks back to where the ox was unloaded.

Can't you see? I don't want to fight or argue with you. I only want to talk to someone, I don't want to be so lonely. Why must you always try to venge your life on me? I didn't ask for it. I don't want to be responsible for it.

He follows with the ox. Why do you defy me every time and force me to lose my temper? Is that your way of humiliating me? All these years I've been self-sufficient; I thought I was. Now you force me, every day, to discover that I've never freed myself from the Cape after all; that, in everything, I'm still controlled by my revolt and my hate. I thought I'd got rid of it. It is agony to discover that it's all been an illusion. But what do you know about it? You think I left it of my own free will. And that makes all the difference.

They carry on with their wordless conversation while he ties up the ox in a grazing spot and she arranges her things for the night. Afterwards, while he has gone off to collect wood, she goes for a swim; and by the time he returns she is once more engrossed in her journals.

For a few minutes he stands watching her. She must be aware of him, but she doesn't look up. After a while he turns away to make their shelter for the night. When he has finished he walks off in the direction of the river.

She looks up to see him disappear among the trees and tries to resume her writing, but she cannot think of anything to say. Irritable, she shuts the book and puts it away with the others. For a while she tries to do some mending; abandoning that too, she begins to walk aimlessly to and fro until it occurs to her to make a fire. Sitting beside it, she listlessly pokes the wood with a stick, abandoning herself to weariness and anxiety.

Why doesn't he come back? Has he taken her at her word and gone off? Well, let him; she'll manage. She'll just follow the river down to the sea. For the time being that is all that's important.

But after a while she drops her stick and gets up. She has already reached the opening in the shelter before she thinks: How smug he'll be if he finds I've come to look for him! She turns back and begins to rearrange their baggage. But after a few more minutes she finally, grimly, makes up her mind and resolutely walks out of the camp, down to the river. Let him think what he will. It's getting late. It's time he started his evening duties.

Emerging from the bushes, she immediately notices his clothes on the flat rock where she sat before – his dirty, tattered clown's suit. For what is he but a miserable clown? Her first impulse is to turn back. But she suppresses it. Determined, she goes nearer and climbs on the rock.

Far away from her, at the downstream end of the long pool, she sees him splashing in the water.

'Adam!'

He looks up, shaking the water from his head. 'What's the matter?'

'You've been away so long, I . . .' She stops.

'I'm coming.'

With long even strokes he comes swimming towards her, the water sparkling on his shoulders. The storks and ibises are still grazing on the opposite bank. In the late yellow sunlight birds are calling in the darkening trees.

Where the water gets shallower he stands up and begins to wade out until it is down to his waist. He stops for a moment, hesitating, looking at her. Once again she wants to turn round and escape. But suddenly she cannot: she does not want to. Defiant, she remains standing, looking straight at him, her head erect, her superiority assured.

With narrowed eyes and a strange, implacable smile he comes nearer. The water glides from his hips. He is lean, angular, but lithe, with a sort of cat-like grace, his body rippling with thin, tight, fierce muscles, the youthful body of a boy. Now she must go. But she stays. The small dark crinkly patch of his lower belly appears above the water. She starts breathing with more obvious effort, stubborn, staring. Today I'll see you as you are. You who always humiliates and insults me. I want to see you in your vulnerable, miserable, shameful nakedness, mercilessly exposed to me: see if you dare. He is coming nearer still. The water eddies round his knees, his muscled calves. Bobbing on his full, contracted balls, shrunken from the cold, ludicrous, innocent, his penis. He jumps on the boulder where she's waiting, still making no effort to turn away or to shield his genitals with a hand.

Bending over, he picks up his clothes, and walks on. For the first time she sees, from behind, across the muscles of his back, across his buttocks and his thighs, the terrible black-purple network of scars and swollen, knotted stripes.

She is aware of panting through half-open lips.

'Savage!' she hisses.

He turns round. Dare he answer? She avoids his eyes, suddenly ashamed of his sex, looking down to his feet. Without a word he walks on, still carrying the clothes over his arm, making no effort to put them on, disappearing among the trees towards the camp.

'Never trust a slave, my child,' said her father. 'You can treat him as well as you can, you can bring him up with the Bible, you may think he's civilised, he may seem as tame as any house-dog. But sooner or later he suddenly shows his teeth and then you discover he's just a wild animal after all.'

Trembling, she sits down. Casting small pebbles into the water, watching them sink. What's wrong with her now? She's seen naked slaves before, paying as little attention to them as to any animal in the Company's menagerie. And what is he but a slave? He has never been a slave so totally as today with that nauseating pattern of scars on his back. Why, then, this weakness trembling in her legs? Why recall his body so meticulously: chest and belly and hips, legs, his penis bobbing on his balls? Why should she even have noticed it? He is, indeed, the savage she called him. She need never fear him again.

Yet it is nearly dark before she finds enough courage to get up and return. Tonight she is afraid of the camp, of the firelight, of his undaunted arrogant eyes.

The first she sees as she enters the small shelter is his clothes: the shirt and trousers torn to shreds and flung across the branches. For a moment, in a panic, she wants to flee. But where can she go? And why? A strange new resignation flows through her: after all, this *is* the wilderness, he *is* the savage, what else does she expect? Through these weeks since his first appearance at the wagon, and especially since their sojourn with the Hottentots, she has begun to believe that he might be different. That, in fact, is what has been most unnerving about him. But now it's all clear, their roles are defined and manageable. If he decides to become violent now, she'll simply have to accept it as part of the risk of her situation. The only thing which surprises

87

and unsettles her is the question: why hasn't he used violence yet? Surely it would have made everything much easier for him, and in the long run even to herself, knowing exactly what to expect and to resign herself to it. The violation of her body, if it had to happen, would have been so much simpler to cope with than all these weeks of wondering and anxiety and uncertainty.

Controlled and outwardly calm she comes into the shelter and piles up the branches in the opening to seal it off. She barely glances at him – yes, he is sitting naked at the fire – goes to her unpacked things and, very deliberately, takes out her journals. Opening the unfinished volume, she tries, or pretends, to write, barely able to control her trembling pen, oblivious of what she sets down on paper.

But soon she finds his silence aggravating, grating her consciousness like a grain of sand in the eye. She looks up; he is watching her. Drawing in her breath, she resumes writing, stringing together random words, drawing the graph of an Amsterdam skyline from memory, listing the names of animals and plants she can recall. Until she becomes annoyed by her own confusion.

She looks up again. 'You may bring me my food when it's ready,' she orders laconically.

'It's waiting.'

'Well, bring it here.'

She deliberately keeps the journal opened on her lap, watching him as he lingers stubbornly. If he doesn't obey this time, it will be proof of open, final, revolt. She is conscious of the danger weighing heavily in the deep silence between them. The moment seems endless.

Then, with an abruptness which startles her, he gets up and brings her food to where she sits: thick milk-roots dug out yesterday and sliced to soak overnight; now he has roasted them: it smells like meat.

He remains standing before her, his eyes unabashedly on hers, trying to force her to say something, expecting it, demanding it. But she refuses. She will not be dominated. Taking the plate, she turns her head away so as not to look at the blunt, obtuse head of his penis, now half-swollen, so close to her.

He returns to the fire. But while she's eating she remains aware of his eyes not leaving her for a moment. And she decides: to stay silent is mere evasion. She'll prove to him that she cannot be intimidated so easily, even if it means direct confrontation.

'Come and fetch the plate,' she orders.

Adam gets up, obeying instantly, but with deliberate insolence. Brooding, defiant, he stands before her.

'Why don't you put your clothes on?' she asks.

It is obvious that this is what he's been waiting for.

'I'm a savage. Savages don't wear clothes.'

'You're behaving like a child!'

'Aren't savages just like children?'

Elisabeth rises to her feet, refusing to look up at him any longer. 'I'm not amused by your little game, Adam,' she says. 'Rape me if you want to. If you think you can get me in your power like that. But if that's what you want, then for God's sake do it openly. Don't skulk around waiting for the dark.'

'What makes you think I want *you*?' he asks viciously, like a snake striking. 'If I wanted you I would have taken you long ago.'

'I'm not so sure.' Her voice sounds uncertain, but she controls it. 'I think you're afraid of me.'

With a sudden jerk of his arm he shatters the plate on a stone between them. She stands waiting. He doesn't move.

'You're the one who is shit-scared,' he says.

'Yes,' she says, restrained. 'I *am* scared. But at least I know what I am scared of. And I don't think you're so sure. That makes it worse, doesn't it? That's why you can't stand me. That's why you're trying to take it out on me.'

What we really fear, she thinks, is this space forcing us inward to one another. It's like the night of the lions again. They stand opposite each other, weighing, weighing; the most insignificant gesture is important, a single word can decide the future. With hate, and longing, anguished, dismayed, they stare at one another. I'm frightened, you're frightened; the night is endless. That's all. If I make a gesture and put out my hand to you, will you comprehend it?

He is the first to turn away. Reluctant; almost meek, almost sad, it seems to her. Perhaps she has 'won' this time. But it is not the sort of victory which proves or decides an issue; it is, in fact, irrelevant. It only complicates everything. And in near despair she asks what she does not want to know:

'What happened to your back?'

'Your people put the cat o' nine tails to it.' He remains with his back to her, while he adds with subdued fury: 'But what about it? It's nothing. It happens every day.'

'Is that why you ran away?'

'What difference would it make?'

'All the difference in the world. You said you left of your own free will.'

'I never said anything. You assumed it.'

'You allowed me to think so. You *wanted* me to think so. You didn't want me to find out you'd run away because you were flogged.'

'Now you know. Are you satisfied now? Have you got me down on the ground?'

'I don't want you down on the ground.'

He swings back to her. 'Why do you keep on asking then?'

'Why did they do it, Adam?'

'I raised my hand against my master,' he says bluntly.

'One doesn't do that sort of thing without any reason.'

'My reasons are my own.'

'You scared about that too?' she taunts him. 'You've taken off your clothes in front of me. What else is there to be ashamed of?'

'Ashamed?' He is shaking with rage. 'It's *you* must be ashamed! You're the one who can't stop asking questions. That's also a way of flogging a man. You women are good at it. Always ready to bring on the salt for the wounds, long after the men have stopped.'

'If that's what you think, you needn't answer my question.'

The wall again, she thinks. Every time. And she turns away to go from him.

'All right,' he says, choking. 'I'll tell you if you want to know. If it'll make you feel proud that you've pried that out of me too.'

She looks round, with a defensive gesture; but now he won't be stopped.

'You wanted to know, didn't you?' he says harshly. 'So I'll tell you. Madam! I raised my hand against my master because sooner or later one reaches a point where one has got to say no. I was his *mantoor*, I had to supervise everything. I even had to punish the other slaves when he ordered it. He had a bad heart, a thrashing would tire him out too much, so he only watched. I never wanted to. Not my own people. But I was a slave, I had no voice against him.' He is quiet for a moment, breathing heavily. 'And then my old grandmother died of cold because I wasn't allowed to deliver her firewood. My mother wanted to go to the funeral, but the Baas refused, he needed her for pruning in the vineyard. So she went off on her own to put away the old woman. And when she came back, the next day, she went into the vineyard as if nothing had happened. Singing.'

He looks past her, into the night.

'And then?' she asks, when he doesn't go on.

'He had her taken to the backyard, to the post. And he gave me the sjambok and told me to flog her.'

'It can't be true, Adam!'

'This time it is the truth,' he says, looking at her as if he wants to scorch her with his eyes. And she stares back, unable to look away. 'I pleaded with him. He refused to listen. I kept on. He grabbed a piece of wood – I was working there, making a table, and he grabbed one of the stinkwood legs – and hit me in the face with it. I wrenched it from him. And I only stopped beating him when he was lying on the ground.'

'And afterwards?'

'Nothing.'

'They punished you and then you escaped?'

'What else could I do? I didn't choose the wilderness because I wanted to. I simply had to. And by now I've learned to stay alive, to survive like an animal. But I'm not an animal. I'm a human being. And I want to live with people again. So I must go back some day: not crawling like a runaway dog, but walking on my own two feet, straight, with nothing to be ashamed of.'

She bows her head.

'How can it ever happen?' she asks.

'It can happen if I take you back to the Cape. Not only to the sea, but all the way, home. Back to the Cape and its Mountain. You can explain to them. If you tell them I brought you back, if you will tell them I saved your life, if you demand my freedom, they'll give it. You can buy me my freedom. No one else can. I am in your hands.'

She stands dumb, unable even to look up.

'Do you understand it now?' he asks in a new surge of anger. 'You needn't fear I'll rape you. If I do anything to you, I kill myself.'

'My safety for your freedom: is that your bargain?' she asks, numb.

'If you see it as a bargain.'

'I asked *you*.'

'Does it matter what name we give it?' He sounds exhausted. For the first time he seems to become conscious of his nakedness again. He turns away swiftly, his maimed back towards her, and returns to his place beside the fire. He adds some more wood to it, then rolls himself in his skins and lies down in the half-shadow on the far side.

Elisabeth sits down, looking at him, that shapeless bundle. How terrible to live on the edge of another's world, aware of the possibility of discovering him. But is it really possible? Dare one allow it to happen? Can one survive it? For how long can a snail exist outside its shell? Why should one try to reach across the flames, into that other darkness, fearing it? Or does that very anguish drive you on?

He has no idea of when she came to sleep. Waking up somewhere in the early hours, he hears her sighing and moaning in the dark. He props himself up on an elbow, listening to her panting and uttering small half-smothered sounds, moving about restlessly, almost frantically, opposite the deep orange glow of the coals. Perplexed and anxious, he rises and goes to her. Only when he bends over her does he grasp what she is doing. With brooding fascination he stares at her hands writhing between her thighs, his throat tautening. He cannot turn away. Independent of his will, his sex begins to stir.

She stops abruptly. 'What are you doing here?' she pants. 'Go away!' Tugging at the blankets in the dark.

He cannot move. Woman: you, wilderness in which to lose oneself.

Huddled in her blankets, she sits up. The glow of the coals hardly gives off any light. All she can make out is the silhouette of his thin body, the shape of his shoulders and his lean belly; and then that threatening, fierce thing jutting out towards her like the erect head of a snake.

Don't force me any farther. Can't you see I'm terrified and hungry, and all I need is peace; I can't bear it any longer, not alone.

He knows he need only lean over and touch her, diving into the moment like deep water. But beyond the moment, vast as the night, is everything of the future: all the impossible possibilities, everything which can be confirmed and petrified by a single gesture, created or destroyed by it.

From his bent position he rises up again and turns away with something like a stifled sob in his throat, back to his place in the dark.

Don't. Don't. Don't utterly disarm me. This is the last freedom I have left.

She utters no further sound. He cannot even hear her breathe. Perhaps she has fallen asleep again; perhaps she lies awake staring with wide eyes in the dark. But he does not turn his head. On the far side of the mound of firewood he sits down, with one of the loading skins of the ox across his lap, and slowly, patiently, he begins to cut himself an apron and a belt.

★

And then the second ox. It started with the storm, one of those violent outbursts characteristic of the Eastern Cape, exposing the deception in the mild and gentle appearance of the region.

At that stage they must have been close to their destination on the coast, probably no more than three or four days away. For some time the weather had been building up slowly, an unbearable oppressive heat saturated with humidity. No movement of air; no clouds either, to begin with – only that invisible clammy heat leaving one drained and out of breath.

They trekked past the fringe of a dense forest, through smaller patches of tall trees – sneezewood, sour plum, redwood and white-wood and blackwood – reaching a long easy slope with thickets of wild olive and saffron, Hottentot's bean, horse-piss bush, wild apricot, ghaukum and numnum and dry-my-throat and the ubiquitous euphorbia. And suddenly the river was below them, breathtaking, broader than any of the others they'd had to cross.

That is the scene as she describes it in her journal. It is easy to presume the rest.

While he is keeping watch for crocodiles she lies down to drink, splashing handfuls of water over her glowing face. In the sweltering heat of the past few days, not finding any water, they've been forced to rely on what Adam could provide to quench their thirst, mainly wild figs and the watery bulbs of *kiepersol* roots. Now, miraculously, there is this broad and swiftly flowing current.

Immediately after drinking she wants to cross the river, but he stops her. The bed is much too treacherous here. They must either trek half a day upstream to a shallow ford or construct a raft for the load of the ox. Moving on in this heat is out of the question, so she resigns herself to staying there, gathering *bibrikos* and tubers at the riverside to tie up the logs he has selected. In the late afternoon, exhausted, they have everything ready.

'Shall we cross now?' she asks.

'Better wait till tomorrow. It'll take us the best part of an hour to get through, and by then it'll be too late to make a proper camp. We need good shelter for tonight: look at that storm coming up.'

Too weary to argue, she resigns herself, but grudgingly, feeling that he is deliberately slowing them down to keep her away from the sea. The sea which, by now, has become a consummation to her, an answer to all problems, fulfilment, utter peace.

As if he is trying to compensate, conscious of her resentment, he

93

says: 'I don't think we'll have any more bad weather after this storm.'

'How do you know?'

'That's how it always is.'

How grateful, she thinks, Erik Alexis Larsson would have been for the information.

She watches him as he gathers logs and branches for the habitual shelter; occasionally he stops, wiping his face with an arm, shiny black stripes of perspiration running over the pattern of scars on his back. As always, she shudders looking at it, revolted and fascinated at the same time. You're tired too, she thinks. It's not only I. Yet you say nothing, toiling away. Why? For my sake? I can't imagine you taking all this trouble for yourself. How did you sleep on all your journeys those many years before you came to my wagon? There is so little I know of you.

Then the wind comes up. At first they are aware of it only as cool refreshment after the harrowing heat: a touch of life breathing against their palms and faces; perspiration turning sticky and cold in their hair. Then the leaves start moving, each tree with its own peculiar sound: the grey rustling of the wild figs, the more delicate, high-pitched music of the yellow-wood with its tiny leaves, the shuddering of the assegai wood twigs, the restless whispering of the underbrush. Heavy branches swaying and creaking. Next, as they look down the slope running down bare and unprotected to the river, the grass suddenly, silently, flattened by a giant hand. The sky is black. Far across the river a single final shaft of sun still transfixes a mountain in unearthly colourless light. Thunder rumbles, dull and dark, still very distant; but it is coming nearer, and over the hills the lightning is dancing like fiery cracks in the sky.

But it is the wind that predominates, thundering over the forest like an animal let loose. Terrified, the ox tramples the ground, straining at its heavy thongs, its eyes showing white.

'We'd better eat while it's still light,' says Adam.

There is some honey left from last night, and he had shelled and fried some Hottentot's beans which they wash down with a small ration of Cape tea. But neither finishes the meal: the wind is too terrifying. In a low, wild roar it comes charging across the veld; the great trees toss and sway; from time to time there is the tearing sound of branches ripped off and tumbling down. The ox is bellowing now, jerking its head against the confining thongs, and every few minutes Adam has to get up and calm it down.

94

It's like the storm the night after Larsson had disappeared, she thinks. No, it's infinitely worse. That night she slept right through, overwhelmed by the futile waiting and the day's long fear: that storm protected her and kept the animals at bay. And then, of course, she was sleeping in the wagon, the canvas firmly tied down. Tonight there is nothing between them and the storm. Except for the trees, the forest.

But soon it is the trees that become their greatest peril. They discover it, both at the same time, when they hear the first shuddering thud in the forest, and the sound of trunks and branches torn and dragged along.

'It's a tree, uprooted.'

And then another; more following, everywhere in the dark, the deep roots torn from their tenacious grip on the earth. Still the wind is on the increase. Now the lightning flickers ferociously, without end, and the thunder booms like falling mountains.

Deep in the timeless night one of the giant yellow-wood trees on the fringe of their shelter is struck by lightning. They hear the blow reverberating through the din, and looking up in terror, see the sky aflame above them. The next moment the enormous trunk comes crashing down right across their shelter, tearing down everything in its way, bursting into flames over its whole length. The wind grabs burning branches, hurling them into the surrounding wood. At the very first sound Elisabeth has jumped up, clinging to him with fear.

'We must get out of here,' he says urgently, shaking her to bring her to her senses. 'Help me.'

'What must I do? Where can we go?'

'Out of the forest,' he says. 'Come on, hold on, hold the ox while I load it.'

'He'll trample me down!'

'Don't let him see you're scared. Speak to him. We haven't got any time to lose.'

Trembling, she tries to control the animal, stroking its nose while Adam loads their things on its broad back.

'Come on.'

He takes the lead. She follows, stumbling, away from the burning tree, out into the open where the wind hits them like a river in flood.

'Over there,' he shouts. Forcing their way through smaller shrubs and bushes where there is less danger of falling branches, he leads her into a tangle of wild olives and euphorbias. They are not even aware of the thorns and twigs lacerating their skins.

And then the rain begins. It is as if the wind, reaching its climax, is simply washed away by a torrent of water streaming down from the black and flashing skies. After all these days of impossible heat the cold is suddenly unbearable, wrapping them in what feels like liquid sheets of ice. Crouching under the tanglewood they hide, pressed against the ox. Adam has removed one of the loading hides to cover their heads, sheltering their possessions with their bodies. And she clings to him, pressed tightly against him in panic, sharing the meagre warmth of her body with his, trembling.

From time to time the wind breaks loose again, and in the distance trees tumble and split open. Brief fires flare up, the lightning performs its St Vitus dance in the clouds; and the rain comes down once more, beating them to the ground.

'Is it never going to stop?' Her teeth are chattering uncontrollably.

So wild is the violence of the storm that she isn't even frightened any more: bruised, thoughtless, beaten, dull, she numbly huddles against him. He has his arm round her, using the other to hold on to the miserable protection of the hide.

'It'll pass,' he says. 'We can only get wet, that's all.'

And at daybreak, with the cold grey light filtering through the black rain, the violence subsides. The rain continues for some time before it, too, diminishes. She remains cuddled up against him, shocked and still. And as the storm abates, exhaustion takes over, flooding her in a great drowsiness. She falls asleep.

The cold forces her to wake up again, soon, for a moment confused about where she is and what has happened; then she discovers him against her, sleeping, his head on her shoulder.

Uncomprehending, she looks at his sleeping face, feeling the shudders moving through his body. Have they been like this all night, so close together, their limbs entangled? Now in his sleep his face is disarmed. No arrogance or threat is left, only exhaustion, silence, distance.

Half numbed with cold, her legs sleeping, she carefully tries to change position. Immediately he opens his eyes, looks up at her.

'Sleep on,' she says, her voice strange to herself. 'You're very tired.'

'It's too cold. We must move about.'

Painfully, they crawl from the bushes, now conscious of every thorn and vicious branch. She looks at the fresh red scratches covering his brown body, as if she's looking at someone she has never seen before.

Everywhere bushes have been blown down and trees uprooted, leaving huge bleeding holes in the red sodden earth. He looks around, his back to her.

Ever since that night when I dared to slake the aching thirst in me I've been no more than a body in your eyes. Our bodies are in our way. But how else can we recognise each other? We are ashamed of our bodies, but they are not ashamed of us. In the storm they comforted one another with the naturalness of logs drifting together in a flood.

Look at me. You needn't say anything. Just look at me, acknowledge me, do not deny what has happened. Give me confidence, give me faith. Can't you see I'm in need of it? If you deny this, then our night was no more than the huddling of animals in a storm, you and I and the ox alike. And I know it was more than that; it was more: it has soaked into us like rain. Admit it. That's all I ask of you. If you deny me that, you are denying me.

'Keep an eye on the ox,' says Adam. 'I'm going to try and get a fire going.'

'Where will you find dry wood in this weather?'

'There may be thickets in the forest where the rain didn't reach. If I can find some sneezewood, it'll burn all right.'

He jogs off without looking at her. Elisabeth stays behind. From the bundle she takes fresh clothes – that, too, is damp in patches, but not soaked as the dress she is wearing. The journals, rolled in skins, are, thank God, dry.

An hour later she sees a thin line of smoke rising tentatively from the forest; soon afterwards he reappears to fetch her. They urge the ox to a trot, working up some warmth in their frozen bodies. The small fire makes her shudder with pleasure. Her hands spread open, she stands waiting while he boils some water and roasts a few sodden slivers of *biltong*.

'We'd better stay somewhere here until the weather's all over,' he says after a while.

And huddle together in the night, pretending, when daylight returns, that it hasn't happened? For how long can one live a lie? A body contains its own truth and will not be denied.

'No, I want to go on,' she says urgently.

'You don't know what you're saying,' he answers curtly. 'We're staying right here.'

'I tell you . . .'

'Who are you to tell me anything?' he asks irritably. 'I know the world round here.'

'Please,' she says, miserable. 'I can't stay here. Why can't we just try?'

'What's pressing you?'

You.

'We must get to the sea.'

'There won't be anything left of the raft.'

No, there's nothing left. When they reach the river, it has risen so high that the lower bushes are submerged. The raft has disappeared, disappeared altogether.

'We'll have to build another,' he says.

'Is it really necessary?' she asks stubbornly. 'Surely the ox is strong enough to swim through with the load. If we take out the stuff that can be damaged by water.'

'Like your books, I suppose?'

'Yes.' She looks in his face. 'I'll carry them myself. You can take the ammunition. And perhaps some of the foodstuff. The rest will be all right.'

'You don't know this river.'

'The ox is strong.'

'And what about us?'

'We can swim.'

He laughs briefly. 'Straight down to the sea?'

'We're wasting time,' she says impatiently. 'Bring on the ox.'

'You're asking for trouble.'

'Do you want me to take over?'

He looks at her, smouldering, then turns away and walks up the slippery bank to where they've left the ox. Grimly he opens their bundle on the ground. She comes to kneel beside him to help him sort their possessions. The journals, the ammunition, the gun and the pistol; as much of the flour and sugar as they can manage, all rolled in a couple of hides. The rest he loads on the ox.

The animal refuses to budge when they try to prod it down the bank. But the slope is slippery and it is impossible to turn back. With its front hooves in the brown water it makes a final futile effort to swing round, then the mud slips out from under it and with a terrified bellowing snort it plunges headlong into the current.

Elisabeth glances swiftly at Adam, sees the narrow, angry line of his mouth, and turns her head away again.

Bearing up under the weight of its load the ox swims away from the bank, carried a little way downstream by the flood; but with its nose and horns above the water it manages to maintain a steady pace against the current until it is only a few yards from the opposite bank. There, so suddenly that at first she cannot believe it, it rears up, bellowing wildly, swings round in the invisible grip of a whirlpool, and disappears. They start running down the bank to see if it will reappear. Only once, a few hundred yards down, they briefly glimpse a dark, bulky thing which may or may not be the ox. Then nothing more.

She has begun to cry, soundlessly, her eyes wide open, her nails cutting into her palms.

'I warned you,' says Adam with almost exultant fury.

It breaks something loose inside her. 'It's you forced me to do it!' she sobs. 'It's you!'

She swings away from him and begins to run on, farther along the bank, downstream, stumbling through the tall wet grass with her long dress. Angrily she picks up the hem to run faster. A few times she slips, or treads in the holes of mice or snakes, and falls down, ploughing through the wet mud. But every time she gets up again, crying hopelessly, running on and on until her chest is burning so much that she is forced to stop. Nowhere in the dirty water is there any trace of the ox, not even when she comes round a wide bend from where she has an uninterrupted view over nearly a mile of the river. *Straight down to the sea.* And all their things; all hers. The pots and pans and cutlery, the remaining food, the blankets, all her clothes.

She stands staring at the water, caught in its evil spell. To jump into those murky eddies and disappear; never to have to struggle any more against everything that's become unbearable, not to have to safeguard herself against him any more, not to try anything or wish for anything or believe in anything any more; just one jump to end it all, to be washed away into the wide sea.

But she can't. I'm too cowardly, I'm too tired. I don't want anything any longer. She doesn't even look up when she hears him approach. All she can do is stare at the flood.

'Don't,' he says, taking her arm.

'How do you know I . . .'

'We'll get through.'

Through her tears she grimaces up at him. 'How can you still talk about getting through?' She tries to wrench her arm from his hold. 'Let me go!'

'First stop crying.'

Suddenly she can no longer bear it. She presses herself against him, sobbing, oblivious, clinging to him, while he steadies her with his arms and tries to calm her down, clenching his teeth.

After a long time she recovers, remains standing with her head against him for another moment; then turns away, ashamed, trying to wipe her face.

'Come on,' he says. 'Before it starts raining again.'

For two more days they hide in the bush, in a shelter of branches to ward off the worst rain. The wind has died down, there is no longer any danger of falling trees. And finally the rain also subsides and the sun comes out again.

He brings her leaves of the chewing-stuff shrub, watching with satisfaction how the sweetish, acrid juice soothes her strained nerves in a gentle euphoria. Once he brings back a hare – caught in a snare, or drowned, or frozen? – and roasts it on the sneezewood fire which he has kept going all the time. After the weather has cleared, they divide their few remaining possessions in two bundles and set out upstream to the ford he remembers from previous treks. There they construct a small raft with a platform for herself and their stuff, and, wading cautiously through the still turbulent stream, he pushes it across.

She insists on looking for the ox first, and for two whole days they pick their way downstream through the debris of the subsided flood, discovering innumerable carcasses of drowned animals – buck and hares, a couple of baboons, even a leopard – but no sign whatsoever of the ox or its load. And in the end she has to accept the inevitable and allow him to turn away from the river again, striking overland in the direction of his distant secret sea.

When you clung to me, crying: was it me you needed, or merely something to hold on to, a body, a prop? When you slept in my arms – do you know for how long I lay awake looking at you, not daring to wake you? – was it only from exhaustion and fear, or because you knew I was holding you? What do you really know about me? What do I know about myself? And if I am so unsure, what else can I do but trek on meekly alongside of you, on to my sea, and then farther, back to your people, to fulfil the terms of our agreement?

'Did you have a wife in the Cape?' she asks once, à propos of nothing at all.

'Slaves don't usually get married.'

'I mean . . . someone – a woman – someone you . . .'

100

'I fucked from time to time,' he says cruelly, looking directly at her.

Her cheeks are burning. 'That's not what I asked,' she says. 'That's not what I meant.'

'What else?'

She stays silent for some time before, her eyes cast down, she dares to ask. 'Wasn't there anyone you loved?'

'No.' But after walking on for a long way, he says: 'Only once. For a short time. A girl from Java. Then she was sold.'

'Sold?'

'It's known to happen.'

'Perhaps you were lucky,' she says reflectively, stunning him.

'Why do you torment me?' he asks vehemently.

'I'm serious.' She is quite subdued. 'It remained intact for you, the way it was in the beginning. You didn't have to stand by and watch it change and get distorted.'

'What do *you* know about it?'

She isn't listening to him. 'Some people only love one another,' she says quietly, 'so that they can always have someone at hand to torture.'

'That's ridiculous.'

'It ought to be. But is it really? I've often thought, travelling on that wagon: love is the beginning of violence and betrayal. Something in oneself or in the other is killed or betrayed.' And then, even more quietly, but with great intensity: 'Didn't I destroy as much in Larsson as he did in me? Poor Erik Alexis!'

'Perhaps you never loved him.'

'Perhaps. But how can one ever know for sure? How can you know in advance? Does one ever know oneself so thoroughly that one can dare to expose oneself?' She shuts her eyes briefly, in horror. 'That is the most terrible thing of all: to give yourself into another's hands, to give him absolute power over yourself, to withhold nothing at all.'

'But if you *don't* do it . . .'

'Then I suppose, you're safe. But then you've forfeited your chance.'

He stares ahead of him, over the shrubby veld stretching out before them, barely billowing, broken by small dense clusters of trees. Yes. Somewhere, somehow, it should be possible to touch someone and never to let go again. To hold someone, not for a moment but forever, in a world where everything is fleeting and painful and treacherous. And for the sake of that small possibility you must be willing to risk everything, to break through, to walk into the night naked. One can

101

stay out if one chooses, one can remain safe. But if it means enough to you . . . He looks at her.

Yes, she would like to say. Yes. Allow me to say yes. But something inside me still clings to that ultimate safety, something inside me is still wounded, I'm still scared. How can I give myself up if I don't know to what or whom?

I desire you. I have to fight against my passion. I want you with me, inside me. But how dare I say yes? The yes I have within me forces me to say no. I do not want to still the arid hunger of my body. I want *you*. And yet I'm not ready for you.

'I had a very good friend at the Cape,' she says as they walk into one of the thickets. 'She was terribly attractive, and very popular. They were rich people, her father was a merchant. Then, quite suddenly, two years ago, she had a baby. At first she wouldn't tell her parents anything about it, but they forced her to. Then she told them the father was one of their neighbour's slaves.' She doesn't look at him. 'They forced her to marry her father's bookkeeper. And the slave was sent to Robben Island for life.'

'Why do you tell me this?'

'I don't know. I just remembered it.'

They emerge from the bush. Among the last trees she stops with a sudden intake of breath, grasping his arm.

'Look!'

He has already seen it.

On the opposite slope there stands a long, low, clumsy mud cottage with a brown thatched roof and a squat chimney leaning against the back wall. A small stone kraal. Signs of fields. Signs of people.

Yet no people are to be found. I can't understand it. Adam thinks there may have been a Caffre raid in the vicinity, it seems they sometimes come all the way from the Fish River. In that case, the people probably fled. Or else they've trekked in search of better grazing. They may yet return. There's nothing wrong with the house: the few windows are bare cavities and there are holes in the dung floor, but it will be very easy to make it habitable again. It's rather squalid, and small, only the two rooms. They must be impoverished farmers. Or perhaps this is all they need.

We found a battered old cooking pot in the backyard, which Adam has managed to mend, and a piece of grating. The fields are in a sorry state, all overgrown with weeds, but he found a few pumpkins.

Now we're staying on, for the time being, although I doubt whether either of us has much hope of anyone turning up. In fact, I'm not sure that it will be of any use if someone did come. Do such people ever go to the Cape? Will I be cared for any better than with him? They may have some clothes, though. There's bound to be a woman in the family.

But it is a strange, suspended existence. Both of us want to get to the sea now, it must be so close. Yet something retains us here. One waits and waits. We don't talk much. At night I sleep in front of the open hearth where he's made a fire, although it isn't cold at all. He sleeps in the other room. We seem to shy away from each other.

Now I'm sitting here on my own, trying to occupy myself. Today he has gone hunting. He left early in the morning. It is nearly five now and he still hasn't returned. It's almost like the day E.A. disappeared. I mustn't think of it, it will drive me mad. If only he returns before dark.

Earlier this afternoon I went for a walk, not far. As I reached the valley, something awful happened. I heard a noise, dogs barking. For a moment I thought it was the people of the house coming back. Then, on the far side of the valley, a zebra came bursting through the brush-wood followed by a whole pack of wild dogs. They swarmed all round him. I could hear him whinny, like a horse. Once he reared up, striking out at them with his front hooves. Then he kicked out with his hind legs. But there were too many of them. He broke into a gallop again. They must have come a long way, for there was foam streaming from his mouth. A couple of them got hold of his flanks and I could see them tearing out strips of flesh. He kept on running. And then they all disappeared over the hill and the sound of the hunt died away.

He must come back. I tremble if I think of what might have happened. Sometimes it seems to me he's like an animal in flight. If only he comes back. It will be dark soon. Such a long journey ahead for you and me. Oh God, oh God.

She stands tugging at the frayed collar of her dress. Nowhere in the house could she find any needle or thread; her own was washed away with the load of the ox. She'll have to tie up the frayed ends, hoping it will not unravel any farther. It's the green dress she originally set aside for her arrival back in the Cape. Now it is all she has left.

At regular intervals she returns to the front doorstep to look out across the valley where Adam disappeared in the early morning.

Perhaps he won't return. He has been very withdrawn these last few days, as if he felt oppressed indoors. If only she can make up her mind. She knows he is staying on purely for her sake, which is the last thing she desires. Yet she finds it impossible to make a decision, to announce unequivocally: 'All right, let's go on.'

For there is something very final about this stay in the miserable little hut of stone and clay and thatch. If the inhabitants return – as he believes they must, otherwise they wouldn't have left everything in such good order – she will take leave of him here. It will be the end of the exhausting trek on foot and the even more exhausting process of thinking day after day, the ceaseless need to be on the alert – not so much against him as against herself.

From the doorstep she looks towards the watery sun drifting on the opposite hills. In the distance four or five hadedas fly past with their death cries; among the karee trees a rain-dove is calling in sweet round notes like drops of water falling. There is no sign of game; they may have been scared off by the presence of people on the farm. This small spot in the wilderness is getting civilised.

She feels unbearably restless. This small cottage with its two bleak rooms, its uneven walls, its hearth and dung floor, the reeds used to thatch the roof: surrounded by the infinity of veld and trees, hills, valleys. And she here on the threshold, caught between interior and exterior. If she turns round and goes inside, the wide world outside calls her irresistibly; but if she goes out to the yard, she feels the need to return to the protection of walls. The wilderness surrounding the building and the small patch of farmland seems much more threatening than when she formed part of it, with no house or wagon to take refuge in, only the futile shelter of an enclosure of branches at night.

If he doesn't return, she will not stay on here. Rather trek into the bush on her own, wandering around until hunger or thirst or animals overcome her.

Is it this he had in mind when he first came to the wagon? To plunder her, to strip her of everything she had left: and then to abandon her? See how you get out of here, it's the fate you deserve, this is how I avenge me on your Cape.

But then, surely, he would not have bothered to care for her, to make fire and hunt for food and bring water and ward off wild beasts and warm her with his body in nights of rain and wind?

She stares across the inhospitable landscape and the endless space touched by desolate wind. Above, the clouds glide past, set alight by the dying sun. But it is so slow, so almost imperceptible that it seems as if the clouds are motionless: it is the earth sailing gently through the wind.

It terrifies her. She turns back into the darkness of the house, sitting down on a log at the hearth. The fire she made a little while ago is burning warm and reassuringly. Leaning her head against the side wall of the hearth, she tries to imagine the life of the house when there were people in it, the sort of people she and Larsson encountered occasionally on their journey. Men with skin jackets and large hats, sitting at their front doors drinking tea or the Hottentot beer of honey and *gli*-roots; bloated, bosomy women inside, a grandmother dozing in front of the eternally blazing fire; children swarming over the floor, wearing filthy shirts, their dusty little behinds bare. Chickens pecking mealies from the kitchen floor or brooding in dark corners under hand-made yellow-wood benches. A handful of cattle outside, tended by a scruffy slave; fat-tailed sheep; noisy goats. Fields swarming with birds raiding the mealies and wheat and sun-scorched vineyard.

Lunchtime: slave women pulling up the backless benches and the few dilapidated chairs (That leg needs mending, says the farmer, it broke under Ma's weight last winter – her hip is still not healed, poor thing, and she's getting so heavy with the water); the family sitting down in strict hierarchy, Pa with his elbows wide apart on the edge of the bare table, pipe in his mouth, hat on his head, teacup beside his left elbow. Samp and pumpkin, sweet-potatoes, sour wholewheat bread soaked in milk, and possibly a piece of wind-dried venison. There is no conversation at table. You brought your knife? Well, use your hands. And here, from the barrel in the corner, brought out specially for the male guests, a tot of husk brandy as proof of hospitality. No one bothers to enquire whether the lady would like some too.

As evening settles in, the old slave woman brings the water barrel, removes Pa's veld shoes with some difficulty and washes his feet with fat-soap, drying them with a rag; then, in the same water, the mother and children have their turns, followed by the guests. Not for me, thank you. The meal, and then Scripture. And after the long prayer, while the slaves are clearing and washing up, the women move to one side – she with them – whispering beside the hearth about female ailments and children with croup, sweet pumpkin pie and the excellence of buchu brandy, the unreliability of servants. The men remain beside the table, with *sopies* and tobacco, commenting boisterously on sheep and cattle, on how you chased the Bushman down with your horse, on locusts and worms, or how you kicked the bloody Hottentot in the balls, and on the hidden meanings of Revelations.

Sleep well. The slaves bed down in the kitchen, the family snugly together in the bedroom on brass bedstead and spare mattresses; the guests are invited to share their room. But if you prefer the wagon, do feel free. Make yourself at home, and don't be shy to ask if you need anything. Oh sorry, the missus is here, too: good night.

My people.

Elisabeth gets up again, with sudden claustrophobia, returning to the front door. No sign of Adam yet. The sun is down; the birds still chattering sleepily. The world has grown enormous, limitless.

He won't return any more.

Perhaps it's better like this. Why should I allow myself to get trapped in you? It isn't dignified. I've fought myself free. I've liberated myself from everything – the Cape, and Erik Alexis Larsson, and my people; my own child; from past and future. I dare not ensnare myself again. For that is what it means. Have you thought something else was possible? – to touch someone and not let go again? But you forgot one thing: we are still human. And so we remain scared, and petty, and treacherous. Look, you have abandoned me.

She wants to return inside, but cannot. The brooding dusk oppresses her, the heavy smell of departed people is nauseating. In near-despair she looks out.

And there she sees him coming back, far away among the trees, carrying a buck on his shoulders.

She wants to cry. But she laughs. Picking up her dress to her knees, she begins to run.

'Adam!' she shouts. 'Adam!'

'What's the matter?' he asks when she reaches him out of breath.

'I've been so frightened,' she pants, ashamed now that he is back.

'Did anything happen?' he asks.

She shakes her head, her plaits swinging over her shoulders. 'No. It was just . . . You stayed away so long. I thought . . .'

'You were afraid I wouldn't come back? You were afraid of what would happen to you?' She hears the urgent accusation in his voice.

'No,' she says. 'I didn't even think of that. I was afraid . . .' She stops. She dare not say it. But she can no longer suppress it. 'I was afraid for *you*. In case something happened. In case you hurt your-self.'

'I'm all right.' He begins to walk on, beside her. It is getting much darker now. They reach the yard. At the doorstep he shrugs off the buck. There is blood on his shoulders. 'I had to go a long way to find something,' he says.

'As long as you're back.'

He squats down, takes his knife from his belt and starts skinning the buck.

She watches him for a while, then goes inside and returns with warm water in the pot he mended.

'You want to wash?' she asks.

'It's been a long day,' he says suddenly.

'It's been endless. You must be very tired.'

'That's nothing.' He gets up, looking at her intently, standing in front of her. She still has the pot of water in her hands. 'It's all the thinking,' he says.

'What have you been thinking then?'

'When I left here this morning I'd decided not to come back. I meant to go away.'

'I know,' she says, trying to read his face in the dark. 'Why did you come back then?'

'You brought me back.'

'We mustn't stay here,' she says with sudden conviction. 'Tomorrow morning we must go on, to the sea. It isn't good to stay here.'

'If you really think so.'

'I do,' she says, quiet and frank. 'I've also been thinking all day.'

She puts down the pot. For a moment she is still unsure. He is waiting for her to move. She tears the lace cuff from one of the sleeves of her Cape dress, soaks it in the warm water and begins to wash him. First his soiled shoulders. He stands motionless, allowing her to have her way with him.

Nothing is stirring any more; the birds in the trees are hushed. It's dark. Only inside the house there is a faint, reddish flickering from the fire in the hearth.

When she has finished, she drops the crumpled rag back in the water.

She looks up at him, quite quiet.

'Take off your clothes,' he says.

She breathes through half-opened lips, relieved of all fear, and experiencing only the strange serenity, not of submission but of acquiescence.

'Adam?' she whispers.

She wants to ask: Who are you?

But one must be able to walk into the night. Not a question of imagination, but of faith.

'I want you naked,' says his voice in the dark.

World provisionally without end. Beyond the undulating veld of heather and heath, and the brushwood of erica and protea, begins the virgin forest: beechwood and elder trees and els, redwood and blackwood, green-grey with hoary moss and ivy and strung with lianas; patriarchal yellow-wood and stinkwood trees, older than Christ.

The open veld is scarred by deep ravines reaching down to streams with long quiet pools and foaming rapids, kloofs so narrow and so deep, so densely overgrown, that from below you never see the sun.

The ravines run down to the sea where the continent ends abruptly. Overland, too, one reaches the coast, suddenly finding oneself on the edge of a dark red precipice stained yellow and green with lichen, decayed into grotesque patterns shaped by wind and water, pockmarked by caves; down to a primeval chaos of rocks and protruding tree-roots, and, in between, small crescents of beaches, sand or shingle.

Sound: the deep thundering of the waves against the resplendent rock of the cliffs; the slushing of water through sluices and gullies and tidal caves; the barking of baboons high up on the cliffside among the trees; the piercing scream of a fishing eagle; the screeching of gulls.

Movement: the primitive simplicity of the sea, wave upon wave, tide after tide, as reassuring as breathing. Tree-tops swaying slowly in the wind. On the wet sand the eager uneven crawling of shells scuttling back to the water; on the rocks the darting of rock-rabbits; above, the gliding and tumbling of gulls in the wind.

They are walking along their small white beach, on the edge of the low tide, directly above the scalloped line of foam, both naked. Rolled up in their cave, unused for the time being, lies her green dress. Her body is brownish in the generous glow of the late summer sun, still a paler brown than his, with her dark brown hair loose over her shoulders; and the pink of her nipples gently brown against the ochre-brown of her small breasts. She swerves away from him, into the shallow water, splashing him; he dashes after her, but she manages to escape. He follows her. With her long legs she runs away from him, but he soon catches up and grabs her waist and swings her round; they tumble down in the sand, rolling, thrashing, laughing, until the low waves begin to break over them, forcing them to jump up, startled, helpless with laughter; children.

'I'm thirsty,' she pants, pushing her wet, salty hair from her eyes.

'Shall we go to the pool?'

It lies on the far side of the rock formation closing off the small bay. Above the broad, foaming river mouth is a quiet pool surrounded by rocks and overgrown with ferns and cycads and moss; sometimes, if one keeps very still, there is a red and green flickering of a *lourie* in the foliage.

The pool is chilly, yet warmer than the sea. She lies down at the edge to drink, then rolls over on her back, looking up at him.

'You're all covered with sand.'

Meticulously, caressingly, she begins to wash him while he stands smiling; a restrained ritual of love; clasping his erection gently in both hands before she goes on. And then it is his turn to wash her clean of sand and salt, unashamedly beautiful.

As he reaches out to help her back over the rocks, a snake suddenly comes gliding past them, swiftly, soundlessly, straight across her foot, a smooth and stunning green. In a lightning reflex he jerks her out of the way, and when she recovers her balance he already stands poised with a stone in his hand. The next moment the broad flat head splits open, crushed and red with blood, the forked tongue flickering its last. Fascinated they stare at the lithe green body coiling and writhing before it stops with a final long shudder rippling from head to tail, its bright green strangely dulled.

'You shouldn't have killed it,' she says. 'It was so lovely.'

'And if it bit you?'

'It was on its way into the bush.'

'A snake is a snake.'

Subdued, they resume their climb over the rocks, back to their beach. As they reach the sand, she stops, pointing.

'Look.'

'What?'

'The way we came: don't you see?'

He looks across the beach.

'No, I don't see anything.'

'That's what I mean.' While they have been at the pool, the tide has

110

turned, foaming in over their footprints, obliterating them. 'It is as if we've never been here.'

'Perhaps we haven't,' he says, teasingly.

'Sometimes I wonder whether I'm dreaming you.' She is more serious. 'And even myself. It's all so impossible, so beautiful. Everything is so remote.'

'Come,' he says. 'It's time for me to fasten my nets.'

Knotted from lianas and vines and monkey-ropes, and tied with tough rushes, the nets are spread out on the sand to dry.

'I'll go and find some fruit,' she offers.

'Not poison-apples again!'

'No,' she says guiltily. 'I'll be more careful today.'

He gives her a playful slap on the behind and stands looking after her as she walks away, brown and bare.

'Savage!' he calls out softly.

She hears it and, laughing, picks up a handful of sand and throws it at him; then runs off. He wades into the shallow water to a line of rocks deeper in the sea: even at high tide they remain above water, a jagged kraal enclosing exquisite sea-gardens and, in the centre, a small oval of fine white sand. But he has to push on now, for if the sea rises much higher, he'll have to wait out there until it ebbs again.

Returning an hour later, carrying one of their roughly woven baskets filled with fruit, she finds him sleeping on the beach in the late sunlight; so still, that at first she's startled, thinking that something must have happened to him. But coming nearer she notices the even breathing motion of his chest, and, once, a slight twitching of his legs.

She kneels beside him, leaving the basket on the sand. He is lying on his side in the fine sand above the highest foam-ridge of the tide, the slack fingers of one hand still lightly clutching a shell.

The intimate landscape of happiness. The ultimately inexplicable quality of it. Everything permissible; everything possible.

His sleeping face on his bent arm. Grains of sand on his cheek and eyebrows. She leans over to blow them off, and hears him breathe, as incomprehensible as the movement of the sea. His shoulders, his tiny nipples. He moves slightly when she touches him, but his breathing is undisturbed. His smooth belly, the dense seaweed of his love-hair. Miraculous life kindled in his penis under her hand, stirring, growing, stiffening, fierce and tender to her touch.

'You're cheating, you're awake!'

'No, I'm still asleep. I'm dreaming.'

111

'I've brought the fruit. I'm hungry.'

'I'm hungry for you.'

'You may have me.'

That is the way it may have been. That is how it probably was. But nothing, she thought, was quite so difficult as the obvious and the natural. To walk about naked when you'd never dared to show an ankle in public. To transcend the thou-shalt-not of a lifetime, to discard an entire education, a way of life, as if it were irrelevant.

Abandoning oneself in the dark to a man's body, slaking the terrible thirst inside one and allowing it to spend itself: even that was quite different from living from day to day in serene and familiar contact with that same body, giving and taking without shame or hesitation, like a picking of fruit. The body of a man, no longer in frantic, furtive spasms in an orderly room or beneath the canvas of a wagon at night, but innocently and permanently present, visible and tangible and available, beside one's own. See how white I am; and you are brown. You're brown like a slave. But slaves steal past on the periphery of one's existence, like pets. And now no longer slave. Man. My man, my own. Bearing on your back and buttocks the hideous scars of a slave. My hands are sensitive and scared to touch them. I have to shut my eyes and clench my teeth. I caress you the way one would touch an open wound. Is it possible to learn to love even scars? To follow their contours with one's fingertip: this is you, your map, your landscape, all mine. It makes me shudder, and from my nausea grows lust; from my lust emerges tenderness. I desire it passionately, tracing the pattern with my tongue, like the track of a snail; I bite you like an animal and am devoured by you.

Was it possible, she wondered, that one could be prepared for it after all, in secret, unknown even to oneself? Remembering: the mulberry tree, her feet wide apart on two branches, the small berries bursting with sweetness in her mouth. She'd thought she was alone. But he had been there too, below her; he must have followed her, stealing into the rustling of the leaves, hidden by them. And then his mulberry hand along her mulberry legs.

He laughed at her when, at times, involuntarily, she tried to shyly cover herself or turn away; it was he who'd first removed the green dress and put it away, laughing at her desperate pleading and her rage and shame. And slowly she'd acquired confidence, defiant bravado. With the breathless, frightened excitement of a child doing something

112

forbidden, she began to experiment: with him, with herself, with the overwhelming newness of her existence. Expecting still, at any moment, the voice demanding: How dare you? Have you no shame? It was so impossible to accept that everything was really permissible. She thought: Forgive me if I'm stupid or ridiculous. Please be patient with me. I'm trying. I'm making progress, aren't I? I'm really not ashamed. Will you promise to be patient? You can be so wild. And yet so like a boy, in your own way even more shy, perhaps, than I, more clumsy, so beautifully clumsy. I love you. I have no other explanation to offer. I love you.

We're living here, provisionally for ever, protected from the wind, in a cave high above the sea, the inner walls blackened by smoke and soot; not from yesterday's fire, but the fires of centuries, perhaps millennia. Here and there, through the sooty crust, one can make out patches of colour – a rusty brown, ochre, off-white, red. And if you look closely in the light of a piece of burning wood, you discover curious little figures of men with bows and pricks, a buffalo hunt, ostriches, elephants with raised trunks, running buck. This is our home: from here we set out on journeys to the edge of the impossible, along moist paths of moss and smooth pebbles, without footprints. Provisionally.

To emerge from the mouth of the cave before sunrise, stopping on the broad rock-lip to look into the world – vast and pale, with the small precise sounds of waking birds and the grey squawking of the first gulls; a haziness on the sea but everything else clear, translucent – and to realise with a shock: here am I, there is the world. And then, perhaps through the slow motion of the sea, to experience the sensation of moving through that world and that space, yet not to touch it anywhere: to remain myself while the world remains the world.

'Come,' he says beside her, taking her hand.

Shivering slightly in the early coolness, they run down the steep slope to warm themselves. Looking back, the cliffs stand burning in the first light, glowing as if lit from the inside. He leads her on, over the rocks marking the end of their beach, and up the narrow twisting gorge they followed on their first day down. He carries the long pistol with its beautifully embossed grip, and a small bag of ammunition; she has the snares she has helped him prepare during their past few evenings beside the fire. Since they lost the gun in the rock-fall they haven't had much meat, hence the snares. And they will need more animal skins before winter.

113

For days on end he has worked on an assegai, first shaping a chunk of quartz found in their cave, patiently and skilfully chipping off flake after flake to form a razor-sharp spearhead, then tying it to a straight light stick with wet tendons, allowing it a week to settle tightly as the tendons dried out. Now it is indispensable for hacking a path through the myriad of thin, tough macchia stems in their way, an almost impenetrable tangle separating them from the real forest. She follows on his heels, struggling with the swaying shoots and the network of intertwined stems remaining behind him, occasionally crying out when a tough young sapling swings back, striking a red weal across her cheek or breast or shoulder. The smaller thorny shrubs leave a network of patches on their legs. Only their feet, protected by the shapeless skins he fashioned for them, remain unharmed. From time to time he stops to pick berries or fruit, showing it to her to test her skill and memory: this is edible, this is deadly poisonous, that is bitter.

Without warning they break through the final barrier of *fynbos*, finding themselves in the high forest. The change is abrupt and shocking. Here is no sun, no tangled undergrowth; only the large heavy trunks of ancient trees, the earth covered with a rustling mat of rotten bark, leaves, crackling twigs, patches of ferns or moss. The silence is absolute, and unearthly. Whenever they stop, so that even the dull rustling sounds accompanying their progress die down, the silence becomes still more awesome, defined by the calls of birds, the scurrying of monkeys among the branches, the sudden high-pitched whistle of a bluebuck dashing off, or the flight of a bushbuck after a momentary glimpse of a brown-speckled body and a flashing white tail.

What amazes her is the clarity of everything. No deep gloom through the absence of the sun, but a luminous reality, as if the leaves themselves are glowing from within, as if earth and trees are manifestations of light.

Intuitively he finds his way to one of the countless game-paths crisscrossing through the forest, following it to a fern-covered stream in a maple thicket. There, spread over a distance of several hundred yards, he carefully sets up the six or seven snares they've brought along, camouflaging them with leaves and splinters of bark.

'What makes you think the buck would choose this one spot in the whole forest?' she asks, incredulous.

'Look at all the tracks. It's obvious they've chosen this for a drinking place,' he says. 'You'll see when we come back tomorrow.'

'Are we going home already?' she asks with open disappointment. 'Why not?'

A *lourie* shrieks close by. Among the trees are bright blobs of red and orange and yellow fungus, there are orchids suspended from delicate stems. The earth is redolent with sweet decay, a gentle green stench. Large butterflies flutter among the leaves and flowers. Something is rustling in the foliage. Silence speaks to them in its innumerable voices.

'It is so peaceful here,' she says. 'I want to stay longer. Can't we go farther?'

He leads her on, along the winding trail, through the green luminosity of the wood. She has lost all consciousness of time.

Once he stops in his tracks, clutching her hand, whispering: 'Elephants.'

'How can you tell?'

He shows her, with infinite patience: leaves plastered against a thick brown trunk, sap oozing from a broken root, branches torn off and tossed away, a cluster of wet, chewed leaves, a trampled fern – and, soon, fresh dung.

'But I can't see anything,' she objects. 'They must be far away.'

With a raised hand he silences her. 'No, they're very close. Step on the tracks.' He points to what she hasn't even noticed: the flattened round marks on the ground, where one may step without causing a twig to crackle or a leaf to whisper.

She still finds it difficult to believe him. But all of a sudden he grabs her wrist. She stops, gazing ahead, but seeing nothing she shakes her head.

At that moment a branch breaks like a cracking shot. Startled, she nearly cries out. The brief movement of the animal's trunk has suddenly revealed the entire brownish mass of its body, motionless among the trees.

'Is there only one?'

'No. Look over there.'

An ear twitching; a long tusk gashing white against the green. Now she sees the bull too. And, gradually, one after another, the whole herd feeding among the trees.

With a long detour he leads her past them, farther into the forest. When she complains of fatigue he finds a pool of reddish-brown water in which to frolic and splash among the ferns. He gathers fruit she has

115

never tasted. And after gorging themselves they lie down to rest a while and sleep.

When, at last, he wakes her, the light has changed. While they have been asleep something must have happened outside somewhere. The green glow of the forest has a venomous gloomy air; the luminosity has disappeared, leaving the huge trunks of trees like dull shadows within shadow, ominous, dumb, large sulking hulks threatening them in the dusk.

A few times she looks round in terror, but there is nothing to see; there is always something invisible.

She has given up all hope of ever extricating themselves from the dark maze when, to her utter surprise, they come upon the first small stream again. In one of the snares a buck has been caught, dangling grotesquely from neck and hindleg – how both got caught in the noose is impossible to tell – strangled, with blue-black tongue and eyes protruding.

Revolted, she hurriedly turns away while he disengages the buck, slits open the belly to remove the guts, and drapes it round his shoulders. Sticky lines of blood trickle down his chest and belly, coagulating in his pubic hair.

In silence they go farther through the crepuscular wood, finally breaking back into the vicious path cut through the brushwood. At least it's lighter here, the clouds above placid and unthreatening.

But she bears the forest with her. Thinking: it's so peaceful there; but the great animals are always lurking somewhere in the gloom.

And back in the safety of their cave, that night, she refuses to have any of the meat he has prepared.

The way you have of studying yourself so intently, with an expression of wonder, as if you find it difficult to believe your own body. Standing in the mouth of the cave to feel the wind breathing against you. Closing your eyes to allow the salt spray of the water to wash over your face. Moving close to the fire where the smoke can whirl around you. Wandering among the tidal pools in the rocks, kneeling for hours watching the silvery little fishes darting about, or worrying a sea-anemone with a limp bamboo shoot, looking up with a guilty blush if I come upon you unexpectedly.

Everything repeats you, in everything I recognise you. In the farthest pool among the rocks, in the curve of a maidenhair fern, the suture of a Hottentot's bean shelled from its pod, the sudden swerve of a gull, a feather's delicate pattern on the sand, small wild calabashes, a swaying tree, the spray of a wave, sea-foam.

The way you suddenly fall silent in the middle of a conversation, looking out across the sea. Your pensive gathering of shells, the most minute ones which I barely notice, the size of grains of sand, but quite perfect, round and pointed, green and red and brown, sheltered in the hollow of your hand and carried to the cave, there stored with infinite care, then forgotten, discarded. Your complete infatuation with water, with washing and bathing yourself, saturating yourself, as if you can never have enough of it. Your habit of talking in your sleep, muttering senseless or incongruous words with a lazy, languid tongue, laughing, or stifling a sudden sob.

And this, constantly: to disappear from cave or beach and wander off on your own, over the rocks to more distant, wilder beaches; along the gorges; even into the forest.

'I want to go with you.'

'No, you stay here.'

'But what do you do all by yourself like that?'

'Nothing really.' Appearing surprised at the question. 'Just wandering about. Looking. Listening.'

'What do you listen to?'

Embarrassed: 'The silence, more often than not.'

And then you're off again.

Why is it so important to you to be alone? Am I not enough for you – or am I too much for you? Are you doubtful, or worried, and trying to hide it from me? Do you think about the Cape when you're away from me? About your people, about one day? If I ask you about it, you simply shake your head. Do you still think I cannot really understand?

Even when I'm with you, inside you, when you close your eyes: is it because you're happy, or because you wish to exclude me?

Returning to the pool beyond the rocks one morning, they find the snake still there: its green changed into a muddiness, the thin body soggy and teeming with maggots and bluebottles. And who would have expected a snake to smell like that? – has it got flesh, then, like man or beast, is there no difference at all?

'You must show me everything you know.'

Patiently, at night or in the daytime. How to dig a hole into a sneezewood log and rub a twig in it to make fire. Where to find the

117

gli-roots you mix with honey to make your heady beer; and how to make a skin bag, with the hairy side turned inside, for carrying liquids. Which berries are edible and how to distinguish them from the others. What herbs to use for fever, and how to stop blood with spiderwebs. How to stand dead still when you see a mantis, so as not to disturb its prayers to the god Tsui-goab. What roots are best to chew for thirst, and how to blend your hash for smoking if you wish to dream with open eyes or feel at peace. How to learn from birds when to watch out for snakes, where to look for honey, when to expect rain. How to read direction in the stars.

How does one cure and prepare a hide to get it soft, and how do you make a kaross? – for the days are still mild but the nights are growing cool, and soon we'll need more covering.

Show me what a woman should do when she loves a man and wants to please him; I have so much to learn.

Show me how to catch a crab without getting nipped. How do you tie your nets, where does one look for ollycrocks and oysters, how does one catch crayfish?

'And tell me about the sea.'

'I can't tell you. You must feel the sea to know him.'

'How does one feel it?'

He studies her for a long time, reflecting. Then, with a slow smile: 'If you want to, I'll show you. Come.'

He pulls her up by the hands and leads her over the beach. The tide has turned an hour or two ago and the water is rising steadily, but he wades in against the waves, holding her hand. Foam splashes against their shiny light and dark brown legs.

'Where are we going?'

He gestures to the small island of rocks deeper into the bay where he usually spreads his nets.

'But the tide is coming in, we won't be able to get out again.'

'That's the only way to feel the sea. When it's all round you.'

They climb up the slippery black rocks. From the top, layers of stone lead down to the inner oval like broad uneven steps littered with pools. Below them lies the patch of sand, finer and whiter than that on the beach, some two yards wide and three or four in length. On the far side it is sealed off by another, higher formation of black rocks.

She has only been here at low tide before, and she looks towards the beach without much confidence. 'How will we get back again?'

'We'll wait for the tide to go out.'

'But that's a long time!'

'Yes.'

From time to time a delicate spray washes over them when the larger waves break against the back rows of rocks.

'I'm not so sure . . .' She hesitates.

'You said you wanted to feel the sea.' He squats down beside a small rock-pool.

'What are we going to do all the time?'

'Nothing.'

Uncertainly she looks at his calm, inscrutable face; then back to the churning water separating them from the beach. The waves are growing visibly.

'If you really want to go back, you can still swim out,' he says. 'In a little while it'll be too dangerous.'

Anxiously she looks at the beach a hundred yards away, and the great red cliffs towering behind, fringed by the forest; the crescent of white sand between rocks and rocks; and their cave, higher up, a black hole in the precipice. A fishing eagle screams its eerie call.

'I'll stay with you,' she says, almost grimly, and comes to sit beside him on a ledge.

The smooth surface of the rocks is covered with a mosaic of barnacles and limpets, some of them ancient, the shells broken and jagged; nothing can loosen their grip. On the bed of the pool periwinkles and pointed snails are crawling, drawing intricate patterns on the sand. Tiny fishes dart from their hiding places, flitting across the sunlit patches, returning to the shadows. There are a few brilliant red starfishes on the bottom, and purple anemones lazily fanning their fringes. Crabs, bright patches of seaweed and, to one side, in the darkest deepest corner, the slowly moving red and white tentacles of an octopus.

They watch in silence, teasing the anemones, trying to catch the quicksilvery fishes in their hands. Like many other times. But different. For in the past their visits occurred at low tide and today they are surrounded by the deeper droning of the sea, rising and swelling. Once she jumps up with a cry of fear as a small splash of foam suddenly breaks over her bare back.

'Got a fright?' he asks, smiling.

'Yes. The waves are getting so wild.'

In spite of herself, she looks back towards the land.

'It's too late now,' he says quietly.

She nods.

He gets up and comes close to her. 'Are you afraid?'

'Yes.'

'That's good. It makes it easier to feel him.'

'What?'

'The sea. What else?'

They stand close together, looking over the rocks towards the deep sea, the incoming waves, swelling and rearing up as if they mean to break right over the black rock-wall, then thundering past on either side, sending the brilliant white foam flying. Through all the cracks and gullies small waterfalls come rushing down towards them, feeding the rock-pools.

'Are you sure we won't be washed away?'

'I don't think so.'

'But are you *sure*, Adam?'

'No, I'm not sure. I've never seen it happen, but with the sea one never knows.'

'But how could you have brought me here if you . . . ?'

'I came with you, didn't I? Whatever happens to you will happen to me too.'

'Are you mad?' she asks, losing control of yourself. 'Do you want us to drown here?'

'Of course not.'

'But why did you let me – why did you let us . . . ?'

'You said you wanted to feel the sea.'

'But not if it's dangerous.'

'How can you feel him without danger?'

'We've got to go back!'

'I told you it's too late.'

'Will it rise any farther?'

'Yes.'

'How much?'

'We'll see. Another hour to go, more or less.'

'I can't wait that long. It's unbearable.'

'You'll just have to, now that we're here.'

'Adam, I'm not going to . . .' She is too upset to continue.

'Don't be ridiculous,' he says calmly.

Hysteria sweeps over her.

'How dare you?' she screams, attacking the lean, tough muscles of his chest with her fists.

He grabs her wrists.

'Let me go!' she shouts at him.

'Not until you stop.'

'Adam, let go!'

He holds on, swaying this way and that as she tries to wrench free. She can barely restrain herself from spitting in his face with helpless rage.

They are soaked by another shower of foam. She gasps for breath.

'Adam, my God . . . !'

'I'm here with you,' he says soothingly, as before.

'I didn't want to die,' she whispers, sobbing.

'Who said you were going to?'

She looks up at him urgently, trying to find hope in his eyes, or merely an explanation, something which will make comprehensible to her what is happening. But he looks back at her, unrelenting.

'What do you want me to do?' she asks, desperate.

'Lie down.'

Once again she tries to resist, but he forces her back until, struggling wildly, she loses her balance. He holds on to her so that she doesn't fall, and lays her down, pressing her firmly against the sand. Furious, but powerless, she succumbs.

For a while he sits beside her, looking down at her, still holding her shoulders lightly. Then he says: 'Elisabeth.'

It is so seldom he uses her name that it touches something deep inside her, in the pit of her stomach, deeper down.

'Adam, what do you want of me?'

'Listen to the sea,' he says. 'That's what we've come for.'

She shuts her eyes, still terrified. Lying here on the sand covering the deeper bed of rock, she seems to be hearing the sea with more than her ears: as if the sound is moving right into her, that dull unending roar, entering every fibre of her, until she can hardly distinguish between herself and the sound. She is so hypnotised by the low thunder of the water that she is hardly aware of him moving beside her, over her; on to her. Instinctively she closes her legs, but he forces her down again, prying her thighs apart with his knee, hurting her. She begins to cry, no longer understanding what is happening. He seems possessed, ramming into her. She goes on struggling as if he were a stranger overpowering her. But in the very act of crying and struggling against him she discovers, shockingly, blindingly, that she is no longer fighting him but actually clinging to him, clutching,

121

grabbing, digging into his body with her fingers. Hearing her own voice like the scream of a sea-bird: 'Yes! Yes! Yes! You must! You must!'

The thunder grows around them. An endless spray comes splashing over the rocks, drenching them. She no longer feels the sudden stinging cold, she is not even frightened any more. She has resigned herself utterly to drowning here. It is the sound of death reverberating through their rocking bodies.

Only much later, after the wild thrashing of his body against hers has subsided and she feels herself slowly shrinking in from that infinity of sound, back, inwards to this patch of sand among the rocks, protected from the sea, she hears him whisper against her cheek:

'It's all over now. It's going down.'

'Adam?'

He moves his arm and pushes himself up on his elbows, looking down at the small moist strands of hair on her temples. 'My name is Aob,' he says. 'Adam belongs to other people. Will you remember that? My name is Aob.'

'Who gave it to you?'

'My mother.'

'What does it mean?'

'It doesn't mean anything. It's just a name. It's mine.'

She doesn't move under him. 'We didn't die,' she says at last, almost, it sounds, with regret.

'No, we're alive.'

'Aob.' She says it softly, as if she's testing the taste of the unfamiliar sound. But she has no will to resist: neither the name, nor him, nor the light, nor the ebbing sound of the sea. There are seagulls over them. Let them be. Let everything be as it is. Let nothing ever change or pass. Together, they drift off into sleep, the deepest sleep they've ever slept together; and only when the ripples of the low-tide wavelets begin to suck and whisper against the sibilant rock do they wake up, and roll over, and return, unspeaking, to the beach.

That night, with the full moon high above the shimmering bay, they suddenly start up in the cave beside their fire: they have both, in the same instant, heard it – the different, ominous change of sound in the sea. From the mouth of the cave they look out across the bay. It takes some time before their eyes get used to the moonlight. Then they see the waves of the spring tide swelling from deep in the heart of the bay, breaking over the black jagged rocks of the little island, flooding

122

it until nothing is left of it and everything lies buried under a moving mass of dark and sparkling water.

'No, it's too dangerous,' he says.

They have left the beach far behind. Here, towards the west, where they are exploring the coast, the landscape becomes increasingly wild, the cliffs running down right into the sea in ridge upon ridge of reddish black rocks: the farthest ridges hazy with vapour against the early sun. In one place there must have been a flaw in the formation causing the entire cliffside to subside in some prehistoric cataclysm, leaving a petrified cataract of boulders all the way up.

'There's a narrow kloof farther on which will take us to the top,' he says.

But she is adamant to climb the breach.

'Look,' she says, 'It's just like huge steps. We can run up in a few minutes. It's very solid.'

'How do you know?'

'I *want* to go up here.'

It isn't really an argument; yet it has a grave undertone. Not active resistance on her part, just the old stubbornness – she acknowledges it almost with joy – reviving in her after the long passivity. You know this coast so well, you're the leader in all our excursions, teaching me everything you know: but you cannot force your will on me in all things. I'm here too. Don't you recognise me? I must pit my will against yours. I insist on going up here.

'Come on,' he orders.

'No.' She scrambles up the first series of boulders, away from him.

'Elisabeth, listen to me!'

With gleeful determination she climbs farther, light-footed, jumping from stone to stone. High up the rocky slope, her legs wide apart to balance herself on an overhanging boulder, she stops to look down at him, her body white against the brown and grey of the stones, with a touch of redness caused by her first exposure to the sun. In this newly won freedom of nakedness, still exhilaratingly self-conscious, it excites her to look down at him like this, defying him.

He follows her a little way, climbing cautiously, hampered by the gun he's carrying.

'Come back!'

'Come up to me. You see how easy it is?'

She turns away again, calling out involuntarily when she stumbles

123

and grazes a knee or when her ankle gets caught between smaller stones. But nothing can hold her back now. Actually, she is so confident that he will be following her, that it comes as a disappointment when she stops to look back again and sees him still standing far below.

'Adam!' she calls.

He waves: come back!

She jumps from her perch to go higher. Not that there is any hurry. She will have to wait for him up there. Having had her way makes her feel a bit ludicrous in the circumstances. But she refuses to turn back.

She is less cautious now; and jumping to another rock, momentarily losing her balance and grabbing the edge of a boulder to steady herself, she kicks loose a few stones under her. For a moment it doesn't seem serious. Then a large rock, hit by the falling stones, is dislodged and tumbles down, setting a spray of sparks flying as it strikes other rocks in its way. And suddenly there is a rumbling below her, a slow shudder all the way down the breach in the cliff wall; and in front of her eyes, wide open with horror, the whole rocky mass begins to move and slide down the slope. She herself is safe, clinging to a ledge of the cliff itself. But everything else is sliding, subsiding, tumbling down in one unending avalanche.

'Adam!' she screams. 'Look out!'

All she can see is a cloud of red dust; and then an eruption of foam as the landslide hits the sea.

He is dead. She knows it. Just like that: violently, absurdly.

And all for nothing. For this senseless urge in her not to yield, to match her will with his. What is it in her that drives her on to this? A yearning for an apocalypse was what he called it, that distant day in the Cape. What was it that urged her to rebel against her parents and marry Larsson and trek into the wilderness with a man she hardly knew and couldn't fathom? What spell was it that was cast over her at the river when she insisted on driving the ox into the flood? And how many times will it still happen? How many more lives will she plunge into an abyss?

She stares down the slope, her fists clenched, her teeth cutting into her lower lip. The dust dies down. In a trance, she begins to climb down, from stone to stone, knowing it's even more dangerous now than before but not caring in the least; almost wishing the avalanche would start again and bury her. Bruising and grazing her naked body, she stumbles on, blindly, down to where the waves are breaking against the foot of the red cliffs.

He is sitting far away from the breach when she reaches the bottom; trying to straighten the twisted metal of the gun-barrel, his face tightly drawn; he barely looks up when she approaches.

Her legs give way under her. She sits down and begins to cry.

With an angry movement he hurls away the useless gun and looks at her. He comes to her and takes her in his arms, holding her tightly against him, waiting for her frenzied sobbing to subside, doing his utmost to control himself.

'It's all right,' he says at last, his voice still trembling. 'It's all over. It was very close.'

'You're not dead,' she whispers.

'No. I saw it coming. The cliff protected me. Skinned my knees when I dived out of the way.' He shows her his bleeding legs. 'But that's nothing. Only the gun has had it.'

'Adam, I . . .' She doesn't know what to say.

'Don't try it again,' he says. 'Next time we may not be so lucky.'

From all our excursions we return, wind-blown, to the cave which closes round us like a fist. This is the space in which, fleetingly, ineffably, we meet and recognise and explore each other. Small miraculous moments when I no longer ask or try to understand what is happening. When it is enough, almost too much to bear, simply to be alive and to know we are alive. In between I must subsist on memories and hope: and both are dangerous. All I know of you I know here. If ever we should go away from here I may lose it. You see, I am frightened. Moreover, the nights are getting colder.

He is sitting with outstretched legs on the lip of the cave, leaning his back against the rock, peacefully smoking his reed-pipe: a mixture of wild hash and herbs. Absorbed, even with slight amusement, he watches her working, cutting up the carcass of the buck in the way he has demonstrated to her, the tip of her tongue protruding from her lips, a frown of concentration between her eyes. Her hands and wrists are slithery with blood, but with a small grunt of satisfaction she finally manages to sever the thick muscle from the bone, cut meticulously along the seams, the bluish membrane covering it practically unscathed.

'Is that right?' she asks, glowing with contentment, as she comes over to him and kneels beside him to show him her handwork.

'Very good,' he says, taking the piece of meat from her, turning it

125

over. 'Only try to cut more neatly along the back, here, where the tendon is joined to the bone.'

'I'll make sure next time.'

'You're coming on very well.' He looks at her kneeling in front of him, and with a sudden movement takes her hands in his.

'My hands are dirty.'

He kisses her. 'That's all right. Blood is healthy.' He opens his hands and looks at them, smudged by hers. With only the suggestion of a smile on his grave face he places his open palms on her bare shoulders. She shudders slightly, but keeps looking bravely into his eyes. Slowly he moves his hands downward, until they come to rest on her breasts, smearing her smooth skin with blood. He sees her bite on her teeth, but she makes no move to resist. Under his palms he feels her nipples stiffening.

'Why do you do it?' he asks at last.

'I don't know. Just because.'

She keeps looking at him, searching, never quite sure about his intentions.

Suddenly he smiles and removes his hands. 'Go and finish your work,' he says.

'I'm tired.'

'You can't stop halfway.'

She gets up reluctantly, taking the biltong from him. 'At home the kitchen slave used to . . .' She stops, guilty.

With narrowed eyes he studies her, but he makes no answer. Crestfallen, she goes back to the carcass and resumes her work.

'Do we really need it?' she asks after some time.

'What?'

'All the game you keep on bringing home.'

'We need the skins. And the meat will be useful in winter.'

'Are we going to stay here?'

'I don't know,' he answers casually. 'Depends on the weather.'

'Adam.'

He blows out smoke, looking at her.

'Aob,' she says.

'What is it?'

'Let's stay here.'

'I told you it depends on the weather.'

'I don't mean for the winter. I mean: for ever. Why should we ever go away from here?'

'I thought you wanted to go back to the Cape?'

'I wanted to – before. Not now. Neither of us needs the Cape any more.' Adding, with unexpected intensity: 'I *can't* go back any more. Don't you understand? It's quite impossible.'

He looks at her, searching and urgent, but doesn't answer.

Almost breathless, she hurries on: 'We're so happy here, we're together, we don't need anything from outside.'

'Will you always think that way?'

'As long as you stay with me. We can live here. We can clean out the cave and furnish it. We can have children. You can teach them everything you taught me. In the daytime you'll take the boys to the forest, or to your nets in the sea; and the girls and I will tidy the cave and make mats and baskets and karosses and things. Perhaps we can find some clay, then I'll try to make pots. We'll fetch water and look after you. At night we'll all sleep together round the fire. We can make music together. We'll gather shells, and lie on the beach, and swim.' She is carried away by her own passionate argument. 'Do let's stay here!' she pleads. 'We don't ever need to do anything else. It would be ridiculous to go away from here, back to the Cape. We've taken all that off with our clothes.'

He comes to her, still with his strange, wry smile: 'Just us two savages in the wilderness?'

'We'll love each other and be good to one another.'

'In that case we may stay here. All right. Until, one day, we'll forget that there has ever been a Cape.'

She looks into the strangeness of his eyes. Is he mocking her? Is he cynical? Sardonic? Or is he just as serious as herself?

On her soft nipples the dry blood has become black and hard: scabs on vulnerable wounds.

The body of the snake is drying out, its skin turned into a leathery flimsy parchment torn in places, frayed by the wind. And through the faded green the ribbed pattern of the inside is beginning to emerge.

It is wild outside – night wind and crashing waves – but inside it's peaceful. Cosy beside the fire, they are reassured by the familiar drawings and colour patches on the walls of the cave; the bats' shrilling almost inaudible, flitting in and out; the wood-pile in the corner; the skins stretched out to dry, the dried ones cured and rolled; the small bundle of belongings they brought with them; her green

Cape dress; the kaross she has completed, stitching together the square-cut skins with leather-strips and tendons; her collection of shells and crayfish and crabs; the horns of buck and a few strings of biltong; a roughly woven basket filled with dried fruit; his tools and weapons. Theirs. And in the circle of the fire, the two of them together.

She is preparing food, roasting fish, frying the large fleshy mushrooms he has brought in from the forest; he is finishing off a crayfish basket.

He looks up: 'What I need is a son to help me on the rocks.'

'You're not taking my children into the sea like that,' she says. 'You'll drown them all.'

'Oh, I'll teach them to swim when they're very small, like little seals. And when we're old they can look after us.'

'I want a son like you.'

'First a daughter,' he says. 'Like you. Every bit like you. I want to see, as she grows up, what you were like through all those years I didn't know you. I'm jealous of everything that happened to you.'

They're drawn into their old game again, dreaming and pretending. Until, through the flames, she suddenly looks at him and asks:

'Do you really think we'll have children some day?'

'Of course.'

'What makes you so sure?'

'I'm a man, you're a woman.'

Before she can restrain herself, she asks, 'That girl you had, the slave girl. Did she bear you a child?'

'How must I know?' he says, closing up. 'I told you she was sold.'

'Of course. I forgot; I'm sorry.'

'Why did you ask?'

'I'd be so relieved if I really knew – that we *could*.'

'But why on earth can't we? You've been pregnant once.'

'Yes. But then I lost it.'

It is the first time she dares refer to it again; the first time she dares admit to him that she has never forgotten.

'I wonder so often what happened to it. What they did to it.'

'What does it matter?'

'It was mine. It was torn from me. It was something of myself they buried in the veld. And sometimes . . .' She shudders. Looking up hesitantly, she says: 'Last night I dreamt.'

'What?'

128

'That they buried me in a porcupine hole. And then it rained and I started growing, like a bean or something, pushing through the earth. I couldn't move my feet, they were roots deep down. I pushed up my branches, screaming for help, but nobody heard, for no one can hear a tree. And I was all alone on that endless plain surrounded by vultures.'

Drawing up her legs she rests her head on her knees, contracted, like a sea-bean.

'It was only a dream.'

'I lost my child. And what's going to become of *me*?'

'You're asking too many questions,' he says.

'Things can't just happen like that,' she insists. '*Why* do they happen? What comes out of it all? Where does it lead to? How can one just live and die like this – and then it's all over? Is that really all there is? Just this?' She looks up in fear. 'Suppose we grow old here and . . . something happens: then no one will even know that we've been here. They won't know that we ever existed.'

'What does it matter? We're here now, aren't we?'

'But I want to know!'

'How can you know? Why should you know? I thought you said you were happy here.'

'But don't you understand? Suppose we *die* here?'

'Perhaps they'll find our bones one day,' he says.

Contemplating the shell, caressing my palm with its small smoothness, ochre on top, almost orange, as if immersed in liquid sunlight; changing to a creamy white below, sloping down into the gently ribbed groove, the secret shimmering of mother-of-pearl inside. Oval, like a small tortoise, but smooth, infinitely smooth, blunt and rounded in front, narrower towards the back, tapering to a slightly elongated orbed point. Perfectly spheroid on top, hard and glossy, glazed, complete unto itself; but turning it over it becomes more penetrable and exposed, the shiny curves folding inward to the narrow slit which housed the snail: vulnerable, naked, trembling, moist. It's such a long time now I haven't seen myself.

The coming of the hunters. The bull had obviously been wounded first, for over a long distance the forest was trampled, with branches torn down, the earth dug up in blood-red trenches, black smudges of blood staining the ferns and trees. He was lying on his left side against a thick yellow-wood trunk, as if he'd propped himself up there before he collapsed, smeared with blood and dung. The front and lower parts of his head were a mess, covered with flies. The trunk had been hacked off, the tusks dug out. It seemed as if an effort had been made to remove the toenails as well, but the job had been abandoned halfway.

Around them the forest was quiet, except for the birds rustling or chattering overhead, bees buzzing in the purple orchids, timid monkeys in the branches.

They risked it out into the open.

'What happened to him?' she asked as they approached above the wind. 'Why is he maimed like that?'

'Tusks cut out. Can't you see?'

'But . . ' She fell silent, not because she didn't want to oppose him, but because she was, suddenly, scared to receive an answer.

He was looking round, frowning.

'Shall we go back?' she asked, almost hopefully.

'We can try and follow his tracks to where he came from,' he offered. 'If you want to.'

'If *you* want to.'

The forest was as bright as it had been the first time, yet it seemed ominous and strange, the openness of its mysteries overwhelming. They weren't even sure what they were looking for, which made it more sinister. What was waiting at the end of the blood trail? More destruction, or more silence? Deeper into the forest they penetrated. It seemed to stretch out endlessly to all sides. How would one know when one had reached its innermostness?

Half a mile beyond the first carcass they came upon a second, lying with its hindquarters in a brook, damming up the water. Once again the head was hideously maimed, the tusks dug out; the small ferocious eyes staring muddily at them through tangled lashes.

'Do you think he's been here for a long time?' she asked, hushed.

'Two or three days.'

'But who could have done it?'

'It's only the people from the Cape who slaughter like this.' In his voice was a dark passion which she hadn't heard for a long time now.

'It may have been Hottentots!' she protested, not knowing why she should.

'Yes. To sell their ivory in the Cape.'

She bowed her head, looking up again after a moment, now with great urgency: 'Whoever they were, they were *people*. So close to us. And yet we heard nothing.'

'We're down there at the sea. How can we hear what's going on in the forest?'

'Two or three days,' she said, reflecting. 'They may have left by now.'

'Yes.'

'What are we going to do?'

He looked back to where they'd come from; and then farther ahead, into the green glow. Dark logs lay scattered in the undergrowth, half sunken into the humus, dumb and heavy, like dead things.

'We can go farther to look for them,' he said.

She wanted to answer: Yes. Farther. Deeper inward. Let us reach the pith and heart of it, penetrating through all the green growth-rings, to the mysterious core of light illuminating it all. Let us find something. Even if we can only approach something, to know it is there, within reach, graspable.

But raising a hand to her breast, looking down at herself, she quietly said: 'I can't go like this – not if there are people.'

They turned back. She felt a curious sadness, almost rebellious against herself. What else could she have done? Yet, by turning back, they'd given up something – something which had very nearly happened, something she'd approached very closely: a feeling, a discovery, a possibility.

Near the edge of the forest they both stopped abruptly in their tracks. What was that sharp report in the distance, so far away that they couldn't even be sure of the direction?

'Was it a gunshot?' she asked.

'Or a branch breaking.'

It might have been a shot.

Almost mechanically they followed their path through the brush-wood and down the gorge, far from the rocky breach and the stonefall of their first excursion. Just in time, before dark, they reached their cave.

He went down to his nets. It was low tide. There were a few fishes; he brought them back.

Smoke came whirling from the cave; she'd already made the fire. But she wasn't at the fireplace when he came in: he discovered her at the back of the cave, beside their bundle, and when she became aware of him, she swung round quickly, overcome by guilt.

'I only wanted to . . .'

She folded up the green Cape dress again, and, avoiding his eyes,

131

put it back with the other things. Then she came to him and took the fish from him, and scraped it with one of his flint knives. When she finally glanced up his eyes were still on her.

'I was only looking,' she said, her cheeks glowing more red than the fire.

'I know.'

'You're not angry with me, Adam, are you?'

'Why should I be angry?'

He went to the mouth of the cave, looking out at the moon rising.

She wanted to go to him, to touch the naked pain in him, to exorcise his sadness and his dull revolt; but she couldn't, there was too much of it in herself. In silence she prepared their food, and he returned to his usual place opposite her. From time to time, through the fire, they looked at each other.

Without finishing his food he returned to the mouth of the cave. She saw the firelight flickering across the dark scars of his back. What are you looking at? What are you listening for? There's only the moon on the water, and the booming of the sea drowning all other sounds.

'Aren't you coming to sleep?'

'Yes, I'm coming.'

They moved in under the large kaross, on the soft bedding he'd gathered in the veld. Lying still beside each other. From habit, his hand started stroking her, a rough caress, questioning, searching. Because she loved him she yielded to him; but she remained absent. Passively allowing him to part her legs, she suddenly felt him contract against her. For a while he lay very still.

'Come into me,' she whispered.

'You're not here,' he said. Not accusingly: neutrally, calmly.

'I want to be here with you,' she said, 'I *am* here.'

'You're looking for the hunters in the wood.'

'How did you know? Why do you ask? It isn't true.'

'The Cape is calling you.'

'No.' She shook her head violently against his shoulder.

'Don't be afraid,' he said, holding her.

'Stay with me.'

'I am with you.'

He felt his heart shrinking, not clearly knowing why. Their small cosy cave suddenly felt so exposed to the night wind; so penetrable by yesterday and tomorrow.

'Hold me tight,' she pleaded desperately. 'I don't know what's happening. Hold me. Don't go away.'

Very early the next morning he went away, just after the reassuring return of the sun. Neither of them had spoken about it: he simply went; and as he left, she handed him a bag of food she had prepared for the road. For neither could tell how long he would be gone. He was wearing his skin apron and carrying the assegai, leaving the pistol with her for protection.

It was a long roundabout route, from the first carcass to the second, following the tracks from there, finding three more dead elephants before noon. Near the last carcass he discovered signs of camping, patches of grass pressed down where people had slept, footprints, a large fireplace with fresh ashes. Some of the ironwood logs were still smouldering. He glanced up instinctively, looking for signs of wind. A sudden gust might set the whole forest alight. But it was deadly still; not even the leaves or the hoary moss stirred.

He went on with a strange sensation, as if time had suddenly obliterated the past few months, restoring him to his endless trail through the land, fired by his own restlessness, rediscovering the tracks of a wagon trek and following them for days and weeks, spying on them from a distance: wagons and oxen, Hottentots, white people, a man and a woman; a woman on her own; waiting for something to happen.

There were two wagons. From the far edge of the forest the tracks swerved back, following an open trail parallel to the route on which he'd set out; so that, coming upon them late on the second morning, their camp was barely a half-day's journey from the coast as the crow flies. Two wagons and numerous oxen, at least forty, with five or six Hottentots, and two white men – one middle-aged, the other quite young, both with wild unkempt beards.

Adam stayed at a safe distance, for fear of being discovered by their dogs. Hiding below the wind, he kept watch for several hours. One of the wagons seemed to be used exclusively for merchandise. A whole heap of ivory, tied up in bundles, lay waiting to be loaded, and piles of dried skins, ostrich feathers, antelope horns. Judging from the bustling activity in the camp they were preparing for departure, probably the next day.

The place held him spellbound, like the first camp of the Larsson trek. But now with more solemnity. And it was with a heavy heart that he finally crawled from his hiding place and set off for the coast. The veld was easy there: heath and proteas and clusters of wild lilies; sparse trees, karee and others, most of them smallish.

It was only when he reached the top of the cliff wall above the green expanse of the sea that thoughts started up in him again. For he knew she was waiting down there and that he would have to report to her. It might be the end. And he was filled with sadness at the attainability of ends. One might drift timeless through the days, abandoned like seaweed to the tide: but in the end you're washed ashore.

High above the cliffs an eagle was riding the wind, looking for something moving below. Almost motionless, it hung in the highest currents, a small cross in infinite space: one day it, too, would fall, dropping like a stone. What appeared impossibly remote, so distant that it seemed irrelevant, suddenly turned factual, immediate. Tomorrow became today; today moved back to yesterday. And the earth remained untroubled by it all: it was like thistle seeds blowing in the wind, insignificant sighs in space.

It was late afternoon by now. The afternoon was morning to the night. And she was waiting.

He needn't tell her anything; he needn't tell the truth. She didn't know a thing yet, she was merely waiting. And whatever he said she would accept. That he'd found a band of Hottentots, ready to set out to the Cape with their bundle of tusks. That he'd found a deserted camp in the forest, but no sign of people. That he'd come upon a wagon plundered by Bushmen, signs of cattle driven off, two maimed bodies he'd buried; no provisions. That he'd found no sign of anything.

You will believe me. Even if you know it is a lie, you'll believe me because we both want it that way; because you are as scared as I am.

Let those two wagons trek through the country plundering as far as they go, planting the beacons of civilisation on their destructive way: you and I shall remain here, in our cave above the sea. Nothing shall disturb us. We'll listen to the gulls screeching at dawn, and tighten our embrace, my bitter root planted deep in you, *doepa* against loneliness. In the daytime we'll gather shells which I shall string round your waist to tinkle as you walk. You'll fish with me and help me bring in my nets, and mend them where the sea has torn them. Sometimes we'll go to the forest and empty my snares and bring home buck for food. I shall see the light and the laughter in your eyes when you taste a fruit you've never seen before. I'll baptise your breasts in blood. And I shall lay you down on the sand again and open you like a starfish, moist as an anemone; and feel the sun burning on the grains of sand on my back where the sweat has dried. I'll play music for you on a reed-flute or a *ghoera*; and you will sing silly little songs with improvised words to keep me company. And we'll be happy, needing nothing beyond ourselves. Believe me. It is true. It must be true.

The eagle, a mere speck in the sky, shot down to its prey below: badger? hare? skunk? mouse? Carrying something in its claws it rose again, rowing against the wind.

With a sigh he started the descent down the red cliffside, following the gorge. It was late.

'There are two wagons,' he said when she came running to meet him on the beach, pressing herself against him. 'One is loaded with things. They're preparing to move on. I suppose they'll be going straight to the Cape, because they've got no packing space left.'

'Only the two white men?'

'Yes. One is middle-aged, the other young.'

'What do they look like? Friendly? Or wicked?'

'Like hunters. Men from the Cape. Rather dirty. Nothing that can't be washed off with water.'

'Do you think they'd try to molest me?'

'You're a woman.'

'I suppose one can keep them in their place, I still have the pistol.'

'Of course.'

'How long does it take to get back to the Cape on a wagon?'

'It's a long way, and there are mountains too. They'll have to trek round the forest. Say two or three months.'

They returned to the cave.

'You'll come with me, won't you?' she asked. 'You can protect me.'

'If they found out about you and me . . . ?'

'We won't let them.'

In the cave he sat down, leaning against the wall, exhausted and depressed. She brought him water in a large abalone shell; and some honey.

Once again she started questioning him, going over everything he'd already told her in detail.

'But can we still catch up with them if they leave in the morning?'

'If we set out early.'

After a while she went to the back of the cave. He didn't look. He could hear her rustling in the half-dark. When she returned she was wearing the Cape dress. It hung down from her, badly crumpled; but in a strange outlandish way he found her beautiful.

'I've lost weight,' she said, inexplicably shy before his eyes.

'You've grown tougher,' he said. 'More beautiful.' Desiring her so much that there came tears in his eyes.

Pensively she stroked down the sides of her dress. 'It's terribly crumpled.'

'We'll get up very early in the morning,' he said no longer looking at her.

She kneeled before him. 'What's the matter, Aob?'

'Don't call be Aob,' he said softly.

'I'll intercede for you in the Cape,' she said emphatically. 'I promised you, remember. I'll see to it that everything will be all right.'

'Yes. Of course.'

'If I allowed this chance to pass . . .' She inhaled deeply. 'It's much worse now than when I had to decide to leave Larsson's wagon. There may never be another opportunity.'

'I know. That's why I told you.'

There was a light of revelation in her eyes. 'You needn't have told me the truth!'

He didn't move.

'Isn't that so? You could have kept it to yourself. I would never have known.'

'But you had to know.'

'Why did you make it so hard for me?' she burst out passionately. 'It would have been so much easier if you'd decided for me. If you hadn't said anything.'

'Easier, yes,' he admitted. 'For the moment. But later? If longing started gnawing at you? If something slipped out accidentally and you suddenly guessed . . . ? How could I?'

'Why can't we stay here?' she asked.

'Nobody said we couldn't.'

'But it was you who wanted to go back, Adam. You said you couldn't live without it, that you were not an animal.'

'I was alone then. Now I'm with you.'

'But can I be enough for you? Will I always be enough for you?'

'One can only believe. Or hope.'

'*Why* did you have to tell me?' she asked again.

'Because they're your people.'

'They're not my people! I was happy here. I still am.'

'It's for you to decide.'

'But what about yourself, Adam? What do *you* want? Tell me what I must do.'

'Since when have you taken advice from others?'

'Help me, Adam!' She grasped his hands, clinging to him.

Somewhere in the night, he thought, two wagons were standing loaded ready to move off at the first light of day, back to the Cape. White bearded men with their oxen and their Hottentots.

Suddenly she asked: 'When we were with the Hottentots and I was ill: why didn't you leave me there and go off on your own?'

'How could I?'

'You didn't love me then.'

'What has that got to do with tonight?' he asked.

'I love you!' she said miserably. 'Oh, my God!'

'Come,' he said. 'We must go to sleep. You'll need some rest if we want to get up early.'

'Why do you say "we"?'

'I said: if we want to get up early.'

She rose and started unlacing the bodice of her dress; then hesitated.

'Why don't you keep it on?' he asked. 'You'd better get used to it again.'

'Do you *want* me to keep it on?'

Without answering, he spread the kaross over the bedding and lay down.

'Come,' he said.

She lay down beside him, like always; yet like a stranger in her dress.

He held her in his arm, his hand on her breast. If this was the end, he thought, if this was really their last night, he should make love to her, unceasingly, till morning, marking her body for good, with scars like his own. But he could not. She was too remote to reach.

Without stirring, he lay awake all night until the first light came filtering into the cave.

Then he touched her lightly, whispering:

'It's time.'

'I am awake,' she said.

'Didn't you sleep then?'

'No.' She sat up wearily, her dress more dishevelled than before. The cool morning air made her shiver. 'Adam . . . ?'

'I'll make the fire.'

137

It was too early to eat. He made some wild bush-tea in the battered old pot they'd brought from the farmhouse; they drank it steaming.

Then he went to his old look-out at the mouth of the cave. The sea-fog lay in a heavy bank against the rising sun.

After a while she came and stood beside him. It was only when he put his arm round her that he realised she was naked.

'Where's your dress?' he asked.

'I don't need it.'

'What about the wagons? And your people? And the Cape?'

'I'm staying here. I'm not going.'

'Are you sure?'

She nodded.

'It may be your last chance ever.'

'I know. I've made up my mind.'

'You're mad.'

'Yes. We're both mad. That's why we're staying here. This is our place.' She gestured towards the sea, the inhospitable pristine world under the forlorn cries of the gulls. 'This is all we've ever had. We're staying here for good.'

It sounded like a sentence, he thought.

And he remembered the great carcasses strewn through the forest.

This morning on the beach, washed out among weed and mussels, cowries, whelks and heart-urchins: a single paper nautilus shell, fragile cradle of forgotten eggs, untouched by all the violence of the waves.

How would they, afterwards, remember the end of that warm season, what would they retain of it? The sun rising later in the morning and setting earlier at night, but almost imperceptibly: mistier mornings and more translucent days, ever more tender around the edges; sad calls of doves, and swallows gathering in great flocks to fly off to the north. A vaster openness opening, as if invisible dimensions were exposed to the light and the lukewarm sun; as if the wind came from farther away and spent itself in emptiness. A more agonising awareness of vulnerability. Longer silences in the long evenings at the fire.

'My mother would have a fit if she saw the stitches in this kaross. I always had to start all over again if the sewing wasn't fine enough. How I hated those afternoons with the sound of the boys playing outside!'

'Don't you ever miss the Cape?'

She looks up, firelight on her cheeks. 'Of course, sometimes.'

The throng of the wine-lease auctions in August; coach rides to Constantia, accompanying important guests from abroad, showing them the flamingoes; the cannon booming on the Lion's Rump, and the flags going up; the bustle on the beach . . . even though her mother had forbidden her to mix with all those common folk at the harbour; the flurry of getting letters finished before the fleet departed to Patria or Batavia; the sound of the clavichord, candelabras, crystal; slaves shuffling past barefoot, carrying laden trays, or fanning the guests with ostrich feathers; Uncle Jacobs and her father playing chess in the garden; rough games with the slave children in the backyard in her mother's absence. Does it still exist? Is her mother still complaining? Has her father withdrawn even more into himself? Are they alive?

'I'm sure you miss it too,' she says defensively.

The stories of his mother and his grandmother: the dancing fire in the craters of Krakatoa; the flaming beauty of hibiscus and lotus, and the scent of jasmine, cinnamon and cloves; Mohammed's flight to Medina, and the glorious crusades of the Crescent Moon. The cynical fatalism of the frail old woman; the naïve emotions of his mother, confusing Christ and Heitsi-Eibib, and the word of God and that of the Master.

'You leading my child astray, Ma Seli.'

'I tell him about the world. I seen the world.'

'From the black hole of a ship?'

'No, long before the ship, when I was young. Padang and Smeroes and Surabaya. I seen it. I was free then.'

'You free now too. The Master he freed you.'

'Can shove his freedom up his hole.'

'Ma Seli, you don't speak so of a Master.'

'Whose Baas is he? Slave of his slaves, is what he is. What can he do without them? You listen to me, hey, Adam?'

'Ma Seli, you stop saying things to my child. Adam, you listen to your Ma and your Master, you see? You don't give ears to that old woman.'

Shavings curling on his bench, the sharp smell of stinkwood in his nose as he chisels the table legs. Fetching wood on the Mountain, looking out across the sea below. The raisins in the loft. Harvest home. Threshing time, late autumn, with the baskets coming in from the vineyards and emptied into the treading-barrels; treading the

139

grapes, holding on to the bar above, dancing, stamping until your legs grow numb: breaking the husks underfoot, feeling the sap trickle through your toes in a sticky soggy fragrant mess; the sweet stream running into the keg below. Rubbing the husks through a mat of plaited cane; pouring the must into the large vats, leaving it there to ferment, foaming and bubbling for days on end. Driving to the Cape on the back of the wine-wagon, perched high on the barrels, flicking your long whip past the flanks of the fat oxen, the dogs jumping and barking on either side. The harbour where they loaded the ships departing to the names of distant places: Amsterdam and Buitenzorg, Texel, and inevitably the Serabang and Surabaya of Grandmother Seli: those barrels of wine trodden by him, off to the corners of the earth, free.

'Yes, I miss it. But it's very far away. And we're happy here, aren't we?'

'Of course.' Her large eyes watching him in silence; questioning, acquiescing, shy.

'Or are you regretting it?'

'Oh no. Are you?'

'Not I. But you often talk about the Cape nowadays.'

'One has to talk about something.'

'In the beginning, when we came here, we never spoke about the Cape at all.'

'There was so much to do. Everything was strange to me, and new, and beautiful.'

'Isn't it any more?'

'Of course it is. But it's different. One has more time to think.'

And so it slipped in, stealthily, as the days turned cool and their defence weakened. Afterwards, it was impossible to tell when they'd first discovered the new stillness of the flaming water-lilies on the dark pools, the new brilliant colours of the mushrooms in the wood, brown and pink, green and white, and splendid vermilion or yellow; impossible to recall at what stage they'd become more conscious of the cry of the bustard in the morning, or the rustling of small partridges in the dry grass; impossible to pinpoint the changeover, in making their fire, to hard, oily ironwood which smouldered much longer at night, the acrid smoke mingling with the ozone of the sea and the warm, fetid smell of lichen and rotting leaves. It all just happened, a gentle metamorphosis. No longer did they run down to the sea at all times of the day to bathe, but maintained only the early morning ritual – and even that was different, a conscious defiance of the cold, gasping for breath in the icy water, thrashing about frantically, rushing out to wrap oneself in the warm kaross to feel the tingling heat slowly spreading through one's limbs again. Only at the hottest time of day did they dare to shed the karosses and bask in the sun in corners hidden from the wind; and he noticed that she was gradually losing her summery tan again, becoming whiter and more frail under her wraps.

There were other shifts, other transitions. In making love, a new urgency seemed to possess their bodies, a more overt violence, a physical compulsion – as if something of the original spontaneous lust had subsided, compelling them to struggle more strenuously, clawing and tearing into each other in search of the receding source of ecstasy. There was something desperate about it, aggravated by the fact that each, out of anxiety and compassion, tried to hide it from the other, frantically trying to prove the constancy of love in the most aggressive ways.

While the game was still possible, they had to cling to it, terrified lest everything disintegrated at a single word or unguarded gesture. And slowly the game itself became a way of living and reacting. But precarious; oh, precarious.

And then the weather worsened. He couldn't understand it. The mild warmth was supposed to last until the lashing winds of August began, followed by the torrential rains of October. But that year something went wrong. Leaden clouds; icy winds; a depressing drizzle lasting for days on end so that they were confined to the cave, sitting in silence at their smoky fire; or talking endlessly, mainly about the Cape, so remote now, so desirable beyond the grey monotony of those wintry days: yearning for it the way they'd yearned for the sea. Otherwise they lay under the large sleeping kaross, deliberately urging their bodies on to passion, struggling and panting; trying to sleep – but not for long, already saturated with it as they were.

The few fine days in between were exquisite, simply because they could go out again, and explore and rediscover sea and veld and forest. Then miraculously, all the joy and faith returned; and their love was nude and new like rocks stripped bare of barnacles.

But those days were rare and vulnerable, and the irritations of the surrounding days began to intrude upon them. There was a passive expectation in them both, a weary certainty that something would, inevitably, happen. They didn't discuss it, but they knew it was simply a matter of time.

When it did happen, it was more sudden and less obvious than they'd expected.

The sky was still filled with loose masses of drifting cloud but it was just possible that it might turn into one of the precious clear days of winter. It was quite early when they set out for the forest in search of mushrooms. Not far from the first elephant carcass – now a scattered mass of bones ravaged by hyenas and vultures and jackals and the wind – it began to rain. At first it was no more than a rustling among the leaves above, a darkening of the light, a general dampness bearing down on them. But soon it grew worse, although they were well protected in the undergrowth below a group of very ancient, enormous stinkwood trees, huddled on a fallen trunk, trying to keep each other warm. The storm had none of the terror of that other night at the river: it was merely aggravating and depressing.

'Do you think it'll last long?' she asked.

'I don't know. Everything is upside down this winter. This morning I was sure it wouldn't rain.'

'Do you think it would be better if we . . . ?'

'What?' he asked, almost eagerly.

'No, nothing. I suppose we're as comfortable as can be in our cave. And it will pass again, won't it?'

'What were you going to say, Elisabeth?'

'Never mind. I'm just irritable because it's raining. Don't pay any attention.'

She looked straight ahead, her breath forming small white clouds.

'Are you very miserable?' he asked.

'Not at all.' She looked at him. 'Why? Aren't *you* happy any more?'

'I don't mind.'

'I don't either.'

They fell silent again, waiting morosely. He looked at the trunk on which they were sitting: a hundred and fifty, two hundred feet long, or more, the end hidden in the undergrowth. On their side it was quite decayed, a slow, destructive rot creeping up the pith of the wood, hollowing it. But where the trunk had been torn loose, a new young sapling was growing from the original roots, as thick as a man's arm. Its own peculiar form of eternity, he thought: his mother would have approved.

It was late afternoon before the storm abated. It was still drizzling, but the violence had ebbed away. The world seemed weary and morbid. They had to go back before it grew worse again.

A hundred yards from where they'd been, a dove-nest had fallen from a tree and three tiny birds lay shivering among the soaked twigs, their yellowish beaks obscenely gaping, uttering pathetic little squeaks.

Elisabeth kneeled to pick them up.

'What will become of them?' she asked.

'It's hopeless.' He sounded annoyed. 'Why the hell did they lay their eggs this time of the year? That's just asking for it.'

'Well, they're here now.'

'What about it?'

'We can't leave them here to die.'

'We can't keep them alive either.'

'I'm going to try,' she said stubbornly.

He was much too concerned about getting back safely to raise any objection. It was dusk before they arrived at the cave, and by that time one of the baby birds had died.

She carried the remaining two inside, in her cupped hands, breathing over them until Adam had lit the fire. He watched her rolling them in a piece of skin, close to the fire, where they lay trembling and squeaking weakly, two hideous little things with prickly feathers and bare necks and soft open beaks.

'You'd better give them something to eat,' he said.

'What can I give them?'

'Try some of the fruit. There's nothing else.'

But the squabs only stared at the food, yawning stupidly. For a moment she looked round in a panic. Then, with a sudden inspiration, she put a piece of dried fruit in her mouth and started chewing it. Leaning over, holding one of the squabs in her hand, she took its tiny beak between her lips, spitting some of the masticated mess into its throat. The bird gave a hiccup, and shuddered, and swallowed; then gaped with wide open beak again. With infinite patience she managed to feed them both.

Shaking his head, Adam roasted the mushrooms they'd brought back with them. Vapour came steaming from their wet karosses. Outside it was still drizzling faintly, there was a final gust of wind; then silence.

When, late that night, he went to the mouth of the cave to look out, the clouds lay scattered in the black sky and right overhead was the moon, looking like the old shoe from which Heitsi-Eibib, in his

143

mother's tales, had fashioned it. He looked round. She was lying beside the fire, the two baby doves against her breast. With a sigh he returned to her.

At regular intervals all through the night she got up to feed the squabs and to make sure that they were warm. In spite of all her care one was dead when they woke up at daybreak.

Just after sunrise she sent Adam out to find some worms. These she squashed in her hand, forcing the pulpy mess into the gaping beak with her fingers.

'This one is going to get through,' she said.

That night she slept more peacefully. But when they got up the next morning the last little dove had also died.

'We can use them for soup,' he suggested. 'There's not much meat on them, but at least it's something.'

'No!' she said, so violently that he looked up in surprise. 'How can you think of it? I fed them myself.'

'What else can we do with them?' he asked, shrugging.

'I don't know. Bury them. Anything.'

She sighed and stopped, as if there was no point in going on; then picked up the two minute, scraggly bodies and went outside. He made no effort to follow her, but stuffed his pipe, waiting for the smoke to calm and comfort him. Outside the sky was clear, but it was bitterly cold.

When, several hours later, she still hadn't returned, he reluctantly went out to look for her.

And now the skeleton lies bare and very white among the rocks of the pool, a long curve of small crescents of bone, each rib shaped perfectly, heraldic on the stone: nothing vague or obscure about it, everything precise and delicate and uncompromising, no longer subject to change, danger, desire or fear, but defined with serene finality, inescapable, and very beautiful.

He finds her beside the pool, away from the beach, with her back turned to the sea: looking up towards the cliffs, where, high up, the land begins.

'Did you bury them?' he asks.

'Yes. Come and sit with me. I've missed you.'

'Why didn't you come back?'

'I was hoping you'd come to me.'

144

'It's cold out here.'

'Yes. But it's so stuffy in the cave. It's very clean here. It's open.'

'You sound as if you felt cornered.'

And all at once, with those words, they reach the moment where they've known for so long they had to arrive.

'Yes, it was cornering me,' she admits. 'I can't breathe any more. It's no use pretending it's different. It will only suffocate us both.'

'What's the matter then?' He knows so well, of course, but she is the one who must say it.

'One can't go on pretending.'

'You think that's what we've been doing?'

He sits beside her, waiting, as if for redemption.

'They're dead,' she says unexpectedly. 'However much I tried to look after them and be good to them.' Shaking her head briefly. 'The world was pretty cruel to them.'

'What's a couple of doves?' he asks, trying to prod her.

And she reacts. 'What are *we*?' she asks with shocking directness, looking at him. 'We don't belong here any more than they did. When the weather was fine, we didn't notice it. We were blind. I know I was.'

'I thought you were happy here?'

'Perhaps it was because I was blind.' She looks down, her hair falling over her face. She pushes it away. 'I thought *you* were happy. And all the time we were afraid to admit the truth. We wanted to be kind to each other. Not knowing it was the surest way of destroying ourselves.'

'And now?' he asks quietly, deliberately.

She laughs, sadly, yet with strange joy. 'So our little paradise was not eternal after all, was it? Just a stop-over.'

'Do you want to go away?'

'It's not a matter of wanting it or not,' she says. 'I only know we must. If we're honest. Nothing else is possible. We've been trying to put it off, but . . .'

'We haven't got much to pack. We can leave today.'

'Yes.'

'Where shall we go?' he asks.

'There's only one destination for us, isn't there?'

He nods without a word.

'We've got to complete the circle,' she says, taking his hands. 'Whatever happens.'

Every time, in going on, there is something of the first venture: a question of faith. Still wet and shaking from the sea which had spewed him out, then tried to swallow him back, he stole through unpaved streets past dark houses and gardens with barking dogs, up towards the familiar mountain, so long gazed at from afar. After a full day's climbing and walking he descended on the far side of the mountain, arriving above the farmyard in the late afternoon. Before dark he had to be inside that large white thatched house, otherwise the big doors would be locked and the heavy wooden shutters of the windows barred.

In the vineyard a swarm of brown women and children were chasing birds; men came down the rows, carrying heavy baskets, singing at the approach of *sopie* time. There was a clattering of milk-pails in the stables. Through the open kitchen door he could see women moving about inside; the chimney was smoking heavily. Beyond the vegetable garden slave girls were gathering eggs and feeding the chickens and the ducks. In the sty the pigs were squealing for the meal of acorns and curds and leftovers.

This was how he had visualised it for months: all activity concentrated at the back of the house, the front deserted. It was still risky, but he had no choice.

He crept along the whitewashed stone wall enclosing the yard, crouching at the front gate, looking round for the last time. Then he got up, his heart thudding against his ribs, his throat taut. Pushing open the gate he went towards the front stoep, finding it difficult to control his legs, conscious of his semi-nakedness. A single challenging voice – 'Hey, what are you doing there?' – and all would be lost.

As he came up the broad steps leading to the stoep, the big watch-dog at the front door suddenly stood up, baring his teeth in a deep throaty growl.

He stopped dead. For a moment they looked at each other.

Then, with quavering voice, he called out softly: 'All right, Bull. All right, Bull. Bull! Come on, Bull!'

The large mastiff came closer, teeth still bared, sniffing at his fingers and his legs as he went on talking, a cold sweat on his forehead.

The dog began to wag his tail, grinning open-mouthed.

'Good boy, Bull.' Adam caressed the huge head. He was trembling with haste to go on, but it was even more important to win the confidence of the dog again, as in the past when they had roamed the farm together.

The front door gave way as he turned the knob. Suppose there was someone waiting in the passage? He pushed the door open and slipped inside. The house was dark and quiet, smelling of beeswax and linseed oil. He knew it so well. The parlour door was to the right. If one of the daughters should be there now, reading or paging through sheet-music . . .

At the far end of the passage a door was opened. Without hesitating any longer he darted into the lounge, panicky, breathing through his mouth. It was deserted. The dark curves of Dutch furniture, a red lacquered Oriental escritoire, the heavy Cape armoire with ornate brass fittings, porcelain and silver behind glass, mats and zebra skins and a lion skin with stuffed head on the broad yellow-wood floor-boards. He hurried to the narrow space behind a settee where he could lie down on the hard cool floor.

From far away sounds came filtering through to him. Dogs barking excitedly – it would be the farmer coming home. Yes: the sound of hooves. Pails. Calves. A child crying outside. The muted sounds from the house itself. Gradually it grew quiet. Shutters were fastened against the lurking dangers of the night, doors were locked. Then the voices of evening prayers, chairs scraping over the floor, a sombre hymn.

Now he felt calm. He was here; he was waiting. It was very dark, so that he had to rely exclusively on his ears. After a long time he ventured it back to the inside door. It creaked as he opened it, and he tensed up in fright. From one of the bedrooms yellowish lamplight still fell into the long passage. Then that, too, was extinguished. Heavy and warm the smell of oil lingered in the passage; a bed creaked, voices continued to whisper for a while, a man coughed. A sigh, then silence.

He waited until he was absolutely certain before tiptoeing to the window to open the shutters. The metal bars squeaked. Once again he

147

froze, but the house remained silent. The moonlight coming in from outside defined the outlines of the furniture.

Down the interminable passage he crept to the kitchen. In the hearth the coals were still warm, giving off a reddish glow. Closing the inside door behind him, he took a candle from the large scrubbed table, lit it at the hearth, and then proceeded to move about quickly and without hesitation. Clothes from the laundry. Too large for him, he'd lost much weight on the island; but it would do. Food. Here were the keys which had once been in his charge. Had he remembered correctly? Yes, indeed, the lock of the chest gave way. A blunderbuss; a bag of ammunition. He unlocked the back door and put everything beside it, tied in an easy bundle.

At last he removed a fire-iron from the hearth, blew out the candle and returned to the inner door. After listening for a moment, he went into the passage, leaving the door open behind him. He was very calm now. This was what he'd been waiting for all the time. His palm grew sticky round the handle of the heavy iron.

This was where, earlier, he had seen the light and heard the creaking of the bed. Inch by inch he moved across the floor. It was stuffy inside, everything was tightly shut. The Cape people were too scared to leave a window open at night.

A dull shine of brass indicated the bed. On which side was he sleeping, on which side she?

He had to come right up against the bed and lean far over to listen to their breathing. In doing so he bumped against a bedside table; glass tinkled, followed by a sudden snorting sound from the bed. Clutching the iron very tightly, he waited.

As soon as the breathing resumed evenly he moved round the bed to the other side. The pillow was a faint pale patch in the dark. Here was the head. Here you lie sleeping. Baas. You who tried to force me to flog my own mother. Baas. You who had me exposed to the irons and the nine tongues of the lash. You who had me banished to the island. Baas. Now I've come back. Try to stop me. Baas!

The iron was raised above his head, poised to strike. A single blow would be enough, cracking open the skull, spilling the brains on the pillow. And another for the woman, should she wake up. To thank you for the salt, Madam.

Today it's *my* turn. This is what you've brought me up for, isn't it? Bred for the land – then banished from it. But I was washed ashore again, like a piece of driftwood; I've come back. Now try to stop me, Baas!

148

But after a long time he lowered his hand again, and turned round, and went out; perspiration on his face; exhausted.

The dogs came running towards him, barking, as he opened the back door, carrying the gun and the bundle. But in a low voice he called Bull to him, and the others milled round them, wagging their tails, whining softly. They accompanied him to the stable. Inside the horse snorted, pawing the ground; pulling up his head when Adam grabbed the halter. Gently he spoke to the great animal, offering him sugar he had brought from the kitchen. Then fumbled in the dark for the reins, pushing the bit into the horse's mouth, tying it up, leading him out.

'What's going on here?' the man asked as he came outside.

He swung round. It was Lewies, his boyhood friend.

'Let me go!'

'My God, Adam! How did you get here?'

'Let me go, I tell you!'

Lewies tugged at his arm. He felt the sleeve being torn off.

'You bastard!'

'Get out of my way!'

'Adam, I'll . . .'

Grabbing the barrel of the gun in both hands, he aimed for the head; Lewies sank to his knees, moaned faintly, and toppled over. Without waiting any longer, Adam jumped on the horse, holding on to his bundle, galloping out of the yard and into the night. Before daybreak he had to be very far away. In spite of the uncertainty gnawing inside him.

'Do you think I killed him?' he asks her.

'How must I know?'

'They must have spoken about it at the Cape. Didn't you hear anything?'

'Perhaps it happened when I was away in Amsterdam.' She shuffles closer to the fire; outside the winter wind is tugging at the skins sealing off their smoky interior. They haven't got very far. After a couple of weeks in the forest they reached this low chain of mountains; and here the cold has cornered them. Along the higher slopes it was snowing, driving them into this deep, low cave where, in order to survive, they are forced to hibernate: waiting, as in some ark, for the world to become hospitable again.

'But can't you remember at all?' he insists.

'Even if I were in the Cape,' she says, 'that sort of thing happened so often, it was so common – slaves assaulting or murdering their masters. All those vagabonds, and drunks, and adventurers, and fugitives around. We had to lock and bar everything at night. Mother suffered from constant attacks of nerves. I remember how I often reopened my windows after they'd gone to bed. Just too bad if something happened, I thought. I couldn't bear the stuffiness. But many nights I got so scared I had no choice but to close the shutters again. You see, being white at the Cape means to live in constant fear. There are so many enemies, and at night they roam about freely.'

'Didn't your father feel safe? Some of his children were bastards.'

'All the more reason to fear them, perhaps,' she says quietly.

'In the end it was his own daughter who rebelled against him!'

'No,' she says. 'I don't think it really was against him. Perhaps it was simply against what they tried to make out of me. It may have been different if I had brothers. If my mother hadn't always blamed me for not being a boy. I can remember how often I thought: to be a boy is everything. To be a girl like me is the worst that can happen to one. Don't do this, don't do that. Be careful, your dress will get dirty. Watch out for your hair. Don't let the sun burn your face. Do you think a man will look twice at a girl who does such things? After all, that was the final aim: to be attractive to a man. No matter what *you* want, your whole life is determined by someone else.'

He smiles with quiet irony. After a while he asks, 'But surely you had power too. You could manipulate men.'

'Oh yes!' she retorts angrily. 'I could turn them round my little finger if I lowered my eyes demurely, or blushed at the right instant, or gently swayed my hips, or if I dared to be so reckless as to show my ankle.' Through the opening in the kaross draped loosely over her shoulder he notices the whiteness of her winter body, breasts, a hint of ribs, her navel, the small tight wad of curls below. 'As long as I was prepared to flirt gracefully, I could get anything out of anybody. Despising them for it, but that was not the point.' She looks into his eyes. 'I could get anything provided I did not presume to think for myself. For that lay beyond a woman's scope, you see. That was something vaguely disreputable, rather irritating, offending their male omnipotence. Can you understand what happens inside one when you grow up to discover you will never be allowed to be anything in your own right? Don't you think it is enough to drive one mad?'

'Yet you married Larsson.'

'Because I thought he would be different. And because he offered

150

me a chance to escape. I thought a man like him, such a famous scientist and explorer, would transcend the petty prejudices of the Cape . . .' She sits tugging anxiously at a frayed corner of her kaross. 'All he ever thought of me was that I was too "demanding".'

'We and our futile little revolts!' he says wryly.

'But why was yours futile? Why didn't you kill your Master that night?'

'I've thought about it so constantly, all these years.'

'Were you scared because he was still your Master?'

'If he'd woken up, or if he'd tried to stop me as Lewies did, I would have killed him straight away. The day he ordered me to flog my mother I didn't hesitate to attack him.' He looks past the fire, to the flapping skins at the mouth of the cave and the darkness beyond. 'No, I was not scared at all. On the contrary. For the first time in my life I was free to decide for myself. It was up to me to kill him or let him live on. In the past I'd always had to obey others. No matter how much I resented it, I had to obey. But that night, all of a sudden, I was free to choose. And I don't know why – but I simply didn't find it necessary to kill him. For two years I'd been planning every little detail of it, cherishing it, sustaining myself with it. Then, when the moment came, it just wasn't necessary to do it any more. That's all. I was free to choose – and I chose. There was no need any more to prove anything, not even to myself.'

'Then how can you say your revolt was futile?' she demands.

'If it had really been successful, I wouldn't have found it necessary to go back now.'

'Adam,' she says. And then, more gently, 'Aob. Are you quite sure it's not merely for my sake you're going back?'

'What difference does it make?'

'I want you to answer me,' she insists. 'I must know.'

'All these years I've been yearning to go back,' he says.

'But you never actually did.'

'Perhaps I wouldn't have gone this time either.' He looks at her. 'But you made it impossible for me not to go.'

'So it is for my sake, after all?'

'I'm not going back only because you can buy my freedom, if that's what you're thinking. But because, without you, I never *can* be free.'

That first night, she thinks, watching him roast some dried meat and boiling *dassiebos* for tea: that first night she sat looking at him like this. It was so dark, she couldn't even make out whether he was looking towards the wagon, or away; and she wanted to call him and talk to him, but she was frightened; his presence both protected and threatened her. And now? Is she more protected or less threatened now that she loves him?

Going to the mouth of the cave she pulls the skins aside to look out. A flurry of delicate moist flakes caresses her face.

'For how long does the winter last in these mountains?' she asks, returning, shivering, to the fire.

'Most years there isn't snow at all.' He brings her food to her. 'We'll just have to sit it out. At least we're sheltered here.'

And, really, it is better being here than in their first cave by the sea. They may feel cornered and irritated, and the days are long and tedious, the nights endless, and she's developed a nasty cough: but still there is the reassurance of knowing that they're on their way, that this is a mere resting-place in transit. One day the weather will clear up and they will trek on. They're not trying to deceive one another any more by pretending it's permanent: they're only hibernating, nothing more. They live in touch with past and future, no longer trying to deny it.

Soon after supper she snuggles in under their sleeping-kaross beside the fire. He brings her a concoction of *ghaukum* leaves picked far below the snowline that afternoon. And listening to the rasping sound of her coughing he busies himself with knife and stones, fire and water, fashioning arrowheads from bone and quartz, and attaching these to assegai-wood shafts. The barbed points are dipped in a mixture of pulped roots and the poison-bag of a half-frozen snake he found on the hillside. It is more than preparation for the future: it is also something to ward off boredom and cold, something to occupy his mind when he feels worried about her illness. She has grown very thin indeed; when he holds her body against his beside the fire she is a deathly white: he can feel her ribs under the smooth skin, the hard protuberances of shoulder-blades and hip-bones; only her cunt is soft and open, like a wound.

In the pre-dawn darkness they are awakened by an unfamiliar sound: the skins flapping and folding in the mouth of the cave, and a body stumbling past them. She utters a muffled moan against his throat, pressing herself against him. Instinctively he rolls in front of her to shield her with his body, in the same movement grabbing a piece of wood and hurling it on the dying coals; by the time the flames begin to spring up, he is ready, the pistol in his hands.

It's only a little buck, wide-eyed against the back wall, shaking with cold and obviously scared to death. Something must have driven it in here – a leopard, or the violence of the wind. On shivering legs it stares at them, aiming this way and that, cornered by the fire blazing between the cave mouth and itself.

Elisabeth laughs with relief, a sob in her throat; momentarily shocked back to a late afternoon in a river, and a small doe seeing her naked.

'The poor little thing has just come in for shelter,' she says. 'Let's go to sleep again.'

He continues to watch their visitor for some time before, reluctantly, he crawls back under the kaross. She is coughing again; and it is already beginning to grow light before she falls asleep once more, quite exhausted. Long before her he wakes up.

The little buck is still there, although the coals have died down long ago. Its eyes still wide open, it lies against the back wall, and the moment Adam stirs it is back on its feet.

He looks round to Elisabeth. She is still sleeping. Without a sound he picks up his assegai and starts shuffling towards the little animal in the back of the cave. It is very quiet outside, the snow smothering all sound in the mountains. Inside nothing stirs, there is only the whisper of Elisabeth's breathing. He goes nearer. The buck is too terrified to move. With a sudden final lurch Adam dives it to the ground, grabbing the prickly horns with one hand, forcing the head backwards to expose the throat to his blade.

A single anxious bleating cry.

'Adam!' she calls out behind him.

He holds on to the buck to subdue the struggling and kicking of its final agony. When he lets go at last, he doesn't look at her. Almost guiltily he skins the small carcass and goes outside to wash his hands in the snow.

She doesn't speak. When he returns, she looks up briefly, and resumes her efforts to get the fire going, her teeth chattering slightly.

'Why did you do it?' she asks at last.

'It's weeks since we had fresh meat.'

'You betrayed it.'

'Betrayed? We've got to stay alive. It's snowing. Who knows for how long we'll have to stay here?'

She looks at him quietly; then nods with a weary little sigh. 'I suppose you're right.' Once again the cough begins to rack her body.

'You must have some of the meat,' he says. 'Will you try it raw?'

She shakes her head.

'Then I'll just scorch it in the flames for you. Please. This weather is bad for you.'

'But the buck . . .'

'It's just meat now.'

'Yes, of course.' Yet she has to shut her eyes tightly when she takes a small piece, hot from the flames; clenching her jaws to force it down.

Her resignation really upsets him more than the explosion he was expecting.

'Try to think of it this way,' he says, without any objection from her to prompt him. 'Suppose it was a lion that came in here last night, and not the buck: then it would have tried to kill *us*.'

'Are we no more than animals then?' she asks, without looking up.

'How can you survive if you're not prepared to be an animal?' She doesn't answer. 'There's something I'll never forget,' he goes on. 'One day I went up the mountain with my Master – when he was my Master. We had to leave early, he was in a hurry; and I didn't have time for breakfast. There was a patch of ground up there he wanted me to clear, to see whether it would be good for an orchard. He stood looking out over the slope while I was digging away. Suddenly he said, "Hell, Adam, just look at it – beautiful sight from here, isn't it?" But all I could think of while I was working there was: I'm hungry. I suppose I would have liked the view too, if my stomach had been full like his.'

She looks up at him, and then down again, coughing. He moves closer to her, holding her, feeling her body contract and shudder.

'All right,' he says. 'All right. It'll go away. I'll fetch you some more herbs.'

And a little later he goes out again, wrapped in his kaross, disappearing into the snow.

Erik Alexis, she suddenly thinks, also shot buck, and birds – all the most beautiful animals he found on their trek – to draw them or stuff them or to preserve their skins, collecting their data to forward to Stockholm one day, so that each specimen would be named correctly. The meat was usually given to the Hottentots. Or, if they'd had their fill, it was buried, to keep hyenas off their bloody trail.

In the evening he returns with new herbs for her cough and milk-bulbs for his own cracked feet. And she feels exultant to see him; cuddled beside the fire it is she who starts caressing him, inviting him.

154

Take me. Let us be animals in our cave together. Soon the winter will be over.

Through days and weeks it slowly begins to thaw outside; the sun returns. Breaking out from behind the dispersing clouds it sparkles on a trembling world, warming it, making it more habitable. Sometimes Adam returns with a rock-rabbit which has risked it out in the open; sometimes with fruit, or dug-up roots, or edible leaves. Her cough diminishes. She is still thin and exhausted, but no longer ill. The snow disappears, the ground dries out again. And one morning, when he comes outside – far in the mountains a dove is cooing with heart-rending urgency – he stands looking out over the valley, and then turns to call her out to him.

'The winter's past,' he says. 'We can go on. We have survived.'

There was no gradual transition between the seasons. It took them several days to get through the mountains; there were no towering cliffs, only a seemingly endless profusion of high hills – yet there was something definite about it, a clear barrier between coast and interior. As sharp as a knife-edge, the dividing ridge stretched across their route and the moment they began the descent on the other side everything was different. The bushes and green hills, the rivers, and densely overgrown streams and valleys had disappeared irrevocably. On this side the country was more even, billowing gently among the hills, with clusters of wagon-trees. For the rest, harsh shrubs growing close to the ground, and grass, white and brittle under their feet. None of the snow melting on the mountains had run down this way. Yellowish and brown, the landscape stretched out before them to the horizon; and when one reached it, the same scene was simply repeated, farther and farther away; with the mountains on their left, and another range gradually building up in the distance to their right, blackish, more formidable than the first.

And the sun was blazing. No gentle changeover from the winter cold of the mountains to mild spring weather: in this long valley between the mountains there was no sign of spring at all, no veld flowers or cool breezes or lush grass to welcome them. High in the white sky the white sun was burning, the colourless and fierce unblinking eye of a bird-god. Trapped among the mountains the heat lay motionless, undiminished even at night, increasing all the time as they went on.

From time to time there was game in the distance, sprinkled

155

sparsely on the arid veld. Ostriches, small groups of springbuck streaming down the hills, their white fans dazzling, guinea-fowl squeaking in the dry grass, a leopard in a sandy spot under white thorns, almost invisible in the dappled sun and shadows; occasionally an oryx with long straight horns and once a herd of buffalo stampeding in a cloud of dust. Once, too, a pride of lions feeding on a gnu, fortunately far away and above the wind.

Their progress was slow. She still felt weak after the inertia of the winter months and the racking cough, and he did not want to break her in too suddenly. There was a long and arduous trek ahead, and a too energetic start might set one back later, when the body would have to survive on accumulated stamina. There were angry arguments about this slow progress; she was impatient and impetuous. But he restrained her, and in spite of her open resentment he ordered regular stops for eating and resting.

Much against her will she was forced to resign herself to it. For on their very first day on the plains the sun overcame her. He had made them Hottentot aprons for the trek, using the karosses for carrying their few possessions, and neglecting to consider the effect of the heat on her bleached body. That first evening she was flaming red all over, the pattern of the apron a shocking white contrast across her hips and thighs. She found it difficult to sleep that night. But she refused to complain, knowing that if he discovered her agony he would trek even more slowly.

But on the second day it became unbearable. Resting for a while among some wagon-trees, he noticed her exploring her flaming shoulders with her fingers, her face contorted with pain.

'Why didn't you tell me?' he asked, shocked by the sight of her glowing body, the tender skin of her breasts blistered.

She clenched her teeth. 'We've got to move on. It's no use waiting here.'

'It will get even worse farther on.' He saw her shudder as he touched her breasts in awe. 'You'll get burnt to death like this.'

'What can I do about it?'

'Why didn't you wear your kaross?'

She undid her bundle and tried to drape the skins around her shoulders, but the mere touch was too painful to bear. Angrily she wiped away the tears forced into her eyes by the effort.

'We'll just have to stay here until you're better,' he ordered.

'No! We still have so far to go.'

'Do you think we'll ever get there if you go on like this?'

Something had to be done urgently before her condition got worse. From the assortment of food he had brought with them, he took some honey and, mixing it with buck's fat, gently covered her body with it. He gave her water to drink and to wash her face, then gathered leaves from the scraggy wagon-trees to lay on her forehead.

By late afternoon she was seriously ill, in spite of his efforts. She found it impossible to lie still, yet the smallest movement was agony: her back, her stomach, her sides, everything was scalded, and to make it worse she was beginning to shake with cold fever.

He covered her with the kaross and went off in search of castor-oil leaves to cure the fever; coming back, he again covered her with the mixture of fat and honey, and forced her to chew some *gli*-roots which made her light-headed and less conscious of the pain. In a half-stupor she continued to groan, mumbling incoherently throughout the night, quarrelling with him, crying from time to time. But at daybreak she finally dozed off, and when she woke up, hours later, the fever had left her.

'We can go on now,' she said, still shivery.

'No. We're staying right here until you're better.'

'But I am!'

'No.'

'Adam,' she said in hopeless anger, 'don't you understand I can't wait any longer?'

'What difference does a week or a month make? If you insist on going on now, I'll have to bury you in a porcupine hole tomorrow and trek on alone from there.'

Once more he used the salve on her and made her drink the half-fermented *gli*-roots mixed with honey so that her euphoria returned; throughout the long day he sat beside her, smoking quietly.

Slowly the worst of her burns began to ebb away. Her breasts were still agonisingly tender to the touch, but on her back the redness was already yielding to a deep tan. Even so, he insisted on staying there for several more days, until he felt satisfied that she was strong enough for going on, trekking for short distances in the early morning and late afternoon only.

For the time being she wore the heavy kaross to cover her from head to foot; and during the days, while she lay resting in the shade, he went off in search of food to strengthen her. It wasn't easy to stalk game in this open country, but on the second day they passed a drinking-place where he managed to shoot a springbuck lamb with the pistol. The tender meat revived her considerably. Unfortunately, in this heat, it was impossible to store much of it. They cooked it all immediately; even so, they had to throw the rest away after a few days.

At least they kept going, which was most important at the moment. There was even a touch of elation in their progress, a strange irrational joy: Look, we're suffering, but we're not defeated by it. We shall survive.

Sometimes when they were resting during the dazzling hours of the day she remembered, with a sense of wonder, her endless discontent in the Cape and on her journey with Larsson. That restlessness, that rebelliousness in her, the interminable quarrels with her mother and her all-too-timid father. Now it was different. She would always remain impatient, driven by the urgency to get things done. But at the same time she experienced a new sense of peace. The timeless existence at the sea had brought her the discovery, in herself, of something she'd never been aware of before: a faculty for happiness. That in itself sustained her through the all-demanding days. I know now that it is possible for me to be happy, I have explored serenity, something inside me has opened wonderfully, I have travelled farther into myself and nothing can ever be quite the same again.

After a fortnight she even found it possible to gradually give up the kaross, walking beside him in the sun wearing only her apron; sometimes not even that. Until the brown toughness was restored to her body, even more effectively than before.

There was something pristine and intensely physical about this experience of walking on and on in the endless valley between the distant mountain ranges: an awareness of limbs – of feet stretching and treading, calf muscles, thighs, the small tendons tightening in the groin; arms swinging, a back straining against the load on the shoulders – surrounded by the violence and stillness of this space, huddled hills bleached in the sun, scorched bushes, stubbly grass, groups of gnarled and weatherbeaten trees, sky. Imperceptible progress, yet, with every new day, every resting-place, a little bit nearer – to something.

Separate objects on the road caught her attention, absorbing her completely, so that she became oblivious of motion altogether. A thorn-tree stump with all redundant bark and softness stripped by wind and sun, reduced to pure wood, a bare hard pattern of indestructible grain. A rock formation corroded through centuries, all sandiness and flakiness destroyed, terrifying and beautiful in its utter stillness, its refusal to be anything but itself. The disconcerting movement of a tortoise, ridiculous on its stubbly scaly legs, the ancient neck stretched forward, the toothless gums exposed, the eyes beady and uncompromising; life reduced to mere motion, hard in a hard land. With the sickening surprise of tender pink meat and strings of eggs inside, when Adam dug out the small senile head with his knife and broke open the shell on a stone.

When did she first begin to suspect that the landscape was familiar? The outline of a hill, the pattern of a mountain range, a specific rock formation, a thicket of aloes or euphorbias, the curious bend in a dry river bed, the red ridges of eroded banks: in the beginning a mere sense of recognition, out of context and too deep for conscious comparison, welling up as from a previous existence. The simple discovery that nothing came as a surprise, that expectations were fulfilled unfailingly, and that – without even thinking about it – the view beyond the next ridge could be anticipated. It was, of course, possible that after two or three weeks the landscape had indeed become predictable. Yet there was this feeling, growing stronger all the time, of knowing it, of having seen it before.

Certainly the barrenness of the region was unfamiliar. But if she ignored the dusty brown and red of shrivelled bushes and bare earth, substituting waving grass, and patches of flowers, and greenery, it did become familiar. It must be the route she'd followed inland with Erik Alexis Larsson. Somewhere they'd entered this long valley, somewhere else they must have swerved out of it again: but this particular stretch she had seen before, trekking in the opposite direction.

The first dilapidated ruin enhanced the impression. Barely a ruin, no more than a miserable little heap of subsided earth and stones and decayed wood. But it had been here when they'd come past on the wagon. In a few more days they should reach another ruin like this. With barely restrained excitement she began to look out for it, not daring to say anything to Adam about it: hoping to first discover it herself and confirm her hunch. But after two days the excitement began to wear off. There was nothing. Unless they'd passed lower down or higher up? The disappointment was almost too much to bear. Not that she could explain what difference finding the ruin would really have made. It was just that she'd missed something. And then, unexpectedly, more than a week later, when she'd long given up hope, they came upon the ruin after all. She realised immediately why she'd been so mistaken in her calculations: they were travelling so much more slowly now. Two or three days on the wagon easily equalled seven or more on foot, the way they were progressing now, walking only in the cooler hours of the day.

'What are you digging here in the rubble for?' asked Adam, surprised.

'I think I've been here before,' she admitted for the first time. 'I'm still not sure, everything looked different then. But I think it's the same place.'

'It's possible.' He shrugged. 'In fact, you could hardly have taken any other way.'

She felt rather foolish, unable to explain to herself why it was so important to her to know. But day after day, as they went on, she continued to inspect their surroundings with great concentration – so intently, in fact, that more than once she stumbled over a branch or stone in her way. Every now and then she turned round to look back: for this would have been the view she'd had of it before. If only she'd been more interested then. But, of course, she had been half-dozing on the wagon most of the time, or curled up in a sullen bundle, allowing the landscape to drift past unnoticed: and now she was walking every yard of it, experiencing every stone, every old broken branch, every moving tortoise, every lizard, every lark in the early morning.

For long stretches she would wander on with her head bowed, scrutinising the ground immediately in front of her feet, looking for wagon trails cut into the hard soil, flattened branches, discarded objects. Something, anything: the barest sign to reassure her that she'd really passed that way before.

But there was nothing. Not the slightest indication or admission by the landscape that it acknowledged her, that it was aware of her. It was like the sea the day they'd found the snake and came back to discover their tracks obliterated by the foam. Nothing. Just nothing.

And yet I know I've been here before. However stern and uncommunicative the land may be: *I* know it. Unless my memory is false? By what am I led, in what do I recognise my past, where do I store all the evidence of my past moments? Only in this body walking on through space? Have I no more than this? How can I rely on it? Is everything really, finally, reduced to faith?

At night she dreamt; in the daytime she walked on, remembering, recalling. A night of festive sound, and music, and people, very far away, beyond doors and walls and rooms. An illuminated garden, an orchestra, people dancing, tables laden with food, laughter, wine, slave girls undressing her; and she naked in the big brass bed, the white embroidered nightdress folded up at her feet. Don't you realise I'm waiting? I want to hang out the sheets in the morning, glad with new blood: look, I've become a woman, I've changed into something different, something new, I have become myself. 'I thought you'd be sleeping.' 'I've been waiting for you.' 'Is that all?' 'What?' 'Is that all – just this?' 'I don't understand you.' 'I don't either.'

You see? I can remember every word. That's how it was. That's how I remember it all: it really happened.

Something forced her to finally discuss it with Adam, to rid herself of everything she had – almost with shame – stored up in her, desiring to look at it with his eyes, objectively.

'The day the lion charged him – I think that was what really decided it; it was our breaking point,' she said.

'But you went on for quite a long time after that, didn't you?'

'Yes. But by then – we were together on the wagon only because it was unavoidable. Everything which happened afterwards was already decided.'

'What do you mean?'

'It was so ludicrous. The lion charging him, Booi killing it right on top of him and nearly getting killed himself in the process. There he was, with the lion on him. And suddenly he jumped up and started running away for all he was worth, scrambling up a sapling which was too light for him. Every time he reached the top, it dropped him back on his feet.' She laughed, but without joy.

'Why should that have been such a shock to you?' he asked.

'I don't know. I don't even think I realised it consciously at the time. Only afterwards. The image of that great scientist, that famous explorer whose name would surely become a household word all over the world – running his arse off like that. The man who possessed part of the world, who knew the names of all things, the crown of creation: there he was climbing up a ridiculous little tree to escape from a dead lion.'

She deliberately wanted to see it like that, to phrase it as crudely and as cruelly as she could. To renew the shock for herself and stir up the initial passion.

After a while, more subdued, she continued: 'You see, when I married him it wasn't only to escape. I wanted to believe in him. I realised afterwards that I should have known it all along. But I *wanted* to believe in him. If I had to accept being a woman after all, if I really had to resign myself to the role I'd been brought up for, then, at least, I wanted to be woman to a man I could respect. He had to be a man, a full human being. If I could be nothing but a woman, then he had to convince me that being a woman was important enough to live for. I didn't want everything to be a gross lie. And then, slowly, it changed. I tried to hold on to it, it was all I had. But that day . . . because it was so silly, so ridiculous, I could no longer deny it.' She wiped the perspiration from her face. 'It's strange, you know: that night it was he who came to lie with me, trying to caress me, one of the rare nights he ever seemed to desire me; he was incredibly passionate, he couldn't control himself. But then it was I who refused him.'

It was the third ruin which brought the final confirmation, not by its similarity with the past but its shocking difference. The first two had been, even in her recollection of the wagon journey, completely decayed, sunken into the earth – melancholy, forgettable signs of people who'd tried to find a foothold in that barren interior and failed, moving on and on, driven through the hard land like tumbleweeds in the wind. But this third one was different. It had been different. When she and Larsson had passed that way, there had been people, she was quite sure of it. If this was the place, it had been inhabited – and they'd camped in the yard. In the evening they'd had pumpkin for supper, scooped from a single communal dish, mainly by hand; and bread soaked in milk; and biltong which the thin man had carved for them. There had been fields outside, beautifully green in the green landscape – but that, of course, had been a year ago – and wooden kraals for cattle and goats.

The people had been more talkative than the others on their journey, more impoverished too, it seemed, but more generous; and they laughed a lot, although Larsson didn't share in it. He found them rather dirty, while they showed very little interest in his exploits. Still, they welcomed the small gift of brandy and tobacco he offered them, and the woman was enraptured by the beads.

The man was white, his wife a freed slave woman. His father – if Elisabeth remembered correctly – had been an important farmer in the Stellenbosch district, planning a great future for his many sons. But this particular son, the third or fourth in the line, had bitterly disappointed him. Not content merely to make use of the slave girls at his disposal on the farm, he'd had the temerity to announce that he was in love with this girl and wanted to marry her. In the end the old man had allowed them to have their way, advancing the youngster enough of his inheritance to buy the freedom of the girl. The only condition was, not wanting to be disgraced in the eyes of all his neighbours, that they had to leave the farm. And so they set out, trekking from one place to the other until, in this valley, as far as possible from the Cape, they settled happily. Here they were determined to stay on, with their four small children and their fields and vegetable garden and their cattle.

But now their cottage was disintegrating; one portion of the roof had already caved in, and the chimney lay broken on the hearth. There were still signs of kraals and withered fields, but that was all.

Fled from the drought? Wiped out by Bushmen? Or had they simply trekked on, forever wandering?

She couldn't even recall what they looked like. Only something of the atmosphere: the lamplight at table that evening, the children sleeping in a row before the hearth, the woman smiling as she fed the chickens in the backyard, the man fondling a lamb between his legs, patiently teaching it to suck his fingers. What did it really matter? They'd been there – if this was really the place! – and now they were gone. It upset her more than the change in the landscape. The flowers and the grass had gone; the people had gone. But when it rained again the grass and flowers would emerge from the dust, like before. The people? She and Erik Alexis Larsson had come this way: now she was the only one to return, with Adam. If one of them were to come back here, years from now, who would it be?

'Sometimes,' she said to him, 'I wonder whether his death wasn't really my fault.'

She didn't pronounce his name; it wasn't necessary.

'What makes you say that?' Adam asked, frowning.

'Didn't I drive him to it? By cutting myself off from him, by not caring any more?'

'He was following a bird,' he said emphatically, trying to coax her from her sombre mood. 'He got lost. What could you have done to prevent it?'

They were sitting on the doorstep of the ruined cottage, having decided to stay over for a day so he could cut them new footskins while they recovered in the shade.

163

She looked out to where the kraals had been. 'This Van Zyl who came with us . . .' she said, not really addressing him. 'It was the same with him.'

'How do you mean it was the same?'

'Haven't I told you about him?'

'All I know was that he was on the trek with you. That he'd lied about knowing the country. And that he made a nuisance of himself, quarrelling with your husband.'

'Yes, he was a stupid fool. But he meant well. He was very young still. I suppose that was why he lied about being a guide: he was so eager to see the world.'

'Did you get along with him?'

'Not really. He was rather tongue-tied. But when one is all alone in the wilderness with no one else to talk to – and him always working on his map and his journals and his collections . . .'

'Did he make love to you?' he asked, suddenly suspicious.

She shrugged.

'What did he do?' he urged.

'It's not so much what he did . . .' She looked at him, her cheeks glowing slightly through her tan. 'We chatted a bit, he would fetch and carry for me, nothing important. But I noticed the way he was looking at me. Constantly. In the beginning it irritated and upset me. I felt like shouting at him to stop it. But gradually, as my husband got more and more involved in his work and had less and less time for me . . . it was almost reassuring to know that at least there was somebody interested in me. Looking at me.' After a pause: 'Perhaps even – desiring me.'

'And then you . . . ?'

'No!' she said quickly. 'I was married. I had my duty. I couldn't be unfaithful to my husband. It's just that – well, it begins to burn one up inside.' Almost defiant, she looked at him. 'It was only a game, a distraction. It amused me and made me feel a bit better. Perhaps that was the worst: that it was no more than a game, not seriously meant at all. To see how far I could tempt him, the way one holds a burning stick to see how close to one's fingers it can burn down before you throw it away.'

He moved against her.

'And then you got burnt?'

'No, I didn't. In fact, nothing happened to me. It remained a game till the end. Accidentally brushing against him as I came past.

164

Allowing him to catch a brief glimpse when I was bathing. But it became too much for him. He demanded more. Suddenly he was no longer content with games. One day he grabbed me. I was scared and began to struggle, and I called out. My husband came running on. There was a terrible fight. Van Zyl managed to tear himself loose and ran off into the bush. And shot himself.' For a while she sat looking at the world growing darker around them. 'It was really my fault. I never meant anything like that to happen, I never expected it. But it happened, and it was my fault. After that there were quarrels all the time. I could no longer stand him touching me. And when he became aware of it, all of a sudden he wanted – what he'd never wanted before. I refused him. He took to wandering off into the woods at all times, and all by him-self. In search of birds or insects. Until he got lost. Do you think that was my fault too?'

'You can't change anything by thinking about it,' he said. 'You're just making it impossible for yourself.'

'But I'm frightened of myself, of what I cannot understand about myself.'

'Don't try. Leave it to me to understand you.'

She thought: for all the others I've been no more than a woman, a game, a toy. You're the first to whom I am a person. That is why I dare be a woman to you. And yet there's something in me I cannot grasp and which I fear.

After the ruin the landscape became even more arid. Previously there had been rare patches of greyish green bushes huddled on subterranean water; narrow streams no longer flowing, but still containing, here and there among the stones, pools of water. Now, as the valley between the mountain ranges began to spread out into ever wider plains, the earth became bone-dry. Day after day there were vultures, sometimes distant, at other times quite close; there was death in the land. Game was getting more scarce. Tortoises, lizards, snakes. Sometimes the cry of a bustard or the screeching of guinea-fowls. Buck or gnus or zebras only on rare occasions. The earth was parched, the sand and rocks burning; erosion ditches lay across their road like gaping wounds.

All the time they kept on believing it would become more green and lush ahead, that the clouds would collect in the sky and bring rain and change the aspect of the world. It was the right season, after all. It had to come, sooner or later – it was only a matter of waiting patiently.

But the sky became more and more bleached as they proceeded, white like ashes; in the daytime the ground was so hot that it burnt their feet through the thick skins they wore. At daybreak there were a few hours they could walk on, and again at dusk. But their progress was becoming more precarious. No longer able to count on finding water every day, they were forced to carry a supply with them in Adam's skin-bag and a couple of calabashes. But it was very little, never lasting more than a few brief laps of their slow trek. It worried him that their energy was running so low. They couldn't risk a long stretch at a time any more.

Once there simply was no choice, when after two full days' walking they'd finished all their water. Now they had to go on, whatever lay ahead, otherwise they would die of thirst right there.

The morning star had just come out when he awakened her. She sighed in her sleep, rolling over, groping for the security of his body next to hers; only then did she realise that she had to get up. There was still a bit of jackal's food left which he'd dug out the day before; they chewed the tough roots for food and moisture, but their palates still felt dusty as they took up their bundles to set out.

'Do you think we'll find water today?' she asked.

'We'd better.' Seeing her clench her teeth in desperation, he touched her briefly, soothingly, reassuring her. 'I'm sure we'll find some.'

In the dawn's comparative cool they progressed swiftly and far, sending up small clouds of dust under their feet. As soon as the sun rose it was hot, with sweat stinging between their shoulders. But they went on. This was the time they usually stopped to rest and eat on other days; today they ate as they walked on: thin strips of dried biltong saved for emergencies. But it aggravated their thirst; they could hardly gather enough saliva for swallowing the bits.

The sun rose higher, hitting them horizontally in the eyes, their shadows jumping jerkily after them, black on the white dust. From time to time he stopped to look round. In the distance, below the northern mountains, specks of vultures were circling. He tried to ignore them, in search of a trickling river bed, a patch of green, anything hopeful. But there was nothing.

By the time the sun was overhead she could hardly go on. Glancing at her, he saw her pale through the tan of her face, perspiration shining on her upper lip, thin wisps of hair clinging moistly to her forehead.

'Want to rest?' he asked.

She shook her head. 'I can go on.'

They walked on, more slowly now, but at an even pace.

Her whole body felt dusty, sticky. She thought: I used to change my clothes twice a day, coming this way on Larsson's wagon. I bathed myself mornings and evenings, because I couldn't stand the dirt. Now look at the filth covering me. Is this really me?

At times it felt as if she no longer occupied her body but rose from it, lightly, gliding out ahead of it or rising up high to look down on herself, her movement: the rhythmic strides of her legs, the swinging of arms, breasts bobbing. Rising higher in the currents of air sustaining her, higher than the mountains, spying on those two specks below moving on and on, like ants.

The sun moved over, striking their shoulders with dazzling nails of light. She stumbled over a stone. He caught her hand.

'Can you go on?'

'Yes. I . . .' But standing beside him she was panting. And when she closed her eyes for a moment, she swayed on her feet.

'There are some bushes ahead. We can rest there.'

'Just for a moment. I'll be all right.'

But soon, watching her in the narrow strip of shade, he realised that she was more exhausted than she'd made him believe. With deliberate, perverse glee he looked up at the vultures in the distance, wondering when they would start drifting this way. For them the plains always had something in store.

'Wait here,' he said. 'I want to look out from that ridge over there.'

'I'll come with you. Really, I . . .'

'No, stay here. I'll be back soon.'

She remained behind, lying on her side, resting her head on her elbow. From time to time she raised her head. There he was on the ridge now. She wanted to get up and go to him. Just another minute's rest. Her head reeling, she abandoned herself to memories of leaves and shade. The mulberry tree. A young girl high up among the leaves, astride on two branches, legs wide apart, her mouth stained by red-black berries. Leaves rustling below, a hand furtively touching her leg under the long skirt she'd pulled up above her knees for climbing. Glancing down: a glimpse of a bare brown arm – it must be one of the slave children she always played with in the garden, disregarding her mother's stern commands. Resuming her silent raid on the tree, picking, thrusting the berries in her mouth, pretending not to notice anything. Moving her feet a little wider apart. Feeling the hand stroke upwards, up to the gentle pulpy parting of her young sex. And the purple stains on her thighs and between her legs when she got home again; and her fear at the thought that it might be blood.

She slept. Waking up, she found that the late afternoon shadows had crept up on her. There was no sign of him. But their bundles were still there, under the tangled bushes.

She swallowed. Her throat felt parched and swollen, her tongue heavy. She sat up, but a spell of dizziness made her lower her head on her knees again.

When she finally got up unsteadily, she saw him approaching in the distance. Running. How could he?

He was shouting something, waving his hand. A sob was stifled in her throat. Water! Had he found water?

No, not water. But two huge ostrich eggs. God knew how he'd managed to rob the nest without being killed by the male bird, let alone how he'd discovered it in the first place. But there he was with the eggs.

On a flat rock from which the day's heat was flaring like white fire, he assembled some twigs and dried leaves and lit them with a spark from his tinder-box. She squatted opposite him to watch. The fire was hardly necessary, the stone was so hot. Carefully balancing one egg on its tip, propped up by smaller stones, he made a hole on top, forced in a blob of fat, then pressed the two prongs of a cleft stick together, into the hole, and began to stir, rubbing the back of the stick between his open palms. Spellbound, she watched, her lips half-opened and cracked, with small dry crusts of blood clinging to them.

It felt like a very long time before he finally said: 'Right.'

Even after he'd removed the egg from the fire, holding it in a piece of animal skin, they still had to wait for it to cool. He broke away the rim of the hole, widening it so that he could blow on the curdly mess inside. It was still scalding, but not able to wait any longer she took the large shell in her cupped hands and began to slurp from it, luxuriously sucking in the half-cooked, quivering egg, burning her mouth, swallowing greedily. Then she handed it to him.

The sun was setting. A new coolness caressed them, drying the sweat on their shoulders and backs.

And suddenly she laughed, almost carelessly, joyful; for now they were fed and their thirst was quenched – and they still had some left for tomorrow. The dark was cool and lovely on their bodies. The day had been hard, but now it was over. They had survived this, too. Life was good and generous; they needed so little.

She thought of her mother's never-ending bickering in the Cape about the two sons in their grave, the barbarous land, the unbearable existence without her family or the music and art of Amsterdam, canals and gables and carrillons, and coaches on the cobblestones; the barrenness of this outpost, a lingering death. You must get away from here, my child, this is no place for civilised people. You're European, you have good blood in your veins, you were not meant to go to pieces in a colony. Here one is always broken in the end.

No, Mother, look: we've found an egg, the land is kind to us, one can live here.

'And tomorrow?' he asked.

'Tomorrow we go on.'

Together they looked at the billowing expanse of the plains under the moon. From very far away they heard jackals cavorting, a hyena uttering its chilling whoop. What lay behind them was of no importance, it was past. This space lay before them, all its possibilities enclosed in the future, on the border of reality. All they had to do, was to say: *I will*. For it was will that opened it, will that made it happen.

'From now on it will be better,' she said, close to him.

'Anything may still happen.'

'No, the worst is past.'

The worst is not yet past. Even she is forced to admit it. That was just a beginning, an initiation, a provisional ordeal. The days remain cloudless and white and hot; the earth is hard-baked, and where there used to be brooks the mud lies cracked in complex patterns. Still there is a hard and hidden compassion in the land which keeps surprising them. Once, when they least expect it, it takes the form of a long pool of water in the wide bed of an otherwise dried-up river among the large bony knuckles of scorched hills. It is surrounded by thickets of mimosa with fluffy yellow flower-balls buzzing with bees. Did not she and Larsson camp here too? She is almost convinced of it: every time this curious discovery of moving in against him, against her previous self – on her way back to the beginning.

This time they stay over for a full week, camping under the trees beside the water, without a single objection from her. In fact, she is reluctant to obey when, one evening, he announces:

'Tomorrow we move on again.'

Refreshed, they continue, reassured by the knowledge that even the desert contains surprises. And for the moment they have sufficient water – two bags, the calabashes, and a couple of ostrich eggs filled to the brim. They are washed clean; their energy is restored.

It takes a single day to get dusty and dry again, and this time there is no sign of water, although they follow the course of the dry river. In spite of drastic rationing their supplies dwindle alarmingly and after a full week they have still not found anything. In the past it never exceeded two or three days.

On the second day after they drank the last water, both of them realise, without having to discuss it, that they have reached another crisis. They have some moisture left to safeguard them against the worst thirst: jackal's food and *kambro* he has dug out, and a collection of bitter fleshy leaves. But that is not enough: it merely suspends the inevitable.

She lies fast asleep when, in the late afternoon, he suddenly notices the small brown bird fluttering and twittering in the dry branches covering the sandy hollow where they have decided to rest until nightfall. His first impulse is to wake her, but he finds it hard to disturb her deep sleep. Perhaps, he decides, he'll be back before she wakes up. Perhaps. He can but hope.

The bird is still twittering in the branches overhead. He gets up, looking down at her sleeping in the sand, then turns to follow the bird on its fluttering, excited way from tree to tree. He has his assegai with him, and his knife; and, of course, the empty skin-bags. Still the bird leads him on, farther and farther away from the dry river bed.

Once he stops to look back. But the bird goes wild above his head, flapping and screeching hysterically. There is no sign of a nest yet, but he shrugs his shoulders and goes on.

It is a long way. He knows from previous experience how unpredictable a journey it can be: half an hour or half a day, it's impossible to tell. But he cannot let this chance go by. Somewhere on these plains there is a hidden bees' nest, and he must have the honey. For her sake, above all.

Dusk begins to fall. He looks back the way he has come. It must be four or five miles now, back to her. Will she have awakened by now? Is she looking for him? Is she terrified? Or will she accept that he'll be coming back and patiently wait for him? He won't reach the honey before dark now, that is obvious. Somewhere here he'll have to stay the night. Perhaps the bird will remain with him, perhaps not – but that is the risk he has to take. If he turns back now, he can still reach her before it is quite dark, but it is highly unlikely that the bird will follow him and then all is lost. And if they don't find food by tomorrow, it may be too late.

Alone under the first stars, he leans against the side of an erosion ditch where he has cleared a space for the night. Somewhere in the thorn-trees above him the little bird is fast asleep. Possibly. It is too dark to see for sure. Faith.

In this complete desolation, keenly aware of her somewhere on these same plains, under the same dark sky, exposed to space, his love is agony and anguish. He never willed or wanted it. But it has happened, and now it has him in its grip.

There was one woman he dared to love when he'd barely reached manhood and she was younger still, lost in this new country, with dreams of Java in her exile's eyes: dreams first revealed to him by his Grandmother Seli, which might account for the acuteness of their impact on his mind. Some of the older men tried to get at her, but he warded them off. At first he only protected her, not desiring anything beyond that, perhaps knowing in advance how futile it would be. Fucking in the dark, all right; relieving one's frustrations, avenging one's rage or passion on another body, all right. But not love. That was too terrible. In the end he couldn't resist it any longer. He tried to, but he couldn't. The smoothness of her skin, her round shoulders, her shy and barely nubile breasts, the pronounced hip-bones of a very young girl, her narrow hands. I love you: I dare not: I love you. I lose myself in you, in the sound of your voice, knowing it's hopeless. Then, one day, just like that, without a word of warning, she was gone. She was supposed to wait for him at the garden gate, with the milk-pails from the cowshed; but she never came. And later, by sheer coincidence, he heard: Oh, but she's been sold, didn't you know?

She. Even here in the desolate dark I dare not think your name, it's too intimate. Forever *she*.

There is a strange, harsh beauty in being, suddenly, alone like this. To weigh. To think. Even more intensely than the night he was away from her, following the hunters' trail. First she, now you. Equally vulnerable, both; with something equally unyielding too. But she was sold. And that is why I have this fear in me about you. For what will happen to you? Dare it last? Is it possible? One is always betrayed.

There was another woman, of course, but she was different. After the old Hottentot crone, cast out by her tribe, had cured him of the poison of the snake, he hunted down her people and spent a year with them, roaming through the land. Took a wife and made her a hut and moved in with her like one of them, a member of the tribe. She looked after him, he provided well enough for her; but that was all. And after a year he found he couldn't stay any longer, he had to go off again. She cursed him in his face and spat at him and clawed at him with her nails. The others merely shrugged and laughed – that was a woman's way – but his own heart shrank in him. It was because she was childless, he explained; which wasn't the reason at all, of course. He simply had to be alone again, equipped with everything they'd taught him, ready for the land, exposed to it. Except for this heart always yearning for the Cape.

And now there is this new woman, Elisabeth, opening the road back to the Cape. But it's a hard country, and honey is scarce.

At daybreak he finds the honey-bird still with him. He smiles. All right, we can go on. An hour later they reach the hollow anthill where the bees have made their nest. Making a fire with two twigs rubbed together, he begins to smoke them out, breaking open the nest with his assegai and his hands, filling his bags. On a stone a little way off he leaves a few honeycombs for the bird before he turns back on a fast trot in the stinging rays of the early sun.

She has spread out their last bit of food on a rock when he arrives at the dry river bed. With a smile she looks up and runs to meet him.

'I've been so worried about you,' he says passionately. 'Are you all right?'

'Of course.' Serenely she looks up at him. 'I wasn't frightened at all. I knew you'd come back.'

'I should have woken you up to tell you before I left.' He holds her tightly against him. 'But you were so fast asleep, and you needed the rest so much. I didn't think I'd be away so long.'

'You're back now, aren't you?' she says quietly.

'I've brought us honey.'

'So we'll get through?' Suddenly there are tears in her eyes.

'Yes.'

Sitting down, he opens the bag and takes out a piece of honeycomb for her. She sits down beside him to eat it from his hand, licking off his fingers.

'What have you been doing all the time?' he asks.

'Just waited. Slept. Then waited again.'

'And you really weren't afraid?'

'No. I thought: if anything happened to you, I would simply stay

172

here very peacefully until I die. I wouldn't worry about anything any more. It's useless, isn't it? It was so quiet. The night was very beautiful, did you notice? In the day one doesn't always realise how beautiful it can be.'

They eat in silence. The honey is too sweet to have much of it; but it brings a surge of new energy.

'Are we going on today?' he asks later.

'I don't know.' She is sucking her fingers. Then looks up abruptly: 'Actually it was good to be without you. One gets too used to one another. You stop thinking. Being all by myself has cleared my thoughts again.'

'What did you think?'

'That I loved you.'

'Was that all?' he asks teasingly.

'No,' she says, her eyes still serious. 'But that was the most important. And because I love you I don't want anything to happen to us. We must get out of this valley so that we can reach the Cape safely.'

'That's what we're trying to do.'

'I mean: we can't just go on like this. All the time we've been thinking it would get better. I really believed it. But the river beds stay dry. Suppose there's nothing farther on: I mean really nothing – no honey, no water, no roots, nothing at all?'

'We'll find something.'

'But it is possible that there may be nothing.'

'I suppose so.' He looks at her searchingly. 'But what else can we do?'

'What lies beyond the mountains?'

'On that side there's the forest.' He points to the south.

'Like the one we knew?'

'Yes, but worse. Almost impossible. All the way as far as Mossel Bay. From there, of course, it's easy.'

'Yes, that's the way we came.' She reflects. 'And over there, to the north?'

'The Karoo.'

'What is it like?'

'I've never been there, I don't know for sure. But I've heard it's very dry, almost a desert.'

'It can't be worse than here. And perhaps it has rained there. Before we reached the Camdeboo they also warned us it would be a desert. But when we came there it had rained, and it was very beautiful.'

'How can we be sure that it has rained in the Karoo?'

'How can we be sure that it hasn't?' she insists.

He shakes his head.

'It can't be worse than here,' she repeats urgently.

'Perhaps it is.'

'If it's all flat we can trek fast and reach the Cape much sooner.'

'Or die on the way.'

'If we go on like this we may also die. And if we try the forest, we may get lost.'

'What do you want to do?' he asks point-blank.

'I want to get back to the Cape.'

'Along this valley I more or less know the way,' he says. 'It's bad, but I know what to expect. Beyond those black mountains I don't know the world at all.'

'Haven't you got any faith?'

'It's a matter of life or death, Elisabeth!'

'That's why I'm talking about it,' she says. 'We can't just go on like two tortoises. We have to choose.'

'And you choose the mountains?'

'Yes.' And she thinks: How very strange, whatever Larsson may have maimed or killed in me, this he has kindled and confirmed – this thirst for whatever lies beyond the mountains.

Leaving the valley also means finally turning away from Larsson. From now on there is no longer rebellion against his memory, but a new movement wholly without him. The anxious excitement of following a half-remembered trail, calculating progress in terms of secret beacons, is renounced. These mountains are a line of demarcation and a bridge between memory and innocence, the half-familiar and the utterly foreign, a dimension absolute unto itself.

Leaving the dry river bed they trek to the foot of the northern range, following its foothills and contours in search of a breach which will let them through. From nearby the mountains appear even more formidable than from a distance, the red cliffs towering in grotesque formations marked by the violence of floods and sun, wind, and landslides. But after four days they find what they are looking for: a kloof cutting through rock and earth to make way for a narrow river of which only the dry bed remains.

It is a strange sensation: not of travelling through the mountains but of penetrating right into them. As they go on, the walls of the kloof grow more perpendicular; below, it deepens into a ravine carved out by prehistoric floods; on either side the cliffs stagger upwards, opening up into chaotic masses of tumbled rocks, or leaning over, almost touching sides, forming a near-tunnel below. It is cooler here, and damp; the rust and yellow of lichen covering the rocks deepen to the moist green of moss. In the river bed pools of cold and crystal-clear water make their appearance.

At first they abandon themselves to the luxury of the water and the exhilarating coolness. But there is something unearthly about their journey: the twisting kloof is cold and stern, dangerous, hostile, not condescending in any way. The mountains where they hibernated were a haven and a peaceful shelter: this great range is a threatening antagonist. In the narrow sliver of deep blue sky high above them they see, from time to time, the specks of eagles or vultures hovering: this is no country for human beings.

But she is adamant: 'Once we're through here, it will be better. It's because it will be so easy on the other side that we have to suffer here.'

'Every time you think we've passed the worst,' he reminds her. 'And every time it gets worse still.'

'This time I'm sure.' She is sucking a spot on her wrist where she has painfully grazed herself. 'One day we'll bring our children back here to show them.'

'Then we'd better have baboons, not children,' he laughs.

'Oh, we'll make ourselves a nice smooth road here so that we can come by wagon.'

'What about sprouting wings? It'll be easier to fly over.'

'Doesn't it say in the Bible that if one has faith one can move a mountain to the sea?'

'Well, why don't you shift it right there now?' he says. 'It can take us with it – all the way to the Cape.'

She chuckles; then sighs. 'It would have been much easier if one really had faith, wouldn't it? In God, or in the Devil. Then one could say: The Devil has put this mountain in our way. Or: It's God's way of afflicting us, or of punishing us.' With new intensity she asks: 'Do you think we *are* being punished for something?'

'For running away from the Cape?'

'But we're on our way back. Surely that should compensate.'

'It doesn't look like it.'

'It really would have been easier,' she sighs. 'Just to resign oneself to what God or Satan has decreed . . . *Let Thy will be done.*' She shakes her head and is silent for a while, before she looks up at him again. 'But for us who have to bear everything ourselves – we must get through all on our own.'

It is as if the strange seclusion in the mountain forces them to discuss what, on the plains, it was possible to suppress.

'Why do you really want to go back?' he asks.

'You know it as well as I do. Because it's better to be there than here.'

'You find it hard to renounce the idea of heaven, don't you?'

'Not heaven. But something better than we have. If it hadn't been for that . . .'

'You see?' He laughs briefly. 'You're still trying your best to change the world by thinking it a better place.'

'Because I'm human.'

'Or because you're white?'

'You have no right to say that, Adam!' Impulsively she thrusts out her hand, holding it next to his. 'Look: I'm nearly as brown as you.'

'Do you think white is a colour?' he asks.

She gets up slowly. 'Do you mean – you're beginning to have doubts about going back?'

'Don't *you* ever have doubts?'

'But we decided . . .'

'Of course.' He takes her shoulders in his hands. 'Do you know that sometimes I wake up at night, thinking of the Cape – and then I cannot go to sleep again?'

'Because you're afraid?'

'Because I don't know what will happen.'

'Will you abandon me?' she asks quietly.

'How can I? Can one abandon oneself? We'll be saved together. Or go into hell together. It will happen by itself: it no longer depends on either of us.'

'I don't ever want to be without you again,' she says.

'Are you absolutely sure?'

She clutches his arms, shaking him, trying to convince him forcibly. 'Why don't you believe me?'

'I believe you. But we're not there yet. We're here.'

She looks up at the cliffs. An eagle is circling above. Then it disappears without a trace and the sky remains unmoved. She thrusts herself against him, blindly, wildly, her small breasts pressing against his chest, his palms open on her hips, moving in a slow caress to the fine down at the bottom of her spine where the swelling of her buttocks begins. She makes a moaning sound, her mouth half-opened, staining his arm with her saliva.

'Adam?' she whispers.

'Why do you call me Adam?'

'It's your name.'

'My name is Aob.'

'For me you're Adam. That's how I learnt to know you. If I called you Aob it would change you into someone else, a stranger.'

'But it's my own name.'

'When you're inside me, sometimes, quite suddenly, yes, then I can call you Aob. But mostly you're Adam.'

'I'm Adam for the Cape.'

With a shy, shivery smile, her eyes unnaturally bright and her cheeks flushed, she moistens a finger in the slit of her sex and touches him on his forehead, between his eyes. 'I'm baptising you again,' she says. 'Now your name is Adam. For me.'

Still standing, supporting her hips with his hands, and with a mere lowering and a thrust of his body he enters hers, his eyes pressed tightly shut; standing almost without moving, clutching her to him with terrible intensity, until she starts whimpering and swaying in his arms and he feels his own climax coming, release, momentary redemption, trembling on his feet, leaning against her.

'Do you believe me now?' she whispers.

'I believe you even if I know you're lying.'

The kloof probes ever more deeply, revealing more and more of the guts of the black mountain in patterns of rock or fern; until they reach a dead-end against a waterfall, a thin white veil of water down the cliffs, evaporating in a swaying spray.

The only way out is up these slippery cliffs meeting behind the waterfall.

What do I want, ultimately? Is it so much? – something permanent in a world of change, something certain in a world of possibilities: I believe all your lies unconditionally. We're naked; we can easily fall to our death; we can break a bone on any stone. Deceit is easy and safe: to pretend to love, to comfort briefly, to go on unhurt. A contract: I shall give you this in exchange for that, a Cape in exchange for freedom – whereas . . . whereas . . . so it is that Adam

177

Mantoor, freedman carpenter of the Lion's Rump, offers his services, quality guaranteed. The lords-of-nine-days may come and go, but I'll stay: artisan at the Cape, respected, free, here's my letter with the seal of the Governor. I, Hendrick Swellengrebel, testify herewith, in the year of our Lord. But is that sufficient reason to return to the Cape? Dare one be fooled by that? I love you, here is my life, I'm holding yours in security: here is my hand, take it, let's jump into the abyss, whatever happens; even if we fall to death, let it at least be hand in hand.

Inch by inch up the smooth wet rock-wall. Slowly: there's no hurry. So close to the stone one notices crevices and knobs and knuckles which never existed from afar. A crack large enough for four fingers; a toe-hold. Dragging up the bundles with thongs tied together. Just hold tight. The spray of the fall sweeps across them, leaving them shuddering with sudden cold. Is it for us the eagle is hovering above? One tends to think of death as something distant and abstract. Here it is so simple and immediate: death is this slippery rock, this root breaking under my grip, this eagle waiting above, this spray in my eyes. Almost reassuring in its nearness: it is so certain and secure, so dependable, so utterly truthful.

Progressing from crack to crack, from ledge to ledge, diagonally up the smooth face of the cliff. Hold tight. If you slip, I fall with you. Even here are signs of life: small lizards, a bird brooding on a nest of speckled eggs, not paying any attention to us.

'Can you manage?'

'Yes. Just hold my hand.'

'Right? Up you come!'

'Thank you.'

Words like pebbles.

For a long time she remains lying on the top ridge, trembling but elated. Then on again, following a narrower, easier ravine to the summit. Before they reach it a movement among the rocks causes them to freeze with fright. Only when the sharp barking sound comes echoing down to them does Adam relax.

'Baboons.'

Following the warning of the leader the members of the pack come scurrying on from all sides, gathering on a high rock-formation to survey the approach of the strangers. It takes some time before they are sufficiently reassured to return to their food-gathering among the shrubs, upturning stones in search of larvae or scorpions, stripping pods and berries and caterpillars from the branches, combing children and comrades in search of lice and fleas.

For the first time since they've entered the mountains they feel relaxed and not oppressed, almost eager for the company of the baboons.

'Once we're up there it will be much easier, going down,' she says.

But darkness overtakes them long before they have reached the summit and they are forced to find shelter among some overhanging rocks a few hundred yards below the baboons.

They are still busy with their meal – the last of their honey, a rock-rabbit he has shot with an arrow, a couple of small fishes from a pool in the river below – when pandemonium breaks out above them. Screams of terror, wild barking, stones tumbling down the slope sending sparks flying from rocks and echoing among all the cliffs of the mountain range. They jump up from where they have been sitting. Baboons come storming past them, fleeing in all directions, mothers clasping their young to their bellies, youngsters leaving trails of shit.

It takes some time before they can make out what is going on. One young male comes galloping straight towards them, stopping in his tracks when he is almost on top of them, snarls and bares his huge fangs and swings round to escape – the next moment a spotted shadow flashes past the rocks where they are standing, overtaking the baboon. They are so close that they can see the mortal terror in his eyes as he screams; then the leopard is upon him, rolling in a cloud of dust. With the sharp sound of a breaking branch his neck and spine snap under the impact. They can see his mouth opening, and blood spouting from a severed jugular vein. An instant later the leopard is on his way up the slope again, dragging the carcass with him, while all the baboons higher up start chattering and screaming, assaulting the marauder with a hailstorm of stones.

Adam discovers it just in time. Pulling Elisabeth in behind the rocks of their shelter, he keeps her out of reach of the stones until the noise subsides. A last few stones come crashing past. Then it is deadly silent, as if there has never been a sound in the mountains.

They emerge from their hiding place, but it is already too late to see anything. The leopard must have disappeared over the nearest hill-top or hidden in a thicket. Of the baboons there is no sign except for the yellow shit marking their flight and the pool of blood where the male was struck down.

'So close to us,' she says, stunned, staring at the blood. 'If we'd gone higher, he might have grabbed one of us.'

'He's gone away,' he says, comforting her; but she can hear from his voice that he's been scared too.

'Did you hear how he screamed? It was just like a man.'

'It was all over in a second,' he says laconically, taking her arm. 'Come. It's getting dark.'

'Do you think the leopard will come back?'

'No. But we can't stay here in the open.'

He leads her back to their shelter.

'You haven't finished your food yet,' he says.

She shakes her head. 'I can't. Not now.'

'Please,' he urges. 'You'll need it. There's another tough day ahead.'

'Tomorrow the baboons will be feeding on the slope again,' she says, staring into the deepening dusk. 'Do you think they'll still remember? Or do they forget very easily?'

He shrugs.

After some time, more collected, she says: 'Perhaps it is better that way, so suddenly. One moment of terror and pain, and then it's all over. It's better than growing as old as that old Hottentot woman and being left in a hole to die slowly.'

'The old woman who found me after the snake had bitten me . . .' he says, pensive. 'She'd also been left by her people to die on the way. But I kept her alive. For months on end I stayed with her, moving on very slowly so as not to tire her too badly. But in the end she died – two days before we reached the new village of her tribe.' He is quiet for a long time before he resumes in the same distant voice. 'I tried to do everything for her which I'd not been able to do for my grandmother. But then she died too. I couldn't understand it. I felt so angry and hurt and rebellious. Long after I'd buried her I tried to keep her alive by thinking about her. But what's the use?'

'*You're* alive,' she says emphatically. 'We're alive. And we're going on.'

'Do you think we'll grow old together in the Cape? Until, one day . . .'

'At least they won't bury us in porcupine holes. Not alive.'

'Is that the worst that can happen?' he asks.

'It's worse than the death of the baboon.'

180

'But we're not baboons.'

'It almost sounds as if you regret it,' she says, trying to sound lighthearted.

'Maybe I do.'

It is quite dark now. They snuggle in under their karosses, close together.

'Tomorrow we'll reach the top,' she says sleepily.

But it is not the top. When they reach what has seemed like the summit there is yet another slope beyond, leading to another, higher, ridge; and then still more, an endless confusion of mountains. Still they push on. They no longer talk glibly about tomorrow, or the other side. They just go on grimly. And at last they come upon a new kloof which also, ages ago, must have borne a river, and following its tortuous course through the mountains, they gradually see the walls of rock recede and dwindle, until one afternoon after they reach the last bend and discover the new land before them, still a hundred feet or so below their feet.

In silence they look out over it, exploring it with their eyes; parched and waterless, with whirlwinds sending small whorls of white dust dancing across the earth and dissolving in the colourless sky; patches of brownish shrubs close to the ground; red koppies like the fossils of giant lizards, ridges, bare stretches, a hazy distance obliterating the horizon.

They do not look at one another. They do not say a word. They can only stare, their eyes wide open.

To turn back is impossible. They have no choice; they must go on.

'I'm going to marry Erik Alexis Larsson,' she announced at table.

'It's completely out of the question!' said her mother. 'I've never heard of such madness.'

'I'm going,' she insisted.

'Use your authority, Marcus,' Catharina ordered. 'What will our friends think of it? A woman in the interior!'

'What's wrong with a woman in the interior?' she asked heatedly. 'What's wrong with a woman anyway? Is it something to be ashamed of?'

'Married to a man with no ambition,' her mother said with unrestrained bitterness. 'Two children in the grave, my two sons who would have made all the difference. Bruised by this land, broken by it. But you, Elisabeth: you're used to a decent way of life, you're held in esteem, you're an example to others.'

'You make it sound as if I'm descending into hell. It's only the interior.'

Hands are lovely, and lovelier still returning from journeys of love. She is holding his hand between hers on her drawn-up knees, her back against the ironstone of a koppie where they are sheltering in the afternoon shade. With a forefinger she traces the pattern of his palm, wishing she knew how to read it (what did the gypsy woman in Amsterdam foretell?). One is supposed to be a lifeline, another a loveline, a third the line of fortune: which is this one breaking off so short? With hopeless love she presses his palm against her lips, wanting to cry. Happiness and suffering are what remains now. To this journey we have been doomed, each of us vast as a desert landscape, pure infinity; interiority. Particulars are for those who are content with facts and faults.

Spread out on the skins of their opened bundles, exposed for inspection:

2 karosses
2 aprons
2 skinbags
3 ostrich egg-shells
1 hunting knife
1 pistol with a small bag of ammunition
6 arrows in a quiver
1 assegai
2 sticks
1 broken cooking pot
1 tinder-box
a small collection of seashells, some broken
3 small bags of herbs
1 bag of honey
an assortment of roots, bulbs, tubers and edible leaves
1 Cape dress

'Can one survive here?'
'Not if one is alone. But if we stick together . . .'
We *must* survive, in this landscape which conceals nothing – red and brown and white nearby, a greyish ochre from a distance, the farthest koppies on the horizon a dull blue. Stones, cheeky ground-squirrels,

praying mantises like dried twigs, occasionally a tortoise. Vultures steadily above; hunting spiders darting among the faded green-blue leaves of bitter succulents growing close to the ground; whirlwinds; sometimes the bare whiteness of bones. Extremes of heat and cold. An hour after rising the sun is like a white coal burning in one's eyes, sending lines of sweat trickling down the dust on one's skin; the earth is too glowing hot to set foot on and one's tongue stirs against a parched palate. Then, immediately after sunset it gets so cold that one has to huddle in a kaross, one's teeth chattering.

On the cracked, baked mud of the dry river bed the old Bushman found him, half dead with thirst; kneeling in the *gorreh* he sucked dirty water from the dust and spat it out in his mouth; the taste of life. And then he trotted off again, into the shimmering mirages, his bow in his hand, and the quiver of arrows over his shoulder. That was what surprised him most of all: not the miracle of the water from stone and hard earth, but that the Bushman, the *Saan*, the despicable *Koetsri*, the dreaded enemy with the arrows, had deigned to offer him water. What else could he do but to take on him the burden of the old woman, trying to take her back to her tribe, later, after she'd saved his life?

Under the salty crust of the dried-up lake – the precious salt, too, is scooped up and stored to be used for meat – he shows her the dark receding rings left by the shrinking water.

'But there's nothing here,' she protests. 'The mud isn't even moist any more.'

'Watch.' With a smile he starts digging, using his assegai. Six inches, a foot, two feet and it remains hard and dry as stone, followed by a softer, crumbling layer; and then it starts getting moist. From deep down, after a whole day's painstaking work, he takes out the turtle which has submerged itself waiting for the next rain to fall: a female with strings of eggs in her belly. They are safe for another day; perhaps, with careful rationing, even two.

She watches him kneeling over the shell to scrape out the meat; horizontally ahead the sun is sinking, bleeding like a thing torn apart by vultures. It looks as if he's praying.

We'll survive, we'll survive. We shall get through. It is the message on your palm. There is always hope.

In the dark pre-dawn they gradually become aware of something happening. At first it isn't even a sound, merely a faint tremor as if, dull and deep, the earth is trembling. Adam is the first to sit up; then he lies down again, pressing his ear to the ground. He motions to her and she imitates him. Slowly sound is added to it, a thunder still too low for the ear to catch up, insinuating itself through the skull and the bones of the body.

'What is it?' she asks.

Adam shakes his head. Perhaps he already has a suspicion, but he isn't sure yet. It is growing lighter round them. The dull rumbling sound remains far away.

By the time the sun rises they can clearly make out a huge, lazy cloud in the distance, spreading almost imperceptibly until it covers the entire horizon from south to north.

'Smoke?' she asks. 'But there's nothing to burn on these plains.'

'Dust,' he says.

Once again he presses his head to the ground, lying down for so long that she gets anxious.

'What is it then?' she asks.

'We must hurry,' he says with sudden urgency, getting up. 'Help me.' He begins to tie up their bundles, his fingers fumbling with the thongs.

'What's happening, Adam?' she demands.

'Migrating buck.'

'But . . .'

'We haven't much time. We must get to that koppie.'

Without waiting for breakfast they set out to the narrow stony ridge half a mile from where they've been camping in their karosses.

On the horizon the red cloud is rising steadily: keeping one's eyes fixed on it, it is impossible to discern any movement; yet every time one looks back, there is a change as it spreads out and darkens and grows more dense. By now the rumbling can be heard distinctly, although still low and even, like the sound of some subterranean landslide.

Hurriedly they scramble up the rocky slope to the highest ridge of the koppie where he flings down his bundle and starts stacking stones to build a short, bulky wall – only two or three yards long, waist high, but hard work in the sun which already beats down on them, chasing up heat-waves from the hard earth. The rocks are huge, most of them too heavy to handle, so that they have to move back and forth between the top of the ridge and the bottom to select the more manageable ones.

After a time something else becomes visible under the moving cloud: a low, unbroken brownish mass approaching over the plains like a solid wall of muddy water – but slowly, unhurried, and quite inexorable.

'Surely all of that can't be buck?' she asks, stunned.

Toiling with the heavy stones, he doesn't answer, barely stopping to wipe the streaks of perspiration from his face or to spit on the cuts and calluses on his hands.

They are buck. Now she can see it for herself. A low, slow mass of springbuck moving across the plains in an endless brown flood.

Adam is gathering wood, stacking it against the wall he has built, still without explanation: dry branches, brittle twigs, decayed bits of thorn-tree bark.

And then the vast herd is upon them. They move at such an even pace that, from a distance, it appears lethargic: but one moment they are still far away, and the very next they are all around them, swirling and eddying in an endless tide of cinnamon-brown bodies, streaked with chocolate, with white undersides, sweeping steadily onward, submerging everything in their way. Directly beyond the wall the tide parts, streaming past on either side, flowing back into one solid mass as soon as they have left the sheltered spot behind. And everything is shrouded in dust, in fine brown powder pervading the very pores of the body, filling eyes and nose and mouth, clinging to hair and eyebrows and lashes.

At first, Adam and Elisabeth remain crouching together against their protecting wall. But after a time, as the flood of brown bodies continues undiminished, they become more confident and stand up. One can touch the passing buck with one's hand, they wouldn't even notice: the moist black eyes staring fixedly ahead, all caught in an inexplicable trance. Now, so close to them, it is possible to distinguish separate sounds in the general rumble: the clattering of sharp cloven hooves on the hard earth, dislodged stones rolling downhill, the gentle grunts of individual buck, the higher, shrill, whistling sounds of others. And under their feet the earth is trembling, an interminable shudder as if the vast plains are feverish in the sun.

'But where are they going to?' she asks, dumbfounded.

'They just trek like this.' He stares at the flood swirling round them: there is still no end in sight. 'Perhaps they smelled rain in the wind.'

After a long time, as she still watches them, hypnotised, he unties his bundle and takes out the pistol. Waiting patiently to select a young male passing a yard from him, he aims, pressing the barrel almost

185

against the head of the buck, and pulls the trigger. The others do not even try to avoid the kicking animal. In fact, Adam has to be quick to rescue the carcass before it is trodden to a pulp.

'Will you cut it up?' he asks after he has skinned the buck.

'What are you going to do?'

He motions to the pistol, loading it again.

'But one is enough!' she protests. 'We can't store so much meat in this weather.'

'Stomach fluid,' he says cryptically.

And with cold-blooded calculation he goes on killing more buck; after a while he doesn't even bother to use the pistol any more and fells his victims with his assegai. Until there are at least ten carcasses heaped up against their wall. And still there is no sign of abatement in the living flood.

She helps him to make a fire. Even that has no effect on the buck passing their shelter. 'If the wall hadn't stopped them they would have come right through the flames,' he says, talkative at last. 'I've seen them at rivers. The front ones are simply trampled down; the others keep on coming from behind, until there is a whole bridge of carcasses damming up the water.'

In the heart of the slowly moving earthquake they roast their meat and have a meal. It is unearthly; even while it is happening she finds it difficult to believe in it. He goes on cutting up the other slaughtered buck, collecting the fluid from their stomachs.

She pulls up her nose at the warm, physical stench.

'You'll be grateful later,' he says, smiling.

'Surely we'll find ordinary water.'

'Do you think they would have been trekking if there had been water that way?'

'You mean . . . ?'

He nods, grimly continuing with his work.

'So it really will be worse ahead?' she demands.

'Yes. Not only because of the water. But because they've now trodden everything to dust. It will no longer be possible to find hidden *kambro* or other bulbs. Now it's a desert.'

She gets up and looks towards the south, the sun directly overhead now: towards the range of mountains beyond the moving plains. And he knows what she's thinking: those are the mountains they have crossed.

Throughout the day the slow-sweeping horde comes moving past.

186

Their shelter is a tiny island on the teeming, living plain, covered by red dust. Adam keeps only the meat of the first carcass which she has cut up, vainly trying to shelter it from the sun under a kaross fastened to the wall. The other slaughtered bodies are hurled back into the moving mass that tramples them into the dust. At last it gets dark. The earth is still shuddering under them. Leaning against the wall, they sit beside their small fire, listening to the night thundering past. The stars are invisible through the dust. It is nearly time for the day to break before the trek is over. As suddenly as the buck appeared, they are gone. The booming sound of their migration begins to ebb away, subsiding to a dull monotonous throb, until only the trembling of the earth remains. Then that, too, disappears.

At sunrise they get up, bleary-eyed and covered with dust, their heads aching. The world is vast and empty, even emptier than before. The cloud of dust hangs motionless over the entire expanse of the veld; not a breath of wind is stirring. On the plains there are no contours left, as if the very hills have been trampled into the earth. There is no sign of low shrubs or piles of dry wood or heaps of stones; just an endless monotony of powdered dust.

'Shall we go on?' he asks.

She doesn't answer; she doesn't even nod.

'I've always believed it would get better as we went on,' she says at last. 'That was what kept me going. Every day I firmly believed: tomorrow . . .'

'And now?' he asks, unnecessarily, bluntly.

'We can't stay here,' she says.

'Shall we try to go back?' He points to the mountains in the south.

'Do you think we'll be able to cross them again?'

He shrugs.

'We'd better go on,' she says.

'Even if you know it can't get better any more?'

Clenching her teeth, she nods, and picks up her bundle.

Through the great emptiness they start walking on, stunned into a stupor. There are vultures in the sky.

A few miles on, the sun already burning relentlessly, they come upon a trampled, bloody, dusty bundle covered by vultures. It is barely recognisable: a portion of skull, teeth, tufts of hair.

'It was a lion,' he says, almost reverently. 'It came in their way.'

'But . . .' It's no use saying anything.

This is that history we spoke about before: do you remember? You

187

didn't want to believe me. You still thought it was something which happened in the Cape and was carried into the land from there. Do you understand a bit more of it now? Of life going its own stubborn way here in the wilderness? Of the suffering of the nameless, the revolt of the humble?

You stand so still beside me. Here are the vultures. Round us there is nothing. You are filthy and covered with dust; sweat has drawn patterns over your burnt face; your hair is caked with dirt; there are lines of suffering round your mouth, and your eyes are bloodshot and scared; your breasts are sagging, your nipples scorched black. Human being reduced to dust. I recognise you. And I have never loved you as I do now.

The ruin is a mere pimple against the bare hill on the scorched and trampled plains, but it lures them like a beacon. It is the first time since the three small ruins on the other side of the mountains that they've come across the slightest sign of human life: and it is the vultures that show them the way.

A cottage of mud and stone, the front half caved in, the woodwork of the roof plundered by the wind; a low stone-wall enclosing the yard half ruined but still standing. It must have been this wall which warded off the migrating buck, protecting the yard. Vultures are circling over the house; a couple are already perched on the torn roof and others have descended to the stones of the tumbled wall. But there are no people. The birds have been lured by the half-decayed carcass of a springbuck on the back doorstep, partly inside the house; and by the dog.

At first it seems as if the dog is also dead, but then it lifts its head – much too big for its panting, emaciated body and sticky legs – barking feebly whenever the vultures come too close. Then they flap out of the way, patiently returning to the dark, slowly narrowing half-circle of waiting birds.

Ever since the passing of the buck the dog must have been keeping watch over the rotting carcass, feeding on it, bit by bit, trying to moisten the dried blood with its tongue.

It struggles to its feet as soon as they approach, baring its teeth, its mouth and sunken eyes swarming with flies. It tries to warn them with a pathetic attempt to bark; then, whining softly, it begins to wag its tail. Adam goes up to him, patting the bony head. The dog must have been left behind when the people of the house moved off: but when was that? And why didn't the dog go with them? Why did they leave

188

their furniture behind, now broken to bits, littering the hard dung floor? It must have happened very long ago. Yet one cannot be too sure: the sun and wind work violently and fast.

First they must get rid of the dead buck. The dog starts growling again and even tries to snap at Adam when he grabs the carcass by the hind legs and begins to drag it away; half a mile from the house he abandons it to the swarming vultures. When he returns, the dog welcomes him with a miserably wagging tail, obviously too exhausted to remain aggressive. Whimpering, it nuzzles Adam's legs, trots off a few yards towards the back of the house, then returns to repeat the process, until, with weary curiosity, Adam follows it. The dog leads him to a few scraggy thorn-trees in a dry ditch running across the backyard; there he discovers a stone well. In rainy years it is probably fed by a fountain. Whimpering steadily, the dog tries to jump on the stones surrounding the well, but its legs are too weak and it falls back.

Half-dazed and eager, Adam peers into the well, but it is too dark to see anything. He throws in a pebble and with a jerky intake of breath he hears the small wet sound of water as it hits the bottom. Tying all their bits and pieces of thong together, he lowers their leaky cooking pot into the well and manages, with patient manipulation, to pull up a small quantity of dirty, foul-smelling water. There is obviously no more than a few inches left at the bottom of the well, but the unexpected discovery sends a choking sob to his throat.

In a surge of joy he pours some of the water into the hollow of a stone for the dog, before he fills an ostrich eggshell for Elisabeth.

She has fallen asleep where she sat just inside the kitchen door. It is the first time since they came across the trekking buck that they've found shelter from the sun. During the week or more that has passed since then, they have had to carry their bundles on their heads for shade; they've even been forced to wear the unbearably hot karosses in the worst hours of the day to shield their bodies from the terrible sun. The supply of fetid stomach-water has kept them going, hers filtered through the hem of the Cape dress to somewhat purify it, otherwise it would have made her vomit. Now, so unexpectedly, there is this precious supply of water from the well.

Burning with impatience, he allows the eggshell to stand untouched for a time so that the worst filth can settle on the bottom before he gently, coaxingly, raises it to her cracked and scalded lips. He sees her move her mouth in her sleep, swallowing; then she suddenly sits

189

up, looking at him in fear and suspicion, unable to believe what is happening.

Without eating anything, replete with water, they lie down to sleep – throughout the afternoon and night, and halfway through the next day, before they are finally awakened by the dog whimpering and tugging at their karosses.

They feel even more exhausted now they've slept, as if the rest has stirred up the silted dregs of fatigue deep inside them, causing it to drift dirtily on the surface of their existence.

Sitting on the doorstep staring out vacantly at the empty world, they strenuously chew the shrivelled remains of the veld food they have saved, sweetened with a mere touch of honey. Elisabeth gives the dog some of the hard, rancid biltong that remains of the slaughtered buck.

For the first time, still in something of a stupor and his head throbbing numbly, Adam begins to explore the house and its surroundings. Coming upon some bones protruding from the caved-in wall in front, he starts digging in the rubble. A human skull. More bones. There may be several skeletons under the mound of dirt and stones. But why bother to dig them all out?

She finds him there and stops, touching the skull with her foot.

'Perhaps the wind blew down the wall on them,' she says, unasked. 'Or do you think it was Bushmen who killed them?'

'If it was an accident there may still be some food around.'

With more interest they begin to search the rubble, but anything edible has been plundered or destroyed. The only recognisable objects they discover are the small skeletons of two children. Unexpectedly, the backyard yields something where the ruined wall has sheltered the little garden: three or four pumpkins which must have been lying there for months, the hard thick skins protecting the fleshy insides; a handful of shrivelled sweet-potatoes; peas in dried-up pods scorched white by the sun – but still edible if soaked in water. It's food. And there is enough of it even to share with the dog.

For days on end they do not move from the house, sleeping or lying listlessly in the shade – but slowly feeling a semblance of energy return, although it hardly stirs up much new hope in them, just dull resignation. There is an eternity behind them, and an eternity ahead. They are weary. But sooner or later they will have to move on.

Under a tattered piece of remaining roof jutting out over a side-wall swallows have made their nest and day after day they watch the birds flitting in and out, returning with worms or beetles; passively they listen to the sqeaking of the baby birds inside. All the time Adam has been waiting, restraining the urge to rob the nest, knowing that that must wait for last: a decisive act, signalling the resumption of their journey. From day to day he puts it off, hankering after the tastiness of the dish, but dreading the decision involved. Until, at last, it cannot be postponed any longer. And one evening, after both the parent birds have returned to the nest, he piles up stones and wood against the wall and climbs up, removing the birds one by one. Holding the small necks between thumb and forefinger he flicks his wrist in a brief circular jerk; that is enough.

Elisabeth takes them inside to make soup, filling all their containers with it. They have a small precious meal, burning hot; and even the dog is treated to a portion, including the delicate bones of the birds. And while they sit on the doorstep with their soup, trying to make it last as long as possible, they both know, without talking about it, that another end has come. This deep subterranean thing driving them on has not yet lost its force.

She remembers the first deserted house on their journey, before they reached the sea: the decisive one. How she was preparing food on the open hearth waiting for him to come back, and how he stayed away until sunset; the pack of wild dogs hunting the zebra, tearing out its flesh as he was running; and how Adam suddenly appeared among the trees with the buck on his shoulders. He was back; he had returned.

'We mustn't stay here,' she said that night; she says now. 'Tomorrow morning we must go on. It isn't good to stay here.'

With their meagre new provisions they set out into the cool bare world before the sun comes out.

The mangy dog comes with them, trotting on their heels.

Adam swings round and tries to kick it. The dog stops, its ears drawn flat against its outsized head, tail between the legs; but as soon as they move on, it follows them again, this time at a safer distance.

Adam picks up a stone and hurls it at the dog. With a yelp it flees from them. But the moment they turn to walk on, it comes hurrying back.

'Why can't he come with us?' asks Elisabeth. 'He took you to the water. He saved our lives.'

'We can't feed him.'

'But he needs us, Adam. He can't survive without us.'

'He'll die of hunger if he comes with us,' he says curtly.

'Perhaps he can find us things to eat.'

'He's too lame and useless for that.'

'Then I'll share my food with him.'

'Don't be bloody stupid!'

He glowers at her, feeling a vicious urge to grab his assegai and plunge it into the skeletal body of the dog. But she seems to anticipate the action and moves in between him and the animal. Neither says anything; to both the situation has become quite unfathomable. Before her steady gaze he lowers his eyes, resigning himself to the incomprehensible: that this disgusting creature has come to represent something to her which he dare not touch without denying a vital part of herself and of what exists between them. Without a word, bewildered and resentful, he turns and begins to stride on; she falls in beside him. And the dog follows a little way behind.

In the rickety shack assembled from the wreckage of ships misjudging the bay and stranded on rocks or sandbanks, old Roloff was working, interminably, on his maps. A wild white mane of unkempt hair; sunken bloodshot eyes, weepy and burning from all the nights under the yellow lamp; three teeth left, two upper, one lower; his arthritic hands gnarled like the claws of a vulture. His shirt-sleeves were frayed; below his unevenly cut-off trousers his legs were bare, the calf muscles bulging as he walked into the dusky shack ahead of one. This was where he lived, with an old Hottentot woman who did the fishing and cooking and shared his bed on the floor, while he spent all his time on his maps. His conversation was a jumble of reminiscences about Germany, which he'd left as a young man; about his voyages as a sailor of the Dutch East India Company; about harbours and women (winking at her), phosphorescent nights on the deep seas, and the stench of the hold; about wild slave-hunts in Madagascar and on the coast of Guinea; and about a long journey through the Cape interior, as far as Caffre Land beyond the Great Fish River, twelve years before.

– Aber zur Sache, Herr Larsson: it was then, you see, back from my travels, that I drew my map, showing every detail of the land, vollständig. You know Kolb's map, I suppose? Forget about it, the man spent all his time in the taverns of the Cape drinking himself kaput, he never set a foot beyond Stellenbosch: have you ever seen a rhinoceros like his? – looks like something from die Offenbarung Johannis. It was his drinking companions who drew those maps of his and told him the stories he wrote down. Schändlich. As for the Abbé de la Caille, verflixt! I don't want to say anything against a man of God, but looking at that map of his one can only hope he knows more about heaven than about the Cape. No, glauben Sie mir: my map is the only one that shows this land as it is.

Nun also, I took it to the Governor, with my compliments, thinking it will earn me a bag of rixdollars for my old age. Gott im Himmel! Here I'm summoned by the Secretary of the Council. Take back your map, he says, by order of Seine Exzellenz. If ever you show it to anyone or dare to make a copy of it, then sofort it is thirty years in chains for you.

Sehen Sie mal, Herr Larsson. From that day I shut myself up here and all I do is to copy that map, over and over. Was sonst, even if it's only for the wind. Überzeugen Sie sich, this whole house is filled with maps, and not a soul may look at them. Perhaps one day, when I'm dead and old Eva has buried me on the beach, this shack will fall in and the wind will blow the maps weit und breit, and somewhere in a bush a stranger will pick up one of them and discover what the land looks like. I mean, how can one sit diesseits of the mountain and ignore what it looks like jenseits? Nicht war? But now you must forgive me, Herr Larsson – liebe, schöne Frau! – I really can't let you have one of them. Suppose the Council finds out about it? Then it's off to Robben Island with me, dreissig Jahre. No, it's better to be patient. I have not so many years still to live, let it rather be in peace. So if you want to find out what the land looks like, there is only one thing you can do, fürwahr, and that is to go and look for yourself. Draw your own map. Perhaps the Governor will be merciful to you. Aber nehmen Sie sich in Acht, the people here are afraid of their own country: they prefer not to know what it looks like. What the eye cannot see . . . das verstehen Sie doch, ja? –

Mapless through space, on to the horizon, not even sure about direction any more, simply following the setting of the sun, in search of the nest where the firebird lays its golden eggs: but does one ever reach it? In the absence of landmarks one cannot even calculate one's progress. All indication one has of going on is the increasing weariness of one's legs, the difficulty to move one's limbs; one's stomach aching, a constant pain clutching one's guts in its long thin fingers, tightening all the time, never losing its grip. One can only go on, mechanically, in bitter resistance to hunger and thirst and to oneself, obedient to this indomitable will which forces one to go on: it would be so much easier to lie down and never to get up again.

First: observation. Now: suffering. It is easier to trek through the landscape of truth than to comprehend it or account for it.

He and she and the thin dog.

Occasionally, the bones of dead animals, half covered by sand.

'Perhaps you and I will also lie here one day. Do you think the land will accept us then?'

'Don't think about it,' he says harshly. 'Think about the Cape.'

She shakes her head hopelessly. 'I've forgotten about the Cape. I can't recall it any more. Sometimes it seems to me I must have imagined it all. All that remains, is here. And I don't know for how much longer I can go on.'

'We *must*.'

'I know we must. I'm trying. But can one really?' She looks at him. Her eyes have sunken deep into their hollow sockets. With a swollen tongue she tries to lick the crusts of dried blood from her cracked lips, but the touch of moisture only makes the pain more acute. She seems to have difficulty focusing her eyes on him in the glare. The pattern of her rib-cage is exposed; her hip-bones are jutting out; it is as if her knees and elbows have become disproportionately large for the thinness of her arms and legs.

'Yes, one can,' he says. He is as thin as she is, and burnt more black. 'We're going to.'

The dog follows them, hobbling on painful feet. She has noticed that when he doesn't know she is watching, Adam stealthily feeds the dog. And to spare the animal's feet he has shortened their shifts, spending the blistering hours of the day under a makeshift tent of their karosses draped over sticks.

Even before they abandoned the wake of destruction left by the migrating buck, the dog, returning from a secret excursion across the plains, had brought them a ground-squirrel it had caught, putting it down at Adam's feet and looking up, its tail wagging gently. She was so moved that she had to turn her head away to hide her tears from him. Almost uncomprehending, he knelt down to stroke the dog's head. Then, the dog still watching, panting, he skinned the tiny animal and roasted it.

Since then, the dog has tracked down other quarry: ground-squirrels, tortoises, once even a secretary bird. And after they swerved away from the trail of dust, it has happened more regularly. The dog has, in fact, become indispensable for their own survival, a strange catalyst to their relationship.

Also, it has lately become possible, once again, for Adam to locate and dig out the rare *barroe* or *ngaap* or *kambro* on their way; there have been succulent plants whose leaves they could tear off, or eggs or larvae they could raid from anthills; gum from thorn-trees; *ghwarrie* berries to turn their heads. Sometimes, at dawn, they could lick the dewdrops from the broad flat leaves of xerophites, or to rob the shimmering webs of hunting spiders of the night's accumulated moisture. But it was so little, so very little. Just sufficient to prevent them from dying, growing thinner all the time, every step more painful: every day a miserable little lease of life renewed, postponing the horizon for yet another day. She has begun to think that, really, this is worse than the absolute emptiness of a desert. There, at least, one would come to accept that death was inevitable, its bitter compassion drawing near. But not here. Here everything remains suspended. Constant postponement, constant motion. No hope of redemption, only the continued ability to go on shuffling over the hard, scorching earth towards the horizon: never really reaching it, never really able to renounce it. And the farthest we can reach out, the most we can hope for, is to wonder whether the horizon we see is really the end.

Once it does seem as if nothing will hold her back from dying any more. For two full days there has been nothing now: absolutely nothing on the absolute veld. Just after sunrise they stop. Adam props the two sticks up with stones, spreading the karosses over them, their blazing little tent for the day. He sits down on the edge of the shade. She lies down. She makes no effort to say anything to him, afraid that he may try to dissuade her. She simply lies down with the serene decision not to get up again. It is not worth her while. One keeps on thinking one can go on; but one day it has to stop. And now that day has come.

In the distance she hears the dog barking, then forgets about it. Dazed and uncomprehending she looks up when she suddenly realises that Adam is talking to her, holding up something the dog has brought. A snake. She shakes her head, unable to grasp his meaning. Concentrating hard, she follows his words:

'We can eat it. It's only the head that's poisonous.'

She shakes her head again.

'No.'

'It's ordinary flesh, like that of any other animal.'

'It's sinful.' Suddenly, uncontrollable, she starts laughing at her own words, not quite knowing why. And only after some time does

195

she realise that she isn't laughing any more, but crying with dry sobs burning in her throat.

Adam cuts up the snake into small bits, scorching them briefly in the flames of the fire he has just lit: just enough to seal off the blood inside. But she refuses to try.

'Please,' he urges her.

'I don't want to.'

'If you don't eat, you'll die.'

'I want to die. Don't stop me.'

'Elisabeth.' Struggling, he lifts her, holding her against his bony body. 'Don't talk like that. Eat. It's food.'

'I can't.'

As if she is a child in need of medicine he prises her jaws apart – she resists for a while, then yields, too tired to go on – forcing a small bit through her clenched teeth.

'Eat. My darling.'

She keeps on shaking her head, but chewing all the same, her eyes tightly shut. She swallows.

'Good,' he says. 'Good. Try another piece.'

Even before she can answer, she begins to retch. The morsel of meat comes out again, horribly bitter of her bile.

'Try again.'

Once again her stomach rejects it, continuing to retch for a while afterwards, like the day they found the body, only worse, for now she is drier inside; there is really nothing which can come out apart from the small bits of meat. She cannot even cry, she is too exhausted.

Then this *is* the end, after all, she thinks. Smiling strangely at the idea of salvation, thin tough filaments of slime clinging to her lips.

But then, after resigning herself to it, an unbearable sadness invades her, too vast for tears.

'I'm dying,' she mumbles through her broken lips, 'and I still don't understand anything. I don't know what I'm doing here.'

He stretches out beside her, holding her.

'Do you remember,' he asks softly, 'the day you asked me about the sea? When I took you to the little island?'

'Yes.' The small fishes and the periwinkles, anemones, crabs in the clear water, and the red octopus, yes, I remember. The sea breaking over the rocks, surrounding us. How can you feel him without danger? You forced me down to the white sand and broke into me, violently, and the sea was all around us; and as the waves came

196

washing over us you spurted into me; and that night the deep water of the tide submerged the island. Yes, I remember.

'Do you remember how we sat on the koppie listening to the buck coming past?'

They even crushed a lion in their way, their eyes staring blindly ahead; death was touchable and beautiful.

'If you can remember that, it'll be easier for you now. Just lie still. You'll hear the land. Don't listen with your ears. *Hear* it.'

'Will you lie on me again?' she whispers.

'If you want to.'

'Don't leave me.'

Cautiously he shifts his body to cover hers. This time they do not move but lie absolutely still. Only her hands move gently, like questions, over the old scars on his back and buttocks.

She hears him breathing against her. In her ears she hears the sound of her own blood. It is as if she is falling asleep, only it isn't sleep. As if she leaves her body and rises up, very high, like a vulture, looking down on them lying in the small shady spot on the plain. The nearer sounds recede. Beyond the cicadas she can hear something different now, more vast, more formidable: silence itself, expressing itself in stones and earth, erosion ditches, koppies, wind-blown wood.

Sometimes I wonder whether I've dreamt you. Sleeping on the sand like a starfish washed out by the waves, a thought born from the water, with sand glistening on your back – sleeping against a breathing mother-sea, your fingers lightly clutching the insoluble mystery of a shell. Your legs twitching like bamboo in a rock-pool. I want to touch you, shyly at first, gently, then more wildly, devouring you, possessing you entirely. You awaken in my mouth. I disappear in the green of the sea. My head is light, spinning, deeper and deeper you pull me into yourself like a tide, in a silent ectasy of submarine beauty. Like a small fish I nibble your neck and your shoulders, your nipples, your stomach and thighs and swelling sex: you are so near I no longer know where you end and I begin, drifting in endless water. And now I'm dissolving, evaporating, like foam or spray or mist, like a small cloud growing until it is enormous, bursting into rain.

You are trying to make it impossible for me to die; you are covering me with your body to keep away the vultures. Silence pervades me, deafening. It has been here before us; it will remain after we've gone. Yes, I remember everything. In my nothingness everything converges: this is what I know, this is what I hear: without me the land

197

will not even know of its own existence. Thank you. For the sake of this remembering I shall have to go on with you. Didn't I say myself: the circle must be completed? In me everything becomes meaningful or futile. It is up to me to decide. This is the freedom you allow me. You want me to explore suffering, not be destroyed by it.

Suffering: it's like the sky through which a bird is flying. And only occasionally, very rarely – an instant in the wind – it is allowed to alight on branch or burning stone to rest: but not for long.

You are with me. I'm touching you. Like among the rocks in the sea; like that evening when you said: I want you naked. Just for an instant. Never more than an instant. Perhaps we can't bear more than an instant at a time. I remember. I shall try to go on. This terrible space surrounding us creates the silence in which, so rarely, preciously, I dare to recognise you and be recognised by you.

Raising her head – when did he move off her and return to the edge of their shelter? – she sees it immediately, realising that that is what he, too, is staring at. On the horizon, just below the serrated line of the last stone ridges: the long glimmering lake. At first she refuses to believe it. Why has neither of them noticed it before? But then, they were so overcome by fatigue when they arrived here this morning to notice anything. They were staring two or three yards ahead, no more: one's eyes are hurt by the constant challenge of the horizon, one becomes more humble in one's progress. She was too exhausted to notice anything at all, and he too concerned about her to look around. But now it is quite clear – and it must have been there all the time. This lake stretching like a broad mirror in the east, surrounded by trees and green hills, by huts and people. So she was right after all about crossing the mountains: there is a paradise ahead. They shouldn't have lost faith so easily. Now they stand ashamed by it.

Crawling on hands and knees she moves to Adam and touches him.

'Do you see it?' she asks unnecessarily.

'Can it be true?'

'Look for yourself.' She is breathing heavily now. 'Come, we must collect our things and go.'

'Shouldn't we wait until it gets cooler?'

'I'll be all right,' she assures him urgently. 'The sooner we start the sooner we'll be there.' She begins to tie up her bundle. 'How far away do you think it is?'

'It's difficult to judge on these plains. We may reach it before sunset.'

The dog lies licking its wounded paws. He has eaten most of what remained of the snake.

'Come on,' she says.

'We must take it slowly,' he warns her. 'You are worn out, and we have nothing left.'

'There will be enough to eat and drink over there.'

And she laughs, with a sob of joy in her throat. Just to reach water again, to dive into it, immerse oneself completely, to wash herself quite clean and feel her body cool and wet, to drink as much as she can hold. To live.

Every now and then he has to hold her back when she hurries on ahead of him. It is a long way to go, and the heat is overwhelming. They must save their energy; she doesn't realise how taxing it is.

Her only response is to point ahead: there, there, don't you see? What does it matter if we arrive exhausted? We can stay there for as long as we wish, until we have recovered completely. And from now on everything will be so much easier, you'll see. The turning point is behind us. We have survived: you have helped me to survive.

He is the first to surmise the truth, but he cannot bear to warn her. Through the perspiration clinging to his burning eyelids he sees the lake shimmer and tremble, the green trees sway, the people moving among the huts. Why hadn't he suspected it before they set out? But one doesn't want to. Perhaps one needs these small explosions of faith to keep one going.

He sees her walking a few yards in front of him, drawing on her last energy to stride on with her thin legs. He can hear her pant for breath. He wants to call out to her, but his voice is a hoarse whisper in his throat. The dog follows them at an erratic pace, running from one shrivelled bush to the next to rest its paws in the meagre shade of twigs as dry as porcupine quills, before risking it out in the sun again.

He feels like crying. He wants to curse. For the first time since they are together he feels his insides contract in real despair.

It is very late in the afternoon when she finally stops, her body heaving, covered with sweat and dirt.

'Is it – very far still?' she asks. It sounds as if her voice is torn, bleeding, from her throat.

He turns away from her.

'What's the matter, Adam?' she asks. 'I'm asking you: is it still far to go?'

'We'll never get there,' he says, unable to look at her.

'Of course we will. Why shouldn't we?'

'It doesn't exist.'

She raises a thin arm to point; then allows it to drop back to her panting side.

'But it's impossible, Adam!'

'No, it isn't. It really is a mirage.'

'If one has no choice but to die,' she says, her voice strained, 'why can't it be violently like that poor baboon in the mountains? Why must it be like this?'

'We're not going to die,' he tries to comfort her.

'I don't want to go on living. I'm too tired. I just don't want to any more.'

'This morning you didn't want to either. But you went on after all.'

'Because we saw the lake. Because, suddenly, there was something to believe in, to keep me going.' She sits down on the burning ground.

'There's a hill over there,' he says. 'Let's go there, it will be easier to stay there overnight.'

'No, I want to stay right here,' she says stubbornly.

He takes her hand to help her to her feet, but she angrily shakes him off, bursting into sobs. It is almost impossible to cry, her chest and throat are too dry, she has no tears; but huddled in a small heap she sits sobbing, her whole body shaking.

'It's not so far,' he pleads.

'Why don't *you* go?' she pants. 'Go back to the Cape. Tell them . . .' She says no more. Even her crying subsides.

He unpacks all her belongings, but there is nothing to offer her, not a leaf or a shrivelled root to chew, nothing. He feels tempted to sit down beside her, to lie down with her and not to stir again: not even to cover them with the kaross, but to remain exposed to the cold of the night and to tomorrow's sun. But the very urgency of the temptation makes him resist. Planting the sticks in small mounds of stone he stretches the kaross over them; then makes a fire and sits down beside it, watching the world grow dark. Opposite him, the dog lies panting. She doesn't stir.

In the distance jackals start yelping and laughing. If there are jackals, he thinks wearily, there must be something somewhere. Hares, buck, a gnu. The moon rises. Clenching his teeth, aching, he gets up. His body is contorted with cramps, his chest aflame.

He covers her with the second kaross.

'Stay here,' he says. 'I'll try to find us something to eat.'

'There's nothing.'

'I'll find something. I promise.'

She shakes her head.

'I'll leave the dog with you,' he says. 'And the assegai. I don't know for how long I'll be away. Perhaps until tomorrow, perhaps the day after. But I'll come back. Do you hear me, Elisabeth? I'll come back with something to eat.'

'Don't go,' she whispers.

'I must. It's our last hope.'

Kneeling beside her, he tucks the kaross in under her, kissing her. There is moisture on her lips; it is like dry pods grazing against each other.

She follows him with her eyes, trying to remember what he said, struggling to unravel her thoughts. Is he going to the Cape? Give my love to my parents. Tell them. Are there people and water nearby? A river in flood. No, the ox has been swept away; it was I who forced it to plunge in. Mind the stones. You can't kill that little buck, it saw me bathing in the stream, it's trusting us, it has come to us for shelter. It's snowing outside, can you feel how cold it is?

What is the dog doing here? Isn't he dead then? I thought a snake had bitten it. An old Hottentot woman sucked out the poison, but she died, too, and was buried in a porcupine hole. Wearing my dress. She had the temerity to pry in my things and steal the dress, not even knowing how to wear it properly, her old dry dugs hanging out. The young girls have long moist love-lips protruding from their slits, she showed it to me, very proud of herself. Nobody is ashamed here, one only needs cover against the vultures. Sooner or later they'll dig him out under the stones. If only one could be pure, bare as a skeleton, like a rock stripped of barnacles. A yellow lantern swinging through my days: we change three times every day, bring me some water. Will you listen to me? I'm used to being obeyed. Never trust a slave, my child. You think a slave is nothing but a woman and a woman no more than a slave. I wish to inform you: I intend to get married. It is not a descent into hell, only the interior. We'll draw our own map as we go on. Sehen sie mal, all I do is to copy that map, over and over. Aber

201

nehmen Sie sich in Acht, the people here are afraid of their own country. Somewhere in a bush a stranger will pick up one of them, blown away by the wind.

They come streaming past you like the wind, it's obvious they don't see anything, their eyes gazing straight ahead: they still believe in a heaven. Look, I'm not afraid. I'm only tired. And he can go on without me: I don't know where he'll go, but he'll be all right, round and round, like on an island.

She must have dozed, for when she opens her eyes again the moon has moved to the far side of the shelter. The jackals are still cavorting in the dark, but very far off. She can no longer see the dog. Those poor children who died in the ruin. Was it really the work of Bushmen? But why destroy a whole household for the sake of a few head of cattle? It doesn't make sense.

Here I am. Destroy me too. Send another herd of buck to trample me into the dust. Lay out my children with me, all those tiny skeletons. One is born with so much suffering: one is so indestructible.

Painfully she sits up to look at the day breaking. Adam is still gone. The day the river carried away the ox, she thinks, she wanted to jump into the flood too, convinced that she couldn't bear any more. How ridiculous! Today, surely, she has reason to destroy herself, yet she makes no move to do anything about it. How is it possible that, with every step into despair, one also acquires more resistance to the one thing which may end it all?

I am tired. I am tired. I do not want to go on, yet I do. How can I allow him to wander through the night, and perhaps for days on end, in search of food for me, if he comes back to find me dead? *You* hold me back, not I.

How much more reason did *you* have for suicide the day your master ordered you to flog your own mother? But you didn't. Day after day you stared at that great free mountain across the sea, yet you did not go mad or destroy yourself. All those months you endured it on the island.

Escaping from the island on the flimsy raft that night: the sound of water trickling from my paddles. It is not the crashing of the waves I remember first, nor the splintering of the wood, but that sound of oars in water – the first, and most intimate, sound of freedom. It was the same that day in front of the Castle. What I recall above all is not the irons or the cat o' nine tails, nor being exposed to all those jeering

202

people, but the screeching of the gulls above me, and their movement in the wind. Even now, whenever my thoughts carry me away from the thirstland through which we're trekking, it's gulls I hear; and as I sink into sleep at night, I hear the water trickling from the oars.

This time there was no water, only a mirage. Will she survive? She seems to have lost all will. I'll have to find something for her, more than just a snake or a tortoise or a wild melon. Would it have been easier if one could pray for help? But to whom? Allah of my grandmother Seli, or my mother's Heitsi-Eibib, or God or Jesus Christ? Names, names. I have to find my way among the meagre things themselves: stone and indestructible roots, earth, plain, koppie, star or moon.

With dogged determination he follows the sound of the jackals. Alone, in the cool of the moonlit night, he can progress swiftly. It is almost exhilarating – but tempered by pain – to be so utterly alone in space, as if the world has grown more limitless in the dark, more absolute, the black shadows of stones or shrubs as real as the things themselves. At the same time it is less crude than in the daytime. Not tender, but more approachable, no longer hostile.

It is impossible to make out whether it is the jackals coming and going around him, or whether the sound itself is deceptive on the open plain. Whatever it is, he seems to be moving in circles in search of it, and it is nearly daybreak before he begins to close in on them. The whole search, he realises, may prove as much of a delusion as the mirage: the sound of the jackals need not mean anything. It may be nothing but cavorting, or fighting, or mating, not a hunt at all. He is prepared for it. But when they become visible in the first light he discovers, with a shock of elation, that his pursuit has not been in vain: three or four jackals have cornered a blesbuck doe against the stone wall of a koppie. She is trying to shield a newborn fawn against their onslaught. They must have found her at a very early stage, for even the afterbirth is still untouched.

At his approach the jackals give way, growling, whining, cowardly threatening, still hovering as close as they can; but when the sun comes out they skulk away. The doe stands eyeing him, sniffing suspiciously. Every time the fawn tries to stagger past her on its long shaky stalks of legs, she hurriedly nudges it back. At the slightest move Adam makes she lowers her long curved horns, whistling a warning through her nose. She is obviously worn out by the birth and the long night's vigilance, but he knows she can still escape with ease.

As she is too large for the pistol, he takes an arrow from his quiver, presses it against the string of his bow and lets fly. It hits her in the shoulder. With an anxious bleat she jumps up and begins to canter off, but within a few yards she stops again and returns to her lamb. Giving furious jerky kicks with her hindleg she finally manages to dislodge the arrow. The smallest scratch is sufficient, Adam knows; the poison is in her. But it may last many hours to take effect, and he lacks a Bushman's energy for stalking her should she run away. Even if she manages to take the fawn with her they can cover a great distance before sunset.

But suddenly he discovers that he is no longer alone. With an excited bark the lean dog comes flashing past him, amazingly agile in spite of its worn-out condition. Immediately the doe lowers her head again, swinging the deadly horns in his direction. The dog is nearly impaled on them. Whimpering, he jumps aside, but a moment later he comes rushing back.

Now Adam can use the pistol, aiming at the same shoulder, to cripple her. She stumbles and falls, but rises again, panting. But the brief lapse was time enough for the dog to dart past her and grab the fawn by the throat. A single jerk suffices.

The doe sinks to her knees again. She must be finished off quickly. Adam doesn't want to waste any more ammunition: there is so little left. And they've already got the fawn. But he wants more than just that. While the dog continues to worry the doe, Adam slips round behind her, grabbing her neck, knife in hand, aiming for the jugular vein.

In a sudden, final, sweeping movement of her long neck one of the fierce horns slashes his arm from wrist to elbow. For a moment he loses his grip. Then the dog grabs her by the nose. That is the end.

Panting, Adam remains on the ground beside the dead doe, his head reeling from exhaustion and loss of blood. The night has been too much for his weakened body. After a long time, groping blindly, he manages to roll the doe over and finds the small swollen udder. Grasping a teat, he milks a thin jet of lukewarm liquid into his parched, gaping mouth, drinking and swallowing painfully but unrestrainedly. At last he pauses for a while, trembling; then forces himself to stand up and fetch his skin-bag to empty the doe's small dugs in it.

His arm is still bleeding badly. Spiderwebs. Fortunately, at this early hour, they are easy to find, sparkling with dewdrops in the dry bushes. He covers the wound with the webs and bandages it with a length of skin ripped from his apron.

Feeling giddy, he first has to rest again. After a while blood begins to ooze through the sides of the skin bandage, but at last it stops. The arm is still throbbing, but he cannot waste any more time. Fumbling with his left hand, he manages to slit open the fawn's belly and tear out the guts. He also rips out the doe's stomach and painstakingly retrieves the fluid from it. After reflection he cuts the hindquarters from the carcass as well: more than that he cannot manage. Lying down to recover again, he allows the dog to gorge himself on what remains of the doe. There won't be much for him later.

The sun is high by the time he gets up again. It will be hellish to travel in this heat but he cannot wait any longer. Far above he notices the vultures circling, his heart throbbing with sudden fright. Is it already too late? Urging on his body relentlessly he begins to trot in the direction of the birds.

She is startled by the vultures. Has something happened to him? But soon she realises that it is round her own small shelter they're circling. Why did it never happen on other days? How can they foresee anything so uncannily? She has no choice but to crawl from under the spread kaross to shout and wave at them before they move away, fading into distant specks, without, however, diappearing entirely.

She lies down once more. Her head feels dizzy. From time to time, as she lies there, everything gets black before her. Painfully she tries to gather saliva in her mouth for swallowing, but it stays dry; her throat is swollen so badly that she can hardly breathe.

It's no use. He'll be too late. I used to be so unyielding, she thinks with wry dejection: I refused to be at anyone's disposal, to become a mere possession like a cow or a wagon or a barrel. Now death is beginning to possess me, without asking my leave. And I cannot resist any longer. For his sake I would like to, but it is no longer possible.

When his shadow falls across her she mistakes it for one of the vultures. She tries to move her lips and chase him away, but can no longer make a sound.

'Elisabeth,' he says.

Since when do such things speak?

'I've brought you food,' he says, sitting down beside her. She can hear him pant and gasp for breath. She smells his sweat. 'Meat and milk,' he says, raising the skin-bag to her mouth. It is lukewarm and sourish from the long day's sun. She finds it hard to swallow. He coaxes her, feeding her with infinite patience, like a baby. After a while she opens her eyes.

She looks up. But there is nothing. God is the emptiness of an endless sky.

The similarity of nature patterns: the shape of a snowflake – the vertebrae of a rocky hill – erosion ditches – a fern frond – the skeleton of a reptile.

It is another lease of life, more decisive than before. They can continue, even though it is in pain. He never complains, but she can see that his wound is worrying him. It has festered; he can barely use his arm. They talk very little. Even that has become an effort.

Something has happened: they have lost the Cape, like something dropped on the way. Neither of them has any expectation left; no hope of ever arriving on a ridge and seeing something different from what they've seen so far. The horizon has taken over.

What remains, is walking itself, pure aimless motion: the swaying of bony legs, the rowing of emaciated arms, the plodding of aching feet swathed in heavy skins, breathing, perspiration forming patterns on the crust of filth covering their skins; the lame dog hobbling behind.

There was a time when you accused me of being too white for the truth. Look at me now. I am black and burnt. And is this truth, then? – this unending suffering, struggling simply to keep moving through space and not to lie down again?

If one of us should give up now, the other would no longer be able to continue.

Increasing listlessness. And a strange sense of amazement about silence and space. In this infinity everything happens for the first time. Our rare words are, every time, the first words. Every daybreak is the first appearance of white light on the empty world. Here is a grain of dust: everything is birth.

In the mountains, that night, I thought: however terrifying it had been, there was something beautiful about the violent death of the baboon. It was like the sordid killing of the bull or the storm in the Bay of Biscay. Because in such moments one knows that one is alive. Dreadful in itself, yet indispensable – these rare moments which keep us going.

But perhaps I was younger then. I needed the sudden violence to shock me into awareness. Now I demand much less, my needs are humbler. In the quiet persistence of suffering I discover again the desperate knowledge that I am. I am going on. Just that. The horizon remains unattainable, I have resigned myself to it. Nevertheless I am going on. Without this despair it would not be possible. Without it I wouldn't even know that I am alive. Because of this despair I love you.

Once there was a paradise beside the sea. We were there: do you remember? And because we have lost it we can believe in it.

Still they go on, through the cold nights and the flaming days. When there is a moon, they trek by night and rest by day, although it makes it more difficult in other ways – it is almost impossible to sleep in the glare; it is hard to find food in the dark.

As long as we don't give up. To go on, to endure, to survive; that is our condition. Not the moments of ecstasy, but the humble persistence which makes such moments bearable.

More and more slowly. His arm grows worse. It is really almost unbearable to shuffle on. Even the dog cannot last much longer. Impossible as it seems, the days are growing ever more sizzling and white. They can no longer proceed in the light at all. But what about food? Only the dog can now provide for them.

It becomes something of a macabre game to try and work out: How much longer? Flesh and blood cannot last indefinitely. There is hardly flesh and blood left, just bone and sinews and leathery skin. Oh, horizon.

In weary serenity, all thought suspended, she walks on beside him. The only answer to suffering – that is why she is still alive – is to be prepared to suffer. Rather than resist one must abandon oneself to it, allowing it to slowly burn into you: into everything inside you which has not yet existed, lending it consciousness: so that, painfully, in the process of being stripped of everything, one can give birth to oneself.

At last another halt, the inevitable halt.

As far as this, then? This sandy hollow is the landmark of the end. She helps him to plant the sticks among stones – his arm is hurting too much – and to drape the kaross over it. When, at nightfall, he makes no effort to get up for the next lap, she accepts that this is, indeed, the end. And almost relieved she lies down and shuts her eyes.

But she has reckoned without his bitter will. He is only waiting for her to sleep, having thought it all out in advance. He refuses to admit

207

even the possibility that they should have come all this way simply only to die like animals on the veld. And as soon as he is sure that she's asleep, he softly calls the dog to him. Struggling to its bleeding paws the mangy creature waddles towards him. Adam rubs its ears and pats the huge head; and the dog wags its tail and with its dry tongue begins to lick his face and hands.

'Lie down,' he says, pointing to his lap.

The dog lies down with its head on Adam's knees.

Holding the knife in his left hand, he continues to stroke the head with his right hand for a while; then folds his fingers over the muzzle.

It won't take long.

With a muffled yelp the dog tries to struggle free when its head is suddenly drawn backwards, stretching the throat for the blade.

It's better for you too.

Blood comes spurting from the severed arteries. Adam's right arm is too weak to hold the wriggling, kicking body down and he has to fall forward to press the dying dog to the ground, subduing its final feeble struggles against his chest and belly. It feels like a woman, it is like love.

He doesn't cry, but there are tears running down his cheeks. He thinks: Now I have raised my hand against my own mother. Whatever follows I deserve – the scourging and the irons under the screeching gulls, the chains, the island, the arid land. I am my own hell.

The buck in the cave she could still accept, however grudgingly. But not the death of the dog.

'My God, Adam!' she whispers hoarsely when, at daybreak, she wakes up in a fever to find him roasting the meat on the fire.

'Don't talk,' he says. 'It's done. Just eat it, you need it.'

'It will be like eating one of us.'

'No. Please.'

She refuses to open her mouth. He tries to force her, like he did with the snake. But with sudden uncontrollable anger she slaps the meat out of his hand.

'I won't!' she sobs. 'I'd rather die.'

'Don't be stupid. It's meat, it's life.'

'He came with us all the way.'

'I tried to chase him away, but he wouldn't go.'

'He saved our life with the fawn.'

'He can save us again today. He was starving to death anyway. Like us. He could no longer catch anything.'

208

'He was ours. He was all we've ever had.'

'You must.'

'Go ahead and eat him if you can!' she cries in despair. 'But don't try to force me. I won't. And then go off alone and leave me here.'

'I did it for you,' he pleads hopelessly.

'Leave me alone.'

'Just try a small piece.'

'No.'

'Look.' He puts a morsel in his mouth, chewing with difficulty, swallowing.

'You're a savage!' she says, shaking with silent fury, 'I hate you.'

'It's no use pretending to be white now!' he flares up. 'Just look at yourself.'

She shuts her eyes, trembling.

'Eat. If you want to stay alive.'

'What is happening to us?' she whispers in a state of shock. 'We can't destroy each other like this.'

'Eat. Else you'll be destroying yourself.'

'I cannot eat his flesh.'

'For God's sake!' he says wearily. 'You'll *have* to eat it in the end. You have no choice.'

She only shakes her head.

It is becoming quite ludicrous, she thinks, on the brink of collapse: every time an extremity, followed by respite, a new effort, shuffling deeper into nothingness. Surely one must have the dignity, sooner or later, to say: Now I refuse.

My mother said: Elisabeth, you're held in esteem, you're an example to others.

And you: How can you survive if you're not prepared to be an animal?

'Give me a piece,' she whispers towards the evening, not daring to look up at him, although she knows there will be no spite in his expression. It's only that she cannot face herself in his sunken blood-shot eyes. Her body revolts against the bit of meat. But she forces a second morsel down after the first has been rejected. Her stomach contracts, but with sheer will-power she keeps it down, lying un-moving on the ground, too sick to stir.

It's madness, madness. Why *bother* to stay alive if it's so easy to give up? It's unnatural. It's inhuman.

Why does she return to life? Why face this new discovery of him

209

after the slaughter of the dog? Why try to live with this new discovery of herself?

'I *want* to die, I *want* to,' she mumbles in a monotonous, distant voice, forcing another piece of meat down her throat, keeping it inside, panting, trembling on the ground – a hideous, burnt and broken thing lying in a bundle, a small bare heap of bones and parched skin, tufts of hair, glowing glowering eyes: a human, living thing.

When the Hottentots arrived three days later they were still there. The meat had strengthened them, but they had not moved on yet, overcome as they were by lethargy and fatigue, worn out by the prospect of facing the same round yet again – the slow decline, the swelling throat, the tongue drying out, eyes tightening in their sockets, the world reeling, the first blackouts; followed by another small supply of meat or plants, an anthill raided, a lizard killed: a new disgusting beginning.

From far off they noticed the cloud of dust rising against the afternoon sun and drawing nearer.

'Buck?' she asked, not sure whether she should be glad about the possibility of new relief, or despairing about the certainty of worse suffering following it.

'I don't think so,' he said, screwing up his eyes. 'Unless it's only a small herd. But perhaps . . .'

'What?'

He didn't answer. For an hour he kept his eyes steadily on the horizon. The cloud approached, still and red and brown, obscuring the eye of the sun.

'It's people,' he announced at last. 'It must be Hottentots on trek.'

'But all that dust?'

'Cattle.' His voice was so low that she didn't immediately grasp the significance of his words.

When it became clear that the trek would pass a mile from them they immediately tied up their bundles and set out across the plain, driven by the same eagerness of the day of the mirage. Once, in fact, she stopped for a moment, a hollow feeling in the pit of her stomach, to make quite sure that it was not another hallucination, before running after him again, panting open-mouthed.

There were fifty or sixty people in the trek: frail, thin men and women and children, grey with dust, accompanied by a herd of cattle and sheep and countless dogs. The cattle were in a sorry state but the fat-tailed sheep could still draw on their own resources.

210

At first the band seemed hesitant and suspicious about the two strangers on the open plain. But the moment Adam addressed them in their own language, their hard-baked faces wrinkled with glee, breaking into smiles. He translated for her; some of them who had mastered the rudiments of Dutch started chattering directly to her.

Yes, they'd been in the Cape: look, here were the beads and copper they'd bartered; they'd had brandy too, and rolls of tobacco, but that was all finished. Now they were trekking on through the thirstland: someone had told them of good grazing land a month from here, to the north.

'Why you not come with us?' one of the spokesmen enquired. 'The world bad back there.'

'No,' Elisabeth said quickly. 'No, we must get back to the Cape.'

'Why "must"?' They seemed baffled.

'We've been on the road for such a long time now,' she tried to explain.

'But we return to the Cape one day,' the Hottentot assured her. 'As soon as the rains he come. Then it's easy trek through here, you'll see. What difference a month or a handful of months?'

'No, we must . . .'

He shrugged, indifferent.

'You don't understand,' she said.

'Is true,' he admitted. 'I not understand.' Then, narrowing his eyes: 'How come a white woman trek through the land like this?' With open curiosity he stared at her: her shrivelled breasts, her prominent ribs and hips. There was no desire in his eyes. She felt no urge to cover herself. What did it really matter?

'Well,' he said at last, clicking his tongue and spitting on the ground. 'You think, and say us what you do. We stay here tonight.'

The women set out to gather wood. Towards sunset the dogs came running back from the veld, some of them with ground-squirrels, a few others with hares or tortoises. For once they were allowed to keep their quarry, since the men had generously slaughtered one of the weakest oxen in honour of the occasion. And they assembled round the fire, eating and chattering, laughing, drinking.

Elisabeth sat apart from them, withdrawn into herself, listening absently as they spoke in their own language.

After the meal they took out musical instruments and in the moonlight the reed-flutes began their breathy shrill, accompanied by the sad monotony of the *ghoera* and the rumbling of the *rommelpot*.

211

With loud laughter and much clapping of hands the calabashes of heady beer were passed round. The young ones were dancing, sending up a cloud of dust over their elders watching and encouraging them from the fireside; the skin-aprons swinging and flapping in the frenzy of their dance. Under their feet the earth was trembling.

She sat watching, fascinated by the intensity and exuberance of their merriment which seemed quite unreal on these plains where everything had been so predictable and silent for so long. In yesterday's sun these same people had been worn out by heat and dust, but now, in the dark, they were dancing themselves back into life, exorcising the silence with their music and laughter, gulping down the sour beer which sustained their ecstasy. For tomorrow – tomorrow would be hard again.

Tomorrow they were going on. She would stand beside Adam and watch the cloud of dust grow smaller on the plains, the noise dwindling, dying away in the distance. And then the dust would settle, too. And it would be exactly as before: he and she, surrounded by the pure anguish of light and space. Only, it would be worse than before, because the memory of tonight would taunt them in their loneliness.

Why not turn back and go with the tribe? In their midst they would survive. Here was meat; here was sour milk and a large supply of honey; here was talk and laughter. What did it matter if it took them another year to reach the Cape? There was a lifetime ahead of them.

But to turn back and face that terrible road again? She was too tired even to think of it. She wanted to be spared the choice. The Cape was so much nearer now than ever before. It was no longer lost: the Hottentots had miraculously restored it to them. Those beads and copper wire came from the Cape; a month ago they had been there. They had seen the Castle with its five massive corners, and the open square with the gallows, the canals running down from the Heerengracht to the sea; they had seen the Mountain from which she'd looked out across the incredible blue of the ocean below; and the houses with their whitewashed walls and thatched roofs, amber or brown or black with age, shelter against the violent South-easter. They'd seen the fishing boats coming in, loaded with galjoen and Cape salmon and red roman and snoek. They'd seen the boats bringing in the sweet red figs and crystal water from the wells on the island, and the loads of blue stone for new houses; the processions of the Governor and the Council of Policy; her father in a coach; *Phoenicopterus ruber*; slaves carrying

212

water from the fountains opposite the cool Gardens; wheat-mills; mulberry trees.

It was true: it existed: only a few weeks from here. They had seen it all, and here they were dancing with her Cape still in their eyes.

Much later they all bedded down in a group, she and Adam pressed against the mass of anonymous bodies in the dark. She inhaled the odour of the rancid fat and buchu powder covering them. But was it worse than her own smell? She pressed herself against the body next to her, oblivious, in her half-sleep, of who it was: they were all together, warming one another against the cold of the night, bundles and bundles of people.

Among all the dark bodies in the dark he had recognised her and pressed her against him. – I love you more than I do myself. This precious instant of togetherness the night allows us is all we have: here is my body, here I am, take me. Whisper in my ear, sink your small white teeth into my shoulder to smother the moan of your joy. Give me a son who will be free one day. You with the memories of Java in your almond eyes and the names of its beaches on your moist quick tongue: in your name lies my salvation, in your darkness everything becomes comprehensible and redeemable. Tomorrow I'll wait for you beside the gate, and later I shall learn that you've been sold at a fair price. Tomorrow all of that will happen, and I shall lose you forever: but in this fleeting night you are eternally mine. –

'Well, you come with us?' asked the spokesman when they started packing up and herding their cattle and sheep the next morning.

She shook her head. 'We must go on. It's not so far now.'

'But is bad.'

'We'll get through. If you can help us with some food.'

'You barter?'

They reopened their small bundles. There was so little. Her shells? No. The pistol and the remaining ammunition? But we need it! Sorry, then we can't do business. All right, take it. Take everything, we have nothing. Just let me keep my Cape dress, and our aprons and karosses, our hand-made assegai, the sticks, the bow and arrows.

In exchange, they received a few bags of milk, half a sheep, and herbs for Adam's wound.

'What is the shortest way to the Cape from here?'

They were all talking together, and pointing. The way we came: straight on.

'Is there anything on the road?' asked Adam.

213

'A waterhole two days from here,' said the spokesman. 'Below a koppie, he look like a lion sleeping. The cattle make it bad. But still water to dig up.'

'Is that all?'

'Ten days from here, a farm.'

'With people?'

'Yes, is people. Honkhoikwa. But the farmer he shoot at us,' he said sullenly. 'He say he not have water for so many people. Curse the cunt of his mother.'

And then they shouted and called and waved. The sun rose, a disc of fire. The trek grew small on the plains; the red dust accompanied them to the horizon. Adam and Elisabeth stayed behind.

'Now we'll get through,' he said.

Ten days from here there was a farm and people.

A few days beyond the muddy water-hole trampled by the cattle they saw vultures again. Adam was the first to recognise the high pile of stones on the plain, one of Heitsi-Eibib's innumerable graves. But the vultures were closer, swarming above an erosion ditch. And even from a distance the stench was unmistakable.

He wanted to bypass it, knowing what to expect. But Elisabeth was curious to see.

'It's the Hottentots' people,' he said laconically, when she pressed him.

'What people?' she insisted, already beginning to suspect the truth; remembering.

They stopped on the edge of the ditch gaping in the hard soil. The bottom was black with vultures; they made no effort to abandon the corpses they were feasting on. The branches and karosses covering the bodies had been torn off and scattered in all directions. Shallow graves had been dug open forcibly. There seemed to be two or three grownups among the dead – old ones, as far as Adam could make out – and several children who must have been too weak to go on.

She grabbed his wounded arm: 'How can we get rid of the vultures?' she asked. 'We must do something!'

'The people are already dead,' he answered.

'Were they dead when they were left here?'

'Not all of them, I suppose.'

'But, Adam . . .'

'Why should it upset you? I told you about it long ago.'

'You said it was the old ones.'

'It's the same with children if they grow too weak.'

She wanted to run down the side of the ditch to scare off the birds, but he held her back.

'There are too many of them,' he warned her. 'They'll tear you to bits.'

'But what about the children, Adam?'

'They're dead too.' He tugged at her hand. 'Come away now.'

The memorial mound of the Hunter God stood opposite the ditch, with calabashes and skin-bags propped up among the stones. Curds, she saw as they came nearer; and honey. Sacrificial offerings, swarming with ants.

She looked aghast. 'But those people were left so close to the mound,' she protested. 'Why didn't they eat this food to stay alive?'

'It's Heitsi-Eibib's food.'

She leaned against the pile of stones. A thin line of ants made a detour round her hands but gradually they became more audacious, shortening the distance, until they came crawling right over her on their way to the spilled honey. She shook her head.

'I can understand about the old ones,' she said. 'But not the children. They were so small, they knew nothing yet, they understood nothing, they had nothing.'

He made no answer.

'We've been together for so long now,' she said suddenly. 'Why hasn't something happened in me yet? Do you think I'm barren?'

'You should have asked the old women for herbs when we spent the night with them.'

'I don't want children from herbs. I want them from you.'

'But they may have been able to help you.'

'It remains empty inside me,' she said. 'Perhaps it's the sun, shrivelling up everything.' Lowering herself down the side of the mound, she squatted in the shade below it, leaning her head and back against the stones.

'What would have become of us if you had a child on the way?' he asked calmly.

'It's true,' she admitted, after a while. 'But once we're back in the Cape . . .'

'What will happen to our children there?' he asked.

'Nothing!' she replied vehemently.

'You once told me about your friend,' he reminded her.

'That was different. The father of her child was a slave. And when we get back, I'll . . .'

'You're taking so much upon yourself,' he said, moved.

She crossed her arms on her chest. 'If only I could be sure about having a child. Children. But I'm so afraid.' She shook her head, swaying her body slightly from side to side. 'It's barren inside me. All barren.'

'There is more than enough time for it.'

'We've made love so many times . . .' Naked, she looked up at him. 'Why should you want a child from me? I'm so ugly. I've grown so disgusting.'

'I love you.'

'The other day you said: "Look at yourself . . . !"'

'That wasn't what I meant.'

'But it's true. Look at me. Look closely. I'm hideous. I'm burnt all over, my skin is covered with wrinkles like old dry leather, I'm filthy, I'm stinking.'

'What about me then? Am I any different?' He took her thin arms in his large thin hands. She looked at the ugly festering wound on his arm, swollen and inflamed in spite of the Hottentots' herbs.

'We've come all the way here,' he said. 'We're still together. We can get through. Surely you know that by now.'

'How can one ever be sure?' she asked wearily.

'Only five more days to the farm. That's what they told us.'

'A farm. People.' There was no joy in her eyes, only fear. 'I can't show myself to them like this.'

'Why not?'

'I can't. I'll have to . . .' Almost panicking, she opened her bundle and took out the dirty green dress she had brought with her all the way.

'No,' he said.

'But you don't understand. I *must*.'

She put it on. It hung down baggily, shapeless. Her bony hands and burnt, distorted face appeared grotesque against it; her hair was caked with grime. Below, her feet protruded, wrapped in the dirty skins.

'What do I look like?' she asked in sudden recklessness, like a young girl going to a ball.

He wanted to close his eyes or turn away; he wanted to cry. But all he could do was to whisper hoarsely: 'You're beautiful.'

She looked at him with a smile. Her eyes became pleading. Slowly her excitement sank away. With a brown claw she tugged at the

216

ribbons of her bodice. 'I know I look horrible,' she whispered. 'Why don't you say so?'

'Come,' he said in a hurry. 'We must push on, it's getting late. I'm sure you don't want to stay here tonight.'

'No.' There was horror in her voice. 'Let's go then.'

He picked up his bundle but put it down again. Looked at her; averted his eyes. Then pulled one of the bags of honey towards him and began to scrape off the ants. Without a word she watched him. He removed the second bag from the grave, followed by the rest of the offerings.

'Aren't you afraid he'll haunt you if you rob his grave?' she suddenly mocked, choking.

'It's only my mother's stories.'

'Every time we pass a mantis, you make a wide detour,' she reminded him.

'It's your imagination.'

'I've noticed it every time.'

He took up his bundle and the bags of food. 'Come on,' he said sullenly.

They walked on, the sun glaring in their eyes. Neither of them looked back towards the vultures or the pile of stones. There was always a final mercy to transcend, a final *No* to pass.

She tried to get used to walking with the dress flapping round her thin legs; her hands felt rough and clumsy against the smooth material.

Five more days, she thought. Five days from here there would be a farm and people.

Arrival and sojourn on the farm. One can imagine how, for days, they'd been scanning the horizon with burning eyes in search of a sign. How the veld continued to stretch out in all directions. How, early that morning, white clouds started gathering behind the first hint of mountains in the distance. How, seeing it, they no longer thought of rest or feared the sun. And then, at last, presumably a flock of goats and sheep grazing among the low dry shrubs, the shepherd lying in the shade of a ditch, hat pulled over his eyes, fast asleep; scorched fields; kraals of stone and branches; and the long, low farmhouse in the distance, with the chimney on one narrow end, a single door, two small square holes for windows. A row of scraggy trees lining the farmyard. Chickens.

Dogs barked. On the shady side of the house a man got up from his *riempie* chair, pushing back his broadbrimmed hat from his forehead where years of shade had drawn a white circle. Unperturbed, he watched them as they approached.

Elisabeth stopped a few yards from the man, Adam hesitating in the background. Still the farmer made no move, his hat on his head, pipe clenched between his teeth. Under his chair stood his half-filled teacup, saucerless. A couple of his shirtbuttons were missing, the dark hair of his chest protruding through the gap. He had a thin bony nose, his eyes were a very pale blue and rather close together, his mouth a moist slit in his beard. He might be any age from thirty to fifty.

'Good afternoon,' she finally said uncertainly, clutching the ribbon on her bodice.

'Yes, afternoon,' he answered, studying her. 'Where do you come from?'

'My wagon broke down in the interior,' she said, with a hint of the old aloofness in her voice. Miserable as she was she held her head high. 'The Bushmen stole our oxen. The Hottentots deserted us. So I had to come back on foot.'

'No one can cross the Karoo on foot,' he said.

'That was all I could do.' Wiping perspiration from her forehead she pushed back the dirty wisps of hair.

The farmer didn't move.

'A few days ago we found a Hottentot trek. They told us about your farm.'

'Yes, the bastards. Wanted to overnight here, can you imagine it? Trampling everything one's got left, drinking up one's water. I told them . . .'

'So we thought perhaps you wouldn't mind to . . .' She stopped as she noticed that he was looking past her towards Adam, his eyes narrowing.

'He's – he's my . . .'

'Yes,' said the man curtly. 'He can go round to the kitchen.'

'But I . . .' She raised her arm in protest, but the farmer misunderstood the gesture and took her hand. It was almost comic.

'De Klerk,' he said.

'I am Elisabeth Larsson.'

'Yes,' he said, with no sign of unbending.

She looked round. Adam was already on his way to the back of the house.

'Mr de Klerk, I . . .'

218

'It's all right,' he said. 'You can stay here until we make a plan.' Turning round, he shouted: 'Lettie!'

A woman in a faded blue dress appeared on the doorstep, barefoot, without any petticoats or hoops, her hair drawn back severely behind her ears, her face weatherbeaten in spite of the bonnet she was obviously wearing all the time. Her age was as impossible to guess as his. But she was pregnant, with a bulge of eight months or more, so she couldn't be too old yet.

'This woman comes all the way through the Karoo,' he announced. 'Name of Larsson. This is my wife. Can you help her with something?'

'Yes. Please come inside.'

On the threshold Elisabeth turned back. 'The man Adam – here at the back . . .'

'The servants will see to him,' the farmer said briefly, returning to his chair where he began to refill his cold pipe.

She wanted to explain, but thought: If he finds out, he may send us away just like this. It will really be better for both of us if I . . .

'Come,' said the woman. 'It's hot in the sun.'

One entered directly into the bedroom with its large brass bedstead, a row of guns against the wall, a few yellow-wood chests, a zebra skin on the dung floor. It was cooler here under the thatched roof with its beams exposed, but stuffy, suffocating.

'You come from far?' asked the woman.

'Yes.' She briefly told her story again, suppressing most of it, not knowing how the farmer's wife would react.

'You got nothing with you?'

She shook her head, sinking down on the edge of the bed. It was covered with a kaross of jackal skins.

'No, this is all I have.'

'I can give you a dress.'

'Thank you. May I have some water?'

'Of course.' Shouting shrilly through the open inner door: 'Leah! Bring water.'

Uncomfortable, they waited until an elderly, thickset slave woman entered with an earthenware jug and a cup without a handle.

Elisabeth hesitated briefly, then took the cup and filled it, and brought it to her mouth with trembling hands, emptying it in one gulp. She drank two more cups before she said: 'Thank you. Would it be possible – to have a bath?'

219

'I'll ask my husband.'

Leaning her head against the post of the bed, Elisabeth waited for the woman to return. When she came in from outside she shouted in the same piercing voice as before: 'Leah! Bring the tub of washing water.' Without waiting for an answer she went to one of the boxes in the far corner where she kneeled down and fumbled for a while before taking out a brown silk dress, crumpled but obviously brand new. 'You think this will fit you?'

'But it's much too beautiful,' Elisabeth protested. 'Isn't there something older?'

'What can I do with a dress like this – here?' asked the woman, getting up with a moan. 'I was keeping it for the christening. But now we've already buried four children under the koppie.'

'You're having another soon. Why don't you wait?'

'No.' The pregnant woman shook her head. 'It's more than a week now the child has stopped kicking.' She gestured towards the outside door. 'I'm too scared to tell him, but I know.'

'Perhaps it will still be all right.'

The woman shook her head again: without grudge or sorrow, almost obtusely.

'I also lost a child in the interior,' Elisabeth said impulsively. 'I don't even know where he's buried.'

'This is no place for white people,' said the woman dully. 'It's just Hottentots and Bushmen and things what can live here. But my husband will never listen.' Almost scared she glanced outside.

The slave woman came in, staggering under the weight of a wooden tub half filled with water. There was a dirty towel draped over her shoulder and a piece of fat-soap thrust into her apron pocket.

'Well,' said the pregnant woman, 'you can have your bath now. I must go to the kitchen. One can't trust these creatures out of your sight. Come on, Leah.'

The water had been used before, she noticed after they had left. It was turbid, with a dirty rim around the side. But she didn't mind. It was water.

She undid her dress. For a moment she stood, self-conscious, wondering whether she should first close the outside door. But that would make it too dark inside. Pulling her arms from the sleeves, she peeled off the dress, wriggling her hips to let it slide to the floor, a shapeless rag on her feet. She kicked herself free and stepped into the tub. It was wide and shallow, one could sit down with ease. Cool and

220

smooth the dirty water enclosed her. She shut her eyes. For a while she sat quite motionless, her elbows resting on her knees, her head on her arms. Water. Water. God.

At last she started soaping and washing herself. Her face, her hair, her body, over and over, until there was very little of the soap left and a thick brown lather covered the water.

As she got up to reach for the towel she noticed a round mirror propped up on a box against the bed. It had cracked diagonally, but was still useful. With a strange, apprehensive sense of excitement she crossed the floor on her bare wet feet and bent over to look at herself. The wrinkles cutting deep into her dry brown skin. Dark blue eyes sunken into the sockets. The short thin nose. The mouth too large, the lips crusted and cracked. The cheekbones more prominent than she could remember. Deep hollows above her collarbones, pointed elbows, her hands unwieldy at the end of her bony arms. The breasts shrunken, mere loose folds in the skin, with large, scabby nipples; her belly a deep hollow between the jutting hipbones. Below, protruding shockingly, her matted pubic hair and the thin beak of her sex. Kneecaps. Narrow feet. If that is me: who, dear God, am I?

Almost with horror, but also with infinite compassion for herself, she turned away to fetch the towel. A movement at the door brought her to an abrupt stop, petrified. When she finally looked up – thin droplets running from her hair and down her shoulders and her spine, like a shudder – she saw the man standing in the doorway, the farmer, De Klerk, still wearing his hat, his pipe in his mouth.

He stood staring at her without moving, even when he noticed that she'd seen him: a pale fanatic stare in his narrow eyes, his jaw white from biting on his pipe.

For several seconds she stood looking at him in silence, her mouth opened in an unuttered sound. Then, because she couldn't think of anything else to do, she crouched forward, raising her hands to cover her breasts.

Immediately he turned round and disappeared against the yellow light of the dying day.

Taking the towel, she started drying herself. She felt nauseous and old, worn-out.

But when at last she went through to the other room, wearing the new silk dress, her hair brushed, she didn't say anything. Only her nostrils flared slightly as she glanced at him sitting at the table with his

221

wife. Outside the sun went down. A young slave girl was lighting the lanterns. Beside the hearth the servants were crouching in a dark mass on the floor – seven or eight grownups and some children; and Adam. For a fleeting instant she looked him in the eyes, and felt like crying. Then she sat down.

The thickset slave woman came in with the tub from the bedroom and carried it outside where she emptied it in a trough – Elisabeth sat watching her through the open kitchen door – before returning to fill it with fresh water from a larger barrel beside the hearth; then she brought it to the table and knelt in front of the farmer to wash his feet, shuffling on her knees towards the pregnant woman afterwards.

'Let us eat.'

There was a dish of stew in the middle of the bare scrubbed table. The man dipped a chunk of bread into the dish and began to eat. His wife followed his example. Then Elisabeth. No one spoke, not even when, after they'd emptied the dish, the slave woman, moving soundlessly on her bare feet, came to clear the table and serve them with cups of bush-tea and a jug of milk.

'Let us read,' said the farmer at last. A slave child fetched a huge brown Bible from a box and put it on the table in front of the man. For a long time he sat paging through it, searching, until he found the place where, presumbly, he'd stopped the previous night.

In the corner of the hearth a brooding hen clucked. A house-lamb was rustling in its bed of straw, then settled down.

With fierce concentration he began to read, nudging the words with a horny forefinger like a dung-beetle on its halting way:

'What profit hath a man of all his labour which he taketh under the sun?

'One generation passeth away, and another generation cometh: but the earth abideth for ever.

'The sun also ariseth, and the sun goeth down, and hasteth to his place where he arose.

'The wind goeth toward the south, and turneth about unto the north; it whirleth about continually, and the wind returneth again according to his circuits.'

He stopped for a moment, looking up. Before his gaze Elisabeth lowered her eyes. With a touch of confusion he returned to the Bible, trying to locate the place he'd lost, his lips parted, drops of saliva glistening in the corners. At last he went on, pronouncing each syllable separately:

'The thing that hath been, it is that which shall be; and that which is done is that which shall be done: and there is no new thing under the sun.

'Is there any thing whereof it may be said, See, this is new? it hath been already of old time, which was before us.

'There is no remembrance of former things; neither shall there be any remembrance of things that are to come with those that shall come after.'

With a heavy sigh he closed the solid book, fastening the brass clasps.

'Let us pray.'

Kneeling on the dung floor, their elbows propped up on the hard benches, they listened to his prayer. Far outside something was rumbling, like thunder; but surely that was not possible.

Among the slaves and servants in the corner Adam crouched, not removing his eyes from her for an instant. Perhaps she was conscious of it, for she kept hers tightly shut. Her hands appeared to be trembling against her face; but it might be an illusion in the lamplight.

There she's kneeling down with you, under the same light: she belongs to you. She is on her way back. The taste of death is in my mouth. I love you: at this moment I hate you. Is it for this I brought you out of the land of the vultures? Only to kneel down again and shut your eyes, your body hidden in a silk dress from the Cape? *I* know how tough and dry you are, how horrible, how lovely. I allowed you to call me by the name only my mother knew. What will happen if I suddenly get up, and put my hand on your shoulder, and announce, 'Leave her alone. She belongs to me?'

The prayer seemed endless. On the horizon there was another muted rumble like a vast herd of buck passing in the distance. At last it was over. They stood up, scraping their benches on the uneven floor. The yellow lamp was burning steadily on the table.

'Your slave can sleep here in the kitchen with the others,' said the farmer. He didn't look at her.

'I . . .' Once again she hesitated, and swallowed, and said no more.

Behind him his shadow seemed enormous on the plastered wall, rising halfway up the thatched roof, distorted and grotesque. She bowed her head in hopelessness. During the prayer she had nearly fallen asleep. Every fibre of her body felt pervaded by fatigue.

'You're sleeping with us,' he said bluntly.

'I'll be all right on the floor.'

'There's place enough, the bed is big.' He looked at his wife. 'Take her with you, Lettie,' he ordered.

Then he went out, probably to inspect the kraals and the yard; to urinate.

'Come,' said the woman. She lit a candle in the flame of the lamp and went on to the bedroom.

'Really, I . . .'

'He said so.'

From the door she looked back. In front of the hearth there was a vague, dark movement of bodies. She could not distinguish Adam from the others.

The pregnant woman sat down heavily on the edge of the bed, sighing as before. As she unfastened her dress and took it off and undid her hair, her shadow mimed her movements on the wall. In her shift she suddenly seemed much younger, vulnerable. She moved in under the kaross on the far side of the bed.

Elisabeth remained standing, her fingers on the bodice of her new dress. But she didn't undo it.

'Aren't you coming?' asked the woman.

She turned away towards the small window opening. Outside it was very dark. It smelled cool and fresh, unlike the mustiness inside. Something stumbled in the yard.

'Take off your clothes,' he said behind her in the doorway.

She looked round. He was standing with legs astride, hands on his hips, looking at her.

Then he came towards her. There was a large dark stain on the dung floor where she had spilled earlier, having her bath.

'What are you waiting for?' he asked.

'Oh, Hans,' moaned his wife from the bed.

'I wasn't talking to you,' he snapped at her.

With her customary sigh she turned her face to the wall.

'Well?' he asked. 'Why don't you take it off?' He put out his hand and grabbed the front of her dress. She tried to stop him.

'What's the matter with you?' she asked blindly. 'I've come here to ask for help. I didn't . . .'

He tugged at the dress and she heard it tear.

'My God!' she cried, helpless with anger. 'If I'd been a man you would have shown me hospitality. You would have given me a place to sleep. Now, because I'm a woman . . .' Her voice was shaking.

'Take off that dress!' he shouted.

She wrung herself from his grip, aiming for the inner door, but with a single move he cut her off, laughing through his teeth.

'Adam!' she called out.

He looked confused. Then he heard the shuffling sound behind him and swung round.

'Get out!' he ordered.

'Don't touch him,' said Elisabeth, struggling to control her voice. 'He is my husband.'

'It's a lie!'

'Oh, Hans,' moaned the woman, pushing herself up on her elbows in the big bed.

'He is my husband,' repeated Elisabeth. 'He's come all the way with me.'

'Leave her alone,' said Adam.

De Klerk gaped at him, speechless. She would never forget that expression on his face: the disbelief and dumb frustration. The unthinkable had crossed his horizon.

Elisabeth stood looking at them, barely breathing. She knew there was no hope if the farmer decided to put up a fight: he could call all his labourers to his side. Everything was balancing between them, very slowly, and around them was the night.

Outside the thunder rumbled once more.

'I could have known it,' he suddenly exploded. 'No decent woman would come here like this. A goddamned whore, that's what you are. We don't mix with your sort. We're Christians here.'

'I only asked for a place to sleep,' she reminded him.

'Take your black stallion and get out of here,' he shouted.

'Not in the night, Hans,' complained his wife, pushing the kaross from her and swinging her feet over the edge.

'You stay out of this!' he ordered.

'She lost her child,' the woman said.

'How do you expect us to go on?' asked Elisabeth, in an angry surge of rebelliousness.

'The way you got here. On foot. Or ride on his back.'

'My father is keeper of the Company's stores in the Cape!' she said, raising her head.

'To hell with the bloody Company!' he said. 'What have I got to do with the Cape? I'm over the mountains here.'

'The Cape can drag you out of here if I went back to complain.'

'Why don't you give them a horse, Hans?' the woman asked. 'That's not so much. Look at the poor woman.'

'Poor woman's arse! Going around with things like that!'

It was at that moment that Adam grabbed him by the shirt. Not the violence of the movement, but the unexpectedness of it, caught De Klerk completely by surprise. Instead of fighting back, he suddenly started pleading, pale with fear.

'Don't kill me,' he begged Adam. 'Think of my wife. She's going to have a child.'

'Will you give us a horse?'

'Yes,' he whined. 'Anything you want. Lettie can make you some food for the road. Just let me go.'

Adam was breathing with difficulty to restrain himself. After a few moments he pushed the man away so violently that he stumbled to the floor. Before he could get up again Adam had snatched one of the guns from the wall.

'Take me to the horse.'

'That thing isn't even loaded,' said De Klerk with a show of defiance.

'Where's the horse?'

The farmer glared at him, then turned to Elisabeth. She looked away.

'I'll go and get the food,' the woman offered hurriedly.

Behind them, as they galloped from the farmyard in the dark, a shot was fired. Dogs began to bark hysterically. There was an outburst of confused, angry voices. Then silence. Reining the horse in to an even walking pace, Adam picked their course through the night. There was a long way ahead; it would be senseless to tire the horse out too soon.

Everything had happened so fast that for a long time neither could say a word. It was an end. A transition. A beginning.

The air was damp on their faces.

'At least you knew me when you needed me,' Adam said, very softly, after what had seemed like hours, his voice completely strange in the dark.

She cowered, wanting to answer, but her throat was too taut for speaking. She could only shake her head against his chest.

'The Cape has come a long way to reach us here,' he said after another silence, with such rare bitterness that it struck her like a whip.

'No, Adam. Don't. You mustn't.' She struggled against the tears. 'I told them you were my husband.'

He didn't answer. She felt his body rigid against her back, sitting on the horse.

'I did it for your sake.' She was pleading openly now. 'Don't you realise? I was scared of what he might do to you if I told him. I couldn't face the idea of him insulting or humiliating you.'

'So he only sent me to the kitchen.'

'I did it so we could stay alive. Both of us. If we hadn't stopped there to rest and eat – what would have become of us? You know we couldn't go much farther.'

'You were prepared to pay his price.'

'I was prepared to destroy myself protecting you.'

He said nothing.

Leaning back against him she yielded to the tears, crying with more desperate passion than he'd ever known in her.

'Oh, my God, oh, my God!' she sobbed when, finally, she managed to form coherent words again. 'Don't let this happen to us. Help me, Adam. I can't bear it any more.'

She was in such a state, she didn't even realise that he'd stopped the horse, that he was taking her from its back, hooking the reins on his arm, holding her in love and dread.

'What is happening?' he whispered at last. 'What will become of us if we no longer hold on to each other?'

She realised that he was crying too, his thin, wounded body racked by terrible sobs, though uttering no sound.

'Adam, Adam,' she pleaded. 'Aob, Aob, Aob.'

Huddled together, they remained sitting on the ground till daybreak. It stayed dark a long time, for the sky was overcast.

'We must never let it happen again,' she said, moving her head against his throat. 'Never. We must be good to one another, otherwise we won't be able to bear it. We're too small. We're too vulnerable. And then there will be nothing left.'

'Come,' he said after a long time. 'We can't stay here.'

For they had not reached the end yet. There were mountains ahead which they had to cross. And then still farther. The Cape was drawing nearer, but they had not reached it yet.

On the hollow back of the old hack the farmer had so grudgingly given to them, they set out. Slowly the mountains rose higher in front of them. They didn't even feel relieved or glad. They only went on: blind and dumb and drained, depleted, beyond disillusionment, through a landscape of naked suffering.

The humidity increased. Soon they could smell it. It was going to rain.

It is raining. Not that it really matters any more. A month ago, even a week ago, it would have made all the difference; but no longer. For the Karoo is behind them, and they have entered the mountains. It is no longer redemption, at most a touch of mercy. Still they abandon themselves to it with primitive lust.

Neither of them even thinks of sheltering from it. The mountains are steep, range upon range; never easy. But there are signs of other treks that have passed this way, even with wagons and cattle – and they follow the broad trail through the hills and kloofs. He is leading the horse, but at regular intervals they stop, turning their faces up to drink the rain, to feel it streaming down their bodies. Her long dress clings to her, wet and heavy, making it difficult to walk, but the sensation of its sogginess against her is exhilarating.

Cavorting like children they chase each other in the rain, leaving the horse to graze; catching and grabbing, slipping, rolling in mud and grass among heath and proteas, lying panting while it pours over them and soaks into them.

When at last they are too tired to go on he opens his bundle, struggling with the tough wet thongs, and takes out a *kambro* he dug on the other side of the mountains. With his knife he scrapes off the outer layer of skin and gives her the gratings, showing her how to rub it into a lather. She wrestles to strip the cloying dress from her, kicking it from her long legs and leaving it in a bundle on the ground. And while the rain continues to stream down steadily over them they soap each other's bodies, washing, rubbing, caressing for the pure joy of it. Slippery and smooth, shiny as otters, they make love on the grass in the rain, feeling themselves dissolve in mud and water, in this no-man's-land between yesterday and tomorrow, between the barren plains and the fertile valleys of the Cape. Here they belong to nothing and are determined by nothing: in the pure play and heaving of bodies they are reduced to simple elements. And when, panting and exhausted, they finally cease to move, they remain on the ground intertwined like tree-roots, their mouths open, while the running water washes them clean of mud and grass.

Nudging his head into the hollow between her neck and shoulder, laughing and relieved, he says: 'You taste like earth and water. You're beautiful, oh God, you're so lovely.'

228

'It would be wonderful to die like this,' she says. 'It felt like dying and living at the same time.'

After a long time he moves away from her, and she thrusts her hips upwards trying to retain him, wanting to cry out with the sudden feeling of loss and emptiness. Drawing up her legs she lies like a hedgehog to retain his warmth in her, her hair spread on the grass, mud-marks on her back.

'It will be dark soon,' he warns, helping her to stand up.

It comes as a shock to them both; what has become of the day? It is dusk already. They'll have to spend the night somewhere here. But there is no shelter nearby, no cave visible in the falling rain, and all the trees and bushes are soaked. Under a slight protuberance they press themselves against the rock, with the horse in front of them to ward off the rain. But the wetness still reaches them. And it is getting colder too. The breath of the horse forms small white clouds in the deep dusk. Crouched in a kaross, they try to keep one another warm throughout the night. For there is no dry wood to make a fire, no warmth anywhere except in their shivering bodies steaming under the heavy skins of the kaross. Now they regret their extravagance, now everything appears excessive and rather childish. The moment which was so perfect in itself, so brimful of life, seems unreal and remote; the ecstasy of his seed in her, her screaming and writhing against him, is incredible and lost. Everything was so eternal, and is so distant now.

Can it never last beyond the moment? she wonders, feeling a cough forming in her chest. The moment of which one believes so confidently that it makes up for a lifetime of suffering. Now it has gone, and all that remains is this night in the mountains – the very memory is unreliable and vague. The moment was so self-contained, but all they have of it now is to know, or to believe, that it happened. And tomorrow?

Shaking with cold they see the colourless day approach; and without waiting any longer they run down the slope to work up some heat. A raging stream down below – brown water and white foam – then up the opposite slope. Keep moving, don't stop. It is late afternoon again before they finally discover a shallow cave with some dry wood inside. Once he has a small fire going he feeds it with damp branches. It gives off more smoke than heat, but it is better than last night's total exposure. She is still coughing, but not as badly as in their winter cave. His arm is in a sorry state, though, even worse in the cold than before.

The rain lasts for two more days befor the sun breaks through the loose, drifting clouds, sparkling on the grass and their wet bodies. They reach a last neck on the mountains. Below them a wide valley fans open to the south-east. In the distance a thin line of smoke from a homestead streaks upward. There is the promised land: they are drawing near. Another week or two, surely no more than that.

Then the horse died. Of poisonous irid appearing after the rains, Adam said. The poor thing didn't have much life left anyway, yet with her on his back it made a considerable difference to their progress. Now he lay on his side, with a huge swollen belly, in a patch of arum lilies.

They sat on the grass beside the dead horse. She was wearing the brown silk dress, dry but badly crumpled after the rain. The small mishap had unnerved them completely.

'Just when it started going better,' she said with bitter resentment. 'Haven't we been through enough already?'

'Perhaps we've been in too much of a hurry,' he said cryptically.

'Why shouldn't we?' she asked. 'We've been travelling for so many months already.'

'*Where* are we going, Elisabeth?' he asked with stunning directness.

She looked at him in amazement. 'Why do you ask such a strange question?'

'Is it really so strange? All the time we've been saying: the Cape, the Cape, home, home.' Almost fondly he caressed the mane of the dead horse. 'Which Cape are we going to?'

'There is only one Cape.'

'It seemed like that when we were far away. That's how we wanted it. But the nearer we come . . .' He was silent for a long time before looking up straight at her. Her hair was stirring lightly in the wind. 'Our Capes are different. Surely you know that.'

'For neither of us it will be the Cape we knew.' She tried to convince him with the intensity in her eyes. 'It will be a new place altogether. To start from the beginning.'

'You think it's possible to start again?'

'But we've already discussed it!' she said. 'Why are you beginning to doubt it again?'

'It's not "again". It's been all the time. On the other side of the mountains it didn't seem so important. It was more urgent just to survive. But now we've got to know.'

'As soon as we get back I shall ask the Governor to pardon you. That's what we have arranged, isn't it?'

'But suppose I really killed Lewies when he tried to stop me that night? There is no mercy for a murderer.'

'Even if you did kill him, you've paid for his death with my life.' She looked at him urgently. 'Adam, why won't you believe me?'

'I do believe you. But I'd like to be more confident about the Cape.'

'You used to say you couldn't live without the Cape any more.'

'I know. But now I must find out whether I can live *with* it.'

'You'll be free,' she reminded him. 'As free as I am. You'll be able to come and go as you wish. No one will interfere with you. You're still thinking of the past too much. You're a new person now.'

'But will the Cape be a new Cape?' he insisted.

'What do you want to do then?' she asked angrily. 'I'm not going without you. But I can't stay here either.'

'I'm not going without *you*,' he said with a wan smile. 'If only you understood . . .'

'You must trust me, Adam.'

'Have you thought about yourself? It may be even more difficult for you. Your own people will disown you.'

'You are more important to me than they. If I am forced to choose – I have already chosen.'

'But once we're there; as the years go by . . . Suppose I notice how you are cut off, how they avoid you in the street, how they turn their noses up at your children, how you become more and more lonely. Do you think I could swallow that, knowing it's all because of me?'

'But there are other white people married to blacks!' Her eyes are flaming. 'Even old Governor Van der Stel – they said his mother or his grandmother had been brown.'

'That was fifty years ago. Things are changing. And it's easier for a black woman with a white man. But a white *woman* . . . !'

'Adam, I promise you . . . ! Please believe me.'

'They'll never forgive you,' he persisted relentlessly. 'If their white women start doing this sort of thing: it undermines everything in which they've got to believe if they want to remain the masters in the land. Don't you realise that?'

'It's you who can't forget about your past suffering. It has wounded you so deeply that you don't even want to admit that another way of life is possible any more.'

231

'Do you really think I don't want to?' he asked. 'My God, do you really think so?'

She bowed her head slowly. The horse lay motionless among the crushed white flowers. Bees were humming in the grass.

'Suppose everything turns out all right as you believe,' he said at last. 'Suppose they do accept us and we live together happily ever after. Then I shall really be free, and I'll owe it all to you. But will it make any difference to my mother? She'll remain a slave on the Master's farm. Will it make any difference to a single other slave in the land? You and I can't do anything to change their lives. The Cape will always remain what it was. At most I'll be an exception to their rule.'

'Then you should never have come back,' she said.

'What else could I do?'

'Do you want to take me there and then turn back and roam through the land on your own as before?'

'That would be worse than the sentence of death. Then I'd rather give myself up to them.'

'But what can we do then?' she pleaded. 'What else is there to do?'

'Nothing. That's what makes it so terrible. Didn't you know that one asks most of one's questions only because one knows they cannot be answered?'

He looked down at his hands, and the long festering wound on his arm, the purple-black flesh flaming angrily all round it. Everything of these past months, everything that has happened, good or bad: neither of us willed it or chose it. We even tried to withhold ourselves from love. We didn't *want* anything to happen. But it did, and we are caught in it; and that is all that matters. And because it has happened, because our possibilities have changed into facts, we can but endure what we have and what still lies ahead. We cannot escape the guilt. We cannot escape the cat o' nine tails and the irons, the sound of gulls in the endless wind. And then, one day, once again the sound of oars in black water and a new beginning? Perhaps that is the most we can ever hope for.

'Come,' he said gently. 'We must go on to the Cape.'

But they reckoned without his wound. The herbs the Hottentots had given him had neutralised the poison for a time, but it didn't heal as it should. Perhaps the strain of their journey through the mountains had aggravated it; or the rain, or something. Whatever it was, soon after the death of the horse it became critical. One long night he

232

couldn't sleep at all, but he didn't want to wake her, she needed the rest. However, when she opened her eyes soon after sunrise she was shocked to see his contorted face and the ashen colour of his cheeks. In spite of his efforts a groan escaped through his clenched teeth. The arm was swollen and black with inflammation. There was perspiration on his forehead. At times he didn't seem to know what was going on any more.

Following his instructions she broke one of their ostrich eggshells and powdered some of it between stones, and propped him up to lick the powder from her hand. But it made little difference to his fever.

The wound itself she gently rubbed with honey, as he'd been doing all the time. But that, too, had no visible effect.

'Is there nothing else we can put on?' she asked in desperation.

'Herb-of-grace,' he said painfully. 'Or wild wormwood, or touch-me-not. That should draw out the fire.'

'Where can I find it?'

'I'll go with you.'

But within a few minutes he had to lie down again, too dazed with fever to go on. He tried to describe the shrubs and leaves to her, and she left him under a tree and went in search of them, gathering whatever seemed useful.

During the last few days they had often passed farms on their way, but deliberately avoided them, as she was apprehensive of how he would be received. So far from the authorities in the Cape the farmers were really a greater menace than the wilderness itself. And yet: if only there had been a farmhouse near them now! But there was nothing.

All through the day she brought him leaves, but none was useful. In the end they started trying whatever she found, bruising the leaves and boiling them in an eggshell, applying the pulp to the wound – as hot as he could stand it – before she set out again.

He remained under the tree, covered by the kaross, his knees drawn up, palms pressed against his head, teeth clenched.

If something happened to him now, he thought, it would really make it easier for her. They were close enough for her to reach the Cape. But his very guts rebelled against the thought. He hadn't come all this way, all these years, to die practically within sight of his destination! He had always survived. When the snake had bitten him he was closer to death than now. When he'd been struck down by thirst, the end was near. Yet every time there had been someone at hand to help, someone who'd known the land. Now there was no one but Elisabeth. And how could she recognise a herb-of-grace or a touch-me-not?

Grandmother Seli, you would have known. All the slopes of Padang were covered by it, you said: all those quivering leaves curling up at the touch of a finger. Different from the Cape variety. Different and more beautiful. Everything you used to know was different and more beautiful: volcanoes, palm beaches, coral reefs, hibiscus and cinnamon and jasmine. Now you lie buried in the Malay graveyard below the mountain. At least they set you free to die. Poor thing, it's so exposed up there, a single row of trees against the wind, so different from the bulky wall enclosing the churchyard of the Dutch.

Was that the day it all began? When the news came of her death, and my mother slipped away to the funeral, and the Baas called me to the backyard? So far, Ma, and no further: all these years you've persuaded me to accept the white man and his laws, one for him and one for us. All we have ever been allowed to do has been to kneel down and say: Thank you, Baas God. But no longer. This is the end. I shall not raise my hand against you. My father and my grandfather I never knew – one dead, the other sold – but you I've known. You washed my wounds and comforted me when I was a child; you've been my mother. Now I take this piece of wood, this beautiful smooth stinkwood I planed with so much care (can you smell the shavings? there is no artisan in the Cape like me) and I bash in his head. All right, let them come for me and take me away. Let them tie me up in front of their stone Castle under the crying gulls. My only regret is that they have sentenced me to no more than scourging and branding. My grandfather Afrika was a better rebel than I. He died here, perhaps tied to this same stake, his bones broken on the wheel: in my death I become a man. I am not worthy of you, old Afrika. Now even less than before: look, here I'm on my way back to the Cape, I'm playing white, I'm going to open a shop and make furniture. They've tamed me and drawn me under the yoke. Forgive me, my Grandfather, Grandmother Seli, Father, Mother. All of you. I no longer know my rightful place. But I love her.

The day I came through the wild figs towards the wagon, after following it for so long, watching them destroy themselves bit by bit: was that my own choice? Or was I chosen? Had everything been decided long before?

It was still possible to turn away then. What concern of mine was a white woman lost in the wilderness? How many others – brown, black, white – lie strewn across the empty plains? Would one more have made any difference?

What did I want of her then? Not her body. One body I had loved before, in the dark among the others, and lost her: that was enough. After that one uses barrenness as an excuse. So what did I want of her? That first evening when she washed herself in the wagon, the yellow lantern behind her casting her black shadow on the canvas – arms above her head, firm breasts, the gentle curve of her belly: no, that was not desire. Not desire only. One learns to control that. Desire is easy, and easily stilled. What else then?

The day she appeared on the flat rock at the river: what forced me to wade out towards her and take up my clothes and tear them to pieces – her husband's clothes, not mine – strewing them over the branches of our shelter? Did I want to taunt or insult or threaten her? But it didn't really concern her at all. It had to do with myself. With how much quaking defiance dare one admit: Here I am, I am human? And how easy to miscalculate!

Did I still have a choice the day I left the deserted cottage in search of a buck, wandering on and on past all the game I found, with the firm resolve to escape and never to return? Or had it already been sealed by then? – To return to everything I feared. To say voluntarily: Here, take me, take my freedom.

And can all that be undone merely because there is no touch-me-not growing in this valley?

With touch-me-not leaves in her arms she returned in the twilight, not even realising that she'd found what she was looking for. They pulped the leaves again and boiled them and applied them, scalding hot, to his arm. And while he lay mumbling to himself in the night she remained watching beside him.

When I was dying of hunger and thirst in the Karoo you went out and found a blesbuck that had protected her fawn against the jackals all night long. You drove her predators off. She must have thought you'd come to save her. But then you killed the fawn, and her too, to quench my thirst with her milk. And to avenge the treachery she slit open your arm with her horns. Now it's your turn. I know I've come too late. If only I'd known what to look for I could have been back so much earlier: these shrubs grow all over the valley. I'm learning so slowly and so belatedly.

Here you're lying helpless as a baby, delivered to me and my handful of leaves. I can go on from here. Within a day or two there will be people to welcome me or abuse me. In the end they'll take me to the Cape. To Mother with her grudge against the world and her dreams of Batavia and Amsterdam. Poor Father with his dead-end life, faithful servant of the Company. There will be parties again, and banquets at the Castle, picnics on the Mountain, excursions to Stellenbosch or Drakenstein, officers to entertain, explorers from other countries. One Sunday, who knows, another bullfight. Life will continue as before: never as before. But how can I leave you here? Even if you died in my arms tonight I cannot abandon you. You stayed with me. You liberated me. You have me cornered in yourself.

You baptised me with blood; I you with the moisture of my love. We have come such a long way on our trek through one another: there has been so much drought, so little to quench the thirst; dead children. But we have also found hidden jackal's food and *ngaap* and elephant's foot; there were ostrich eggs, and honey on a dead god's grave; there was buck's milk and a slaughtered new-born fawn. And there was a forest and a sea. Don't ever forget that. There was a paradise. There was. And for that reason you must live on: Adam in the sweat of your brow. And I. This is how it happened. This is how it is. We are.

If you recover I shall cherish your life. I shall no longer be vain or try to fight for myself. Humbly, I shall try to protect you from the disillusionment and hate of every day. Till death us do part. Don't die.

'Sooner or later you've got to die, man, whether you want to or not,' said the old man with the network of purple veins covering his nose and cheeks, his green eyes laughing at her. He sat with legs apart on the *riempie* chair to leave room for his rotund belly in the expensive brocade waistcoat brought from Patria a month ago. 'That's why one must lead a decent life, you see. The Devil is keeping watch day and night. And if he catches you sinning, he takes you down to the pool of fire and brimstone, to everlasting destruction, with wailing and gnashing of teeth.'

'I don't want to go there, Uncle Jacobs,' she said, pale, her throat contracting. 'Although I wouldn't mind just to have a peep.'

'A terrible sight,' he proclaimed. 'The beast with seven heads bearing the scarlet woman on his back. The screaming and crying of the damned. Much worse than the criminals tortured at the Castle. And it goes on for ever and ever.'

'Don't frighten the child like that,' reprimanded her father sitting on the opposite side of the small table they had set down in the shade of the mulberry tree. 'Your move, Stephanus.'

'But I want to hear all about it, Father.'

'It's not fit for young children,' he insisted, annoyed.

'It's better to know it and be warned,' said Jacob, putting a hand on her shoulder. 'Don't you agree, Elisabeth?'

She nodded. He moved his hand down her back, allowing it to rest on her bottom for a moment. Aware of what was coming she began to breathe a bit faster, moving her feet slightly apart in anticipation and a thrill of fear.

'One of these days the young men will start courting you,' he said, running his hand down her legs. She stood pressed against his chair. Her father, opposite, was concentrating on the chessboard.

'Elisabeth isn't thinking of such things yet,' he said irritably, without looking up.

'You're at an age when a young girl is so easily led into temptation, so it's better to know beforehand what to expect,' Jacobs continued, unruffled. From the low hem of her dress his hand was moving slowly upward, over her calf and the back of her knee. 'This is your move, Elisabeth. I want to see whether you can remember what I taught you last time.'

She moved a horse.

'You should have watched your father's bishop,' the old man scolded her gently. Moving his hand higher he pinched her lightly on the inside of her thigh. 'And if the young men can't behave themselves you'll keep them firmly in their place, won't you?' he resumed.

'Yes.' She nodded, breathless.

Her father executed a move.

'You again, Elisabeth.'

She studied the board, biting her lower lip; then moved a pawn.

'That's better.' A gentle caress of approval. 'You see, a young girl's most precious possession is her chastity. Don't ever forget that, my child. You know what is by far the best you can do? Leave all those upstart suitors and come and look after your old uncle. I'll treat you like a little princess.' His hand had reached the top, touching the small tendon of her groin.

'Yes, Uncle Jacobs.'

She didn't stir against his knee, her face a flaming red, unable to explain why she allowed him to have his way like that. It wasn't intimidation: the dear old man had never been anything but gentle towards her. She needn't even discourage him with open protest or gesture: the slightest movement of her body away from him, closing her legs, would not only prevent his explorations but undoubtedly finally discourage him. It was something entirely different. Not embarrassment in the presence of her father, but a curious elation for the very reason that he was present – sitting directly opposite her, reacting to her uncertain moves, unaware of anything; the temptation of danger which left her trembling, the proximity of fire and brimstone. And once again she moved a piece on the chessboard, conscious of his finger brushing the down on the lips of her sex.

'Now keep an eye on that castle of your father's. One must be very alert in this world. Else you get caught.' Repeating the gentle caress of her mound with almost loving warning. 'Then all your pawns end up in the pool of fire.'

'It's only a game, Stephanus,' said her father.

'Chess is a very serious sort of game, Marcus. That's why I want Elisabeth to learn it from an early age. It prepares one for life, it teaches one to keep one's eyes open. You must admit it's not easy for a young girl to go through life unscathed.'

'And how did you manage to get through it all unscathed?' enquires the old farmer, keeping one eye on his wife who is pouring the tea the slave woman has brought in.

Elisabeth shrugs. 'It just happened like that,' she says, 'And this man protected me. He's been with us for so many years, one can depend on him for everything.'

'You're lucky,' says the old man, stirring his tea. 'One can't trust today's slaves any more. An ungrateful lot.'

She sits with downcast eyes. (Forgive me that I have to play this game again – for your own sake, to get you safely home.) What really surprises her is the ease with which she has learned to lie; a question of experience.

'And you say it happened just over the mountains?'

'That was where the Bushmen attacked the trek, yes,' she confirms.

'And then lost your husband too. Poor child, you're so young still.'

Elisabeth does not look up. The old woman sighs, parting her heavy legs to sit more comfortably. A few flies are buzzing round her head but she makes no effort to chase them away.

'Yes,' says her husband. 'We're all exposed to the mercy of God. And He does chastise one severely. But we can't complain, it's only that the cattle are dying in a heap. Poisonous irid, that's what it is. After the rains, you see.'

'We lost our last horse like that.'

'Yes, you can't stay out of the Lord's way if He's looking for you. I still think it's because of all the Company's sins that we're punished so hard. The farther one can get away from the Cape the better. Look at us. My wife and myself and our seven sons came to settle here – and today we're all alone. The children gone over the mountains, farther and farther away. No stopping them. You may just as well expect an ant to sit on its arse.'

'Actually I only wanted to ask you . . .'

'Yes, that's what you said. Want us to help you to reach the Cape. Yes.' He takes another sip, sighing. 'Only it's such a bad time of the year. I don't really know.' He gets up and goes to the door, looking out towards his fields and the mountains on the far side of the valley, a hazy lilac in the late sun. 'It's the fruit season now and the grapes are just beginning. The labourers are on their feet from before dawn to after sunset. I tell you, it's a full day's work keeping an eye on them.'

'Perhaps you know of someone else . . .'

'No, no, don't misunderstand me. We'll help you. Poor child, to be a widow at your age. Only it's hard to spare someone right now.'

'I'll pay for it,' she offers, restrained.

'Good God, no, don't think of it. How can I ask for money for a favour?' He returns to his chair. 'What have you got to pay with anyway?' he asks with barely concealed curiosity.

From the floor beside her chair she picks up the gun Adam stole when they left on the horse that night.

'Mm,' he says reflectively, taking it from her to inspect it carefully, peering into the barrel, testing the flint, caressing the butt. 'Mm. Not a bad gun at all. I don't suppose you've got anything besides this?'

Without a word she takes up her dirty bundle and undoes the thong. The two people watch eagerly as she unfolds the filthy skin, then sit back with obvious disappointment.

'Nothing else?' the old man asks.

She gets up, standing before him, thin in her crumpled dress, her hair plaited on her shoulders, her head raised.

'All I have left is myself,' she says.

'No, no, that's all right,' he answers hastily, avoiding his wife's accusing eye. 'I told you we didn't want anything. One should help one's neighbour, shouldn't one? And I suppose we would have sent a wagon to the Cape in any case, in a week or two. I have some feathers and eggs and ivory and stuff my eldest son brought over the mountains some time ago. So we'll just send the wagon a bit sooner. It's no trouble at all. Thank you for the gun anyway.'

There was something unreal about travelling on the wagon, perhaps the strangest lap of their whole journey. All those months they had trekked on foot, through the forest and over the mountains and across the burning plains; even at times when their motion had seemed mechanical it was still up to them to keep going, to decide when to stop or when to change direction, when to go faster or more slowly. Now they were sitting on a wagon subjected to the rhythm of the slow oxen plodding along, with no control over their progress any more. They were carried through the days as if towards a fate to which they had resigned themselves in advance. Elisabeth in her dress, newly washed and starched and ironed by a slave girl on the farm, Adam in a linen shirt and knee-length trousers that had grown too small for the old man. The clothes had an effect of estrangement on them. They felt ashamed to look at one another, as if they had just discovered that they were naked.

On the driver's seat sat an old slave, Januarie, trailing the long hippo-hide whip across his knees, his eyes partly obscured by the brim of his hat. The oxen seemed to know the route by heart – through a narrow gorge to the lush valley of the Land of Waveren; then changing their course to due north, following a broad wagon trail all along a winding river which brought them to the dark and amber billowing hills of the Swartland; and from there back to the south, aiming for the huge granite domes of the Pearl Mountain. Once there, all that remained would be a few days across the barren stretch of the Cape Flats to where the blue of Table Mountain would slowly be defined more persuasively against the blue of the sky.

Unreal. Because at night she had to sleep on the wagon while Adam joined the old driver under its belly. Even in the daytime their meetings had to be contrived in such a way as to appear coincidental. They dared not let the old man become suspicious. Would it really matter? By the time he was back on the farm to tell his story they would be safe, his freedom confirmed. Yet something restrained them. Fear of what Januarie might disclose on the Cape market; but

240

also reticence, a need to maintain intact what had so long been theirs alone. For her there was something in it of a bride's withdrawal before the wedding. It was so close now, and so unavoidable: she wished to safeguard, in those last few vulnerable days, the dream of virginity. It would so soon be over. And for him, perhaps: On this last journey to which I've resigned myself, unable to prevent it, the old driver's presence has rendered you untouchable again; I must maintain that illusion, I must even, momentarily, believe in it myself. Soon I shall hold you in my arms again and recognise you. For the moment there is a curious necessity to guard this distance between you and me. It is unsettling; yet strangely comforting.

Unreal. As if now they were moving forward but the earth was slowly sliding backwards under them, returning to the past, resisting the future which was brushing their faces like wind, although the air was windless. This, he thought, was like the springbuck flooding past them on the plains, drawn towards their fate with large and unseeing eyes.

Unreal: back. Here the hills, covered with dark rhinoceros bushes, were unfolding around them, but by tomorrow they would already belong to the past.

'Do you often come this way?' Adam asked the old driver.

He first finished chewing his quid, spitting the tobacco juice over the rump of the rear ox, before he replied: 'From time to time. Three or four times a year.'

'Do you like it in the interior?'

'Yes. I got a good Baas. We grew up together, him and me. That's why he always send me back to the Cape, so I can see my wife. She was sold before we left. And she getting old now, so it's good to visit her. One never know when will be the last time.'

'If you'd been free . . . ?'

Januarie uttered a small whinnying laugh. 'What shall I do being free? The Baas he look after me. I won't know what to do with myself if I was free.'

'Were you born in the Cape?' He couldn't explain why he kept on questioning the man. Perhaps it was only to pass the interminable hours of the day while she lay in the back, dozing.

'Not born, no,' replied Januarie. 'I came with my mother from Madagascar. But I can't remember nothing. I was too small then. Better that way.' With another chuckle. They went on in silence for some time. Then he asked: 'You glad to get back home, hey?'

241

'Home?' asked Adam, surprised.

'The Cape.'

'Oh yes, of course.' He stared ahead, repeating slowly, 'Yes. Home.'

'You been away a long time now?'

'A very long time. I've almost forgotten what the Cape looks like.'

'He always look the same, *mos*. All these years I been seeing him. New houses, streets, churches and things. New gallows the other day. But he stay the same.'

'Have you ever been to the Island?'

'Robben Island? Never. Don't want to neither.'

The moving sound of the water dripping from the oars in the dark.

'You was in trouble?' the old man suddenly asked, prodding.

'No,' said Adam quickly. 'I just . . . went there sometimes to load fruit or water.'

Januarie looked at him with wise old eyes, chuckling. 'Why you try to hide what happened, hey?' Stuffing another quid into his mouth. 'Heh-heh, I was a real bastard in my time, too, don't worry. All the beatings I got. But one get easier when you get old. Your blood lie down. It's no use.'

'My blood will never lie down,' he said grimly.

'You still young. You'll see.'

'You're allowed to come all this way on your own,' Adam said suddenly. 'Haven't you ever tried to run away?'

'Run away?' The watery eyes looked startled. 'Where I go to? I belong to my Baas.'

Adam said nothing.

'Tell me,' Januarie demanded. 'You: will you now run away from your Madam?'

For a long time he didn't reply. Then, tersely. 'Of course not.'

'You see?' said the old man smugly, chuckling.

The wagon went on, swaying unevenly along the ridges of the trail they were following.

'You go take the lead for a while,' ordered Januarie. 'These oxes walking today as if they got a *sopie*. And I want to get the Pearl Mountain before dark.'

Self-conscious in his new clothes, he went to the front to lead the team. The days were falling away now, he thought. Would his mother still be on the farm? Was she still alive? And the Baas – and Lewies? Would they still remember him in the

Cape? But they never forgot. And if Lewies was dead they would demand his blood from him. He'd paid for it with her life, she'd said. Please trust me, Adam. I want you to be happy. It is so near now.

'You're so quiet,' he said, almost awkwardly, when, later, he went round the wagon to sit with her. The front flap was closed; the driver couldn't see them.

'I'm not feeling very well,' she said evasively.

'Are you ill?'

She shook her head; she seemed pale. 'No. I suppose it's just the movement of the wagon. It's so slow. And it never stops.'

'The driver said he wanted to reach Pearl tonight.'

'Then it can't be so far any more, can it?'

'Only the Cape Flats. By tomorrow we'll see the Mountain. And in three days – perhaps four, with this load . . .'

She nodded, her eyes cast down, her legs swinging over the edge of the wagon. Under the wheels small clouds of dust were turned up and remained hanging in the air behind them.

'Are you unhappy?' he asked.

'No. Of course not.'

He kept watching her, waiting for her to slowly raise her head and look at him. 'I can see you're not really happy.'

She said nothing.

'Elisabeth.'

She shook her head. Her eyes were burning. Does happiness exist then? Or is it only something you yearn for? No! I have tasted it and plumbed it, it does exist, I know it intimately. Paradise exists. Even though one may only see it in fleeting moments, even though it is always threatened.

'I'm sorry,' she whispered, pressing her head against him. 'It's just so strange to live apart from you these days. Once we're there . . . I am happy. Really, I am.'

'No, my girl,' her father had said. 'Your thoughts aren't with this game at all.' For a moment his hand had hovered over the chessboard before he put it down to sweep all the pawns from it. 'What's the matter then?' he asked.

'Just the excitement of a bride-to-be,' she evaded him, trying to smile.

'You don't look excited at all. This past week your mother has had to lie down ten times a day. But you . . .'

'I wanted to be with you this one last time,' she confessed. 'That's why I said we must play chess. You're so busy otherwise.'

'From tomorrow you'll have a husband to keep you occupied.'

'Yes.'

'And a good man he is too. I'm satisfied. But I'll miss you, of course.'

'We won't be away for ever.'

'But when you come back . . .' He smiled sadly. 'You know what the Bible says about "one flesh . . ." '

'Is it true?' she asked impulsively. 'Was it like that for you? Is it really worth so much that one wants to sacrifice everything else in the world for it?'

'You mustn't think of it as a sacrifice,' he protested. 'After all, one chooses it freely.'

'How free is one to choose?' she asked, impetuous.

'It was you who simply confronted us with the fact that you were going to marry Larsson,' he reminded her.

'That's not what I meant,' she said irritably. 'I want to know whether it's possible, whether it works? To be one flesh. To have nothing left of oneself.'

'My darling girl . . .' He hesitated.

'What happens when one opens one's eyes one day to discover that it has all been a mistake? That one has never been together at all? That all the time one has been living next to each other like two wagon trails running parallel and disappearing on the horizon . . . ?'

'It's common for brides to have doubts on the eve of their wedding,' he tried to reassure her. 'Your mother was just like you.'

'Why can't you be honest with me?' she demanded.

'But I'm telling you . . .'

'One does something with open eyes. You're absolutely certain your eyes are open. But it's like dreaming that you are awake. In the end you do wake up to find it's all been a dream . . .' She reflected. 'One does it because one believes in it, because it seems right. Even if it means going against the rest of the world. You think you're creating a new world for yourself. For him and yourself together, one flesh. And then, one day . . . What happens if one opens one's eyes to find one is still alone? And all they can say to one is: You see? We warned you, but you wouldn't listen. Now you must bear the consequences . . .'

'Now you're exaggerating, Elisabeth,' he said, almost annoyed. 'I'll get you something from the doctor.'

'What did you do the day *you* woke up?' she asked with deliberate cruelty.

He glanced at her, and lowered his head. 'How did you know?' he asked almost inaudibly.

'Don't you think anyone can see it?'

He shook his head. 'We wanted to be happy. We tried. I swear. Her family was against it, they said I didn't belong to their class. She was accustomed to a better sort of life. I was only a man from the Cape, my father had rebelled against his Governor. We decided we'd show them. We would not allow them to interfere with our happiness.'

'But why did you fail then? If you were really so serious about it?'

'I don't know.' He sighed. He was looking much older. 'Must something specific happen? It just comes about. One day one simply discovers that the world is no longer what it has seemed to be.'

She looked down at the empty chessboard.

On an impulse he got up and came round the table to her, taking her shoulders in his hands. 'Elisabeth, please. I don't want you to have these doubts. You dare not fail too. Ever since you were a little girl I could see you had a real spirit in you. My mother's Huguenot blood. My father's rebelliousness. Don't let them get you down. I believe in you, do you hear me?' His hands were trembling on her shoulders. 'It's enough that I've made a mess of my life. You must succeed. Something beautiful, something worth while. Not just for your own sake but for mine as well.'

Pressing one of her hands on his, she stared in front of her. 'But is this the way to do it? To get married. To become one flesh. What will be left of myself?'

He shook his head, giving a small wry laugh. 'You've always wanted to have things your way. You're so stubborn.'

'Because it's *my* life!' she said. 'I can't allow anyone else to dictate to me. I'm not just a woman, I'm a person. I want to mean something. I don't want to die one day knowing everything has been in vain.'

'Are you really so terribly unhappy, my darling?'

She looked down at the board again.

'Perhaps we should rather have finished the game,' she said, sighing. 'Talking doesn't get one any farther, does it?' She got up and looked him in the eyes. 'Please don't pay any attention to me. I'm just a silly girl getting married tomorrow. I am happy. Really, I am.'

The wagon rode on. They sat in silence. After a while Adam put out his hand and laid it in her lap. She covered it with hers. Creaking and swaying, the wagon went on its way.

This I shall fight for, she thought. To keep it intact. It is ours. Until today it has belonged to us only: in a few days' time it will be exposed to the world. But I shall fight for it. To be one flesh. Why else have we come this long way? It cannot all have been in vain. We shall survive; together. All this time we've been nothing but man and woman, two people alone in the wilderness. From now on the Cape will try its best to make us white and black. She closed her eyes tightly. This man sitting next to me, whom I love; this stranger I know so well.

No: we must no longer question it or wonder whether anything may have turned out differently. It is unworthy, and irrelevant. What has happened, has happened because you are you and I am I. If we'd been different we would have acted differently. We ourselves have determined what has happened and what will happen from now on. The land has made it possible. Therefore we have no right to regret anything.

The innocence of a girl in a mulberry tree.

'If it's all right for Madam we outspan here tonight. Then we can go to the market early in the morning,' says old Januarie, hat in hand.

He has been driving the oxen in long shifts to cross the Cape Flats in three days: now, the sun setting behind the mountains, they are just outside the town. In the distance one can see the sombre stonework of the castle. Glimpses of white houses among orchards. Beyond, the purple-green kloofs and cliffs of Devil's Mountain, Table Mountain, Lion Mountain. Down below, the wide sweep of the bay. During the past few days the Mountain has been rising almost imperceptibly on the horizon, more and more blue and formidable in its self-sufficient silence. Now they are here.

'Are you sure we can't go on tonight?' Elisabeth asks, eager but hesitant.

'But where will I stay for the night, Madam? I go no place in the Cape.'

'We can walk from here,' says Adam next to her. 'We're near enough. If you want to.'

'I don't know.' Suddenly she feels bewildered. 'It's so close. All the way I couldn't wait to be here, but now . . .'

'I know. But we can't stay here in the open either.'

She looks up at him, questioning him with her eyes. He makes a gesture with his head, indicating the sea. She does not immediately

246

understand what he has in mind, but accepts his decision. Her limbs are numb, there is a heavy lump in her stomach, she feels nauseous.

'I can take Madam in if you want me to,' Januarie offers patiently.

'No,' she says, 'We can walk.'

'Will Madam find her way? There's many houses.'

'I'll be all right.' She smiles briefly. 'You forget: it's my home town.'

'Yes, Madam.' He rummages in the things in the box under his seat and takes out a piece of biltong. 'You take this for the road. To chew on. It is farther than Madam think and you may feel hungry.'

'Is there anything left for you?' she enquires.

'No. But it don't matter. I can eat at the market in the morning.'

'I'm used to being hungry,' she says. 'You keep it.'

'Madam is a woman.'

'Keep the food, Januarie. We'll manage.'

The old slave bows gratefully.

They start walking. This time they aren't carrying anything at all, not even a bundle or a kaross. They need nothing. Without speaking they walk in among the milk bushes. Suddenly they are alone again.

From here I left an eternity ago, with two tent-wagons each with ten oxen, and twelve extra, four horses, eight dogs, fifteen chickens, six Hottentots; with Hermanus Hendrickus van Zyl and Erik Alexis Larsson. And here I arrive again, alone. Poor Erik Alexis Larsson. Poor Hermanus Hendrickus van Zyl. Neither of you could outlast a woman. Is it a curse I'm carrying with me?

The town itself is very regularly built and quite small, about 1000 *toises* in length and breadth, including the gardens and orchards, by which one side of it is terminated. The streets, cutting the quarters at right angles, are broad, but not paved, this being unnecessary owing to the hard nature of the soil. Many of them are planted with oaks. None of the streets have names, excepting the Heerengracht, which runs alongside the large plain opposite the Castle. The houses, mostly uniform in style, are handsome and spacious, two storeys high at the most: the greater part of them are stuccoed and whitewashed on the outside, but some of them are painted green: this latter colour being the favourite colour with the Dutch. A number of the best houses have been built from a peculiar sort of blue stone hewn by prisoners from the quarries of Robben Island. A great part of the houses are covered with a sort of dark-coloured reed (*Restio tectorum*) which grows in dry and sandy places. It is somewhat more firm than straw, but rather finer and more brittle. The popularity of this thatching in the Cape must be ascribed to an effort to avoid the grave accidents which may result from heavier roofing being ripped off by the notorious 'Black South-easter' winds raging in this region.

As soon as the wagon had disappeared behind the milk-bushes they swerved to the right, leaving the open road behind, towards the sea. Over them the dusk was deepening. A swarm of flamingoes came past, a rosy cloud, in the direction of the marshes beyond Devil's Mountain.

Back on the beach where I was born the night the sea washed me out with the wreckage. *You* said: One had to complete the circle. *You* said: Come what may.

The tide was out, the small waves sighing on the wet sand, smelling of seaweed and bamboo. They walked in the shallow water, leaving no traces, following the curve of the bay. It was getting darker still. There was no moon. The stars came out. First Khanoes. Then the sky was covered with them. The Milky Way, The Cross, the six lights of Khoeseti.

At last they arrived directly below the town, in the open, walking hand in hand. The water came lapping over their feet, icy cold in spite of the balmy evening. One could see the yellow specks of lights, dull window patches lit by lamps. Was that music, on the border of audibility, pulsing somewhere in the night? Perhaps a ball at the Castle, officers in full regalia, ladies in hoops, poudre de riz, roses, slaves carrying silver trays and crystal bowls, the best imported burgundy. It might be a hallucination. The only certainty, here, was the moist sounds of the sea; tiny shells crackling under their footsoles.

This was close enough. They walked out on the beach, still holding hands not to lose one another in the dark, and sat down higher up where the sand was dry and soft, and warm with an afterglow of the day's hot sun.

Do you remember the night of the lions, and how infinite the world lay brooding round our tiny shelter? And then, driven by insane hunger and disregarding the thorns and the fire, they came bursting through the fence, trampling everything, sending the oxen

248

stampeding into the night; devouring one. These stars were above us then.

They sat close together. There was no need or urge to speak. The silence was dumbfounding.

Remember the day at the river when I came upon you where you swam and you came out to me, naked? You forced me to look at you, to acknowledge you. I feared you and desired you; I feared myself. Always this incalculable thing in myself, this secret unexplored interior.

And the day of the bullfight at the Castle, opened with a prayer. He was so full of life, rippling with muscles; and then all blood and dung. And purified of all passion I went home.

Now we are stripped bare like the skeleton of a snake.

It was she who started caressing him, so quietly that there was no discernable transition from their stillness to the slow and subtle movement of her hands on him. When he became aware of it he whispered:

'Take off your clothes.'

They could not see each other at all. The night was absolute. But they were naked again, the unfamiliar clothes removed. He held her against him, her hands resuming their gentle exploration. After a time she pushed him over on his back, pressing his searching hands down on the sand. Comprehending, he acquiesced. In a strange way it seemed obvious that he had to be passive, submitting to her lovemaking.

Love? Nearness and night.

Through their subconscious the sea rose up as her caresses grew more intense and wild. I want to store up everything about you inside me forever. Whatever may happen in the future, this is ours; it will last.

It is so beautiful to die.

'Aob,' she whispered against his cheek.

Lying so still together, we are travelling more intensely than ever before.

Who are you? I have never known anyone better. Yet you are altogether strange to me.

In the early dawn they ran into the water, washing each other, gasping for breath in the shocking coldness. Shivering they ran out on the beach again and dried themselves in the sun. Then they dressed and went to the lower slope of the Lion's Rump, entering the bushes where he was to wait for her. She would go on ahead to arrange everything. And then return for him. It would be so easy to confirm the freedom already gained.

In our winter cave a small buck came to shelter from the cold or from a beast of prey. And you killed it: you also killed the dog; our child. One has to learn to live with betrayal. You said: it was meat, it was food, we would die without it. At first I didn't want to. But in the end I ate with you. Without it we would not have survived, I think. You were absolutely right.

One can imagine him waiting there in the bushes with their semen smell in the sun, for hours. Watching the movement of the indolent clouds approaching over the Mountain, and the hood forming on the summit. One can imagine the wind starting up, increasing, tearing at the branches of the bushes where he crouched.

And later he would hear, within the fierceness of the wind, the sounds in the distance, coming nearer. He would get up now, eager and anxious.

Then he would see them coming towards him from the distant town, with the high Mountain behind them, in the wind. He would search for her among them, but in vain. For a while he wouldn't comprehend. But then he would realise, and accept it. He would not even consider an alternative any longer: it had been given from the beginning.

He would stand up in that wild wind, his arms folded serenely on his chest, waiting for them to come and get him: all those men, the soldiers with their horses and their hounds.

It would have been very still in him as he stood there waiting for them to ask, like her in the beginning: *Who are you?*

Come, he would think, breathless in the wind. The land which happened inside us no one can take from us again, not even ourselves. But God, such a long journey ahead for you and me. Not a question of imagination, but of faith.

September 1973 – June 1975

André Brink

One of South Africa's leading Afrikaner Writers

Looking on Darkness

'A novel of stature that explores our cancerous condition more persistently than any other novel has done before, and without benefit of anaesthetic.' *Alan Paton*

An Instant in the Wind

'It is difficult to see how any South African novelist will be able to surpass the honesty of this novel.'

World Literature Today

Rumours of Rain

'It both enriches our understanding and increases our knowledge of the world we live in.' *Spectator*

A Dry White Season

Winner of the Martin Luther King Memorial Prize, 1980.

'The revolt of the reasonable . . . far more deadly than any amount of shouting from the housetops.' *Guardian*

A Chain of Voices

This novel transforms a political statement into a compelling and moving artistic achievement.

'A triumph.' *The Times*

The Wall of the Plague

'Particularly powerful and affecting . . . subtle and suggestive.' *Literary Review*

Flamingo

ANDRÉ BRINK

States of Emergency

States of Emergency is directly inspired by the present crisis in South Africa. It is a moving and compelling attempt by one of the country's foremost voices to find artistic expression for the pain and misery of a country at war with itself.

'*States of Emergency* is a quiet, thoughtful, highly intelligent book, packed with literary and intellectual allusion.'
Financial Times

'Allusive, contemplative, fizzing with ideas, it is a pragmatic, paradoxical, playful book, political with a diminutive "p", offering an infinity of endings . . . this book is a triumph, to date Brink's most ambitious and possibly his most dangerous.'
Glasgow Herald

Flamingo

Roy Heath

The Murderer

'A notable study of paranoia, remarkable for its psychological insight and the restraint of its climax.'   *Guardian*

The Murderer won the 1978 *Guardian* Fiction Prize.

A haunting Guyanese trilogy

From the Heat of the Day
One Generation
Genetha

'A combination of narrative skill, ingenuity of plot and marvellous, vibrant dialogue.'   *The Listener*

Kwaku *or the man who could not keep his mouth shut*

'To be good, God knows, is enough to ask; to be astonishing into the bargain is a bonus.'   *Guardian*

'A Soldier Schweik in Civvy Street.'   *TLS*

'A paradise of cartwheeling words and images.'
New Statesman

Flamingo

E. Annie Proulx

Heart Songs and Other Stories

The nine stories in *Heart Songs* introduce a unique, new voice in contemporary American fiction. The settings are small New England blue-collar towns; the characters are the dispossessed working class confronted by an influx of Yuppies from New England cities; and the themes are the traps people set for one another, out of malice or naiveté, premeditation or misunderstanding. The stories in *Heart Songs* play on all keys – loneliness and lunacy, dead-end humour, country music, and the saving grace of trout fishing. E. Annie Proulx writes of her New Englanders' pinched lives with the understanding and irony of a northern Faulkner.

'A new writer of such unarguable talent that it is not a question of "promise" but of performance.'
Vermont Sunday Magazine

Flamingo

Flamingo

Flamingo is a quality imprint publishing both fiction and non-fiction. Below are some recent titles.

Fiction
- ☐ Rich in Love *Josephine Humphreys* £3.99
- ☐ City of Blok *Simon Louvish* £3.99
- ☐ Deep Diving *Stephanie Conybeare* £3.99
- ☐ States of Emergency *André Brink* £3.95
- ☐ Rock Springs *Richard Ford* £3.95
- ☐ The Silence of the Sirens *Adelaida Morales* £3.95
- ☐ Playing Foxes *Helen Dixon* £3.95
- ☐ Blue Eyes, Black Hair *Marguerite Duras* £3.50

Non-fiction
- ☐ A Pike in the Basement *Simon Loftus* £3.95
- ☐ Solitude *Anthony Storr* £3.95
- ☐ A Leaf in the Wind *Peter Hudson* £3.99
- ☐ In the Land of Israel *Amos Oz* £3.99
- ☐ Taking it Like a Woman *Ann Oakley* £3.95
- ☐ Feeding the Rat *Al Alvarez* £3.95
- ☐ Uncommon Wisdom *Fritjof Capra* £4.95

You can buy Flamingo paperbacks at your local bookshop or newsagent. Or you can order them from Fontana Paperbacks, Cash Sales Department, Box 29, Douglas, Isle of Man. Please send a cheque, postal or money order (not currency) worth the purchase price plus 22p per book (or plus 22p per book if outside the UK).

NAME (Block letters) _____

ADDRESS_____

_____

_____